# Buried
# DEEP

by Penny Grubb

# Buried
# DEEP

by
Penny Grubb

Cover design by Heather Murphy

ISBN: 978-1-909163-51-5

To George naturally, and to my indefatigable band of beta readers
Dot, Linda, Stuart, Madeleine, Avril, Sue and Danuta

# acknowledgements

My thanks for invaluable help and suggestions from Hornsea Writers. (www.hornseawriters.com)

Thanks also to Tia Croftts and Susan Hunt at Fantastic Books Publishing for their editorial input.

# prologue

Annie Raymond snapped from relaxed to full alert, senses tingling. And for a moment she couldn't be sure why. Her target Damien Marks hadn't moved from his table in the window of the restaurant down the street, nor had he taken his phone from his ear. Crowds still bustled in all directions drawn by unseasonal sunshine.

It was Annie's first ever visit to York, and it had been an unexpected destination. Until just now she'd felt more like a tourist than a private investigator, her attention focused on the riverbank, intrigued by the casual way people brushed past the chain link fence and sat on the edge, their legs dangling over a sheer drop of several metres to the flowing water.

Marks had told his wife he was on his way to Chelmsford today, but had then led Annie 200 miles north. She'd followed him on and off for a year and a half, uncovering secrets in his working life, but not the other woman that his wife suspected. Several times, she'd gone to the trouble of getting close enough to listen to his calls. Early in the surveillance, an arrangement to meet a Miss Price had her on her toes but the woman proved to be an elderly estate agent, and property deals were his legitimate business.

Watching him a moment ago, fiddling with his phone, breaking bits off a croissant, throwing an occasional glance towards the street, she'd wondered if it were some sort of midlife crisis; an urge to roam at random.

Leaning on a wall, acting the tourist, she let the gaze of her camera phone roam along the mix-and-match, old-and-new of

York's streets. Whilst it panned high above the crowds to a second storey jutting out; the flat brick wall of a converted warehouse; the modern glass expanse of a smart gallery, Annie's stare crisscrossed the crowds. And with an inner crow of satisfaction, she homed in on a woman strolling down the street towards her target's restaurant from the other direction.

Was she about to find the elusive lover? Certainly this one was more the right age and bearing than the aptly named Miss Price, but something in her gait was wrong. It was too deliberately unconcerned, too measured. And as Annie watched, the woman walked past the restaurant window, her head turning neither right nor left. Marks didn't react, didn't seem to see her as she strolled by.

Annie, still the tourist, lowered her lens to follow the woman's path along the pavement towards the bridge over the river. Click …

A couple walked off the bridge towards the woman. They passed each other. They didn't speak; they didn't exchange even the glance of strangers brushing past. Click … Click … Click …

Before they were anywhere near, Annie knew the couple would enter the restaurant. She glanced back towards the lone woman who paused and leant her head discreetly to one side, perhaps talking into a hidden microphone. Her quarry chatted on into his phone, oblivious to the byplay as the couple settled themselves at the table behind him.

Annie melted into the crowds, needing complete invisibility to think this through. Damien Marks's wife was right. He was up to something. But it cost money to send three plainclothes officers to watch one man. This was nothing to do with an extramarital affair.

# chapter one

Billy inched the tractor forward feeling a flutter in his chest as the giant offside wheel sank in the soft earth. Then it climbed, righting itself, and he blew out a tiny sigh. Razor-sharp judgement kept these beasts standing tall, and this close to the edge the minutest of errors would spell catastrophe.

Cool salt air blew in off the North Sea, the swish of waves on the shale way below gave a background beat to the roar of the engine and incessant squawks and squabbles of the gulls close behind. Hands steady on the controls, Billy stretched forward to peer at the rut left by a winter landslip. In less than a minute he'd be the other side of it, back on solid ground, the field ploughed to its edge like it should be. Inside his head, he smiled. Outwardly, his face showed no emotion. The gang with their metal detectors would be delighted. A new strip of ploughed earth that hadn't been disturbed in decades. He ran his tongue round his lips. They'd dried.

The old man might pretend to be shocked, but he'd be pleased, too. He'd laugh that cracked laugh of his. *You old soak, Billy, so you did it, did you?*

She wouldn't laugh though, the old man's daughter, that slip of a girl fresh out of college, marching in giving the orders, like she knew more than they did about the land they'd farmed between them for decades. He and the old man always bantered about this stretch. He'd say, 'How about it?' and the old man would nod and say, 'Good idea, Billy. Good idea.' Then the cracked laugh would wheeze out and he'd add, 'You know what, Billy? Let's leave it, just for this year.'

Not the girl, though. She had to barge in with her swearing, shouting that she didn't give a flying eff how many fingers he lost, she wasn't having her machinery put at risk. *Her* machinery, mind you. Things would be done her effing way now if they wanted roofs over their heads. She'd seemed to include her father the way Billy remembered it, but surely even a little bitch like that wouldn't turn out her own flesh and blood. He resented the reference to the three short stubs that accompanied his left thumb and forefinger. He'd tried to tell her, a man who'd had a tractor topple on him didn't let it happen a second time, but he wasn't good with words, not when he was all het up. She'd growled at him that she'd break his effing neck herself if he effed up her new tractor.

His mind skipped over the changes she'd brought in since she'd burst back into their lives. She might not have to turn anyone out. If everything were done her effing way, the farm would be bankrupt in a year.

He eased the beast forward, hands steady as the huge vehicle tossed him one way and then the other as it bounced in slow motion into that rut and out again.

As he felt the wheels pull forward towards familiar ground, he saw the split deep in the clay. The weight of the tractor bouncing into that rut had ripped the ground apart, a gash running sideways towards the headland.

His half-hand pushed against the lever, sudden shock coursing through him, as static exploded from the radio.

'What do you think you're doing, Billy!' snapped her voice, filling the cab, disorientating him.

His head whipped round as though expecting her to have materialized beside him. He stared out across the field, bewildered. Thirty empty acres stared back.

Her yelling rang in his ears. He didn't reach for the radio. His insides had turned to jelly; his heart beat hard enough to burst out of his chest. Mechanically, he let the tractor roll on until its huge metal tail was clear of the danger area, then he stopped it.

There was no urgency to his movements. It was as though he watched from outside himself, just as she was watching while she shrieked at him to get a move on; to pick up the effing radio and tell her what he thought he was playing at.

He realized she must be right up on the top road with binoculars to be able to see him so clearly. She'd gone to some trouble to spy on him.

'I told you not to go near the edge.' Her shout crackled through the radio. 'And don't you dare get out of that cab! Pick up the radio, Billy! Now!'

She hadn't told him not to go near the edge; she hadn't actually said it.

Climbing down, he barely felt the sharp tang of the sea breeze. It was as though he'd been wrapped in an invisible cocoon. Her words meant nothing; the trouble he'd be in for ignoring her meant nothing. He stumbled as he picked his way over the churned earth. His half hand reached out to the giant plough blades to balance him as he walked back.

He noted that even she with her swearing couldn't compete with the fat plume of scavenging gulls clustered round the metal tail of the tractor. They shrieked at his incursion, flapping out of his way, then swooping back in, screaming defiance as he walked a few paces beyond the reach of the machinery and stopped to stare into the split earth.

Bit of an old toy, he tried to tell himself. Nothing more.

But the old man had kept him off this stretch for years, and she with her swearing had taken the trouble to come and spy on him.

No cocoon around him as he stumbled back towards the cab, tears coursing down his cheeks, following the deep lines etched into his skin. And I've not cried since I were a nipper, he thought.

Static from the radio began to balance and then drown out the squabbling seabirds. She was still at it. Effing this ... effing that ... What you effing crying for, Billy?

That was a keen pair of binoculars she was using wherever she'd stationed herself.

As he reached into the cab and picked up not the radio receiver but his mobile, the swearing took on an air of disbelief.

'Billy! Pick up the fucking radio! Billy ...'

And he did. He opened the channel so she could hear his call.

# chapter two

Detective Superintendent Martyn Webber elbowed his way through the door letting it slam behind him, no thought for the fabric of the elderly building, no thought for anything but a child's body buried out in the back of beyond. A mix of emotions fought for dominance; angry irritation bubbling to the surface as he glared round the room. Three of the four desks were unoccupied. The lone DC, Ayaan Ahmed, stared so hard at his computer screen he might be watching a disaster unfold. This deference to his bad temper annoyed Webber all the more, especially as he saw the flush creep up Ahmed's neck.

'Found either of the Cochrans yet?' he barked.

'Uh … not yet.' The young DC jumped and stared up at him, half rising from his chair.

Webber wasn't without sympathy for the lad, dumped into this shambles of a makeshift team already hanging in limbo between strategic restructuring and the sabre sweep of public sector cuts, but he wasn't in a sympathetic mood. It didn't help that the lad seemed frozen half-standing.

'Get on with it then,' he snapped, releasing Ahmed to sink back into his chair and grab the phone. 'How long does it take to track down a woman and an 80-year-old guy? They're not even on the run, for heaven's sake?'

'We're not talking ancient history, then?' The voice of retired Detective Chief Superintendent Len Klein came from behind him, its owner making a gentler entrance to the office, shrugging his way out of a heavy overcoat as he stepped in.

Webber spun round to stare at the man who'd been his boss years ago, and met the ghost of a raised eyebrow that admonished him for his bad mood. He felt a grin break across his face as he realised he'd counted on running into Len Klein; and that a part of his ill-temper was born when he'd arrived to find Klein, now on civilian hours, had left for the week. He returned his ex-governor's look, the acknowledgement of shared experience, and stepped forward to slap him on the shoulder in welcome. 'Good to see you, Len, but how come you're here? You civvies can just close the door on these things; enjoy your weekends.'

'Believe me, Martyn, when the grapevine started buzzing about a body ... a kid's body at that ... I kept my head down and I was off the second that clock hit five. We were just settling down with a DVD when word came that you'd been shipped in from York. I thought I'd just pop back and see how you'd shaped up; see if any of the lessons I taught you ever made it through that thick skull of yours.'

Webber smiled. *Ignore loose horses*; that had been the first piece of advice Klein had ever given him. It must be twenty years ago. They'd been heading past York racecourse after one of the big meetings when the animal, head held high, trailing bits of leather, trotted across their path. 'Ignore it,' Klein had ordered, 'or you'll be all day hanging on to the thing.' He and Klein had been a good team in the old days, but if they were to work together now, their roles would be reversed. He wondered if he could get his head round being Klein's boss. Or indeed how Klein would feel about working under one of his own protégés. They hadn't parted on good terms when Klein had left York but if any bitterness remained Klein would have stayed away.

'How's Julia?' Webber asked.

'I'm sure she'd have had your balls for earrings if I'd not had my tea, but she doesn't mind watching a film on her own, so you're safe for now.'

'Give her my best.' Webber smiled. Julia Klein had clearly mellowed to be letting her husband off the leash so easily. If the row had been just between him and Klein, they'd have made up years before, but both Melinda Webber and Julia Klein had got their teeth into it, leaving a seam of resentment that had never healed, neither husbands nor wives recapturing the easy friendship they'd once shared. Hearing the click of the phone behind him, Webber turned back to Ahmed. The rough edge had gone from his tone as he asked, 'Any luck?'

Webber noted that Ahmed, probably in response to the exchange with Klein, had swung to the far extreme of being totally relaxed in his company. The young DC wobbled his hand in a yes-and-no gesture and said, 'I've tracked down the father, but I'm afraid it looks like the daughter's taken off.'

'What …? Why?' Through his bewilderment, Webber felt anger rise. He hadn't come across from York just to find this was all to do with the Cochrans. He was here on the assumption it wasn't.

'From the top, son,' said Len Klein. 'Who've you talked to? What have they said?'

Webber made himself sit on the edge of the desk as he listened to Ahmed talk them through his calls, chipping in with a query when the DC's focus threatened to shift to Klein. Glad though he'd be to have Klein on the team, he would make it crystal clear from the start who was in charge.

A promising young guy, Ahmed, he thought as he listened. If he'd been on hand when the initial call came in, they might have saved some time. Uniform had gone out to the Cochrans' farm after bringing Billy Judd in, but found it deserted. Judd, hysterical and not making sense, had been no help. Nor had the neighbours because there weren't any. The place was in the middle of nowhere. Ahmed, using brains not brawn, had called up an old woman who'd run the post office in the nearest village. Though long retired, she knew the Cochrans, father and daughter, and had directed Ahmed to the pub where old man Cochran spent his Friday nights. Ahmed had already called up the landlord to make sure of his man and then let uniform know. More concerning was that he'd learnt the pub was awash with gossip about a body they should know nothing about. The man who was due to marry Cochran's daughter was there, 'face like thunder' with a wild tale of Janice Cochran having reneged on their plans to go to town and get wasted. Instead, she'd raked through cupboards for her passport saying she had to catch the ferry to go and see mates in Amsterdam. Ahmed, a model of efficiency, had already put in the necessary calls to their East Yorkshire colleagues. 'We might have missed them at the dock in Hull,' he told Webber, 'but they won't be out of the Humber. We'll get her if she's on it.'

'Good work,' said Webber, moving towards the whiteboard where there hung half a dozen photographs of Billy Judd's find partly obscured by the deep ruts in the earth. Side by side, held to the shiny surface by magnets, they told him nothing. It was always the same. New photographs either horribly gruesome or uselessly bland held on to their secrets. It was the familiarity of having them there for days, weeks, sometimes months that turned them into old friends, took the edge off the awful images and allowed connections to spark. He looked back towards his two colleagues and blinked as a shaft of evening sunlight speared through a high window. The glimpse of a blood red sky reflected uncomfortably against his thoughts and emphasised the gloom deep within the room. 'Can we have some lights on? Does this godforsaken place run to electricity?'

Again, Klein's expression admonished him as Ahmed leapt up to turn on the lights.

'We were hoping for ancient history, Martyn. You know how it is?'

Webber nodded. He knew. He'd arrived at a station collectively holding its breath, praying that the pathologist would declare the Cochrans' field an ancient burial ground of the sort the Holderness clay threw up from time to time. He'd also arrived expecting to interview a young boy, having been told that the 'farm lad' who found it was in 'a bit of state'. The 'lad', Billy Judd, was knocking 80 and so hysterical at every attempt to talk about what had happened, Webber feared he'd have another death on his hands if he didn't tread carefully. He'd pulled a female officer off the desk to organise tea and sympathy in the hope Billy could be calmed to coherence.

Ahmed chipped in. 'It never looked likely, Len. The old guy was rabbiting on about flesh and blood. And just look.' He pointed to the photographs.

It jarred on Webber that the young DC treated Klein as an equal, but he wouldn't have known Klein in the job, just in his post-retirement role looking after the PCSOs. 'Looks like the so-called blood is probably paint,' he said, 'but it's a recent corpse. Poor little blighter.'

'You wonder though,' said Klein. 'Judd's been in farming all his life, I should think. Must have seen death a thousand times.' He nodded towards the board. 'What do we know about it?'

'We'll get more from the full post-mortem,' Webber told him, 'but we know she's a girl about eight or nine.'

'One of the plough blades sliced off the left arm,' Ahmed added. 'That's what's freaked Judd. He thinks he might have killed it.'

'Her, not it,' murmured Webber. 'Right, we need another go at Mr Judd. I want to know how word got out. Let's hope tea has a calming effect on him. He must have drunk the place dry by now.'

'Shall I join you, Martyn?' said Klein.

'Uh … no. Would you stay here and field calls, Len? And let me know as soon as we get either of the Cochrans in. Ayaan, you're with me.'

A tiny part of him wondered as he spoke whether Klein would simply laugh and pick up his coat, saying he hadn't come back to play office boy, and if there wasn't a proper job for him, he'd head back home to his wife. But he just said, 'I'll see if I can dig out any useful background on either of the Cochrans.'

Webber let out a tiny sigh of relief that there'd been no sign of resentment from Klein, but he hadn't chosen Ahmed simply to stamp his authority on the process. Ahmed had shown a useful feel for the players in this little drama.

Klein rubbed his hands together as though to warm them and strode across to the board where he pulled out his glasses and peered at the photographs. 'Poor little blighter,' he echoed Webber's words. 'Any idea who she is? Do we have any matching mispers? I can't see her face in any of these. In fact–' He stopped abruptly and turned to face Webber. 'Why have you been brought in, Martyn? Does someone think we can't cope over here?'

'It's not that.'

'Then what? Why don't these shots show her head?'

'There are no matching missing children reports. I know that because we looked into it two weeks ago. And they don't show her head because it's in York. That's why I'm here, Len. It's my case. We found her head two weeks ago.'

# chapter three

Webber stared through the glass at the lined face of Mr Cochran, sitting where Billy Judd had sat until ten minutes ago. Cochran leant back, ostensibly relaxed, another octogenarian, but this time anaesthetised by several pints of beer. Webber watched closely as Klein and the female officer who'd calmed Judd probed about the day's events. After eight decades, he thought, you must have things to hide, but were they of any interest? Cochran made no bones about having told Billy Judd to keep clear of that stretch. 'Like every year,' he'd added. 'Madness to go that close to the edge.' Webber believed him. He'd known from the off that Cochran couldn't be involved with the murdered girl.

The door behind him opened and the ghostly reflection of Ahmed's face, disembodied in the two-way mirror, hovered by Cochran's.

'I put Billy Judd in a cab,' Ahmed said. 'He's going to his niece in Cayton Bay.'

Webber nodded. Once he'd been sure of both Cochrans, he'd let Judd go. They'd had all they could from him and there were no stories he could spread that weren't already circulating in the east coast pubs.

'Are we going to Hull tonight, Guv?'

Webber shook his head as he smothered a yawn. First thing in the morning would be soon enough to drive down there to interview Janice Cochran. She'd made things easy for him by assaulting two ship's officers and one uniform as she'd been plucked from the Pride of Rotterdam on its way down the Humber estuary towards the sea.

A night in a cell might persuade her to spill whatever sordid secrets she hoarded.

He listened to Klein's questions, razor-sharp, delivered with a smile, and was glad he'd said nothing about the body's missing hands, probably cut by the plough blades and flung away from the makeshift grave. Severed hands would resonate badly, unearthing memories for Klein of his last big case; it must be a decade ago now. Klein had got his man, seen him behind bars, before accepting a divisional post over here in Scarborough to see out his last stretch before retirement. Webber hoped the hands would be found quickly and the unfortunate similarities would slip unnoticed under Klein's radar.

Cochran's initial wariness had evaporated and he'd drunk enough to be careless in his answers, but he was relaxed now, confident he was in the clear. Klein probed, but whatever Cochran was hiding – and he sure as hell was hiding something – Klein couldn't rattle him. Webber had seen enough. He was no longer interested. Two weeks ago, the girl's head left high and dry on receding flood waters had unleashed huge resources, the more so when a link popped up with a two-year old case 800 miles away in Geneva. Circumstantial evidence to start with but everything began to coalesce as they crammed a year's work into the two weeks following. They'd been so sure they had the killer in the crosshairs. One week ago, he seemed poised to lead them to the rest of the body. Yet, he hadn't. He'd somehow spirited the rest of her to the North Yorkshire coast. The crimes screamed recluse; events had begun to hint at accomplices, but Webber couldn't believe it to be anyone connected to the florid-faced man in front of Klein. He toyed with leaving Janice Cochran to his colleagues here and heading back to York, but the fact remained she'd taken off when Judd had unearthed the body, and her father's one moment of wariness had come when he'd been asked about her.

◉ ◉ ◉

It was a little after eight the next morning as Webber and Ahmed arrived on the outskirts of Hull and met their first traffic queue.

'It'll be chocka all the way in at this time,' said Ahmed, 'but don't worry, I got them to bring her to Tower Grange. We'll be there in five.'

Webber's hand had been poised to slap on the siren, but he held back at Ahmed's words. The guy was almost presciently efficient. He liked him better, the more he saw of him. As they slowed behind a tall van, Webber felt the vibration of his phone before its ringtone sounded. Slipping it from his pocket, he glanced at the screen and smiled. Carol Ennis was the pathologist who'd agreed to drop everything to get the earliest possible look at the body. It would be the continuation of a post-mortem she'd begun two weeks ago on the severed head, one that she still couldn't complete, not until they found the girl's hands.

'Speaker-phone,' he told Ahmed, passing the handset across.

'Carol?' he raised his voice to counter the rumble from the vehicles around them. 'Martyn here. What have you got for me?'

'Nothing official yet, but I thought you'd want a heads-up. I heard you were going to interview a suspect this morning.'

'No, I'm afraid not. Possibly a witness, but it's a long shot.'

'It looks like the killer used a knife. Cause of death probably a deep stab wound to the lower abdomen.'

'Any idea what sort of knife?'

'Long blade, I'd say, and wide.'

As the call ended, he heard Ahmed blow out a sigh. 'Who'd do that to a kid? Straight across, here, Guv, keep in the right hand lane. Nearly there.'

'God knows, but never stop asking the question, Ayaan. Never fall into thinking it's routine.'

As Webber pulled up outside the station, Ahmed pointed. 'That's one of the guys who got her off the ferry. Is it OK if I get a quick word?'

'Sure.' Webber left Ahmed to jog round the side of the building as he marched in and up to the desk to introduce himself.

He learnt that Janice Cochran was already waiting with the duty solicitor in an interview room. 'Christ! She's a firebrand. The lads said they couldn't hear the drunks fighting over the racket she made. You on your own? Shall I find someone to go in with you?'

Webber looked around but there was no sign of Ahmed. 'Yes, if you would.'

'Tommy! Get over here. DC Tommy Marchant, Guv. He'll look after you. Tommy, Detective Superintendent Martyn Webber, over from York for the Cochran woman.'

Marchant was a stocky man with an air of unruffled calm, older than Webber expected from his DC tag. He ambled over to join them. 'We'll need flak jackets for this one.' He offered his hand which Webber took in a brief handshake.

'Let's get moving,' Webber snapped. 'I've no time to waste.'

Janice looked bleary-eyed and dishevelled. She pushed out her lower lip in a sulky pout as they entered the room. The duty solicitor, sitting next to her, was a slight woman who cast a nervous glance at Janice as Webber and Marchant sat down. Glancing at the clock, Webber clicked on the recording equipment and announced the interview underway. Janice spat out a 'Yeah,' to his query as to whether she understood she was still under caution.

His opening questions were innocuous enough, but met with blank hostility. Janice 'knew nowt', and had 'nowt to say'. Beneath the surface, Webber seethed with frustration, but to Janice he showed only the face of someone content to sit here and interview her all day and all night. Bit by bit, he chipped away at her brittle anger, making sufficient headway to pull out an admission that she ran her father's farm.

'And where were you off to on that ferry last night?'

'See me mates. I often go. No law against it, is there?'

Webber wondered how many trips would show up if he were to

order an audit, which he wasn't about to do.

'And what was in that holdall you took with you?'

Her head shot up; she glared venom at him. 'I never did. You're making that up.'

'Your fiancé told us you did,' Marchant put in mildly.

Webber saw Janice deflate. It had been a well-timed intervention, though not an entirely truthful one. The information had come second hand from Janice's father and the pub landlord who'd spoken to Ahmed. And where had Ahmed got to, anyway?

'Huh! What does he know?' Janice slumped back into the chair.

Not enough to steer clear of you, thought Webber, but before he could ask his next question, the door opened and Ahmed looked in. 'I need a word, Guv.'

Janice heaved a theatrical sigh and rolled her eyes heavenwards. Webber suspended the interview, smiled at Janice and left the room pulling the door closed gently behind him. Had he slapped Janice hard and slammed out, he felt it would have been better for his blood pressure, but he closed his eyes for a second and took in a couple of deep breaths before turning to his colleague.

'You need to see this, Guv.' Ahmed all but pulled him down the corridor. 'I chased up the port and the ship last night. They were really pissed with her. She did real damage. In the posh bar, too, so they were keen to nail her. Look what they've got.'

'Just tell me, Ayaan. No guessing games. I'm not in the mood.'

But Ahmed rushed to a desk and spun the monitor away from the group clustered round watching it, and faced it towards Webber. 'They sent this through from the CCTV. Hang on, it's just after this.'

Webber watched the narrow walkway, dusk throwing a filmy curtain over the image. A couple walked into view, swaying as the ship lurched. The man grabbed the handrail; the woman's hand went to her head as a gust tipped her hat askew and they wobbled out of range of the camera.

'Now,' said Ahmed. 'Look.'

The resolution wasn't great, but the lone figure was unmistakeably Janice Cochran, a holdall in one hand, fighting to make her way along as her hair blew across her face. She threw a quick glance behind her, ripped open the bag's zip and shook it wildly over the rail. Webber leant close to peer at the image. Wads of cloth and paper sailed out, some whipping back to hit Janice who tore them aside, and in amongst the flurry something flew free of the ship and vanished out of shot.

'I'll replay it.' Ahmed used the mouse pointer to grab the slider and pulled the video back. Again, Webber watched Janice empty her holdall over the edge and he cursed. In the fraction of a second as the object broke free of its encompassing wads of paper and cloth, he caught the unmistakeable glint of a blade. A long wide blade.

# chapter four

........................................................

Webber and Ahmed stood side by side looking out across the Humber. The tang of salt and seaweed swept in off the estuary making them screw up their eyes against the sharpness of the breeze. For no good reason except that he wanted to chase away the image of that small broken body, Webber's thoughts turned to his ex-boss whose retirement home lay close to this same crumbling coast albeit many miles further north. Before the row, he'd been Klein's confidante, had heard all about his wife's desire to retire to a bungalow by the sea. Klein had hated the idea to start with, but then all his energy, mental and physical, had been swallowed in one of those cases that every officer dreaded; a maniac snatching children off the street. Klein had seen the killer gaoled, but the stress took its toll, and within months he'd taken a post in Scarborough and moved with Julia to the coast. Webber wondered if Klein had returned to a civilian post to lay the ghosts of his final traumatic months in the job. If so, a child killing on his patch was the last thing he needed. He looked out again across the water. He wasn't short of reasons to want to wrap up this case quickly, but he'd add Klein to the list.

Somewhere, in the same swirling currents that destabilised the Kleins' retirement home, lay the knife Janice Cochran had thrown overboard. The image of her frantically flapping the holdall to empty it sat uncomfortably in Webber's head. He felt trapped by it. He couldn't hotfoot it back to York with that unresolved. He'd asked for a search of the ship on the off-chance the knife had flown back aboard lower down, except Janice had chosen her spot well. There'd been no lower deck for it to return to and even if it had stuck temporarily, the journey across the North Sea would have knocked it adrift. The thought depressed him. They were looking at the place she'd jettisoned it, but it might be out in the ocean by now.

'We can get an exact location for the ship from the time recorded on the CCTV,' Ahmed was saying, 'then we can …'

Webber let the young DC's voice wash over him, the words meaningless. He wasn't sure why he'd come out here except to get away from the confines of an unfamiliar station and the unvoiced resentment at his leaching their scarce resources to pluck Janice Cochran off the ferry. He'd faced the same silent annoyance in Scarborough when he'd ordered a search of the Cochran's farm. But he'd had no other choice, even though he was certain the Cochrans were a dead end. He should have brought Klein with him, not Ahmed. They'd have bounced ideas off each other, found a way to make sense of what had happened. But he didn't want Klein in Hull, getting involved, picking up gossip, raking over the embers of that long ago row. His history with Klein was just that; history. He shook it out of his head. For all the evidence, his gut knew it wasn't the Cochrans. It had never been the Cochrans. They were too stupid. He'd clocked that much in one brief encounter with each of them. But most murderers are stupid, said the voice in his head. It's why we catch them. Stupid, spur of the moment actions that leave a trail as wide as a highway.

'… you reckon, Guv? And shall I get on to a dive team?'

'What?' He turned his attention to Ahmed. 'No, no dive team.'

'But Guv, it's the murder weapon.'

He smiled as he shook his head, imagining the reaction of his Hull colleagues who had a home match and a Saturday night looming. 'It costs an arm and a leg to drag a small pond, Ayaan. Can you imagine what it'd cost to search this lot?'

'But Guv, it's a kid …' Webber listened as Ahmed's brain went into overdrive, listing gadgets and gizmos from underwater metal detectors and satellite tracking to public appeals to raise money to conduct the search.

'Let's work out if it's the murder weapon first. If it is, there'll be forensic at the Cochran's place. How's your geometry?' He laughed at the look on Ahmed's face, knowing the lad thought him off his head. It was good to laugh; it had been a good idea to come out to this spot, away from the bustle of the city, just to be able to relax a little. 'Get the stills. Get some exact measurements from the ship; length of that stretch of rail, that sort of thing and we'll get as near as dammit the size and shape of the blade she chucked out there.'

'Match it with the pathology, you mean?'

'Right, and I don't have to bust my budget on a pointless search. Now, there's someone else I want to interview informally. While we're on the way back, I want you to ring and get them to get this woman in. A Miss Andrew.' He busied himself with the car keys, to avoid looking Ahmed in the eye as he handed the business card across.

'A private investigator?' Webber heard the disbelief in Ahmed's voice.

'I'm not going to employ her. Her firm was involved in a missing child case. I want to make sure there's no link.'

'But all missing children are logged. There's nothing to match–'

'Just organise it, Ayaan,' Webber snapped, giving Ahmed a glare as he twisted in his seat to reverse the car round to set off back into Hull. He maintained a stony silence to avoid the interrogation Ahmed was clearly itching to give him. The fact was that although the Hull private investigation firm had taken on a missing child case, he knew the child had turned up. He also knew it would take an impersonal request to persuade her to come in to the station. If he phoned her himself, she'd play games.

Back at base, he put in a Skype call to his team in York, hoping to hear they'd unearthed something concrete. They had a single promising suspect; a man who'd started as one name on a long list of people present in a key location at a particular time. Then research into his movements had begun to flag him present in other places at other times. It was all circumstantial but when they'd heard he was on his way to York, the adrenaline had begun to pump. He had no legitimate business interests to take him so far north. Would he lead them to the murder site … to the rest of the body? He'd done neither. He'd wandered around York like a tourist, spent a couple of nights in a B&B, then headed back south and stayed there. A week later the call had come from the North Yorkshire coast about Billy Judd's find. If their prime suspect had been to that stretch of coast, he'd done so before he was under surveillance, and if he hadn't, he was rapidly losing his prime status.

When the desk sergeant came to tell him his visitor had arrived, Webber nodded curtly. 'I'll be along in a minute.'

Then Ahmed was at his elbow. 'That case, Guv. The missing kid. I had a quick word with the PI. The kid turned up. It can't have anything to do with–'

'Have you worked out the dimensions of that knife yet?' Webber cut across him.

'No, Guv, I haven't had a chance yet, because–'

'Because you're too busy sticking your nose in everywhere. At least get your own jobs done first.' The knowledge he was being grossly unfair to Ahmed hardened the edge to his voice. He watched the young DC slink off and in his mind's eye saw Klein's face, reproving him. As he walked towards the interview room, he was aware of a background murmur. He didn't try to meet anyone's eye and was pretty sure he'd see nothing but glances sliding away if he tried.

As he opened the door, the woman who'd been standing with her back to him, turned. His gaze took in her willowy form, the imperious tilt of her head, the pout of her lip as she said, 'Detective Superintendent Webber. You wanted to see me.'

He eased the door closed behind him, but before it had quite clicked home, she marched up to him, pressed her body on to his and snaked her tongue between his lips. Desire flooded through him, overwhelming everything but the need to grab her, pull her close, return her kiss fiercely. In a moment of insanity he knew he just had to lock the door and he could have her right here on the edge of the desk, right in front of the mirror. She wouldn't care if they had an audience. But it was the thought that Ahmed might be the other side of the glass that pulled him up. Ahmed reporting back to Klein, who would take the gossip home to share with Julia … who had once been a friend and confidante of Webber's own wife back home in York looking after their baby, and who would find a way to get the bad news to where it would do the most damage.

Gripping his visitor's shoulders tightly, he moved her away. 'Uh … Miss Andrew.' It was a struggle to keep the breathlessness out of his tone. 'Christa. Thanks for coming in.'

He back heeled the door closed behind him and pushed her towards a seat the wrong side of the desk, while he sat facing the glass. They'd have crowded in there to watch, he'd lay money, but he could only pray there'd been no one there to start with. He threw a couple of bland pleasantries at her, barely conscious of what he was saying. At least this way round, they couldn't see her face, couldn't see the way she choreographed her responses with sultry glances, half smiles and the tip of her tongue tracing the line of her lips. She knew what she did to him and she revelled in it.

'One of your guys told me it was about that missing kid we looked into; that there might be a link with a missing girl. But our missing kid turned up and it was a boy anyway.'

Webber had to swallow against the dryness in his throat before he could respond. 'Yeah, it was some similarities in the case that made me think of it.' He couldn't concentrate. It was madness to have called her in here. He'd kidded himself that by bringing her in pseudo officially, then what he was going to do with her later would be less of a betrayal to Melinda; that it would just be something else the job had pushed him into rather than something he'd deliberately sought out. The trouble was that Christa Andrew had a way of getting into his head that drove out all caution and common sense. Not that it was his head calling the shots when she was within reach. He closed his eyes for a moment.

'I was across in York last weekend,' she was saying.

'Oh yeah?' He should have walked right in, shut off the glass panel, locked the door … let them think what they liked. Again, he breathed deeply, his gaze flicking to Christa's and away again as she taunted him, her expression saying she knew just what he was thinking.

'Yeah, I was catching up with an old friend who was in York for a couple of days. Annie Raymond. D'you know her? She's a private investigator, too. She used to work in Hull.'

He shook his head.

'Now, Martyn, if I'd just thought, I could have been in touch … introduced you. You could have told Annie all about your missing kid.'

'I don't think so, Christa. I'm not planning to employ you. I just …'

'Just wanted to see if I had anything you wanted, is that right?' He held her gaze, fighting to keep his expression uninterested. 'So, do you have suspect?' she went on. 'It sounds like a nasty business.'

'We're following a number of lines of enquiry.' He gave her the stock response and wondered how on earth to wrap up this conversation with any shred of dignity. It was crystal clear he'd brought her in for no good reason. The lads behind the glass must be pissing themselves.

'Bit of a wild goose chase that's brought you here, though, Martyn. I mean Janice Cochran's not a likely candidate, is she?'

Webber felt shock prickle his skin as his head shot up and he glared at the blank glass wall. If there were anyone there listening, let there be no mistake that he'd have their balls for leaking this. 'Where the hell did you get that, Christa?'

She gave a half-shrug, half-smile and raised her eyebrows in a wouldn't-you-like-to-know gesture. He was reminded that she could infuriate him just as much as she could excite him. 'Oh well, never mind,' she said. 'You're here now. I suppose you'll have to stick around a day or so.' She leant forward, resting her elbows on the desk, cupping her chin in her hands, holding his gaze, her eyes full of promises. 'Go on, tell me, Martyn. You've someone better than Janice Cochran in the frame, haven't you? Someone back in York, yeah? Hey …' She paused and tipped her head to one side for a moment in thought, then said. 'Don't tell me it's a guy called Damien Marks. That would be priceless.'

Webber stared at her. He hadn't talked to anyone about the case details. He supposed Klein or Ahmed might have been in touch with the incident room in York, but if so, why didn't he know about it? And even if someone had let Janice Cochran's name slip, they surely wouldn't have … He spoke through gritted teeth, his voice low, hard. 'What the fuck do you know about Damien Marks?'

Christa looked momentarily taken aback at his change in tone, then she shrugged again and laughed. 'He's the guy Annie Raymond was hired to follow. His wife thinks he's playing away. It's why Annie was in York.'

# chapter five

Webber emerged slowly from a deep sleep. For a second he felt amazement that baby Sam had slept right through. His mouth curved to a smile prior to turning towards Melinda with the intention of taking her in his arms. Then he was jerked fully awake by the unfamiliar give in the mattress and silky feel of the sheets. The morning light streamed through the uncurtained window. Automatically, he orientated himself in the unfamiliar space, letting out a groan as his back protested a night on too soft a mattress. The other side of the bed was empty but the pillow held the indentation of Christa's head and he could hear water running from the bathroom. Thoughts of home made him uncomfortable. He pushed them aside because he felt good … relaxed … buoyed up by a night with Christa. He needed someone like her now and again. It counteracted the shitty turns the job could take. And she meant nothing to him, no more than he meant to her. If he were honest, he knew she invested even less than he did in their relationship. She'd drop him like a hot brick if he were to retire or find himself in a less senior role. They were good for each other and he could handle the risk. It was no worse than the clandestine shots of hard liquor Klein tipped down his throat behind Julia's back.

His thoughts turned to the previous day, to how Ahmed had been completely gobsmacked that he'd come out of the interview with Christa with something concrete. The others hadn't been watching, hadn't even cared. He'd set Ahmed on to digging some info on Christa's mate, what was her name …? Annie Raymond.

It had been strange to see the atmosphere change when her name cropped up. They knew her. She'd worked in Hull some years ago. Knew of her anyway. They'd pointed Ahmed to a couple of officers who'd known her well. He was interested that they seemed to rate her, and wondered if it would be worth his time to interview this Raymond woman himself.

So Damien Marks's wife was having him followed. Christa said it was the usual suspicious spouse setup, the sort of thing that Christa and her lot did routinely. Was that really the reason? He'd kept his team clear of Marks's family but maybe it was time to get close. If she'd turned her husband over to a private eye, perhaps she'd talk to the police about her suspicions. He pulled the second pillow across under his head, watched out at a clear sky where a trio of gulls darted squabbling into view and he sighed. The tentacles of this enquiry reached ever further.

OK, Christa's mate worked in London, though there'd been precious little to find about this London firm. It was run by a woman called Pieternel; the sort of name that stuck, but she'd been invisible to an impromptu search and no one could remember her surname. He would make a call later, brief someone to go and have a word. Klein and Ahmed could be trusted to tie the loose ends with the Cochrans. On second thoughts, perhaps he'd leave that side of things with Klein and take Ahmed back to York. He'd be a useful addition to the team. A single hint of a link and he'd be right back, but there wouldn't be. The blasted Cochrans were playing some game of their own. He felt his fists clench as though to will Carol with her autopsy kit into finding enough for him to show that what Janice Cochran threw overboard was not the murder weapon; to snip off that loose end. But a bolt of frustration welled up. How could it not be the murder weapon? Janice Cochran had spied on Billy Judd and the moment he'd uncovered the body, she'd stashed the weapon and made for Hull. How could that be coincidence? It was what Ahmed was thinking. It was what they were all thinking.

Circumstantial, he'd said several times to a chorus of incredulous comment. Weird behaviour, suspicious, clearly indicative of a crime having been committed, but not this one. Whatever the Cochrans' role, it was no more than a bit part. He'd yet to tell Ahmed what the team in York already knew. This young girl probably wasn't the first victim, and if they didn't move fast he had a horrible feeling that she wouldn't be the last.

◉ ◉ ◉

Eleven year old Olivia marched up the hill, eyes forward, striding out enough to make believe she barely noticed Ryan's hand grasping her upper arm forcing her along. If she kept a fraction ahead, it was just as though she wanted to go up here, almost like he was her boyfriend. He wasn't, though, and she didn't even want him to be. He was Ryan, Year 7, a whole year older than her. Olivia hated him, really hated him. Before she'd only hated him in the way you do when someone you like won't like you back. She'd only told him about the ghost house because he wouldn't take any notice of her otherwise, but she wished she'd kept quiet.

The grass slapped wet against her trouser legs, the damp seeping through to her skin. Her mother would go mad if she came home all muddied again. Ryan was selfish, making them walk side by side so only one of them could fit in the narrow tyre track. She glanced down and saw it did him no good. His trouser bottoms were well muddy, too. Serve him right.

She hadn't talked since they'd got to the wild bit of the track. She'd meant to. Her plan had been to talk and talk, to scare Ryan enough that he'd change his mind, but he hadn't sounded scared and in the end she'd started to scare herself so she'd shut up.

The hedgerows began to close in. They had to scramble where it got steep. Leaves rustled like someone was the other side of the hawthorn. It had done the same thing the time she came here on her own. Now she heard it again she thought maybe it was because of the way the hedge had grown tall and tangled just here.

Ryan paused. He was scared now; he thought someone was following behind the hedge. She shut her mouth on 'It's OK, it did that before. It isn't anything,' because he deserved to be scared and it might be enough to turn him back. Only it wasn't. They arrived at the top of the rise.

Through the tall grasses, the house nestled in its bit of a hollow. If there was nothing there, Ryan would crow and tell everyone. They'd all be on at her for making things up. But in a sort of a way it would be worse if there was something. She was sort of sure she'd made it up … not quite made it up, but made it sound bigger than it was. She'd gilded it, that was it. Her Auntie Enn always told people she gilded things. Always gilding the lily, our Livy.

She was going to whisper, 'Over there … the well,' but he was already walking towards it, so she didn't say anything.

# chapter six

..........................................

Annie Raymond pulled into the side of the road as her phone buzzed an incoming call. She glanced at the number on the screen.

'Hi, Heidi. Thanks for getting back to me,' she said to Damien Marks's wife. 'I just wanted to let you know I'm out of range if he decides to go walkabout.'

'Why? How's he been during the week?'

'One odd trip last weekend. He went to York, not Chelmsford, and I might have found something up there. I'm on my way now to see someone.'

'Who is it? I knew it!' Heidi's voice snapped to attention.

'No, no. it's not a woman. I'm not really sure what it is. I'm trying to find out. While I was in York, I met someone I used to work with, a private investigator who works in Hull. Let me make some enquiries and I'll get back to you.'

Annie thought back to the weekend in York. Once she'd known Marks would stay a second night, she'd called Christa Andrew. They'd fallen into the habit of sharing coffee or a meal whenever Christa was in London or Annie travelled north. This time they'd established themselves in the Lighthorseman, an imposing pub on a corner site that overlooked the place Marks was staying. Annie had noted the word Chelmsford in the name of a nearby guest house. It fitted the model of inadequate alibis with which he equipped himself on his extra-curricular jaunts.

He'd been an easy target to follow as he'd wandered the city's streets, but she thanked heaven she hadn't dropped her guard once she realised she wasn't the only one tracking Marks.

It was professional suicide for a private investigator to step across the line into police territory. But it had given her a whole new perspective on her quarry. For the police to spare that level of resource, he was in bigger trouble than she'd dug out in her months of following him.

Later that night, she and Christa had seen the official surveillance team clock off when Marks was well settled in his B&B. And Christa had advised Annie to 'leave the bastard to it and get some sleep. You look all in'. Annie had smiled false acquiescence but resigned herself to a night in the car, cat-napping in sight of Marks's billet. Waiting and watching; two of the things that private and official investigation had in common. Marks had given her the slip late at night once before, and she wouldn't let him get away from her a second time.

Annie had worked for Heidi on and off for close on two years. Heidi had had no money to start with, only suspicions to stoke her determination to get to the bottom of what her husband was up to. She'd booked a single hour of Annie's time.

Annie had spent 50 minutes following Damien Marks to a conference venue. Before slipping in with the crowd, she'd taken a few shots of his car, particularly the front seats which were littered with documents. Inside, she'd seen him sign in, greet his colleagues and head off with the crowd to the main hall for the opening address. Watching the stragglers slip through the double doors into the big hall, she'd checked the time and decided Marks was probably on the level for today at least. He'd been on the phone throughout the drive, but she knew nothing to suggest his calls weren't above board.

On a hunch, she'd walked round the perimeter of the venue instead of straight to the car park. And there she'd seen Marks emerge from a back entrance. He'd marched to his car and sped off. If she hadn't had another job to go to, Annie might have given Heidi some free time and followed him further, but had had to content herself with watching him disappear.

'And no one was with him, no woman?' Heidi had asked when Annie met her later.

'He was on his own when he left, but …' Annie had shrugged. Who was to say where he'd headed, who he'd met or how long he'd stayed away? And that was it. Case closed and filed on an indeterminate result.

But within a fortnight Heidi was on the phone and money was no object. 'Things are looking up for the business,' she'd said. 'And I'm not having some other cow get her claws into his money.'

Since then, Annie had followed Damien Marks many hundreds of miles. And apart from one incident he'd been an easy target to track. That once had been when he'd slipped out from his hotel late at night during yet another of his interminable conference attendances and she had only spotted him by chance. Because he'd taken her unawares she hadn't been able to follow him and could only log a gap of four hours where she didn't know where he was.

That incident apart, the case had seemed a simple one after Annie had tied together the information she'd found from a number of background checks. Marks, a founding partner in the firm, had sold out his interest a year ago and become just another employee. His salary had plummeted accordingly. A man with business difficulties who kept the problems from his wife. He wasn't the first and Annie felt that Heidi would be a sympathetic spouse once over her anger at being kept in the dark.

'Sold out!' she'd screamed. 'But that business is our future.'

'Got out at the right time, I'd say,' Annie had showed her the paperwork she'd unearthed. There had been a speculative land deal in Eastern Europe a couple of years previously that could have netted millions, but the timing had been unfortunate, an economic downturn tangling with difficult local politics and bureaucracy.

The firm was now in serious decline, not looking to be a good bet for anyone's future.

Only a handful of people knew that Marks's new position was a result of his having sold out. It had taken Annie far longer than it should to work it out, but as far as she could tell no one had replaced him in his senior role. He had become one of the team of travelling ambassadors and salespeople.

'So where did the money go?' Heidi challenged her.

Annie sank back into the soft leather of the new settee in the Marks's living room. 'When we first met, you were struggling,' she pointed out. 'Then you splashed out on all this.' The furniture gleamed. Fresh flowers stood in a vase on the hearth, a voluptuous burst of colour against the designer tiles of the new fireplace. Annie knew Heidi well enough to know she was no more enthusiastic for housework than Annie herself. Hired help had polished this room to a showroom sheen. 'I suppose you had debts.'

Heidi nodded. 'All paid off. How much did he get?'

Annie passed across the sheaf of papers. 'Don't spend it like water,' she said. 'The firm's in a bad way.' She'd returned to the office to close the file again on a solid result.

There had been a gap of two weeks before Heidi's name reappeared in Annie's inbox. Heidi had been busy with a spreadsheet matching the dates of her husband's pay-out with his salary cut and with the face he presented to her.

*The money must have run out at about the time he told me the bizz was going through a bad patch. Has it picked up again? Has he had another pay-out? Can you check the firm's records? I can't work it out. See attached.*

After a moment's thought, Annie had emailed back.

*Why don't you ask him? I'm sure he'll be relieved to come clean about it.*

Heidi had answered by phone. 'I know what you said. I've almost had it out with him a hundred times, but something keeps holding me back. There's just … Oh, I don't know. Please, just check the money for me. I want to know if it makes sense.'

Annie had given the task to a junior colleague and had heaved a weary sigh when he reported back to her that it didn't quite tally. Again she had picked up the phone to Heidi. 'It sort of makes sense,' she'd said. 'At the time you reckon the money ran out you struggled for a couple of months on just his new salary. Then he had a rise. Quite a hefty rise.' She read out the figures her colleague had teased from the secretive firm.

'Oh, well,' Heidi had sounded upbeat. 'That explains it. They fobbed him off with a nothing job. All that travelling. And he's shown them what he's made of.'

'Well ...' Annie had hesitated. Marks had been drawing his huge salary for almost a year but there was nothing in the records to justify it.

'But still ...' Heidi's voice had taken on a tentative air. 'I don't know. Look, maybe I'm being stupid, but there's something. I want you to follow him for a few more weeks. Everywhere he goes when he's not at home. I'll email you his itinerary.'

'Heidi, I've been on his coattails for months. If anything was going on, I'd have found it. The only woman he's met more than once was an elderly estate agent called Price.'

'Can't you bug his phone?'

'Not legally, no.'

'Please, one more month. And don't fob me off with one of your juniors. I want you on it.'

So Annie had retrieved the file, taken a deep breath and hoped this really would be the end of it. One more confirmation that her husband was doing nothing untoward except keeping business secrets from her and Heidi would have to make the decision: have it out with him or accept the situation and make the best of it.

Then Marks had set off for Chelmsford, saying that late meetings would mean overnight stays, and had led Annie 200 miles north to York.

After what she'd seen there, Annie had already strayed from her remit. She'd let Marks head off for home unaccompanied and had turned to past contacts. From the years she'd worked in Yorkshire in her early career, she knew two detectives who were based in York and decided to look them up. They'd been pleased enough to see her and to share a couple of beers, but had skilfully avoided her fishing about Marks. The one thing of interest was a Detective Superintendent Webber whose name was mentioned ostensibly at random soon after Annie had alluded to Marks.

Webber, Annie was told, had had contact with a private investigator working for the Thompsons in Hull. 'You used to work for the Thompsons. Do you know her? Christa Andrew.'

'When I left, they were on their own. They were going to get in temps, not employ anyone else full time.' It was the exact truth, though it masked the fact that it had been because of Annie that Christa Andrew had originally travelled up from London to help out on a case in Hull. And it had come as a huge surprise to everyone, not least Christa, that she'd cleaned up her act and stayed on.

Annie had turned the conversation, not wanting to embroider the lie, but had squirrelled away the knowledge that the big cheese in York, the one whose name had popped up when she'd allowed Damien Marks's name to slip out, was a Detective Superintendent called Webber and that he was someone known to Christa.

It might have been coincidence that Webber's name had been the one to crop up in almost the same breath as Marks's, but she didn't think so. She'd intercepted the ghost of a glance between her two companions and knew that her name was going to be carried back to the heart of whatever it was that was going on. That was fine. She knew where the line lay between private and official investigation and she would cooperate as and when she should. But before anyone caught up with her, she intended to find Christa and quiz her about Webber.

◉ ◉ ◉

'Martyn, come on. You said you'd give me a hand. They'll be here in an hour.'

Webber looked round to give his wife a smile. She stood in the doorway, the baby on her hip. 'Sure. Just give me a minute. I need to look something up.' He tipped his thumb at the computer as he spoke and wrinkled his nose at them. His son's face broke into a grin and he squirmed in his mother's arms.

'Fine.' She marched across and plonked the boy in his lap. 'Sam can help you. Then get his bath run, will you?'

Webber gave his son a conspiratorial wink and settled him on his knee facing the screen. 'I'm after a couple of private detectives, Sam. Are you going to help me find out about them?'

Sam gurgled assent and banged his fists on the keyboard. As he eased him out of range, Webber blew on to his son's neck making him squeal. 'There's a turn up,' he murmured. The database was telling him that Annie Raymond's father had been in the job; a sergeant in the Strathclyde force and not that long retired. 'I wonder what turned her to the dark side,' he said. The baby stared up into his face.

'Now, how about some images.' He manoeuvred the mouse. An anonymous avatar popped up. It had been the same everywhere. It was annoying not to get a picture of her, but he'd dug out something of her history. The online record was thin on detail but she seemed straightforward.

'Is Sam in the bath yet?' The question came as a shout from the kitchen, but he clicked away from the current screen as he heard Melinda's voice. He didn't want to be seen gathering intel on female PIs.

'On our way,' he shouted back, pausing to see if she would come and check.

Sam had caught hold of a wire to one of the machine's small speakers and was pulling it across the table. While he was occupied, Webber had another quick recce for Annie Raymond's boss.

Pieternel, she was called. He didn't have a surname but he'd match her via the firm and what he'd dug out on Raymond.

It should have been the work of seconds, but again he kept running up against glitches in the databases. And no images. He supposed PIs would work hard to keep their faces under wraps. All that covert surveillance. But he couldn't seem to get a handle on her at all. He needed her full name. Everything he accessed to get to the firm had Raymond's name on it. OK, this Pieternel woman had to be licensed or she couldn't operate. He'd get her from work tomorrow.

His mind went back to Friday evening. It had been good to see Len Klein again. Klein's last big case before he took that sideways move to Scarborough and then retired had been a child murder; multiple murders it had turned out. He hugged Sam closer. Sam struggled in his arms, tugging at the wire. The victims of Klein's old case had been waifs and strays, children who were almost feral existing at the edges of society. He'd had Klein's old case file out after the severed head had washed up, half wondering about copycats and recalling something about anniversary killings. He'd found a stash of press cuttings, one that went into gruesome detail about the injuries the killer had inflicted. He remembered stalling on it, puzzled; hadn't recalled Klein's team dealing with anything like this, yet it was familiar … then he'd seen it was older than the rest, way older, harking back to different murders in a different age. Murders he knew quite a lot about. He'd been volunteered to act as an expert witness for a documentary put together by a local TV company. He'd thought it would be interesting, something different, but mainly it had been tedium. The highlight had been to spar with Christa Andrew, another expert on the panel, though he'd found her greatest expertise was nothing relevant to historical crime. He pushed her out of his head. She wasn't a distraction he needed tonight.

Someone in Klein's team must have considered the idea of a copycat of those faraway crimes, but the old reports had talked about hands severed and then crossed on the victims' chests. *Extra fingers make extra hands for extra prayers.* Severed hands had figured in Klein's case, maybe that was why they'd taken a look at this older one, but the killer hadn't done anything ritualistic, simply stashed the body parts in a sack that some poor sod of a CSI had unearthed when Klein finally ran his man to ground.

Klein's notes had dismissed the anniversary theory as journalistic sensationalism and the similarities to Webber's own case had been superficial. He'd talked it through with Chief Superintendent Farrar. Klein had got his man, eventually. A recluse with no family who'd died in prison just a couple of years ago. It must have brought it all back to Klein when he'd heard the child had been decapitated. Webber looked down at his son who had the speaker grasped in both chubby fists and was chewing on it with fierce concentration. Klein's case was over ten years ago. Webber hadn't been part of his team, but he should have been more sensitive when he'd talked to Klein on Friday.

With tighter policing techniques these days, he hoped to see this culprit behind bars more speedily than Klein's who, with shades of the Yorkshire Ripper enquiry, had been the subject of more than one interview before becoming a viable suspect. That wouldn't happen this time, not on his watch.

He looked again at the database listings on the screen, then logged out of all the systems and shut down the machine. Sam squirmed in his arms and began to grizzle. The speaker dropped to the floor with a thud. Webber pulled the baby towards him and blew into the soft skin of his neck turning his gripes to giggles. He grinned at his son as he stood up, throwing him lightly into the air – proper shouts of laughter now.

Melinda's voice, 'Martyn, I can hear the water isn't running. If you don't get a move on you'll still be bathing Sam when they arrive. And don't expect me to come and take over.'

'Come on, Sam,' Webber said. 'The Governor's getting stroppy.'

# chapter seven

Just over a fortnight after her first ever trip to the city, Annie was back in York. She passed the guest house where Damien Marks had stayed, drove down Fishergate and onto the A19. Christa had given her a series of can't-miss-it landmarks to guide her through the outskirts, the final one being a pub behind which she would find a police station. And there, Christa had been fairly certain, she would find Detective Superintendent Webber.

Not wanting to park her car where it would be clocked on the police CCTV, she turned down by a small pharmacy into a street of imposing three-storey townhouses. She walked back towards the main road, flanked by the Georgian red brick walls that seemed a feature of this end of York.

Her meeting with Christa had convinced her that she had better find Webber before he came to find her. Apparently Webber had paid a visit to Hull after the discovery of the child's body that had been hitting the news all week.

Her favoured theory was that Marks had got himself too close to someone in whom the York police were interested. Perhaps they expected the mysterious someone to go to meet Marks and that was why they had watched him. Not closely enough, though.

Christa for some unfathomable reason had mentioned both Annie's and Marks's names to Webber, and Webber had reacted angrily. Annie had felt a measure of empathy with the policeman. She herself had experienced a burst of annoyance at Christa's loose tongue. If she'd ever had the option to back away quietly, it was gone now.

The official team would be coming to find her and it would be foolish to be on the back foot when the inevitable encounter came.

A paved path between stretches of manicured grass led the way to a square brick building. It was busy inside. She'd thought her entrance would create a mini drama, something that counted as an event in amongst the everyday bustle of a Monday morning. But no one paid her any attention. She took her place in the queue, half listening to the stream of queries and problems that were laid in front of the unflappable middle-aged constable at the desk.

'My name's Annie Raymond. I'm a private investigator. I'd like to see Detective Superintendent Webber,' she told him when her turn came. 'It's to do with Damien Marks.'

Again she experienced a minor let-down that her words elicited no reaction other than a mechanical response. She was invited to take a seat whilst her message was conveyed. She sat watching the tide of people in and out, feeling the rush of air as the door opened and closed. Some minutes later she heard her name called and went back to the desk.

'Miss Raymond?' said a tall female officer, looking Annie up-and-down with a piercing gaze.

Annie nodded and smiled trying to read the woman, wondering for a moment if she might be quizzed here in amongst the hubbub of the reception area, but the woman said, 'Would you come this way?' and opened a door leading to a staircase, as she added, 'Detective Superintendent Webber will see you in the incident room.'

Annie weighed these words. Seeing the incident room would be useful. She would at least get to know the nature of the incident in which Marks had somehow become tangled.

The woman pulled open the door to a large open-plan office. At once the noise hit Annie's ears. The space teemed with activity; the underlying hum of conversation punctuated with an occasional shout; the quiet clatter of keyboards; the buzz of dozens of fans keeping internal electronics cool. Squinting through the crowd, the woman at Annie's side said, 'That's Webber over there,' as she pointed to a large man leaning across a desk, one hand resting on the surface as he and a second man studied a computer screen.

'Just stay put here,' the woman told her. 'He'll be with you in a mo. Have a seat.' She waved to a small plastic chair and then strode off.

Annie took in the bustle, the people, the activity. She'd been held carefully at the edge of it and her amazement must have been plain, but at the same time her instincts kicked in. See everything. Gather information. Not all of the whiteboards had their backs to her. She caught a glimpse here and there of photographs even though there was no paperwork close enough to read. Realization seeped in. This wasn't the noise and clamour of a general office. This was the incident room. She was looking at the deployment of massive resources. Her heart plummeted to her feet. Whatever Damien Marks was involved in, no matter how peripherally, it was huge, it was nasty, and he was in big trouble.

# chapter eight

Webber was aware of the door opening. He'd been waiting for it. He and Ahmed watched the window on their screen that showed the view from the surveillance camera. Annie Raymond was a small blonde woman, nothing like he imagined a colleague of Christa's would be. A bit of a nonentity. Ahmed too had tried to look her up and failed to find any images online. Webber's snap judgment was that she would be one of the smug ones, but not too bright. He doubted she would have anything for him but he had to try. And if he'd underestimated her, all the better, she might be able to help. Frustration welled up in him at their lack of progress. Marks's trip to York had seemed such a promising development. It had to tie him in somehow, given all the other evidence, yet he'd done nothing except a bit of sightseeing and a few enquiries in estate agents that were proving to be innocuous. But if Marks's real mission had been put off by a stupid private investigator clumping along behind him, Webber was prepared to roast her over an open fire.

It was at his explicit orders that she was left stranded at the periphery of the action and ignored. He wanted her to experience the feel of a real operation in progress to highlight her inadequacy. As he watched, her discomfort was obvious. She stepped sideways and slid on to the plastic chair placed deliberately to seat her full on to the camera. He studied her features, saw tension rising within her as she fidgeted, glancing around as she tried to slide the chair backwards to be less obviously stranded in the middle of an open space. Do what you like, he thought, as he saw her half rise, awkwardly struggling out of her jacket. You're still in the frame.

'This is the detail from the second estate agent,' said a voice in his ear and, keeping the camera's image in his peripheral vision, he turned his attention to more important matters.

◉ ◉ ◉

Just stay put, the woman had told her. Annie looked around as she sat obediently on the flimsy chair. She clocked the camera but didn't look directly at it. The chair, an uncomfortable distance from the wall, stranded her like an exhibit on show. So they wanted her to feel awkward and ignored, did they? Fine. She could act awkward and ignored with the best of them. She fidgeted a little, whilst taking in the bustle and absorbing the layout of the space. The attention of the people who'd been noticeably ignoring her was beginning to stray for real. They were busy. Webber's stare had not once turned her way, but in case that screen he studied with his colleague was the other end of the camera lens trained on her face, she kept her head lowered, squirmed just a little, made heavy weather of struggling out of her jacket, and watched for her chance.

She reached in her pocket, pulled out her phone and fiddled with it without registering anything on the screen. A quick glance showed her people intent on their own tasks, uninterested in her. Webber and his colleague had been joined by a third man, their attention wandering from the computer monitor.

She moved the chair just a little as she turned to drape her jacket in an untidy bundle over the back of it, and slid smoothly downward as she did so, ducking away from the camera's beady eye, and moving quickly towards a bank of filing cabinets to intercept a middle-aged woman with half a dozen cardboard wallet files tucked under her arm. Annie knew she had no more than seconds, but a focused question might pull out some useful information. She had to try because she didn't think she'd get anywhere close to the heart of this operation again.

Putting on a bit of a smile as she rested her hand on the open drawer, she ventured a 'Hi' of greeting, then had to jerk back as the cabinet drawer slammed shut within a whisker of slicing her fingers. The woman thrust her face uncomfortably close to Annie's and hissed, 'If you think no one here knows who you are, think again. I do and I'm a friend of Melinda's. They have a young baby. You should be ashamed of yourself.' With that she marched away.

Annie froze in shock at the woman's attack. What? Who was Melinda? What baby? Was this about the Hull case? Then she pushed aside the woman's hostility – something to worry about later – and turned her gaze sharply towards Webber. The three men were still talking, not looking her way. She had a few seconds more. The whiteboard nestling close to a nearby desk provided a degree of cover. In two strides she was beside it, her fingers sliding forward to flip over the top page of a stack of paper. It was a photocopy of a newspaper cutting, a very old one. The writing was faded and hard to read. She leant close staring intently trying to make sense of the words.

*Child killing … Brutal slaying …*

A sudden movement stood the hairs at the back of her neck to attention. Her mouth dried. She'd focused on the page, forgotten to watch her back.

◉ ◉ ◉

Webber stared aghast. He'd kept the CCTV image at the edge of his field of vision as he'd listened to the detail about Marks's visit to the estate agent. Then something snapped his attention back. That wasn't the woman sitting in the chair, it was just her coat.

He stared across the wide space. For a moment he couldn't see her at all, but then watched in horror at the sight of her turning papers on a desk. He didn't know where to target his anger. At himself for the lapse or those who were nearest to her, or the Raymond woman herself for outwitting him. Had he really underestimated her or was she just a nosy cow like most in her profession?

Within seconds he was across the room, crowding her, pleased to see her start with the shock of his sudden appearance, a guilty flush creeping across her face as she whipped her hand away from the paperwork.

One thing was for sure, he wanted everything she knew about Marks as quickly as possible so he could be rid of her. Now he'd spooked her, he would follow up with the sort of threats that PIs hated to hear, being always in fear of seeing their licences revoked.

'What the hell do you think you're doing?' he snapped, wondering if she would answer with stumbling apologies or defensive justification. In either case, he was ready to ride roughshod over her.

'You want to know about Damien Marks.' Her tone neither acknowledged nor challenged his authority, but simply ignored it. It took him aback. The part of him that wanted to jump down her throat for her unauthorised prying suddenly felt petty. She was right. Marks was the priority. When he didn't speak immediately, she said, 'I clocked your guys following him, a man and two women outside that restaurant down by the river.' She held up her phone so he could see the photograph.

He was surprised at that. He'd sent a good team after Marks. OK, he would keep her here long enough for a proper interview. Maybe she would have something for him after all. Deliberately he lightened his tone. 'You're based in London aren't you?' As she nodded, he went on, 'We could have sent you Marks's itinerary and saved you a 400 mile round trip. It wasn't very interesting.'

At the look she gave him, Webber felt the crawl of something over his skin. His vague wondering about whether he'd underestimated this woman took a sudden turn into solid certainty. It was as though she'd arrived in disguise, yet he knew that all she'd used to fool him was his own preconceptions. Before he caught the sense of her words, he was raising his hand to call Ahmed over.

'No, you couldn't,' Annie Raymond told him. 'Because he didn't do anything out of the ordinary until almost 3 hours after your lot clocked off.'

# chapter nine

Annie found herself outside the square brick building, the turmoil of what she'd heard leaving no solid impression of the steps that had brought her down from her interview with Webber. She took a quick glance back and then strode away, wanting to feel distance between herself and what she'd seen. He'd wanted to shock her at the enormity of it and he'd succeeded, but he'd also wanted every last detail she had on Damien Marks and there'd been no choice but to tell him everything he asked for, because if Damien Marks were involved in this in any way, she had no legitimate reason, professional or private, to keep it from him.

The main road was quiet now, the morning rush hour gone. Annie walked across, heading for the side street where she'd parked her car. At one point, Webber had appeared to trust her; he'd handed her snippets of information he hadn't needed to; asked her to keep them to herself. She assumed he was testing her, seeing how much her promised confidentiality was worth, but wasn't sure how he thought he'd get to know if she spilled the beans, which she intended to do as soon as she could find space to report back to her senior partner. Every word of the morning's events would go to Pieternel.

The only time she'd held back was when he'd pushed for information on the company. 'You have to go to my senior partner for anything on her or the firm,' she'd told him, proffering her card. 'Ring that number and ask for Pieternel. If she's not there, she'll get back to you.'

'Pieternel who?'

'Anything on her or the firm, you'll have to ask her.'

Webber had given her a hard stare then turned to grilling her on Damien Marks; his movements; how long she'd been following him; where he'd gone and why. There were certain dates he'd homed in on and really turned up the heat. She hadn't been on Marks's heels on every occasion Webber wanted to know about but those she had, Webber had pressed for a second-by-second account.

She'd challenged him on being disappointed in her answers. 'It's as though you want to fit the evidence to show that he was involved in this killing. He might have nothing to do with it.'

'Someone did it,' Webber had shot back. 'I want to find out who and I want them in custody before they do it again.'

Their eyes had met briefly and for a moment shared some common ground. If Heidi's husband had done this, Annie too wanted nothing more than to see him locked away. But he wasn't involved. He couldn't be involved. She and Heidi between them couldn't have missed something as big as this.

What now? She couldn't report this to Heidi. What would she say? There's a brutal child killer out there. Damien was in some of the wrong places at the wrong times. They're putting two and two together and seem to think they're close to four.

But what about Christa? Annie wanted a confidante closer to hand, but Webber knew Christa, and Christa had a loose tongue. He'd asked about 'the Thompson Agency' and 'that woman who works for them' fishing, Annie thought, for how well she knew them herself. Webber had interviewed Christa when he'd been in Hull. Christa had told her it was about a missing child case that the Thompsons had taken on. 'It's nothing,' Christa had said. 'Our case was a boy. He turned up.' Having at first dismissed the idea of a link between Webber's interest in Marks and the child killing that had brought him to Hull, Annie now knew better. Her next move was to get back to Christa and find out all she knew.

Half a dozen customers lounged over their newspapers or chatted quietly. Christa stood at the bar watching the barman pull on the handle to deliver their creamy beers. At the far side of the room Annie squirmed to get comfortable on the hard leather seat, gagging for a good bitter after her drive over from York to Hull.

She wanted information that Christa would probably give her willingly, but a drink would oil the wheels. She gave her a smile as she returned with two brimming glasses.

'So you found him OK?' Christa said. 'I thought that's where he'd be.'

'Yes, I ended up in the interrogation suite for the best part of two hours. Where do you know him from? Did he used to work in Hull?'

Christa shook her head. 'It was a TV programme. I got the Thompsons involved in this documentary not long after I came to work for them. If you'd stuck around a few more months, you could have been in it, too. Great for business. Crazed Killers of Yesteryear, something like that. I was the expert PI, telling them how a private investigator would have gone about things a hundred years ago.'

Annie narrowed her eyes. 'What do you know about the history of private investigation?'

Christa shrugged. 'They had a researcher. And they had Webber. He was the copper with the interest in old crimes. They said the chemistry between us worked well. What I didn't know, I made up. No one seemed to mind.'

Annie had to bite down on a moment of resentment. Christa was just a chancer who'd landed up in the profession; it wasn't lifelong ambition that had brought her here, as it had Annie. She tipped her glass savouring the smoothness of the liquid as she listened to Christa expand on her plans to digitize the whole of the Thompsons' archive and throw out the rows of filing cabinets that had gathered dust for years. 'Most of the old cases are done and gone, thank God.' It was a good idea. Annie would never have been able to persuade the sisters into anything as radical, but then she'd never managed to develop such an easy relationship with them as Christa had.

Annie swept her tongue over her upper lip removing the foamy moustache. 'He's a prickly character, isn't he, Webber? I feel like I've done a few rounds in a boxing ring.'

'Yeah,' Christa barked out a short laugh. 'He's a bit of a weirdo.'

Weirdo wasn't the word Annie would have used, but now Christa was off again about how she'd persuaded the Thompsons to shell out for a specialist firm to come in and cart out all their old paper records for confidential disposal. She seemed strangely uncurious about Annie's meeting in York. 'Anyway,' she broke into a gap in Christa's recital. 'You know the case Webber wanted to see you about when he was over here?'

'That was nothing to do with anything.'

'Yes, but it was–'

'It was nothing, Annie. Our missing kid was a boy who turned up months ago. Webber was clutching at straws, that's all.'

Annie hid her surprise. She hadn't expected Christa to get defensive over an old case. 'So how are the Thompsons?' she said, changing tack. 'You seem to have them well in line.'

'Yeah, they're good. Need a bit of pushing to spend money sometimes, but we're doing OK.'

'I'll call in and say hello. Seems a shame not to touch base when I'm this close.' And while I'm there, she added silently, you're going to show me that case file.

# chapter ten

Annie picked her way past the graffiti-covered remains of a corrugated iron fence. She'd expected to find a traveller site, but beyond the fence lay an expanse of bare earth strewn with shards of wood and rubble, its perimeter marked with concrete blocks and bits of flapping ribbon inscribed, Keep Off. Three figures in hard hats headed across from the far side, packing away some kind of measuring equipment as they walked.

It had been a thin file. A couple of sheets of paper and a contract signed Syeira Franklin in a round childish hand. Christa and Syeira had met twice, the second time to close the case because Syeira had no money.

'No money!' Annie had been appalled. 'You closed a missing child case because she had no money?'

'He wasn't missing, Annie. His father had him. And anyway, I did chase her up a few days after that. I rang and spoke to her. He'd brought the boy back. She didn't want anything to do with me. What was I supposed to do?'

Christa had been uncomfortable. She knew she'd skimped on the job. Sometimes, it wasn't just the money. Annie had let it pass, but had been determined to suss out the detail for herself. The file was painfully thin on useful data. The mobile number Christa had used was no longer live. Christa didn't think Syeira had been married to the boy's father, but hadn't discovered his full name. In the file he was simply Will. Precious little detail on the child, either. Syeira hadn't wanted to tell Christa anything, not even a name; she'd just wanted to know how much the job would cost. If Annie had known this at the time, she'd have asked Webber, but now assumed there'd been uncertainty over the sex of the murdered child as her body turned up bit by bit. She could surmise from his initial interest that Christa's missing boy must have been about eight years old at the time he disappeared. And the address Christa had written down had turned out to be this derelict wasteland.

The three overall-clad figures were close enough that Annie could distinguish their comments as they came closer. 'If isn't fit with last one ...' 'Are we to t'right 'ere or to t'left?' '... I aren't sure ...' She identified accents from Hull, from further south in Yorkshire, maybe Sheffield, and from Eastern Europe, possibly Latvia.

It was clear she had waited to speak to them and she moved forward expecting some acknowledgement. As they swapped light banter and laughed, Annie realised they would walk right past her without a word or glance. She stepped forward into their path and said, 'Hi.'

'Nowt for you here, love.' They didn't break stride, didn't look at her, just brushed her aside and carried on talking to each other.

'Oy!' said Annie, annoyed. 'I want a word.'

At that they stopped and faced her. 'If you're after causing trouble, we'll have the police out. Is that what you want?'

'What? No! I just want to ask you about this site. I'm looking for someone who used to live here.'

'Ah, he promise marry. And he done runner?'

Annie kept a grip on her anger. She spoke in measured tones. 'No. I'm looking for information about someone who used to live here. I'm a private investigator.'

'Oh, right, you shoulda said.' And there was a subtle shift in their body language from admonishing a recalcitrant child to allowing her into their adult bubble to talk. 'If it's bad debts you're after, you've your work cut out. They're long gone.'

'Gone where?'

'Back where they come from, let's 'ope.'

It was unclear whether they didn't know or simply didn't care enough to think about it. 'It's not a bad debt,' she told them, hoping to jolt them out of their indifference. 'It's a missing child.'

'Bloody 'ell!' 'Stole child?' 'When …?' 'The bastards!' '… you get police …'

'No!' Annie looked from one to the other of the flushed faces in front of her and jerked her thumb over her shoulder indicating the cleared site. 'One of their children went missing.'

'Oh right … one of them … you could try t'Council. They're t'ones who moved 'em on.'

And although a level of impersonal sympathy remained in their voices, the fire about the missing child died as quickly as it had flared up. One of them … It didn't matter anymore.

Annie watched the trio walk towards their van, chatting, forgetting all about her. She looked back at the barren earth, the concrete blocks placed to deny vehicle access. Across the street., a river of brightly dressed children burst out of a single storey building on a rising tide of voices and spread themselves around a fenced and tarmacked yard. The two adults amongst the throng moved to and fro, attracting clusters of children who gathered around them and then scattered. Batons appeared, swinging in the air, shrieks matching the striking of balls that traced high arcs, some clanging dangerously close to the top of the tall railings. Annie watched for a moment and then set off towards them. The missing child had been of school age.

◉ ◉ ◉

'The school secretary says she'll see you.' A young woman labelled Layla, assistant to Head of Year, ushered Annie along a deserted corridor. The cacophony outside became a muffled babble that permeated the building as a low continuous beat. Layla had come to unlock the door for her after an exchange by intercom. The air held an aftertaste of paper and ink, food and people, subtle but unmistakeably the smell of school. It took Annie back over the years, made her mind superimpose the walls of a gloomier, colder space. She glanced around. Maybe it was her adult eye that saw the contrast, but she didn't think her school had ever been this bright or welcoming, even though its doors hadn't been barred to visitors. The feel of a warm welcome died at the entrance to an office where a severe middle-aged woman labelled School Secretary looked her up and down, before chipping off a 'Thank-you, Layla,' to Annie's companion who then melted away. With the window behind her, the woman sat in a position of power, sunlight glinting from her tight iron-grey curls.

'I understand you're making enquiries about a family from the traveller site.'

'Yes, I'm trying to trace a couple who lived there. Their child went missing for a while. That is, I don't know if they both lived there. Syeira Franklin and Will. Only I don't have his surname. Their son would have been eight or nine when ...' Seeing the woman about to interrupt, Annie hurried on, 'All I wanted to know ...'

'I couldn't poss–'

They spoke over each other and both stopped, the woman's attention snapping to something over Annie's shoulder. 'What are you doing, Layla?'

'Just getting the workbooks.' Annie caught a glimpse of Layla stretching to a high shelf in a cupboard in the corridor outside the room.

'All I really want to know is that the child's safe.'

'I can't possibly give out information to anyone who walks in off the street.'

'No, no, of course. Um ... I just wanted to be sure that ... I've just talked to someone working on the site who didn't know where the people had gone. Well ... he said maybe back where they'd come from, but they didn't seem to know where that was. I just wondered if someone here might have an idea.'

Abruptly, the woman stood up. 'Come with me,' she ordered, marching out of the room, moving so fast that Layla with her workbooks had to spring aside. Annie hurried in her wake. As they turned a corner, the upper halves of the walls became windows letting on to classrooms either side. Deserted now, their occupants racing about in the open air, the rooms showed signs of recent activity, tiny chairs askew, bits of paper, multi-coloured displays covering every wall.

'Here.' The woman threw open one of the doors and waved Annie towards a wall of badly drawn people, horses, carts and houses under a sign in a round childish hand, Gypsies and Travellers. 'We do this project every year with the Nightjars and Blue-tits classes. We teach them about ethnic travellers. Have you any idea the problems that traveller children have in schools, why so many of them leave without even being able to read and write? Well, it doesn't ... didn't ... happen here. Did you learn about different cultures when you were at school?'

'Uh ... yes, I think we did,' said Annie, surprised into a flash of memory. She didn't recall any traveller children, nor any racial tensions around skin colour or religion. 'We used to give the English kids a rough time,' she blurted out, adding, 'I was at school in Argyll.'

'Yes, well, most lessons miss out traveller culture. You wanted to find out where they'd gone? Where they can. Some will have joined family in other parts of the country. Others might have found other sites. But no, I doubt any will have gone back in the sense you meant. A good many who lived there have never had another home.'

'I don't know what I meant.' Annie felt compelled to defend herself against the scorn in the woman's voice. 'I was just repeating what the guy told me. Why were they evicted?'

'Planning permission turned down. It usually is for travellers, which leaves them in a bind because Councils are no longer obliged to provide sites. It's all there.' She pointed to a mock scroll filled with handwriting. 'The 1554 Egyptians Act ... the Caravan Sites Act ... the Public Order Act.'

Annie studied the display, paying no attention to its contents but looking for the names of the children who'd created it, hoping to see the surname Franklin so she could at least know the boy's name, but each piece of work was signed simply 'by the Nightjars' or 'by the Blue-tits'.

'Do you remember a child going missing?' Annie asked, watching carefully for any reaction. 'Syeira and Will's boy.'

'Aged eight or nine, did you say? And how long ago?'

'Within the last year.'

The woman nodded. 'I thought that's what you'd said.' Her voice hardened. 'Did you think someone would fall for a tall tale like that, give you information on the strength of it? There was no missing child. There wasn't even a traveller child of that age, boy or girl. I don't know what you're really after. I assume you're a journalist. No.' She held up her hand to stop Annie's denial. 'Not interested. I just hope you might have a think about what you've seen here.' She jabbed her finger at the display before turning abruptly to the door.

Annie followed, perplexed. The woman knew Syeira and Will she was sure, but she'd seen no reaction at all that led her to suspect the woman knew anything about the missing boy. Yet until recently this had been a settled community clearly with strong links to the school. Had Syeira been spinning a line to the Thompsons? And if so, why?

'Layla,' the woman called. 'See our visitor off the premises.'

Annie murmured a thank you to the school secretary's back as she disappeared into her office, then followed Layla who marched smartly in front of her making no attempt to continue the friendly chat they'd shared on the way in.

After punching in the code to unlock the outer door, Layla

stepped outside as if to make doubly certain Annie wouldn't try to sneak back in. Annie's thoughts were across the road at the cleared site. It was unlikely there'd be anything left to find, but it was always worth a proper look. She went to step away, only to feel a jolt of surprise as her arm was gripped tight.

'Syeira was my friend,' Layla hissed. 'I couldn't help her when she came back, but I want to help her now, only I don't know where she is. Do you know?'

'Here.' Annie pulled her away from the door, away from the windows. 'I'm trying to find her. Tell me about her. Quickly, before anyone comes.'

'This is where they went, but they ain't there now.'

Annie took the proffered scrap of paper, looked at a hastily scribbled address. 'This is where Syeira went with Will?'

'No, she never went nowhere with Will. That's where she went with her Mam when she left here. Near on ten years since.'

Annie ran through a lightening calculation. 'When Syeira was pregnant?'

'Will just went off. He didn't want nothing to do with her, not till he came back and said he had a right to his child. That's when she came to me for money, but I didn't have nothing to give her.'

Annie glanced up at the building. They were out of sight of prying eyes from the windows but someone would come looking for Layla soon. 'He took the child, didn't he?'

Layla nodded. 'She wanted to pay someone to go after him.'

'Did he bring him back?'

Layla looked puzzled.

'Did Will bring the boy back to Syeira?' Annie urged, knowing they were on borrowed time.

'The boy?' said Layla. 'There was no boy. Syeira's child was a girl. A dear little girl.'

# chapter eleven

Webber sat in his office, feeling hemmed in by the piles of paperwork around him; all the things he was supposedly dealing with that could never quite make the transition to done. People had been giving him a wide berth so he could assume his bad temper was showing. It was that woman, the PI from London, waltzing in here with her smug tale of Marks and his late night trip. What the hell sort of world was it when private investigators could spare the resource for round the clock surveillance and he couldn't?

And what had she actually told him? Basically that Marks had left his guesthouse for long enough to have driven to the North Yorkshire coast to dump the body. But when he'd finally sat her down to get every last detail, she'd told him Marks hadn't put a foot outside York the whole night.

The only good thing to come out of this case was that he'd repaired the breach in friendship with Klein. He wondered if the same might happen between Melinda and Julia. He'd never much liked Julia Klein but she and Mel used to be close. Like Mel said the other night, they might finally get to see Len and Julia's retirement home. He'd heard from others who'd visited that it was quite a grand place.

The clock showed him it was barely four. Did he stay here surrounded by useless paperwork or return to Hull and be on the spot to see what was happening there? He needed something to get rid of the tension inside him. Not that he'd let her availability be the deciding factor, but if he were to head for Hull, there was no harm in giving Christa a ring.

Olivia perched on the top bunk in her bedroom, hands tucked under her knees, facing the window. The window with the best view on the estate. That's how come she'd ended up with the loft conversion and not the bigger bedroom in the proper upstairs. Her mum had made it sound like something special when they'd had the conversation about Auntie Enn moving in.

She remembered saying, 'I'd really like to have the loft room. Can I? Auntie Enn can have my room. And there won't be so many stairs for her.'

Her dad had shaken his head and said, 'Oh, I don't know. I'll think it over.' But he and Mum had been in a good mood, laughing at something. Then he'd said, 'I've thought about it and I think Olivia's right. It'd be a good idea. But only if Mum says OK.' Her heart had sunk at that because her mum was bound to say no, but she hadn't. She'd still been laughing, and she'd said yes.

The excitement was still there deep inside; the thrill of a new place to explore, all her own. And a special blue shade round the light that made it glow like a space ship. Whenever she could, she left it on even when she wasn't here. You could see her light from up on the hill, a kind of shimmery blue that made the window look like it belonged to someone special. And a new bed because her old one wouldn't fit up the stairs to the loft. Not new from a shop. It was an old bunk bed from Auntie Enn's cellar. It didn't have a bottom bunk, but like her mum said, that made it better because she could have the underneath for a den. Her mum tacked a curtain across. Her friends thought it was cool but the truth was she didn't spend too much time under there when she was on her own. It was dark. She spent her time on the top bunk, at the edge so her head didn't hit the slopey bit of the ceiling. That's how come she got to know what her mum meant about it being the best view on the estate, out across the roofs of everyone else's houses and with a glimpse of that track out beyond.

Sitting here now, she couldn't help wondering what would have happened if her mum had said no and she'd stayed in her old bedroom. Auntie Enn wouldn't have spent time on the top bunk, that was for sure. She wasn't even very good at getting up out of a chair. So Auntie Enn wouldn't have watched that tantalizing glimpse of the track; wouldn't have seen the ghosts with their wobbly lights searching in the rain. That's how she'd thought of going up there in the first place; how she'd come to know about the ghost house at all. It had seemed such a good idea for getting Ryan to take notice of her. It was funny about ideas. The moment they worked, they weren't such good ideas after all.

She'd been going to tell Ryan her secret, but she hadn't told him at the finish. Because she could tell he was going to steal it and make it his own. He'd looked in the well. It wasn't her fault if he hadn't seen what she'd seen. She'd said to her mum that Ryan seemed to know all about it. And her mum had said, what the house on the hill? That's where his auntie works. Olivia hadn't known that. She wondered if it was Ryan's auntie, Mrs Fairclough, who had been at the school concert. The thought of Mrs Fairclough's horrid starey eyes made a shiver go right through her.

When Ryan had pulled out his torch and shone it down into the blackness, the water in the well had been so far down it had been lost in the dark. Olivia didn't think he could have seen the ghost, cos he didn't go funny or anything. She'd gone funny when she'd seen it and been on her own.

It had been the day after the rainstorm that flooded the school, that's why she'd been there. The water in the well had been proper boiling, like an angry beast fighting its way out. Then she'd seen the ghost. Anyway, she'd seen its hands. All grey and yukky with loads of fingers, they'd seemed to leap at her from the swirling water and she'd turned and run for her life before they could reach right out and pull her in.

Ryan had been back without her. He didn't know she could see that bit of the lane from her bedroom window, but she could and she'd seen him. She'd run out and chased after him, arriving at the top of the track so breathless she forgot to be scared. He wasn't at the well so she'd marched right up to the house. She'd heard voices. One of them sounded like it might have been Ryan's. That day she'd been cross enough that she almost pushed in through the door.

And now Ryan wanted her back in the secret and not to tell anyone else. Echoing her father, she'd told him she'd think it over.

'I'm still thinking it over,' she'd told Ryan again today. And strangely, he'd been OK with that. Ryan was waiting for her to decide.

As she sat on her bed thinking it over, an idea began to form. Someone had been in there talking. And even if it wasn't Ryan, it wasn't ghosts. Ghosts didn't talk, not normal talking like she'd heard. Her mum was right. Her mum said there weren't such things as ghosts. But Ryan didn't know it. She'd seen a frightened look in his eyes. He still thought there were ghosts.

Olivia smiled. The plan she'd had all that time ago was coming right in another way. It was Ryan wanting her to do stuff now, not the other way about. She was the one who could do the pushing around. When people saw that Ryan did what she wanted, they'd all have to do what she wanted. She tried to imagine being bossy with Ryan in front of her friends. It didn't really seem like she'd have the nerve or that he'd do anything except push her over and walk away. And yet … maybe she couldn't just do it, but she could sort of build it up in advance. Auntie Enn was always going on about building things up in advance. She'd tell Ryan she'd do what he wanted but only if he bought her a Kit Kat at break time and she'd tell everyone that she'd told Ryan to bring her a Kit Kat and they'd be amazed when he came right over with one.

Then she'd have to do what he wanted. That made her shiver a bit and have to sort of swallow because he wanted her to go back to the ghost house with him.

# chapter twelve

It was late afternoon before Annie arrived back in Hull.

'Did you find what you wanted?' Christa greeted her. 'What are you back here for?'

'This,' snapped Annie, marching to the filing cabinet, yanking open the drawer and pulling out Syeira's file.

'Hey! You can't walk in here and …'

'Just watch me!' Annie flicked through the few sheets, aware of Christa's glare and of footsteps from behind. Pat Thompson had hurried along at the sound of angry voices.

'Why didn't you follow this up?' Annie raised her voice to cut off the protest she saw on Pat's lips. 'And why didn't you pass anything on to that copper, Webber? This could be the murdered child.'

'No, it couldn't.' Christa was smiling now, sure of her ground. 'They're looking for a girl. That was a boy.'

'It wasn't,' shouted Annie. 'Syeira's child was a girl.' Even as she felt the anger boil inside her, she made herself take a mental step back to stare closely at both Christa and Pat. Their shock was for real. They hadn't known.

'But … She told me a boy … How …?' Christa floundered, lost for words.

'And what about when Webber came asking questions? What did you tell him? Why did he come to you about it? Why the hell did he let it go without checking?' She caught the ghost of a glance spear from Pat to Christa. 'What?' Annie rounded on Pat. 'What did you keep from him?'

Pat cleared her throat. 'I don't think our Detective Superintendent's attention was ever on the case. He's grown quite fond of his visits to Hull since his venture into television.'

'Yeah … well …' Christa spoke defensively. 'Not done us any harm, has it?'

'On the contrary.' Pat rolled her eyes heavenwards and turned to leave the room.

'What …?' Annie looked from one to the other of them, a memory surfacing of an angry face in a police station in York.

*If you think no one here knows who you are, think again. I do and I'm a friend of Melinda's. They have a young baby. You should be ashamed of yourself.*

'Oh for God's sake! You're shagging him.'

'So what? He's useful.' Christa laughed. 'I told you the chemistry worked.'

'I suppose Melinda's his wife.'

'How come you know so much? And what's up, you gone all moral in your old age?' Then the smile vanished from Christa's face as she stared at the file in Annie's hand. 'You're not serious? I told him we had a missing child case, but it just gave him an excuse to get in touch. He likes to mix it up. Likes to be on the edge of being caught the whole time. It'll all end in tears but I'll have bailed out by then. I told him it was a boy. It's what Syeira said to me. And that he'd been found. I did try, Annie. When she came back and said she'd no money, I didn't just chuck her out. I asked questions and that's when she told me the father had brought him back to her. I suppose … Thinking back, she wanted me off her back. She wasn't very convincing.' She looked down and blew out a sigh. 'What can we do?'

'For starters, do you have any way to find her? She and her mother have not been at the place that's on the file for years. They moved away when Syeira was pregnant. I've got the address where they moved but as far as I can tell, it's on an estate that's been bulldozed.'

'I'll check it out.' Christa held out her hand for the paper.

'Just find her, Christa. And don't hang about. I need to catch up on my day job. I'll use your back office, OK?'

Annie didn't wait for permission before marching through and shutting the door behind her. Christa hadn't done enough. A vulnerable young woman had come to her to report a missing child. She knew she should have done more. It was bad conscience that hadn't wanted Annie digging too deep, that and the affair with Webber. The stupid git, Annie thought angrily. She wasn't the one who'd missed the obvious. He had. Syeira's child was sure to be alive, well and maybe even with her parents, but someone should have checked. Webber, besotted by Christa, hadn't even glanced their way.

No one disturbed Annie in the cramped back office. She rang Heidi but there was no reply so she tried Pieternel and gave her an indignant account of Christa's carelessness. Mid-recital there was a tap at the door.

'Hang on,' Annie said to Pieternel as Christa put her head round.

'Syeira Franklin's mother died about two years ago,' Christa said. 'And it sounds like Syeira had a breakdown. She was taken to some kind of a unit. I'm assuming Castle Hill, but I haven't tracked her there yet.'

'And the child? She would have been taken into care, I suppose?'

Christa nodded. 'We'll find her, Annie.'

When she was alone again, she returned to her call. 'Pieternel, it looks like Christa's on to Syeira, but can you have a look for Will?'

A heavy sigh met her words. 'Annie, we can't right the world's wrongs all on our own. And we can't do it on fresh air. Who am I billing the work to, Heidi Marks?'

'No, we can't do that. It's …'

'It's her husband who's led you down this track. Why shouldn't she pay? Oh, all right then, but if I can't turn him up easily I'm not spending forever on it. You don't even have a surname, do you?' Another audible sigh. 'Give me what you've got.'

After ending the call, Annie sat in the encroaching gloom checking through her emails, not wanting to return to the bigger office in case it was taken to signal that her annoyance had subsided, but after half an hour, feeling cramped and uncomfortable, she heard the sing-song tone of Christa's mobile. That would do as an excuse and she pushed her way back through.

While Christa spoke into her phone, Annie picked up the thin file. She'd promised Layla that she'd get word to her when she found Syeira. She hoped it was a promise she'd be able to keep.

'Aw, jeez, that's terrible ...' Christa's voice cut across her thoughts. 'The poor kid. I had no idea.'

As Christa clicked off her phone, Annie's mobile rang. Pieternel. As Annie went to answer it, she looked the question at Christa.

'Syeira died,' Christa told her. 'Poor kid took an overdose. Almost a year ago.'

'Annie,' said Pieternel's voice in her ear. 'Does this sound like the right Will? I have him down as Will Stanley.' As Pieternel rattled out a list of dates and places, Annie mouthed at Christa, 'The daughter?'

Christa shook her head. 'There was no child with her.'

'Yes,' Annie told Pieternel, 'That's the one. Will Stanley? That didn't take you long. Where is he?'

Pieternel heaved a sigh. 'You're going off beam again, Annie. Getting into territory we won't be able to bill for. I've no intention of giving days to it.'

'No, no, I realise that, but it could be important–'

'I know it's important, Annie, that's why I'm getting back to you. Go to that detective superintendent tomorrow, give him whatever you've found and then we'll be wrapping up the Marks job. And is Will Stanley definitely the guy you're after?'

'Yes, where is he?' Annie asked again.

'He'd dead. He hanged himself. Just under a year ago.

# chapter thirteen

Annie jogged down the street, the beat of Hull's morning rush hour building around her. The physical exercise lightened her mood, but she couldn't shake off her irritation. She wanted to be cross with Pieternel for carping on about money all the time, but Pieternel's barbs about obsessional behaviour hit too close to home. So she focussed her annoyance on Webber instead. Why did he have to choose this morning to locate himself here? York would have been easier, but she was determined to get him face to face. It wasn't enough to tell him what she'd learnt. She had to know he'd listened. She jogged the last few metres to the blue and white rails that outlined the entrance and was taking the three stairs in a single stride when she saw Webber himself heading down the pavement away from her.

'Detective Superintendent Webber!'

As he turned at the sound of his name, she saw his eyes widen at the sight of her. She also saw he had his phone to his ear. He spoke into it and then summoned her with an impatient gesture. 'Come with me but I can only give you a minute.'

His tone was not hostile, just impersonal. Annie became aware they were under scrutiny from inside the blue-framed windows that enclosed the foyer. Her heart sank as she recognized two faces she'd known years ago when she'd been based in Hull. They were in amongst the general bustle and the wrong side of the glass for her to acknowledge them, and anyway, Webber was walking away, talking into his phone again. The body language, the covert glances all told the story. She remembered her reception in York. She was being labelled Webber's bit on the side and he either wasn't aware of it or didn't care.

◉ ◉ ◉

Webber felt both surprise and annoyance to see it was Annie Raymond who had called his name. To have taken the trouble to track him down here meant she'd found something else she wanted to pass on personally. His experience of her so far had shown a level of conscientiousness that made him uneasy. He didn't want her to be good at her job because much though he wanted a killer off the streets, he didn't want to hear that some two-bit amateur had found something else his team had missed.

Having spoken, he strode off down the street, throwing just one backward glance. He saw her hesitate and look towards the station before she turned to follow him. The rumour mill pulled in another gobbet of data to chew on. It was only a matter of time before the gossip filtered through to Ahmed and thence to Klein, and it would suit Webber just fine if the rumour that landed in Klein's lap was about Annie Raymond because he could deny that with both truth and conviction. He turned his attention back to his phone.

'Sorry, Carol. I was hoping for a chat but something's come up. Give me the headlines and I'll ring you later.'

He marched down the length of the building, crossing the road to the pedestrian walkway that skirted Queen's Gardens. He was aware that Annie Raymond caught up with him as they moved into the shadow of the Gosschalks building, its pastel shades and geometric contours rising above them, looking out over the waving branches of the trees in the park. He ignored her as he carried on towards the BBC building at the end of the block. It was the nearest café and he supposed he should offer the Raymond woman a drink as she'd come this far out of her way. In his ear, Carol Ennis was giving him an outline of the official report she was about to email across to the team. There were no new surprises. The body and head matched up. Just the hands left to find. They hadn't turned up in the churned soil at the cliff top. He thanked her briefly and said goodbye, muting his phone as he slipped it into his pocket.

'OK,' he said, giving his companion a brief look. 'Let's sit down.'

She stomped behind him through the revolving door and across to the small bar at the far end of the space. Annie Raymond shook her head impatiently as he turned to ask what she wanted to drink. Instead of sitting at one of the tables, she waited until he'd paid for his coffee and then ordered her own. He shrugged. She'd do just fine as cover.

'Have you identified the child yet?' she rapped out as they sat down.

'We're still–'

She spoke across him. 'Because I've been looking for a girl about the right age who went missing just over a year ago and I can't find her.'

Suddenly she had his full attention. 'Who?'

'You know who,' she snapped. 'The child Christa Andrew was hired to look for.'

'But that was a …' The words were automatic and faded as he spoke them. Christa's missing child. He'd never checked. But that was just a handy excuse, he wanted to say. It wasn't a serious lead. Even Ahmed had taken Christa's word that it was a boy and that he'd turned up. But he couldn't lay any blame on Ahmed. He'd as good as warned the lad off. His eyes focused again on the woman across the table, watched her sip hot coffee from the cardboard cup, saw the contempt in her face as she glared back at him.

'It was a girl,' she said.

'But why did Christa Andrew tell me it was a boy?'

'That's what the mother told her, for whatever reason, but it was a girl, taken by her father.'

'And ...? Maybe she's still with her father.' Webber's mind raced through scenarios.

'The father's dead,' Annie Raymond told him. 'The mother, too. Will Stanley and Syeira Franklin. Suicides. Not together, but within months of each other. I don't know why. Syeira's mother had died. She'd lost her child. She was alone. The guy, who knows? They were travellers, both of them.'

Her face blanked for a moment as though something had caught her attention. 'What?' he prompted.

'Nightjars and Blue-tits,' she murmured. He glanced at the window but saw only pigeons. She blinked and seemed to pull herself up. 'I saw some appalling statistics recently and it just struck me they'd been researched by very young children. The suicide rate amongst travellers is sky high at the best of times. With Syeira's mother gone, there was no family left to miss her. I don't know about Will Stanley. And I've no idea what happened to the child. All I know is that she disappeared and I don't have the resources to search for her. Here.' She slapped a page of notes on to the table in front of him. 'Names, dates, as far as I could find them. Look, for all I know, she's safe in a foster home somewhere, but if she didn't turn up again, I'm not sure there was anyone left to notice.'

Webber put out his hand for the paper, pulled in a deep breath and closed his eyes for a moment. Please God, let the girl be safe. He couldn't bear to have missed something this big. He'd never thought of his affair with Christa as a betrayal. Not really. And certainly not a betrayal of his own child. But what if it had turned into a betrayal of someone else's?

'Ah, there you are, Guv. Sorry to interrupt.'

And there was Ahmed standing over him, casting a sideways glance at Annie Raymond.

'What is it, Ayaan?' He was aware of Annie Raymond's discomfort, but happy to have her dangled as a red-herring, a rumour without foundation as he would later prove to Klein.

'You're not answering your phone, Guv. They've been trying to get you from York.'

He nodded. 'It's OK. The official report's in. I've already spoken to the pathologist.'

'No ... uh ...' Ahmed threw a meaningful look at Annie Raymond, who jumped to her feet with an alacrity that surprised Webber.

'Go ahead,' she said, walking away from them. 'I have a call to make.'

'I don't think that was all,' Ahmed said, his voice low. 'But there's something else. You know that Len went out to the Cochrans' place. He wanted to ... um ... I'm not sure really, but anyway ...'

'What? What's he found?' Webber prompted, impatience beginning to take hold.

'Uh ... There's another body.'

'What!' Webber's exclamation was loud enough to turn heads. He took a moment to pull himself together. This couldn't be happening. He knew from the hundreds of man-hours that had gone into this case that it couldn't be the Cochrans. They simply could not have got things that wrong. 'Another child?' he asked.

'No, an adult. A man. No ID as yet but it's early days. They've only just ...'

Webber felt relief flood through him. For form's sake, he summoned an expression of regret for the newly-found corpse, but it was OK. Somehow it was two unrelated cases colliding. It had to be. It happened from time to time. Maybe this would turn out to be the ancient burial they'd all hoped for the first time round.

Annie Raymond still lingered tactfully over by the window that looked into the recording studio. 'I'll come back with you now,' Webber told Ahmed as he clicked the York number into his phone.

'Martyn? Where've you been?' The excitement underlying the voice in his ear sent a shiver up his spine. 'You're gonna love this.' As he listened to the news they'd been bursting to tell him, he felt his shoulders relax and a smile curve his lips.

He gave Ahmed a grin and kept his voice low. 'We've got the bastard. At bloody last.'

Grabbing the notes Annie Raymond had left for him, he waved them in her direction as he and Ahmed hurried out. 'Thanks,' he called across.

◉ ◉ ◉

Annie Raymond watched them go, making sure she met the young guy's stare unflinchingly as he nodded a goodbye. Once they were out of sight, she took her hand away from the side of her head, abandoning her pretend call. Webber, the insensitive dolt, hadn't seemed to realise how their meeting must have looked. But even as she asked herself why she should care, she remembered the venom she'd met in York and felt a moment of unease.

Returning to the table she'd shared with Webber, she lifted her jacket from the chair. Taking a handful of coins from one of the pockets, she bought herself a refill and sat back down again. From the other jacket pocket she drew out her phone and clicked off the record function. Plugging in her earphones, she sat back to see what Webber and the young guy had had to say to each other.

# chapter fourteen

..................................................................................

Radio Humberside's morning show played on around Annie as she listened to the recording twice through, then relaxed as she looked out over the formal gardens with their central fountain, remembering the incredible sight of the water frozen in towering stalagmites one harsh winter. After a while, she took up her phone again and replayed it. The beat leaked through from the studio behind her as background first to the young guy and then Webber's voice in her ear.

*There's another body ... no, it's an adult ... Cochrans ...*

This stuff about the Cochrans was nothing to do with her, though Christa had mentioned the name. More worrying was the change in Webber's tone from impatience to triumph when he'd ended his call.

*We've got the bastard ...*

The other side of the conversation hadn't been audible. Annie had seen him lift the phone to his ear, but wasn't sure whether he'd made or received the call. Glancing through the darkened glass panels, she saw a man take off a set of giant headphones. Two figures entered the studio. They talked in mime and then sat as the song faded and the DJ replaced his headgear and began to speak, his words coming from the speakers in the public space.

Webber had taken her seriously. He would track down Syeira's daughter. Annie had been on Damien Marks's heels every step of the way at the time of the girl's disappearance. She'd made sure of that from the dates Layla had given her that matched those in

Christa's file. If Syeira's daughter and Webber's unidentified body were one and the same, Heidi's husband was out of the frame. Mission accomplished. It was a pity she hadn't found out why they'd targeted him in the first place, but if push came to shove, her surveillance records would be enough to clear him.

Her train of thought paused for a moment on the puzzle of why Damien Marks was being paid so much to be so busy doing so little. But she and Pieternel had no need to manufacture work these days. It was time to call a halt, time for Heidi to move on. And as though tuning in to her mood, her phone vibrated to life showing Heidi Marks's number on the screen.

'Annie, is that you?' Heidi sounded at the edge of panic. 'Where are you? I need you to come round.'

'I'm afraid I'm 200 miles away at the moment, but I'm on my way back.' Annie heard clattering behind Heidi's voice, a background rumble that she couldn't identify.

'200 miles! But Damien's here … was here. Why weren't you following him?' Although still wound up, Heidi kept her voice low.

'I'm in Yorkshire, Heidi, trying to find out what sort of trouble he might have been in with–'

'I know!' Heidi screeched. 'But you should have been here to stop them. What is it? What sort of trouble is he in? You said they were investigating a child's murder. That's nothing to do with Damien. You know that.' Annie heard the sound of knocking, and heard a woman's voice call out, 'Mrs Marks, are you OK? Could you come out here now?'

'I'm come out when I'm good and ready!' The volume of Heidi's bellow took Annie unawares. No mistaking the anger and upset in her voice now.

'What's going on?'

'They're searching the house,' Heidi's tone became dull, defeated. 'I've locked myself in the shed. I keep the mobile in here so Damien won't see that I've called you. How soon can you be here?'

Annie's mind raced across possibilities. What did she need to know right now? 'Heidi, where's Damien? You said he was there. Where is he now?'

'They took him away.'

'Did they arrest him?'

Heidi sighed. The knocking sounded again. 'Mrs Marks!' the voice called with less sympathy and more authority this time.

'Oh, I don't know. I suppose so.' Heidi said.

'Heidi, it's important.' Annie injected authority of her own into her words. 'Did they arrest him? Were you there? Did you hear them say they were arresting him?'

A pause. Then an irritable, 'Oh, all right. I'm coming out now.' And to Annie, 'Yes. Yes, they did. Damien Marks, I'm arresting you on suspicion ...'

'Suspicion of what, Heidi? It's important.'

'How should I know? I was screaming at them to leave him alone. They said ... I think they said ... They said suspicion of murder. Annie, he didn't kill anyone. He's not a child killer. You must know enough about him to know that.'

Annie found herself nodding. Though how could she know for sure? What did she really know about Damien Marks? Then she pulled in a breath. She had to be quick, to get what she needed from Heidi. 'Did they give a name? Did they say who?'

'Uh ... I don't know. No. No, they said person unknown or whatever the phrase is.'

There was one thing Annie knew for sure. At the time that Syeira's daughter had disappeared, Damien Marks hadn't had a glimmer of a window wide enough to go out and do murder, nor to dump a body hundreds of miles from his home. If Syeira's daughter were the victim, Damien was innocent.

'Heidi, listen to me. Go out to them. Cooperate. Tell them everything, including that you hired me. They know anyway. And yes, I know that Damien didn't kill the child.'

'Stick with me, Annie. You've got to help.'

'You need lawyers now, Heidi, not a private investigator.'

'I know, but I need you to keep doing what you're doing. Prove that he's innocent. They don't go this far … they don't arrest someone without good reason. He's been set up, Annie. It's those so-called colleagues of his. You've got to find out.'

'Heidi, they're going to break in if you don't go out. It's far better that you cooperate. Go on. I'm still on the job. I'll be down to see you as soon as I can. I'll ring, but I'm turning off my phone now because I'll be driving.' *And because I don't want to take their call just yet*, Annie added under her breath. 'Go on,' she urged.

'I don't know if I can face it, Annie.' The defeated tone was back.

'Go out there and be strong,' Annie ordered. 'Even if it's just an act. You're going to need all the practice you can get.'

Annie sat looking at her phone after ending the call. They'd be on to her soon enough wanting chapter and verse of her dealings with Heidi. In fact, it might be a good idea to move from this location just in case Webber sent someone for her.

*We've got the bastard …*

He must have been talking about Heidi's husband. And yet … The fact it was Webber talking implied it was the murdered child case, and she knew that wasn't Damien Marks. Could it be coincidence? Did Webber have other suspects and had Damien been arrested for something else altogether? She drew in a breath. Murder. Heidi had said suspicion of murder. What else could it be? She brushed off Heidi's suggestion about a set up by Damien's colleagues, but then paused. What were they paying him for? What was that huge hike in salary all about? It had happened before she'd started following him. She needed more information.

She took the long route back to the car park to avoid passing the police station, ignoring the vibration of incoming calls on her phone. At the car, she checked through the list. A number she didn't recognize and Pieternel. OK, Pieternel could handle things but she'd get on to her to let her know the latest as soon as she had a moment. It wasn't Pieternel's number she clicked into her phone.

'Christa, it's Annie. I need you to find something out for me.' She told Christa what the young guy had said to Webber about a man's body found at the Cochrans. 'Find out whatever you can for me, but in particular I want the date and time of the murder.'

Damien Marks might not be a child killer, but he hadn't been arrested for nothing.

# chapter fifteen

Friday morning, as she stood in Heidi Marks's kitchen waiting for the kettle to boil, Annie's mind turned to Christa. When they'd met on Wednesday afternoon, Christa had shown herself more than keen to find information for Annie and had immediately sought Webber out. Hearing he'd returned to York, Annie thought she'd have to wait, but a vitriolic series of text messages that same evening, beginning with 'You bitch, Martyn should be home with his wife,' indicated that Christa had caught up with Webber and was getting to work on him. Someone with access to case files, and thus her mobile phone number, had again added two and two to make five.

Thursday morning, Christa had waltzed into the Thompsons' office, looking dishevelled but cheerful. 'They've brought your guy to York, got him banged up there, did you know? And thanks for whatever you put them on to yesterday, Annie. Our Detective Super is a lot of fun when things are going well.'

Annie had shared a glance with Pat Thompson who sat at the desk flicking through files. 'Spare me, I've not had breakfast. I suppose you realize they think it's me he's playing away with.' She'd held out her phone so Christa could read the poisonous texts.

Christa laughed. 'You want to watch your back.'

This had elicited a guffaw from Pat. Trying to hide her annoyance, Annie had asked Christa what she'd found.

'Yeah, it's your guy,' Christa had told her. 'He killed the kid'

'No, he can't have. He …'

'They've found forensic linking him to the body.'

'I heard the body was dismembered,' Pat said.

Christa told them how the child's head had been found in York, followed two weeks later by the rest of the body in a field in North Yorkshire. 'Except the hands,' she'd ended. 'They're still looking for those.'

'They've worked bloody hard to keep that out of the news,' Pat commented. 'The papers just talk about a body found over here.'

'Luck to start with,' said Christa. 'No missing kids. They thought it was an ancient burial ground or something, and what with all the in-fighting over the flooding and whose fault it was … local elections and so on … it didn't get air time. They kept it under wraps once they found out. Not sure why. I've some stuff for you, Annie. It might be in there. I've not been through it.'

Hands? Annie had let Christa's words sink in. A headless body … hands cut off … Something had played at the back of her mind. She'd heard something like this before. And not so long ago. It wouldn't come. She'd turned back to Christa. 'It couldn't have been Damien Marks. I was on his heels when the girl disappeared, and ….'

'What girl?' Christa had asked. 'They've no ID yet.'

That had stopped Annie mid-sentence. Christa was right. Marks's innocence of that particular murder depended on the victim being Syeira and Will's daughter. 'There was another killing,' she'd said. 'He talked about the Cochrans. What was that about?'

Christa had brushed it aside. 'He wasn't interested. Said it was nothing to do with him. Just gave me a hard time for knowing about it.'

Now, watching the kettle boil in Heidi Marks's kitchen, Annie felt she was trying to outrun a tsunami, having dodged Webber's calls for a day and a half. She made the coffee and carried the tray carefully, balancing its matching cups and saucers as she shouldered open the door to the Marks's living room where Heidi sat, wringing her hands, darting worried glances towards the window. It was a measure of her distress that she'd let Annie loose in the kitchen at all.

'I hope you haven't left too much mess,' Heidi said fretfully. 'I can't seem to think straight. I don't know what's the matter with me.'

Annie gave her a sympathetic smile as she handed over the cup. 'It's shock,' she said. 'It's no wonder you feel out of sorts. Your husband was arrested on Wednesday and you've had your house turned upside down. Just be thankful his arrest has stayed under wraps … anyway, the link to Webber's case. You don't want the press banging on your door. Drink this.'

As Heidi's gaze slipped momentarily to the coffee cup in her hand, Annie glanced up over the woman's shoulder to the picture window. It framed a neat patch of lawn bordered by flowerbeds and a short stretch of thick bushy privet that obscured the path to the front door. No protection from the press siege that was sure to come. Annie herself was on borrowed time as far as Webber's team was concerned. They'd been trying to get to talk to her for a day and a half now. She'd kept them at bay with messages and missed calls, but would have to concede defeat soon. The ripples of the case had hit Yorkshire and bounced back as far as the London office. Pieternel had told her about a visit from detectives wanting the Marks' files, but had clearly had something else on her mind that she wouldn't mention on an open phone line.

'Coffee grounds all over the show, I suppose,' Heidi muttered. 'He's not a killer, Annie. He's not a child killer.'

'No, I know. He's no child killer.' Annie heard herself put emphasis on the word, child, and hurried on, 'Now drink your coffee. We need to talk.'

Annie sank into the cushions of the settee, eyeing the wide computer monitor on a desk beside her. Christa had come through with more information than she'd bargained on and her eyes ached with reading long documents on a tiny screen. It would be wonderful to hook up her phone and have a proper look. But for all she knew the Marks's living room was packed with tracers and had been recording the Marks's movements for months. She was thankful Heidi had kept their emails and calls to her own mobile, but it hardly mattered now. All the surveillance records would have to be handed over, even if Pieternel climbed on her high horse and demanded the correct seizure warrant before doing so.

'Tell me everything,' she said to Heidi, only half listening as she heard again the events of the visit, the arrest and the search.

Outside, a squabbling flock of birds tumbled from the bushes and out of sight. It would be a media pack before long. She should warn Heidi, see if she had somewhere to go for a few weeks.

But Heidi seemed to gain strength as she talked. The tearful edge to her voice was gone. In the middle of her indignant recital about the damage done to the floor in the airing cupboard, she tipped her cup and stared into its depths for a moment before getting to her feet. 'Refill?' She held out her hand for Annie's cup, then marched out. Annie didn't think she'd left any mess in the kitchen, though it all looked ragged from the search. Ironic, she thought, that she could carry out a fingertip search of almost anywhere without leaving a trace but people always seemed to know when she'd been in the kitchen. Maybe she should approach culinary matters in a more professional frame of mind.

She thought back to the day before, when Christa had told her what Webber had said. Feeling a sudden curiosity about him, Annie had asked, 'What's he like? I've met him twice. I thought he was cold … manipulative. What do his colleagues think of him?' If she had to conduct enquiries of her own, rekindle old contacts, it would be useful to know this stuff.

'They respect him,' Christa had said, 'but he's not much liked. Guys he works for want him behind his desk, not out and about so much. He's always carping about his Chief Super, a guy called Farrar. He tells me his team wants a governor who's not afraid of being hands-on. Not my impression, though. I think they see him as a meddler, not letting them get on with it. I wouldn't want to work for him. But he has a reputation for getting results.'

'And he has no conscience about leaking stuff to you?'

'Not at all.' Christa had given Annie a big smile. 'Not least because he's no idea he's doing it. He thinks the traffic's all the other way. Here, plug your phone in. I've some files for you.'

Even thinking back to what she'd seen downloaded on to her phone made Annie's heart lurch. She needed it either in her head or in some secure storage and not in her pocket. Collated via Christa's unique and illegal toolkit, she had a list of long jpeg files of varying legibility comprising a stream of documents, statements, emails, letters, that she had yet to study in detail. No way would she go anywhere near Webber while she had that phone on her.

Annie knew she'd spent enough time with Heidi. If Webber were desperate to find her, he might be receiving reports about her whereabouts right now. Was it paranoia to think Heidi might be under that level of surveillance? She ran her gaze all around. The computer monitor gleamed blackly at her. The TV reflected the light from the window.

A child's severed head found in York, washed up somewhere in the aftermath of a flash flood. The torso fifty miles away on the coast. And no hands. It matched something she'd seen recently. But what and where?

# chapter sixteen

Pieternel perched sideways in the window seat, her glance straying to the car park outside, where the smooth walls of a windmill dominated the tiny space. Annie saw her colleague peer up at the four latticed blades. She'd already asked, did it work or was it for show, and Annie had assured her she'd seen those huge sails turning years ago, during the time she'd lived in Hull. It was Pieternel's first visit to the city and Annie had chosen a venue not too central, not too out of the way. Somewhere no one, Webber included, would think to seek them out.

'The Mill,' she'd said. 'Holderness Road. You can't miss it.'

The fallout from what had been a routine surveillance of an errant husband had certainly caused ripples. The police had been in touch with Pieternel. Annie's work for Heidi Marks wasn't front and centre but it had given them an awkwardly high-profile bit part in Webber's case. Although, if that was all that bothered her colleague, Annie knew this meeting would be conducted by phone or Skype. Something had plucked Pieternel right out of her comfort zone and brought her 200 miles north. Annie had watched her every move from the moment she'd arrived ten minutes ago. She hadn't recognized the car, had barely recognized the woman climbing out of it. Poised, every nerve ending on alert, total awareness of everything and everyone around her. It was the old Pieternel re-emerging from the veneer of the successful businesswoman of recent years.

'Coffee?' she'd greeted her, heading inside without waiting for an answer. It was always coffee first.

'Tell me everything I don't know about the Marks case,' Pieternel said. 'The arrest and all that.'

Annie related all she knew then passed her mobile across to Pieternel to show her the set of files Christa had provided. Pieternel let out a sharp intake of breath as she flicked through, then handed back the phone. Annie knew that a loose cannon like Christa Andrew was the last thing she wanted to have to worry about.

'She hasn't kept copies, has she?'

Annie shook her head. 'She's not that daft. And it's not her case. She owed me ... Well, I guess she felt she owed someone for taking her eye off the ball. The missing kid.'

'And the guy she got them from, Webber, are you sure he doesn't know she has this stuff?'

'Hell, no. That's his job down the swanny. You don't know how slick Christa can be. She can hack into anything.'

'I do,' Pieternel commented dryly. 'I taught her.'

Annie nodded. She'd half forgotten that Christa had been Pieternel's contact long before she'd met Annie or had anything to do with the Thompsons. 'The thing is I want to analyse this stuff properly, get it in my head. I want to find out what they've got ... what they think they have on Damien Marks. It's in here somewhere. But I daren't carry it round with me and I daren't upload it anywhere.'

Pieternel patted the briefcase on the seat beside her. 'I've a laptop and tablet. We'll do it here. Just enough to get a handle on where we need to dig. A couple of hours, OK? I'll get the guys on it to do a proper job when I get back.'

The pub began to fill up as lunchtime approached. Cooking smells wafted over them, but they had the far corner to themselves. Annie plugged in the leads and began the file transfer, saying, 'I'll be relieved to delete it all off the phone.'

'That phone's not safe, Annie. I don't have the tools here to erase it properly.'

'Don't worry, I do. Webber's not getting his hands on this.' Annie imagined Webber's dour face becoming sourer as he listened to the recording she'd made of him.

'Before we go any further, Annie, there's something I need to tell you.'

Annie sat still and let her eye meet Pieternel's. Now she would learn what had been worth a 200 mile journey for a face to face meeting.

'Someone broke into the office two days ago.'

'Broke in?' Annie was surprised but it wasn't a first, despite Pieternel's ideas on security which were built around mistrust from every angle. Years ago, Annie had questioned the level of paranoia, but Pieternel had told her she'd been cornered once in her life and was determined it would never happen again. Even the serving of a seizure warrant the previous year hadn't been enough to uncover any but the superficial files Pieternel kept as a barrier against discovery of the detail she insisted her operatives recorded. A break-in – and Annie envisaged a shattered window and shards of glass across the floor – would have messed up the office but lost nothing significant.

'Someone was in the office after hours,' Pieternel said, holding Annie's gaze.

That had happened before, too. Employees slipping back in to use the office as social space when they'd been short of more convenient cover in a spell of bad weather. They'd been caught out by Pieternel's movement sensors. But nothing trivial had brought Pieternel all this way.

'I assumed it was a couple of the guys using the place to sleep. Saving themselves the trouble of a long trip home when they'd been out on the piss. Anyway, nothing disturbed. I was set to have a word, but I hadn't got round to it when your guy Webber sent his friends along. All very civilised, asking about your work with Mrs Marks and would we like to hand over the files. So I said, of course.

I mean not that they were giving me a choice. They were ready to camp out until we handed over what they wanted, but I'd no reason not to.'

'No, no, that's fine.' Annie read a slight defensiveness in Pieternel's tone. You didn't just hand over a colleague's files in the normal run of things, but this was different. 'Not a problem. It's a child killing. I wouldn't have expected you to do anything different.'

'Except they weren't there.'

Annie's gaze shot up to meet Pieternel's. 'Of course they were … I haven't …'

'Yeah, yeah … that was my first thought. Your piss-poor record keeping. There was nothing in the office. I had to download and print out a new set for them. Then of course they get interested in the computer and want to have a closer look at that.'

She knew Pieternel wasn't worried about losing a PC to officialdom; its hard drive was no more than an e-version of the superficial records that should have been printed and filed. Virtual cover for a complete electronic record held securely off site. But it wasn't her own slipshod record-keeping this time. The Marks's file was definitely up to date.

'Once I was rid of the boys in blue, I got our lot in my office and gave them the third degree about coming back in after hours. I assumed they'd brought people with them, had some sort of party and trashed stuff. But they swore it wasn't them. So we dug out the CCTV and we watched an empty office at night; empty the whole night through, that is, which was weird because my sensors had recorded someone in there. Then we spotted one of the screen savers, you know that one with the swans?'

Annie nodded.

'There were those swans at nine o'clock. There they still were at midnight. Then at two in the morning they flipped to a waterfall. Problem is it doesn't stay on those swans for five hours. It changes every few minutes. And it blanks out anyway after it's been idle long enough.'

Annie stiffened. Swans … waterfall … that wasn't right. 'It doesn't go from swans to waterfall. That isn't its sequence.'

'I know,' said Pieternel. 'That camera had been stopped for five hours. And someone had been using that PC right before they set the camera running again. Smooth as anything. The whole office had been done. Good and proper. A real professional job. They'd been everywhere, but we were running things under UV before we could catch a trace of them.'

Annie whistled softly. A professional job indeed.

'They missed the real stuff.' Pieternel paused and Annie read in her face that there'd been a moment when she hadn't been sure even of that. 'But they were good.'

'What else was missing,' Annie asked. 'Other than the Marks's files?'

'Yeah, well, that's the thing. Nothing. Heidi Marks wiped out of everywhere they could get at. Nothing else touched.'

'But why?' Incredulity and something close to fear fought for dominance in Annie's mind. That they'd somehow been caught up in a murder case, a child murder at that, was bad enough, but there was no angle that made sense of a clandestine raid on their offices. 'We've been cooperating. I might not have been easy to track down these last couple of days but I went to him in the first place. I handed over everything I had that might be relevant.'

'It didn't feel official to me, Annie, not unless we're talking Security Services. When Webber's team wanted the stuff, they walked in and asked. If they'd wanted it sooner, they could have walked in with a warrant.'

'They didn't get everything, though, did they?'

'They don't know that. And my hunch is that whoever came round fiddling with the cameras that night doesn't know they haven't got everything. What's worrying me is what I gave

Webber's guys. I handed over a copy of a file that someone thinks they disposed of a week ago. If it was anyone official, or pseudo official, they'll get to hear about it and they'll know they didn't get everything. They'll be back.'

'Why would it be official? Who gains by destroying the evidence that Marks is innocent?' Annie stopped abruptly. All questions had answers. It was just a case of having sufficient data and following the chain of logic. Pieternel briefly met her eye, then glanced at the table where her laptop and Annie's phone lay tethered by a short snake of a cable. They had to mine the results of Christa's hacking and hope to hit pay dirt, because without new information to divert it, the chain of logic was heading somewhere nasty.

# chapter seventeen

Annie felt Pieternel's eyes on her as she deleted the files from her phone. 'That won't do it, Annie. And I don't have the tools here to do a proper job on it.'

'I do, I told you. I'll see to it before we leave. Now let's have a look on a decent-sized screen.'

Pieternel disentangled the laptop and tablet, tucking away the leads in her pocket. Annie glanced round. The pub was still busy with lunchtime customers, but the bustle had not reached their corner. She picked up the tablet and sat back. Pieternel's stare was intent on the screen of the laptop. Annie knew Pieternel would be looking for a link between the Marks case and the raid on the office. Annie intended to focus her efforts on finding what Webber had on Damien Marks. This was better than a tiny phone screen but she felt frustration build. She wanted it printed and spread about on the tables, pinned to the walls, where she could flick her gaze from one document to another and seek out the links that must be there. She took a moment to envy Webber his incident room and his whiteboards, then she began to read.

For a long time, she went mechanically through what was in front of her, not analysing or evaluating just trying to give her brain the space to see a bigger picture emerge from mounds of detail. After a while, the format of the witness statements with their recognisable headers pushed themselves to the fore. Here was something she could use to make sense of the chronology.

'Tell me again, where did he go?' Pieternel's voice cut across her concentration. She looked up unsure for a moment if she'd been reading and absorbing this stuff for seconds or hours.

'Who? What have you found?'

'Damien Marks. The night you followed him in York after Webber's team clocked off.'

Annie thought back, experiencing the same puzzlement she'd felt at the time. 'He drove to an all-night services and sat there for hours drinking. Hot drinks, not alcohol. Then he went back to the guesthouse.'

'You told Webber?'

Annie nodded. 'He made me show him on a map.'

'Did you follow Marks inside?'

She shook her head. 'I was going to, but it was too empty and all guys. I'd have had a spotlight on me going in amongst them. I got my car up off the road so I could see him the whole time.'

'What did he do?'

'Not much. He spoke to the guy at the counter as he was served. He's café-guy in my notes. Then when he turned away from the counter he almost walked into a man queuing behind him and they did that brief nod and smile thing. I called him sorry-guy. But that was it. He didn't talk to anyone else. He wasn't even on his phone. He sat at a table, flicked through the menus and stuff. Every time anyone moved, he watched them, but then so did everyone else. It was the middle of the night. There was precious little to look at.'

'And you were there the whole time?'

Annie paused as she reran the scene in her mind. 'The guy he nearly bumped into, sorry-guy, didn't stay long. When he left, I followed him to the corner of the building and I took a couple of shots of the rest of the cars. The other guys looked like they were set for the night, dozing in the café for the warmth I suppose. Eventually a second guy left. He's second-guy in my notes. I followed him to the car park too. So Marks was out of my sight for … what? A matter of a few seconds each time. And he stayed put, elbows on table, chin in hands. In the end, he got up and walked out. He scrunched one of the flyers in his hands as he came through the door and flicked it at a bin. Then he was back round to the car park, in his car and back to the B&B.'

'What did Webber have to say about all this?'

'Was I sure it was Marks? Did my photos of the cars show the licence plates?'

'Do they?'

Annie shrugged. 'Not sure, but I'd listed them anyway. There were only four. It's all in my notes.'

Pieternel glanced at the screen in front of her. 'He'll have matched them to owners by now. I wonder if it's in this lot. How long was Marks in there?'

'Exact times are in my report but it was well over three hours, nearer four.'

'And that was it?'

'More or less,' said Annie. 'When I saw him heading for the car park, I went and fished the flyer thing out of the bin. I wanted to see what he'd thrown away. It was just a bit of a scribble, a half done sketch of a house. Odd shaped place with old-fashioned chimneys. Like a rough draft for an estate agent's thing, but badly done, homemade. Something someone's started and abandoned halfway through. Webber has the original now, but there's a scan in the file.'

'It's in Marks's line, isn't it? Property sales.'

'Yes, but not that sort of thing. He's into commercial properties. Why did you ask anyway, what have you got?'

'Not sure,' said Pieternel. 'I think I'm getting to grips with what they had on Marks to start with. They looked really hard at some of the places he'd been. I wondered if that would turn out to be somewhere he'd been before. It isn't, though, not that I've found yet. If I find the why, I'm hoping it might give me a clue about what's so sensitive about the case.'

Annie felt a smile curve her lips. Pieternel hadn't intended it, but she was also following a trail that ought to end in why Marks was arrested. Her own focus on witness statements was beginning to slot into place, too. From the point of view of the witnesses it was a fragmentary record about who had seen Marks where and when. It was a trail that led far and wide – a hindsight tracking of Marks's movements. Her own testimony would clear him – if the victim were Syeira's daughter – but something else had damned him more recently. She remembered Webber's reaction. *We've got the bastard.* It hadn't been surprise in his tone, it had been satisfaction. It wasn't brand new information. Something he'd had brewing had paid off.

She went back over a clutch of statements whose purpose seemed to be to corroborate events and sightings from earlier. Her mind built a picture of Marks as one suspect in a huge crowd, something to do with attendees at a conference in Switzerland. She couldn't catch the why. That must have been spelled out in earlier documents, before Marks's name had been isolated. It looked like Christa had hunted down documents containing Marks's name from wherever she'd gained access. They must have appeared in random order and she'd cobbled them together as quickly as she could. Maybe there was no time to copy into a searchable format that wouldn't have left a trace. But the picture was slowly appearing from the morass of detail. Marks had been one of many before meticulous investigative work began to spin off the targets one by one. His presence at the original conference was just a piece in the puzzle. Nothing incriminating was recorded. These were routine statements taken from bystanders, hotel staff, events managers, even bus passengers at one point. Banal stuff, but so much of it.

*… I was called to the desk just after 14:00. The man had booked into the hotel and had asked for help with his luggage. I remember him because he only had one small suitcase, but it was heavy. I joked with him that it was full of gold …*

*… the whole crowd of them came in the bar. I can't say if he was there or not …*

98

*… I remembered the man because he had a problem with his ticket. I translated for him. It was the 4.15 pm on the last Thursday of the month. I can be sure about that because I always catch that bus …*

*… Mr Marks registered for the seminar on the Monday morning with most of the other delegates. I don't remember him registering, but he signed the form and took his badge …*

No hard evidence in any of it, but Damien Marks was the last man standing when all the others fell out of the picture. Serious resource across several countries had put this together. There was a tantalising reference to documents having turned up, and some lost CCTV footage. What had Christa said? *They've found forensic linking him to the body.* Whatever access Christa had managed, it didn't include lab reports or pathology. Annie wondered if Marks's guilt or innocence would come down to a straight contest between Webber's lab people and her surveillance records. And how would her surveillance reports, detailed though they were, stand up against the compelling nature of forensic science?

'I've found you in here.' Pieternel's voice cut into her thoughts. 'Webber's checking your story about the missing kid. They're struggling for an ID.'

'Unbelievable,' Annie said, 'that a child can slip off the radar so easily.' Webber had moved quickly for his enquiries to have been caught up in Christa's sweep. She hadn't liked him any more than he'd liked her but it was reassuring that he'd followed her leads. Marks's fate might hinge on how meticulous Webber was prepared to be.

'Elliot and Sanger,' she said to Pieternel. 'Have you seen either of those names?'

'Not yet. Why? Who are they?'

'Witnesses. Just bystanders who were caught up in a general trawl months ago, but important enough that they went back to see if they could get more from either of them once they'd homed in on Marks from other angles. I'd like to get a look at their second statements.'

She blew out a sigh. 'I've never missed a search function as much. I'm going cross-eyed. I'm going to have to stretch my legs. More coffee?'

Pieternel nodded. 'Where are you up to in that file? I'll have a quick recce while you're getting the drinks. It'll be a relief to have something definite to look out for.'

'Page 112,' said Annie, adding, 'a few more hundred to go,' as she stood up and headed for the bar.

When she returned, Pieternel accepted the steaming mug and said, 'Elliot appears on pages 120, 186 and 333. Sanger's on page 120 as well. I didn't spot him again. No guarantees.' She pushed a torn beermat across on which the numbers were scribbled. Annie grinned. She took pride in her own speed-reading abilities, but she was an amateur beside Pieternel. No guarantees of course, and to have been through the whole file so quickly Pieternel had put enormous faith on her subconscious to tell her when to hit stop on what must have been a lightning scroll through several hundred pages. No guarantees, but a shortcut to this part of the trail.

Sanger's appearance on page 120 seemed to corroborate his absence from the rest of the document. He had died since making his original statement. Annie glanced outside. The windmill with its huge sails sat peacefully dominating the adjacent houses. It was nothing. Sanger was just a bystander who had happened to remember Marks on a bus. The fact of his death was noted without anything to give rise to suspicion.

She told Pieternel, who said, 'There must be hundreds of people referenced in this lot, Annie. Statistically, some of them will have died. Any hint they think there's anything odd about it?'

'Well … no.' Annie paused as fragments of past conversations played in her head. 'They speak several languages in Switzerland, don't they?'

Pieternel held her gaze for a moment, then said, 'Give me the details, I'll look him up.' Annie scrolled back to the original statement for Sanger's full name and address.

Elliot, a bartender, had been tracked down. In his original statement he'd been asked to pick people out of a posed group photograph to identify who had been present in a hotel bar on a particular date. Another conference social. It had been somewhat random. He'd picked out a number of people who definitely weren't there – a man with a shock of red hair, another wearing a suit of electrifying blue. *If he was there, he wasn't in that suit.* And he'd picked out the ones he remembered for sure. *He bought the drinks ... he was drunk by 10 o'clock ...* Marks wasn't identified in either camp.

Second time round, they had CCTV images that Elliot had been asked to study. *Was this the full group? Was there a corner hidden from the camera's eye?* It became clear that Marks hadn't been there that night. So where was he? They were very interested but Annie couldn't find out why. This looked like the point Marks began to distinguish himself from the pack. August just over two years ago. It was before she'd been following him, before Syeira's daughter had gone missing, but the statements were from much later – they tracked him in hindsight and were lucky their witnesses had remembered as much as they had. They'd tracked a lot of people in hindsight until Marks began to stand out.

Annie removed her gaze from the screen, her mind allowing in the image of what was at the heart of everything – a small incomplete torso in a shallow cliff top grave. 'Pieternel, you know how the kid's body was cut up. Have you seen anything like that in the press recently, other than the stuff about the case?'

'It's been all over the news since they plucked the kid out of the cliff.' Pieternel's gaze remained on the screen in front of her as she spoke.

Annie shrugged. 'Yes, but not about the way it was dismembered. They've kept that quiet, but I've seen something. Not the press reports. But I can't remember what.'

'While you've been following Marks?' Pieternel sat up, her attention caught.

Marks had to be innocent. She couldn't have missed something this big. Yet where else had she been these last few months but on his coattails? On countless occasions she'd peered through his car windows at documents lying out in view, taken any number of photos. What exactly had she seen and when? Why couldn't she remember? And how had she missed the link?

'And anyway,' she said. 'Why would you remove the head and hands from a body?'

'To prevent identification? Delay it, anyway.'

'But the girl was eight years old. Her fingerprints wouldn't have been on file anywhere. She hadn't even been reported missing.'

'Then for no rational reason I can think of. Will Heidi Marks keep you on? I don't want to drop this case until I know why we were targeted.'

'If she can afford to. It's lawyers she needs now. It depends if they stop paying him now he's been arrested. Can they do that? Can you stop someone's salary if they're arrested for a major crime?'

Annie thought she had better warn Heidi of the possibility, and wondered again about Heidi's assertion that Damien was being set up by one of his colleagues. Was that possible? Certainly in one of the statements a colleague of Marks had been equivocal about whether or not he'd seen him at a particular event. It was all circumstantial and frustratingly incomplete but there was a pattern of a net closing. Even discounting a colleague with a grudge, Damien had clearly not been where he'd claimed to be on at certain times. The bartender had no axe to grind. Nor had the guy on the bus. She'd kept tripping on references to Marks's bus trip and wondered where they thought he'd been going and why it was so significant.

'I can't get any more out of this today. I'm not taking it in. And I need to get back to Webber before he gets to me. I don't want to give him any excuse to label me uncooperative. He'll be a bear with a sore head if he has a press pack to deal with. He's a bad-tempered git at the best of times.'

'OK.' Pieternel shut down the laptop and stood up, stretching her arms. 'I'll set one of the guys on to some of these loose ends.'

'Why are they so interested in that day two years ago? That's months before the child even went missing.'

'You're assuming it's the same child.'

Annie tipped her head in acknowledgement. It kept coming back to that.

'Now,' said Pieternel. 'Let's see you wipe that phone clean. Fifty quid says you can't.'

'You're on. Soon as I've rung Webber.'

She was put through to the incident room, but Webber himself didn't come on the line. And as far as she could tell her call didn't spark exceptional interest, but yes, Detective Superintendent Webber would like to see her. Could she come to York? And no, no need for her to come in over the weekend. No point, there'd be no one to see her. How about Monday? And would she bring all her files on Damien Marks.

'I need to ring Heidi,' she told Pieternel as she ended the call. 'They won't see me till Monday. And they'll have had to charge Damien or let him go before then. They don't think we have anything.'

'He already knows you were on Marks's tail when the girl disappeared, right?'

Annie nodded. 'But he doesn't have all my detailed logs. I suppose he thinks his forensic evidence trumps my surveillance record, but it can't. I'm beginning to wonder about what Heidi said … about him being set up.'

'What's the child's name?' Pieternel asked.

'The mother kept it from Christa and I missed my chance to ask Layla. No one else I've talked to can remember.'

'If this is the murdered child and you wreck their case against their prime suspect, they're going to get very interested in us. Still,' Pieternel shrugged. 'forewarned and all that.'

Outside in the car park, Annie delved in the boot of her car for her toolkit then moved behind the bulk of the sloping walls of the windmill to avoid prying eyes.

Placing her phone on the ground, she gave it a sharp thwack with a wrench. Bits skittered across the tarmac surface, radiating from the bent and crushed casing. Annie gave it a second whack, then prised apart what was left, fishing out the circuit board and SIM. 'An unfortunate accident,' she murmured, 'but I think these are parts of the wreckage I failed to retrieve. You take them and get rid. You owe me fifty.'

'Huh!' Pieternel tossed the fractured parts in her hand. 'I could get data off these.'

'Yeah, but Webber couldn't because he'll never get his hands on them, and you're not going to waste time doing it just to prove a point.'

'OK, I'll put it towards your new mobile.' Pieternel paused for a moment. 'When you said you'd seen something like it before, what was it exactly? Newspaper reports, official documents, coroner's stuff?'

'I wish I knew.' Annie spread her hands wide in a gesture of helplessness. 'Whatever it was, it barely registered. But I know I saw it and it wasn't about the girl who was found in the field. It was different … the same, but different.'

'So maybe there was an earlier crime.'

'Then why was there no reference in all that lot? Oh!' Annie stopped on a gasp, holding herself absolutely still as the memory dropped back into place. 'It *was* an old story,' she said. 'Way too old to have anything to do with Damien Marks.' She felt herself alone in the bustle, no one watching as she uncovered a copy of a newspaper cutting, its writing faded. *Child killing … Brutal slaying* … Then Webber had been at her elbow, in her face, mad at her for meddling. 'I saw it in York,' she told Pieternel. 'In the incident room.'

# chapter eighteen

.........................................................................

'You're so lucky,' Stacy said, the envy in her voice made it almost breathless. It even made Olivia feel a bit short of breath to hear it. She, Olivia, was the one with the invitation. Not Stacy, not Emmeline, not even Ava. Olivia watched Stacy turning the card in her hand. She felt butterflies in her stomach. She knew it ought to feel so good to be the one who had the card.

Stacy's face was in shadow in the corner of the den under the bunk bed, but her eyes almost seemed to shine. 'You're going on Ryan's birthday trip.' Again the words came out like a whisper, like they leaked out without Stacy even meaning to say them. Stacy turned the card back and forth. Olivia watched intently. This wasn't quite what she'd imagined. She'd imagined that Stacy would have turned the card just once, back and forth, and then ripped it to shreds so Olivia couldn't go. She'd had it all planned. She'd keep out of Ryan's way until afterwards. Then she'd say, I couldn't go 'cos Stacy ripped up the card. Her insides felt uncomfortable again, because they'd all say that was no reason not to go, that she could just have told on Stacy and gone anyway, but it would be too late by then. All it needed was not to tell anyone, and not to see Ryan till it was all over. That brought another flutter because it might mean missing school again without telling her mum.

It was so strange the way it had all happened just like she'd wanted and now it was all wrong. Some of the boys from Ryan's year had had a real go at him when he was talking to her; calling Ryan girlie and calling her a baby. Ryan just hit out at one of them and went right on talking to her. 'You keep quiet,' he'd told her. 'Those ghosts can come right out and get you if you don't.' She remembered how she'd nodded her head as she looked at his eyes, all cold and empty, but at the edges she could see other things. She could see Emmeline and Stacy with their mouths open and she could see the boy Ryan hit scrambling to his feet, blood pouring from his nose; his friends looking all scared.

It was the first time she'd seen how hard and cold Ryan's eyes were; first time she'd seen him not care what the other boys said. She'd done all those things to make him take notice of her but she'd not seen what he was like. Only now she had what she wanted. Ryan talked to her even when other people were there. It was almost like they were going about together properly. And she didn't know how to get away.

'You're so lucky,' Stacy said again, and Olivia knew she wouldn't ever get pushed around by Stacy again, or any of them.

Olivia had words in her head. The words were: *I don't want to go.* But how could she say them? Instead, she said, 'Ryan's not the same when you get to know him.'

'Isn't he?' Stacy looked at her like she'd said something wonderful but she hadn't meant it in a good way. Then Stacy said, 'Ryan's mum said to my mum that Ryan's changed. He's like a different boy.'

'Did she?' That was interesting. Olivia had never thought of it that way round. She thought she'd been wrong about Ryan. She hadn't thought about him changing.

'Ryan's mum says it's his age,' Stacy went on, but Olivia didn't think so. Now she knew she hadn't been wrong about it, she knew just when he'd changed. It had been since she told him that there was a secret at the ghost house.

◉ ◉ ◉

Annie hadn't expected Webber to let her anywhere near the incident room in York after last time. But she found herself ushered upstairs by a woman who told her Martyn Webber would be free to speak to her in a few minutes. She was interested to note that she'd been promoted to someone allowed to hear his name unadorned by rank. She was relieved, too, that her companion didn't radiate hostility. She'd worried that rumours about her and Webber might have spread through the entire place by now. As they entered the big space, Annie's eye was drawn at once to the corner where Webber had caught her flipping through papers. It had all changed. No desk there anymore, just a blank whiteboard, its surface smudged by inadequate cleaning. There'd be no chance to pry this time. The woman couldn't have stuck closer had they been handcuffed together.

It wasn't just the position of the furniture that was different. The early light made sharp lines fusing the screens and desks. Flashes of cold colour burst from reflective surfaces as the sun caught them, drawing the room's occupants together as though they were all attached to an invisible network. The space seemed emptier but with a more resolute sense of purpose. Everyone focused on his or her task. Every conversation looked serious. No small talk over cups of coffee. They'd passed some sort of milestone, made their arrest, amassed their evidence and would see their prime suspect in court.

When she'd finally got through to Heidi, it had been to find that Damien had been charged at about the same time she and Pieternel were talking about him on Saturday afternoon. Her original intention of convincing Webber that Marks was not his man had become a mountain to climb. Webber could only be looking to her for corroborating evidence. But of what? He knew she'd been following Marks. He might not like it but he knew she was good at her job. She and Heidi between them could account for every second of Damien Marks's time when Syeira's daughter had disappeared.

There was only one answer. She'd been wrong. The victim wasn't Syeira's daughter. Webber had the authority to release hospital records, to check DNA profiles. It was both a good and a bad result. Annie was determined to leave with solid confirmation before she contacted Layla. The promise she'd made played on her mind. Bad enough that her news about Syeira would be the location of a grave, but how much worse to have to tell Layla that the murdered child in all the papers was Syeira's daughter? Again she told herself, either Marks was a child killer or Syeira's daughter was the victim. Either … or. Not both.

Webber called her over, pushed forward a chair and asked if she'd like a drink. When she shook her head, he followed her cue and got straight to business. 'Your records on Damien Marks. Your boss gave us copies of the files but I understand you have some detailed surveillance records.'

Annie pulled a USB pen drive from her pocket.

'These cover …' She tipped the device on its side to show the inscription and read out the dates, watching him as she did so. These were the dates that covered the time Syeira's daughter disappeared. He must know that. 'Read through them,' she told him. 'They account for every second … well, near enough. The only times I wasn't watching him was when he was at home with his wife. In fact, the Wednesday of that week …' She heard herself prattle on, annoyed because he was looking through her, because she had to hold the pen drive out for several seconds before he reached for it.

'Thanks.' He signalled to someone over her head.

'I'm not saying there wasn't the odd ten minutes where I couldn't swear to his exact whereabouts, but I know that …' She wasn't getting through to him. His eyes had glazed over. He wasn't even hearing her anymore.

Footsteps approached and she looked up to see the young guy she'd seen with him in the BBC building in Hull. His appraisal of her then had been curious, but this time he shot her a dagger of a glance before turning to Webber. 'Miss Raymond's surveillance records,' Webber said, passing the pen drive across. 'Take them across to the team for checking, will you?'

The young guy took hold of the pen drive, then said confidentially to Webber, 'They've emailed those … uh …' He tipped his head towards Webber's PC whilst shooting Annie another filthy look. Webber pushed aside the mess of papers on his desk as he pulled forward his keyboard. The blank back of the monitor faced Annie. She watched as the two men spoke in shorthand that made no sense to her. *Is that the one …? Yes, and that was the previous day's … there and there …*

At the edge of her vision, a familiar shape caught her eye. Webber had disturbed the heap of documents on his desk. One of the papers now showing was the flyer Annie had given him. That incidental piece of paper Marks had screwed up and thrown away. Someone had scrawled something on it, but the words were obscured.

Her hand shot out and grasped the edge of the pen drive, almost dislodging it from the young guy's grasp. Their fingers touched. 'The dates are written on the side,' she rapped out, staring into his eyes as he flinched away.

'Yeah, OK.' He snatched his hand away from hers, exchanging the ghost of a glance with Webber. Annie sat back and lowered her gaze. The whole move took less than a second and was just enough to push the papers aside a fraction more. It was an address. Someone had written an address against that half-drawn picture of a house.

As the young guy turned to go, he shot her a contemptuous glance. Webber, too, treated her to a glare. She wondered suddenly how badly she'd hurt his pride by following Marks in York after his crew clocked off. And would Heidi's husband suffer all the more because she'd punctured Webber's ego? But he'd followed up what she'd given him so far. Even that flyer. She wanted to tell him, we're quits now. I wouldn't have chased up that one at all.

'We'll check it all out,' he told her, his voice bland, his face neutral.

She nodded. She believed him. 'The body you found isn't Syeira and Will's daughter, is it? She's nothing to do with it. It can't be her or you wouldn't have charged Damien Marks. I don't need you to tell me who it is, but please just confirm to me that it isn't her. Syeira had a friend. Uh … I need to let her know. She'll want to track down the girl.'

She had Webber's attention now. There was something different about the way he watched her. 'You've saved us some time and I should thank you for that.' His voice was serious, that same expression in his eyes. 'We'd have got there in the end but … thank you. And I'm sorry, but the child *was* Syeira Franklin and Will Stanley's daughter.'

Disbelief fought inside her to find a voice. 'But … Are you sure? It can't be … It …'

'Will Stanley had a record,' he told her. 'And the hospital had histology samples from Syeira Franklin. Given the circumstances, we fast-tracked it. I'm afraid there's no doubt.'

Annie watched him pause, watching for her reaction, giving her the space to speak. When she said nothing, he went on, 'So, this friend of Syeira Franklin's. How was she involved?'

Annie recognized what she saw in Webber's face. It was sympathy. She felt irrationally angry as though he'd tricked her into lowering her guard. 'The surveillance records.' Her hand opened as though to show some vestige of the pen drive the young guy had carried away.

'They'll show you were on his heels every second of the relevant time, am I right?'

'Well, yes.'

'So he couldn't have done it, is that it? I told you, don't worry.' That sympathetic edge remained. 'No one's looking to bang up the wrong man. Mr Marks will get a fair trial.'

'But you believe he did it.'

'I wouldn't have had him arrested if I didn't.'

'But if my records show he was nowhere near the girl when she disappeared …'

'I'm sure they will and I'm sure his defence team will make the most of them, but if you want my view, your Mr Marks won't see the outside of a prison cell for a very long time. Now I'd like to know more about this friend of Syeira Franklin's.'

Annie slumped back in the chair. She was in a cul-de-sac. Was Webber telling her he believed her evidence, but he still believed Marks to be guilty. She'd missed something. She glanced up at him. Whatever he knew, he wasn't about to tell her. Could Christa get him to spill the beans? And now she'd have to tell him about Layla who had nothing to do with anything. No point holding it back. There was enough in the records they'd had from the office to follow the trail. There was one thing she could try and as he wasn't about to leave her to wander about the place unchaperoned, it would have to be a direct approach.

'Last time I was here, I saw some press cuttings, really old ones. What were they about?'

The last vestige of sympathy vanished from his face. He leant forward. 'We're grateful for your help, Miss Raymond, but let's not push our luck.' He paused whilst staring hard at her, then sat back. 'You were telling me about Syeira Franklin's friend.'

She looked into his eyes and knew he wouldn't disclose anything about those cuttings. 'The child,' she blurted out. 'What was her name?'

He looked surprised. 'Didn't the friend tell you?'

'Uh … No, I didn't ask. I think she thought I knew. Can't you at least tell me that?'

'Myra. Her name was Myra.'

For a moment neither of them spoke and she felt an unexpected empathy with him; the bond of a senseless murder, the need to find justice for three people who had no one else left to care. But he didn't want her meddling, and he'd been foolish not to tell her about the press cuttings. They wouldn't be hard to track down even if all she could remember was the layout and the lurid headlines. *Child killing ... Brutal slaying ...*

# chapter nineteen

Annie's plan was to check out the address she'd seen on the flyer on Webber's desk, then to head south, calling in to talk to Layla Johnson on her way back to London. She could research the newspaper cuttings herself, but Pieternel was better placed to gather more information on the two witnesses she had identified from Christa's documents; witnesses who were peripheral enough to the investigation that she wouldn't be noticed if she found and contacted them but who had been key in placing Marks in some particular location a little over two years ago. Annie wanted more detail on what they'd been asked.

The first obstacle to her plan came when she looked up the address. It would take her the wrong way through York and wouldn't leave time for a diversion to find Layla. She decided it wasn't her main concern. Priority was to go south to speak to Layla before Webber found her and then to head back to the office to talk to Pieternel and then Heidi.

The day continued to irritate her. Traffic chaos on the M1 meant the planned diversion took far longer than she'd allowed for and at the end of it she couldn't find Layla anyway. Monday evening found her back in the London office, dozing in a corner, tired from all the driving and frustrated by a day of dead-ends. She was roused out of her lethargy by Pieternel who crashed into the office, saying, 'Ah, there you are. I've a lead on whoever was skulking about in here the other week.'

'Who?' Annie sat up.

'Someone who works freelance for one of those pseudo-official security outfits. We've either blundered into some sort of national security investigation or got ourselves the wrong side of someone with serious money to burn. Any ideas?'

Annie tried to fit the theory to her conversations with Webber. She'd had no hint of anything other than a murder enquiry in his head and said so.

'And how about that woman you were after? Did you speak to her?'

Annie shook her head. 'Layla Johnson, no I couldn't find her. Now Webber'll get to her first and she won't give me the time of day if I ever do track her down.' She shrugged, but felt annoyed for letting Layla's existence slip out. It had been careless. 'Anyway, he can't stop me digging out those press cuttings for myself, but I wish I'd spotted a date. And did you get anything on those witnesses?'

Pieternel nodded. 'As much as I'm going to get, yes.'

'Good. We might get to know where they think Damien Marks went that day.'

'Isn't that the date to look for your old cuttings?' Pieternel said.

'No, they were older than that. Way older. Too old to have been to do with Marks at all. But I saw so little of them. I'm going on the layout of the page as much as anything. I've an idea it was the Daily Mail, but that might have been an impression not anything concrete. And something about it said broadsheet, not tabloid.'

'Was the Daily Mail ever a broadsheet?' Pieternel asked.

Annie nodded. 'I'll check when it went tabloid. Before Marks was born I should think. But why were those cuttings in the incident room in York?'

'Any number of reasons,' Pieternel said. 'Wrapping paper from something … member of the public sending stuff in. Why are you so sure they're important?'

'Because Webber knew exactly what I was talking about when I mentioned them. He'd have done better to pretend he didn't know what I was on about, or at least to hesitate. I'm wondering about some sort of copycat thing. No idea if it'll help on why they're so certain it's Marks, but it might. He was so sure ...' Annie paused as she thought back. 'It wasn't that he was dismissive of my evidence, just that it didn't trump whatever he had on Marks.'

'When are you seeing Heidi again?'

'I told her I'd go round tomorrow morning.' Annie looked across the deserted office. She saw two swans gliding against a peaceful backdrop on one of the screensavers. As she watched, the screen blanked. A rustle of paper brought her attention back to her colleague.

'This is the paperwork on the witnesses in Switzerland,' Pieternel said. 'There were six in that set, not two. One of them was Marks's colleague, so we should steer clear of him, but the others were locals; nothing to do with the conference, just bystanders, people living in Geneva at the time; the man looking after the bar who semi confirmed that Marks wasn't with the crowd that night; another of the passengers on the bus, along with the one who died. They didn't chase up the one who'd died, by the way, other than finding that out. They didn't do much to track down any of them, just interviewed the ones who were there for the taking. They were lucky to find any witnesses that long after the event.'

'More a non-event,' said Annie. '*Did you see this guy on a bus four months ago?* Anything odd about the death, by the way?' She took hold of the papers one by one as Pieternel handed them across.

'No, but I've got someone looking out the death certificate. What they were doing, some months after the event, was tracking Marks's movements that particular day. Going back to witnesses they'd interviewed before they were targeting Marks or anyone, but I couldn't get what they were looking at ... why they were so keen to know who'd been where ... or why they targeted that conference. Second time round, it was the barman they were after mainly, to confirm Marks hadn't been in the bar that night. They had a cursory look for the other witnesses. They found some of the conference people … found the second bus passenger. The other two were estate agents. They weren't re-interviewed. I'm guessing they got what they needed first time round; that Marks visited a particular property maybe, not that I can get an address. Some of the references are annoyingly vague, they reference documents that Christa didn't get.'

Annie's glance was drawn again to the monitor where the swans had been swallowed into darkness. Its black sheen gleamed at her.

'That address you got this morning,' Pieternel said. 'Have you followed it up yet?'

'I've looked online. It could well be the same house that was sketched on that flyer. It's on the outskirts of York, but too far to take a detour this morning. I'll look when I'm next up there, or I might ask Christa to check it out. So if they were interested in a particular property in Geneva just over two years ago, then we might dig out one of those estate agents and have a word. They won't be hard to find.'

Pieternel nodded. 'That's what I thought. I'll set one of the guys on it. They can ring tomorrow. We want a French speaker, don't we? Is that the French-speaking part of Switzerland?'

Annie shrugged. 'Geneva's a bit of a melting pot I think.' She assumed that Pieternel had already had several people working on this to have dug out so much from the mass of detail that Christa had given her. This wasn't the time to say that she wouldn't allow it all to be billed to Heidi. 'What are the chances of finding that second bus passenger?' she asked. 'It doesn't sit right to me that someone had to help Damien out with the language. Maybe it wasn't him. Maybe that's the root of a misidentification.'

'It was the passenger who died who said he'd helped Marks.'

'Yeah, but maybe the other one overheard whatever it was. It had to be something memorable for anyone to recall it after all that time. In fact, it's stretching it a bit to get a positive ID on a stranger in those circs.'

'We can try, but I'm not sending you off to Switzerland unless you go on Heidi Marks's budget.' Pieternel's phone beeped as she spoke. She glanced at it then murmured, 'Too bloody late to read on a phone screen,' and got up to flick on the monitor opposite Annie. Instead of swans, it came to life with the froth of a tumbling waterfall. Pieternel reached forward for the mouse to fire up the email. After a moment she said, 'It's confirmation of the IDs from those cars outside the services place near York where Marks went in the middle of the night. Nothing new.'

Annie felt her eyebrows rise. There was something reckless about having this stuff arrive in an office that was recently combed through and that had already been targeted by the police operation. She watched Pieternel open a web browser and saw a map appear. 'What are you doing?'

'I'm just wondering if …' Another beep interrupted her. 'Hang on, there's something else. That's efficient. It's the death certificate. I'll print it. But just look at this, Annie, and tell me if it looks familiar.'

'I'm looking, and yes it does.' Annie stared as Pieternel homed in on the house she'd looked up herself just a few hours ago. 'It's the address that was on the flyer. Where have you got it from?'

'It's where one of those cars was registered. Give me a moment and I'll tell you which one.'

Annie reached backwards to pull the single sheet from the printer as it whirred through into the tray. Half an eye on Pieternel, she read through the words. It wasn't a death certificate as such, but a brief report on the circumstances of the witness Sanger's death. *Long-standing heart condition … dead some days before anyone found him … loner … no family …*

'It's the one you clocked as sorry-guy's truck,' said Pieternel. 'It's registered to that address.'

'I suppose …' Annie screwed up her eyes as she tried to recreate the scene that night. 'It could have been sorry-guy's bit of paper.

Marks just happened to pick it up. They didn't speak apart from ...'
Her voice died away. Had she missed something?

'You'd better quiz Heidi on that address tomorrow.'

Annie nodded. Her thoughts exactly. 'Do you have a name?'

'The car's registered to a woman. Hannah Levine.'

'Oh, please don't tell me I'm about to uncover Damien's clandestine affair. That would be rich ... Oh shit!' Her train of thought came to a crashing halt. Her gaze was on the page in her hand, but the words weren't making sense. She thought about the pen drive she'd handed across to Webber. 'My surveillance records don't clear Damien Marks. Of course they don't. I haven't been thinking straight. I'm too bloody tired.'

The page focussed again in front of her. *Have I missed something?*

'Hang on a minute. What the hell ...?' She closed her eyes and shook her head as though to clear it. 'Pieternel,' she held out the page. 'Am I going mad or what?'

'What are you talking about?' Pieternel frowned as she took the paper. 'What's this to do with your surveillance of ... Oh!'

Pieternel's sudden exclamation ran an ice cold shard through Annie. She'd hoped to hear Pieternel tell her to get some sleep; that she'd knackered herself with all the driving; that she hadn't missed anything; that she could go to see Heidi in the morning as planned. In the background, the frothy waterfall dissolved into a rolling green landscape.

'Get working on your cover story, Annie. This is going to drop us right in it. And you'd better get some sleep. You're going to York again in the morning.'

# chapter twenty

A knock sounded on the open door. Webber looked up to see Ahmed standing there.

'It's Annie Raymond, Guv,' Ahmed told him. 'She's in reception. She says she's found out something about Damien Marks from two years ago. She wants to speak to you.'

'Her again?' Webber felt surprise. He thought he'd seen the last of the Raymond woman. 'OK, you'd better go and get her. But don't leave her on her own. I don't want her rummaging through stuff.'

Webber let his pen trace a thin line around the few notes he'd been making on Heidi Marks. Annie Raymond's surveillance records had turned out to be more robust than he expected. They didn't … couldn't … trump his forensic evidence, but it disturbed him. There was something not right about the set-up she worked for. Her boss's online tracks were troublingly sparse and hard to follow. Professionally doctored online tracks always held a smell of MI5, but that was absurd. Raymond and her cronies were two-bit investigators who made their money out of other people's problems.

When Ahmed came back with her, Webber waved them both in and motioned for them to sit. He looked Annie Raymond up and down. The sun shone through the blinds at an angle making shadows where good psychology would have put light. He'd have preferred to have a bright disk of sunlight behind him and know that his face was obscured from view.

'We're very busy,' he opened, 'but I suppose you haven't called in again for nothing. And by the way, are you still working for Heidi Marks?' When she nodded a yes, he added, 'She can't think much of him if she's still looking for another woman.'

'Heidi is convinced her husband is innocent,' said Annie Raymond. 'And she's asked me to help prove it.'

He exchanged the ghost of a smile with Ahmed. 'And are you expecting to do that?'

'My problem is that I'm not in a position to do that. You are. Don't get me wrong. I've no interest in seeing him walk if he's done it, but since you ask, I don't think he has.'

'That's come from your months of following him, has it?'

'Not really. I was relying on the surveillance records to start with; to prove his innocence, I mean. But I realised yesterday that they don't. To be honest, I got too wrapped up in the detail of it after you arrested him. The time when the Myra Franklin disappeared isn't really relevant, is it? We know who took her. It was her father, Will Stanley. If Damien Marks was involved, it was later.'

'But you're still convinced of his innocence, are you?'

'Yes, but I can't prove it.'

Webber suppressed a smile. Any minute now she would tell him she had a hunch. 'Go on,' he said.

'Heidi thinks he's been set up ... framed ... by his colleagues because of some sort of business feud. And no, I didn't think much of it as a theory, either. Heidi's convinced he's innocent and she has to find a reason, but now I've found something ...'

Webber glanced at Ahmed, meeting his eye. They exchanged a look. Annie Raymond was strangely uncomfortable, hesitant. He lifted his hand from the desk to glance at his watch. Her gaze followed the movement and then she looked up at him. He couldn't read the expression on her face, but had a sudden premonition that she was about to come out with something he wasn't going to like.

'I had to look further than my surveillance of her husband,' she said. 'I had to start looking at the things that you had been interested in from a couple of years ago.'

A spark of anger. 'How the hell did you get information on our enquiry?'

'I asked around.' Her voice was quiet, her eyes lowered. He wasn't fooled. She had no intention of saying more, but she was telling him that she wasn't about to make a fight of it if he wasn't. OK, he thought. Not yet. Not today. But she needn't think she was in the clear. Her and that boss of hers back in London with their scant online footprints. Just let him get this enquiry out of the way, and he'd chase them down.

'You wanted to know if Damien Marks had been on a particular bus two years ago, just over. You found a couple of witnesses. One of them remembered Damien having some bother with his ticket. He helped to translate. The other one witnessed the exchange. You were pretty lucky to find anyone because it was months after the event. And later on, you went back to get corroboration from the second witness. The first one had died.'

She paused but Webber wasn't going to trust himself to speak. He was aware of Ahmed, sitting slightly behind her and not trying to hide his look of horrified fascination. She was telling him things she could not have found from just 'asking around'.

'It struck me as odd,' she went on, 'because Damien Marks is quite a linguist. Why would he need a translator?'

'You think it wasn't him,' Ahmed cut in.

She turned her head briefly to acknowledge his question, but aimed her answer at Webber. 'It's more complicated than that. The witness who said he'd done the translating, I checked up. Here,' She reached into her pocket and pulled out a sheet of paper. Webber watched her place it on the desk and spin it round so it faced him. She pointed to the salient dates. 'Your guys interviewed him on that Thursday. They checked him out. There were no problems. Why would there be? He was just an incidental bystander. Months later, when you were going back to re-interview, he turned up as having died in the meantime. A shame but nothing sinister. It was a natural death. He was one in a long list. Easy to see why no one gave him a second look.' Webber watched as she raised her eyes to meet his. 'He had no family, no close friends,' she said.

He was ahead of her. Ahmed was still floundering. Webber felt a hollow carve itself out inside him as he cut in to complete what she was about to say. 'No one clamouring for paperwork.' He pushed the page towards Ahmed as he spoke. 'Assuming Miss Raymond's dates are correct ...' He would check but with no real hope of catching her in an error. 'At the time of his first interview, the witness Mr Sanger, was already dead.'

# chapter twenty one

The day had become overcast, threatening rain, dark enough that shadows shimmered like wraiths in hidden corners. Annie had taken the time to eat, drink and recuperate and was ready to take her chances in the encroaching dusk. She'd learnt not to fear ghosts a long time ago. It was the living who posed real threats. She rummaged in her car boot and slipped a few things into her pockets; picklocks, gloves, balaclava. Her intention was just to take a look, but it didn't do to be unprepared.

She'd worked to impress Webber with the quality of her surveillance, but a frank appraisal was worrying. She'd been tired even before she and Christa had parted company and she'd settled herself for a night watching Damien Marks's guesthouse. 'I never lost sight of him for a moment,' she'd said. But she had. She'd followed sorry-guy and then second-guy round to the car park. Small gaps each time, but gaps in which Marks might have spoken to a third party. How long? Sorry-guy had strolled off picking at his teeth, climbed into his truck and turned to rummage about in the back as she stood in the shadows noting the vehicle numbers. It might have been a couple of minutes before she'd returned. Marks hadn't appeared to have moved. Then she'd followed second-guy and watched as he'd pushed past the truck and climbed into his own car. No, that was wrong. There'd been a vehicle and a gap where there'd been two vehicles, sorry-guy's truck and Marks's car. Second-guy had walked through the gap, but it was a measure of how tired she'd been that her memory wouldn't replay a sharp picture of the cars themselves. Maybe the address Webber had unwittingly provided would come up with some answers.

She walked along the street without dawdling but without undue hurry. Most of the houses she passed had drawn curtains; some showed figures flitting back and forth. She concentrated on being no more than a forgettable someone going by. A narrow lane took her between two of the houses. If she was right, this would take her close to the back of the address on the flyer. She glanced round to see if she was observed. The house on one side had tall hedges enclosing its back garden; the other showed lights behind closed curtains and an eerie blue glow from its attic window. Looking ahead, she could see that the narrow road held its tarmac coating just far enough to lead beyond the houses, then it gave way to shale compressed into dual tyre tracks but with scant evidence of regular traffic. In bad weather it would be impassable.

The twists in the track and its high hedgerows hid her from view as she climbed higher, but there was a stretch where she could look back on the housing estate. Only the attic windows lay in direct line of sight and it would take sharp eyes to spot her up here in the gloom. The eerie blue she'd seen below lit up an uncurtained window, but with no sign of movement from within.

Webber had been furious at how much she knew but he'd kept a lid on it. For now. He hadn't tried to hide that he'd seen the enormity of what she was saying. She'd wondered beforehand if his official reaction would be to doubt her evidence, but he hadn't. He'd assumed her to be right.

And what about Damien Marks? It had taken the events of the past few days to jolt her into taking an objective look at her months of surveillance. The exercise was uncomfortable as it highlighted the peculiarity of his movements. He'd been bought out of the firm he'd helped to establish, re-employed in a junior role, come close to bankruptcy, then been awarded a sudden salary increase, but done nothing to earn it. Blackmail was the obvious answer. He had dirt on his former partners. She wondered how she'd managed to miss it. Not that there was a shred of real evidence, but what other answer could there be?

She stopped on the narrow track and peered ahead. Not much to see from here. She was hemmed in by the tall hedges and could hear the whisper of the breeze in the fields either side. It sounded almost like footsteps matching her own.

Sorry-guy had already been there before Damien arrived. Had he got up deliberately to join the queue behind Damien? Or had he simply been going to the counter for a drink? Why had he been there at all when his house was so close … or anyway the house where the truck he was driving was registered? There was an easy enough answer to that. He'd been hungry. Annie remembered his heaped plate. He'd done nothing but eat. He hadn't spent time sketching. Had he dropped that half-sketch from his pocket? Had Damien picked it up because it was there, because it was something different to look at? Webber had gone to the trouble of matching it to an address. Was that significant or just attention to detail?

As she reached the top of the track, the house began to define itself out of the murkiness. At first it looked derelict, a square dwelling cluttered with ad-hoc outbuildings and extensions. As she stepped closer, keeping to the shadows, she could see that although shabby the main structure was in good repair. The ground became unpredictably uneven as she left the track. She slowed as she crept forward, not wanting to use her torch until sure the house was empty. Her confidence ebbed as she came closer. There were no lights, no sounds, no shadows at the shaded windows, but the nearer she came the less abandoned the house looked and the more it screamed *fortress*.

Two choices: march round to the front door, ring the bell and brazen it out. Or keep to the shadows, get in close, see what she could see. If there was something sinister here, it would be a dangerous move to confront the occupants with her nearest backup in the office 200 miles away. On the other hand, to be caught creeping around the property wasn't a great idea either. Chances were there was nothing of interest, but before she left, she would take as good a look as she could without undue risk.

As she moved forward into the shifting shadows, the walls took shape into a messy spread of interlocking bricks. The main structure's age was apparent in the tiny hand-made blocks. A patch of darkness between her and the nearest building morphed into the circular brick walls of a well.

Why had Webber gone to the trouble to identify this place from a screwed-up sketch that hadn't even been finished? If it had no significance, why had the paper been sitting on his desk? She wondered suddenly if part of Myra Franklin's body had been found here. A shiver ran through her unrelated to the falling temperature, but there was nothing here to suggest a recent police search and if they'd found body parts, there would have been plenty of signs – cleared ground, the remnants of tape.

The last vestiges of sunlight were gone, but the rising moon provided a silver sheen and as she relaxed to let her eyes adjust, a route forward suggested itself. An uncurtained window gleamed blackly. It might lead nowhere but a deserted outhouse, but if it were unlocked, it could be a way in to the heart of the house. She wasn't sure what she was after, but didn't want to leave without some idea of whether or not this place had a role to play. Nor did she want to stay in York tonight, but wasn't sure she had the energy for the journey back to London. There was always Christa, a short drive away in Hull.

Just before committing herself to a scurry past the well, she saw it. High on the wall. Barely visible. Just a quirk of the rising moon catching the gleam of a mirrored surface where there should have been nothing but centuries-old bricks and mortar. A lens. CCTV or an alarm system. She held herself still as she stared at it. Did it signal there was something to hide or was it just a show to keep vandals away from an isolated dwelling? She stepped backwards, not giving up on the window, but searching out a safer track. She had her back to a wall now, tendrils of some kind of creeper pressing into her. There was a more circuitous route round under the cover of the undergrowth and the deep shadow of the outbuildings.

Out of sight of the high lens she peered into the gloom struggling to make sense of a dense shadow that nestled in the angle between the path and one of the outbuildings. The half-light played tricks with her vision. As she watched it, the pool of darkness seemed to grow. She blinked and looked again … then froze as the shadow swelled, sprouting fat tentacles. Shrinking back into the ivy-covered wall, Annie fought against an irrational dread that played childhood nightmares in front of her eyes. There was nowhere to run as the black tendrils reached out, growing in size and length, a many-limbed monster emerging in front of her.

Her hands clasped involuntarily at the poisonous leaves, raising a mini dust cloud to dull the air and engulf her in decay. She struggled to stay calm, immobile. What was it? Her stare remained glued to the apparition as it wrestled silently in the dusk. And then a blaze of light erupted from the ground, a blinding flash that flared and died leaving images writhing in front of her eyes. A shower of bits rained down from the creeper as she pressed into it. The monster shrank as fast as it had grown, becoming two ordinary shadows pushing their way out from some subterranean entrance.

'Didn't I tell you!' She caught triumph and complacency in the sibilant hiss from by the wall.

'It's not,' whispered a second voice. 'There's no such thing as ghosts.' It was the voice of a young girl.

She held still as they shook themselves down and walked away. 'There is.' It was a boy's whisper that carried on the light breeze. 'But they don't come for you if you don't show fear.'

Then the girl looked back. Annie's heart thumped heavily in her chest. Moonlight lit the girl's face; her eyes seemed to stare right into Annie's. Then she was gone, scampering after the boy, swallowed into the darkness. Annie felt the rough brickwork of the wall scraping at her clothes as the soft voices melted into the night leaving her alone.

# chapter twenty two

Webber glanced at the clock and saw it was already mid-morning. The video call had lasted longer than he'd anticipated. The big screen closed into darkness, swallowing his far-off counterparts. He turned to Farrar at his side, seeing his own feelings reflected in his boss's face. They'd scaled a mountain, come within sight of the summit, hauled themselves the last few painful inches only to find it had been a mirage. The real summit lay far ahead of them shrouded in mist.

'Better we know, Martyn, than have it come out a decade from now when the killings start up again.'

'Who's to say they'll wait a decade?' Webber muttered as he stood up and reached for the light switch. The gloom that enhanced the image on the screen lay heavy now that the call was over. 'But yes, of course you're right, John.' He conceded the point, knowing it was the last thing he wanted, understanding suddenly and viscerally the temptation to lose evidence, to shape things to fit the suspect who they all knew to be guilty. Only they didn't. It wasn't Marks. It had never been Marks. And the days of that degree of evidence manipulation were gone; for gophers like him at any rate. Someone, somewhere had manipulated evidence with precision and efficiency, showing a level of skill that shouldn't be available to anyone not on side. He was tired. He'd told himself it would look different in the morning, but if anything it looked worse. He wondered where Christa was and if he could find an excuse to slip across to Hull this evening to find her.

'That young lad you brought across from Scarborough, Martyn, he's to go back.'

'It's not him,' Webber said. 'I'd stake my career on it. He's a good detective, knows his stuff.'

'That's as maybe, but there were no leaks before he arrived, and I'm not taking the chance. You should have brought Len Klein with you in the first place. I know you've had his old case files out.'

Webber looked up, surprised. 'I needed to check. There were similarities, but he got his man. The guy's dead. It's nothing to do with our case. And anyway, he wouldn't come. He's retired now.'

'He would. And he is. I've spoken to him. He'll be here later today and he'll work under you, but Ahmed has to go. As soon as Len gets here, we'll brief those who need to know, but for now we keep this tight.'

Webber felt his fists clench. They'd gone over his head, questioned his judgement. He stared at the blank screen. No comfort there. The recent call had brought nothing but more bad news. 'How could they have missed those witnesses?' he snapped. 'It's a murder enquiry, for God's sake!'

The only answer was a quizzical glance. He knew that no one had missed anything through carelessness. The dummy witnesses had all been walk-ins, apparently conscientious members of the public responding to requests for information. Their IDs had all checked out and they'd been too incidental to have created red flags when their paperwork caught up and declared them to have been dead at the time they made their statements.

He'd be sorry to lose Ahmed. He knew it was nothing to do with him. He'd better keep an eye on the lad to make sure no fallout damaged his career. And in some ways it would be a relief to have Klein on board. He'd always been a steadying hand when things felt to be out of control. Webber pulled himself up. He was the boss these days, not Klein. It would be up to him to be the stabilising force.

◉ ◉ ◉

Late afternoon found him back in his office with five others: the Chief Super, Len Klein and three trusted colleagues. It was crowded and stuffy in the small space, but the door was shut. Through the glass partition he could see the rest of his team milling about and wondered if he imagined the pall of unease that hung over them. Certainly, the euphoria of an arrest was gone. For Klein's benefit, he gave them a more detailed background summary than they needed.

'Are you saying Marks was deliberately set up?' Klein looked troubled. 'That's taken some organisation.'

'Not only Marks,' Webber told him. 'We now have a dozen dummy witnesses. Someone was setting up as many of those conference attendees as they could, knowing we'd check them all, hoping one of them would fall through all the hoops and keep us busy for long enough for the trail to go cold. They've gone back to the hotel but frankly the chances of finding anything useful after all this time are remote.'

Klein shifted in his seat and looked round, glancing through the glass to the people beyond. 'So Marks is completely out of the frame?'

Webber assumed Klein had been told about the private investigators and the leaked information. Maybe he was wondering which one of them out there had said more than they should. Klein must know it wasn't Ahmed. 'Oh, I didn't say that,' he replied to Klein's question. 'He might have been targeted to draw us away from someone else, but his behaviour since then hasn't been exemplary. He's involved now even if he wasn't then, even if he has no idea what he's got himself mixed up in. Involved enough to lead us to the perpetrators with any luck.'

'You think they're copycat killings, don't you?'

Webber shrugged. He'd never liked the theory. But it was Farrar who answered. 'We're keeping an open mind on it, Len. We had your old files out months ago.'

'You should have called me in as soon as you realised, Martyn. You never said a word.' Webber was surprised at the sharpness in Klein's tone and wondered if he was taking on a measure of responsibility, somehow blaming himself. There was no need. Klein and his team had played their part in finding a killer and putting him away. Webber saw the old press cuttings in his mind's eye, and superimposed on the memory was Annie Raymond's face as she asked about them. Interfering bitch! He knew the thought was unfair. Without the interfering bitch, Marks would be on his way to a life sentence and a new killer would be at large to celebrate another anniversary. Was still at large, he reminded himself. As though Klein had plucked the thought from his head, he rapped out, 'And how about these private investigators? It sounds to me as though they might be mixed up in it.'

'We'll throw the book at them, Len, don't worry, but they've cooperated to date, and we might have missed the dummy witnesses if it hadn't been for them. Even so, we hope we've stopped the leak.' Webber felt a buzz from the phone in his pocket and slipped it out to look while he answered Klein. It was a text. It looked innocuous and would mean nothing to anyone else, but he deleted it anyway and felt himself relax. Christa would be waiting for him.

◉ ◉ ◉

Stacy was at the corner again so Olivia would have to walk home with her. She was usually there these days. She told Olivia straight out she'd asked Ryan if she could go on his birthday trip, too, and Ryan hadn't said no. Olivia knew all about it because she'd been there. Only when Stacy came along, Ryan had shoved her behind the shed and said to keep quiet while he got rid of Stacy. And he hadn't said no. He'd said he'd think about it. Then he'd said, 'Clear off,' and Stacy had run away.

Olivia had asked her mum about ghosts. Her mum knew about things like that and she'd said for definite there weren't any. Only in films, and they weren't real, they were pretend. So Olivia asked about ghost hands. She'd pointed at the TV where there was a real stormy sea all waves and froth and she'd asked, 'If there were hands in all that swirly water, would they be ghost hands?'

Her mum said it would be a trick of the light, not ghosts. And Auntie Enn said, 'Or dead men's hands,' and her mum had said, 'Enn!' real sharp and gone and got Auntie Enn's tablets.

When Olivia got home, it turned out that Ryan had got his big brother to go round to her house while she was at school. He'd talked to her mum and dad about Ryan's birthday and her mum and dad had said yes. When they told her, she could see they expected her to be really pleased, but Auntie Enn said, 'Ooh, I don't know, Livy. You're right young for boyfriends. And look at her, you can see she doesn't want to go.' She hated being called Livy and Ryan wasn't her boyfriend, so that had kind of given her an excuse to stamp her foot and say, 'He's not my boyfriend, Auntie Enn, and don't call me Livy.' Then she'd shot out and upstairs to her room.

On the way up the stairs, she heard her mum say, 'Must you always take the gloss off things, Enn. It's a small group from the youth club. It's not just Olivia. They'll be well chaperoned. She'll love it.'

She'd made a mistake; she shouldn't have shouted at Auntie Enn, she should have told her mum she didn't want to go. If she'd only known that Ryan was sending his big brother round, she'd have shown her mum the invitation card and told her she didn't want to go, then her mum would have put it right when Ryan's big brother came here. She clicked on the light with the blue shade so she could see to pull the invitation card out from the den where she'd hidden it. Then she climbed up on to the bunk where she sat to have a think about it all. She knew that Ryan's big brother worked at the place Dad worked, so that would have been another thing to make them say yes. And anyway, they all thought she wanted to go.

She'd have to find another way do it on her own. Like Auntie Enn said, *You help yourself in this world; no bugger else will*. It made her mum real mad when Auntie Enn said that. It made Olivia giggle a bit thinking about it. it was funny how Auntie Enn got things right like her not wanting to go, but then still messed things up like making her laugh about *no bugger else will*. Because when she thought back to it later, it was Auntie Enn's fault that she was sitting on the bunk giggling and holding the invitation in her hand when her mum walked in, so her mum thought she was happy about going.

The big problem about doing it on her own was what she'd worked out. If there were no ghosts then she didn't have to go. All she'd needed to do was pluck up the courage to tell Ryan, and then put up with Stacy and them being horrid about it. She'd been really close to it the last time they'd been up there. She'd even said about there being no such thing as ghosts. But then she'd looked back and there'd been a face in the ivy. It was the hardest thing in the world she'd ever done not to show fear so it didn't come after her. It was a very still face with eyes that stared right at her. No trick of the light and not a dead man's face either.

◉ ◉ ◉

Webber was aware of Klein watching him as he packed things away for the day. Maybe Klein thought it odd, given what had happened; thought he should be staying on into the night, like the long shifts they used to share. His ex-governor's voice echoed in his mind from across the years. *Focus on what's important … stop at nothing to get a psychopath off the streets … ignore loose horses …* He smiled as the memories crowded in. 'We're stalled until we get Marks back on the spot,' he said aloud.

'You could have had him brought here today.'

'If you want the truth, Len, I'm not ready. We're keeping the DPP informed but we're not even close to withdrawing charges at this stage, not with the forensics.'

Klein shook his head. 'It's not looking good.'

'He wasn't the key player,' Webber said. 'And if you discount the witnesses, which we have to, we've lost even a circumstantial link to the body two years ago, but he had to have been involved in the recent one.'

'How long can you keep the link under wraps?' Klein asked.

Webber shrugged. They'd been careful. The first body made news in Geneva; theirs hit the headlines here. There were more reasons to keep quiet about a link than advantage to be gained from advertising it. It would be ironic if it leaked out now it looked likely they'd been wrong. Klein slipped on his glasses and pushed them to the bridge of his nose as he peered at the papers on Webber's desk. 'Now's the time to hit him, Martyn. When he's still shell-shocked from the arrest. If he genuinely had nothing to do with it, then he'll spill his guts.'

Webber nodded. 'I know, but I want that report back from Geneva first.'

'Has it occurred to you that it might have been Marks himself who engineered the witnesses? It's a great bit of insurance. Maybe it was something he would pull out of the bag during his trial. It takes the rug from under everything.'

Marks himself setting up the dummy witnesses? Webber reached across to pull down the blinds. On the face of it, he found it hard to credit Marks with that level of scheming, but somehow after the past 24 hours, all bets were off when it came to what things looked like on the face of it. Indicating to Klein that he should step back into the main office, he pulled out the keys to lock the door, which was another first during this enquiry. Yesterday, he'd had an upbeat team basking in the smell of success. This evening, he was leaving behind him a veil of suspicion and morale on the floor.

'You should have told me, Martyn,' said Klein as they walked together towards the stairs. 'As soon as you suspected. It was my case. I know more about it than anyone.'

'But it's not, is it? Your killer's dead.'

'But you think this one's a copycat or you wouldn't have had my files out.'

'Your killer's dead, Len,' Webber repeated. 'We were just exploring all the avenues. You wouldn't expect us to do less.'

'And what about these private investigators? What's their role?'

Webber frowned. 'They're cooperating. They came to us. There's no evidence to say they're involved in any crime, certainly not a murder.'

'Those walk-ins in Switzerland looked like they were cooperating, too.'

'We're on it, Len!' Unease made him snappy. He thought how they'd tried to follow Annie Raymond's boss online; tripping over small glitches in the databases; the picture always incomplete. He saw Raymond herself sitting in that chair, her form morphing into a jacket slung over the back while she pried into their records. If he followed them across virgin snow, he had an idea they'd leave no footprints. Slick professionals or dodgy dealers? They might be both. And even if they had their secrets, they weren't dead women walking.

'They don't like dealing with us any more than we like dealing with them,' he said. 'But we're on the same side on this one.' As he spoke the words, he wondered why he was so sure. Yet he was. They hated the way his enquiry had shone a light on their operation, but they would put up with it to catch a child killer. Once the perpetrator was behind bars, they wouldn't wait around to share the champagne. They'd try to fade back to invisibility. Well, he'd see about that when the time came.

'We might be in the middle of nowhere out by the coast,' Klein said. 'But the gossip leaks back, you know.'

Webber laughed easily. 'You're harking back years. Things have changed. There's nothing wrong now except this blasted case.' He saw uncertainty flicker across his ex-governor's face. Klein had had time for an update from Ahmed; time for his own quick check on Annie Raymond who was proving the perfect decoy.

'I just want to be sure you're not doing anything foolish. Me and Julia, we were close to you and Mel. We don't want to see you throw away something precious.'

'So will you bring Julia across? Come round for an evening like you used to. You still come to York, don't you?'

'Well, not really … not since Julia's aunt died. She was the only one we were really close to.' Hanging unvoiced between them was the knowledge that the Kleins' trips to York had been as regular as once a week for a long time after Len's retirement, but they'd steered clear of the Webbers. 'Maybe if I end up staying on more than a few days, I'll see if Julia'll come over.'

Webber knew he should be pleased, but he'd made the offer sure that Len would decline. Melinda would be pleased to see Julia again, but only because it had to mean a tacit admission from Julia that she'd been wrong. He wasn't sure how he felt about the sharp-eyed and sharp-tongued Julia Klein back in their lives. 'Where are you staying tonight?' he asked, assuming that Klein would be driving back home.

'With you. I begged a bed from Melinda earlier. Has she not told you?'

Webber shook his head, and made himself relax. 'I haven't had a chance to speak to her this afternoon. Julia's really letting you off the leash.' A tight smile met his remark. He wasn't fooled. Klein intended policing his movements both on and off duty. 'You want a lift?'

Klein shook his head. 'I'll take my car. I don't want to end up stranded if you're called out.'

As soon as he was alone, Webber phoned home. 'I'm sorry. I had no idea he'd land himself on us. I'll have a word with John soon as I can, see if I can get him a billet somewhere. We need him here but I expected him to commute.' He smiled at her reply. She was right. Len was getting on in years. He wouldn't want to be driving on dark country roads.

When he arrived home, Klein was there before him. Melinda was doing her best to give an old friend the welcome he expected from years ago, but years ago there'd been no teething problems and wet nappies, no endless round of chores, no leaden tiredness from the demands of a young baby.

'We'll have to put you on the couch, I'm afraid,' Webber greeted him cheerfully. 'No spare room anymore.'

He kissed Melinda, took the baby from her and went to sit with Klein who surveyed the couch with obvious dismay. Webber tried not to laugh at the way Klein watched him as he jiggled Sam on his knee, interleaving conversation with them both.

'We didn't think copycat, Len, not at first, but we looked out the old files. ... What d'you want, Sam, your teddy? Here you are. Gonna give him a hug? ... It's the anniversary thing ... Oops, I see. We're playing that one, are we? Give Ted a punch on the nose.'

He laughed as he reached to retrieve the fallen toy. Sam giggled too as he made the furry toy leap in the air.

Klein, perching on the edge of a chair, looking as lost as if they'd begun to speak Swahili, cleared his throat and began, 'You know I never bought into the anniversary thing ...' when Melinda's voice interrupted, calling Webber to the kitchen.

'I thought I had potatoes in. I was going to bulk these out, but ...' She made a helpless gesture as she indicated the boxed M&S ready-meals that along with home deliveries had been her salvation after colic, night feeds and then teething had made ordinary living a thing of the past.

'You do these for you and Len. I've to nip out later, anyway. I'll get fish and chips.'

She looked up at him gratefully. 'Are you sure? We haven't even any bread in. Will you be late?'

He pulled a face. 'Depends what I find. Could be. Only don't say anything to Len. It's an old contact of his that I've tracked down. I don't want him feeling pushed out, but I don't want him in the way either.'

She nodded as the baby grizzled and reached out. 'No, you don't,' said Webber. 'You're going to stay with me while your mummy sees to our visitor. I'll get him bathed and ready for bed.'

The creaking of the chair followed by footsteps announced Klein's arrival in the kitchen doorway. 'Anything I can do to help?' he asked.

'Thanks, Len,' said Melinda. 'Can you set the table? Just for two of us. Martyn has to go out. And put the kettle on if you fancy a cuppa.'

Webber knew she would have decanted the food from its foil containers so Len might be fooled into thinking she was still into home-cooking, but now he'd seen the evidence, she wouldn't bother. Klein's face was a picture. Webber saw the disappointments stack up; tea not beer, ready-meals not home cooking, a hard couch to sleep on. He wouldn't be back for a second night.

'Never mind that, Len. Come with us. We'll show you how to wash away the cares of the day. Bath time with baby Sam. That right, Sam? Shall we show Uncle Len what we can get up to with a waterproof alphabet?'

Sam gurgled his acquiescence, Melinda shot him a smile across the baby's head and Klein, dumbstruck, turned to follow. He and Julia had no children. Whilst they were up there getting soaked, Webber would have a few words with Klein. Melinda wasn't to be bothered either with idle gossip from work or with hints about home cooking. He would remind him that the tribulations of babyhood were outside his experience. Melinda had enough on her plate.

Webber stayed until they'd eaten. He made them both coffee and then excused himself. Melinda looked happy and relaxed. He'd tucked baby Sam into bed himself and for a wonder, the boy had allowed himself to be lulled to sleep by his father. Klein still looked stunned at the domesticity surrounding him, but Webber was sure his words over the bathtub had not gone unheeded. Melinda returned his wink behind Klein's back and followed him to the door.

Satisfied he'd left each of them suspicious enough of the other's motives that there would be no soul-searching heart-to-hearts about him, Webber smiled as he leant forward, rubbing his nose gently against Melinda's before meeting her lips in a soft kiss that said how much he loved her. It was no lie. It was to her benefit, too, that he didn't stay around this evening. The case had wound him up too tight. He'd only been able to play the model father because he knew he could let go, get rid of his pent up emotion later with Christa. This way, Melinda had the best of him; she didn't have to put up with him being restless and snappish. He would return home in the small hours, a caring husband slipping quietly into bed so as not to disturb her.

◉ ◉ ◉

Annie faced Pieternel across a table by the window of the restaurant in the Premier Inn tower in Hull. Pieternel's gaze took in the wide sweep of the Humber, the strings of lights outlining the bridges and tidal barrier, taming the river Hull where it met the estuary. 'Doesn't look like the same place,' she said. 'You know, with the windmill?'

Annie nodded. 'It is though. Same city.'

'I don't know what I expected but it wasn't this.'

'Everyone says that.' Annie picked up a menu and scanned it. 'The food's good here, so take advantage of Hull prices while you have the chance. Are you staying over?'

Pieternel nodded. 'I've booked a room here. You?'

'I'm staying with Christa. Have you got any further with who raided the office?'

'Yes, and the more I find, the less I like it. Your Detective Superintendent's going to come after us, isn't he?'

Annie nodded. 'He wants the rest of my surveillance files, too. I'd like to hand them over, but how?'

'If you do, we have to make out it's a set of files you hadn't got round to uploading. If word gets back that they didn't get rid of all the Marks files from the office ...' Pieternel's voice tailed off as she turned her gaze to the panoramic view beyond the windows.

'It won't only be Webber coming after us,' Annie finished the sentence. She thought about what had been done in the London office; of someone setting up the witness Sanger. She didn't want anyone like that stalking her. 'I'll have to make up some story about lost files, lost phone. He won't like it.'

'That's a thought ...' Pieternel began, then stopped as a waiter came to take their order. She took her time interrogating him on the no frills salmon steak before choosing Mediterranean skewers. Annie picked the meatball Bolognese. The man scribbled on his pad, then retreated. Pieternel watched him walk away before she went on, 'Suppose you hand over your wrecked phone to Webber and he gets the surveillance records off it himself. I could get you a mangled circuit board and SIM with just enough info retrievable. Then if word gets back, it's just that they got the data off your phone.'

Annie looked at her colleague while she thought this through. It was a dangerous game, deceiving someone like Webber, but they'd been pushed into a corner. If Pieternel could engineer a way to get the data to Webber, it would be worth the risk. There was something in those records that she'd missed, but it had to be something she didn't know enough to see. Webber had access to all manner of official records she couldn't get a sniff at.

'Tell me about the house?' Pieternel said. 'Was it the one on the flyer?'

Annie told Pieternel of her visit in the encroaching dusk. 'Yes, it was the one. I didn't think so at first. I couldn't see anything clearly when I first got near it.'

She described the lens high on the roof. 'Not deserted then?' Pieternel said.

'No, it wasn't, but it might not be anything sinister. The place has been discovered by the local kids.' She explained the way the two children had emerged from an ancient coal chute. 'It must have connected to a coal bunker at one time. It was a good distance from the house. I doubt it's had any use in decades, well, except by the local kids. It opened from the side of the path. Neat. You wouldn't have known it was there. They'd left a corner not quite closed. Maybe on purpose so they could get back in, but I closed it. There was a light down there but not right at the bottom. It made it impossible to open the shutter without throwing a huge shadow out across the yard. To be honest, I wasn't keen to go in that way, but I could have. And if they have kids breaking in, it's no wonder they have security.'

'So there's nothing to it?'

'Well, I'm not sure. I went right round to the far side, the proper way in. It has a driveway, gates. That's where I could see the shape of it, those old-fashioned chimneys. It matched the flyer. Oddly enough there were still no lights showing from inside. The only light I saw was when that cellar cover was opened.'

'So maybe there wasn't anyone there. It was just the kids put the cellar light on when they went in.'

'Oh, there were people in there all right. I'd just about decided the place was empty and I thought I'd take a photo. So I clicked the camera and ...' Annie paused on a shiver, remembering how the horribly bright flash of her phone camera had coincided with the background rumble of voices. 'I thought I'd been spotted,' she said.

'But nothing happened, so I got up as close as I dared and there were definitely people in there. I couldn't work out which bit of the house they were in. A man and woman. He raised his voice at one point. I heard him shout, 'For God's sake, Hannah!' and then he quietened down so I didn't hear the end of it. She spoke too but I couldn't make out the words. Her voice was quiet ... frail.'

'Hannah Levine?'

'I suppose so, but I don't know what it has to do with anything. Next thing I heard footsteps crashing down the hallway and I hot-footed it back round to the track.'

She pulled her new phone from her pocket, flicked through for the photograph and passed it across. Pieternel glanced at it and said, 'Yeah, that's the house on the flyer all right.' Then she lifted the phone to the light as she studied it closely. 'I see what you mean. There's something about it more stronghold than country cottage.'

As Annie took the phone back, it buzzed to life, showing Christa's number on the screen.

'Annie? You coming round tonight?'

'Yes, later. Is that OK?'

'Sure, but Martyn's on his way. I thought you might not want to run into him.'

'Too right! I'll find somewhere else.' She looked across at Pieternel. 'Webber's on his way to Christa's. Let's hope there's a spare room here or I'm sharing with you.'

'That's great!' Pieternel reached out and plucked the phone from Annie's hand. 'Listen to me, Christa. You're to get him on to Annie's surveillance records and ...'

Amazement robbed Annie of the power to move for a few moments as she listened to Pieternel rap out instructions. Then she snatched the phone back. 'Ignore her, Christa. You'll do nothing of the sort. We can't afford to ...'

'No, it's OK, Annie. You might be in luck. He's not staying over so he won't be falling asleep. Once he's good and relaxed, that's when he talks. But what's my story? How do I know about any of this stuff?'

Annie's immediate reply was prevented by the arrival of their food. A thought crept into the small delay. Why not? There was so much they needed to know. Why give up the chance? 'I suppose I might have told you about handing over the surveillance records. Then I'd likely have said what happened to my phone.'

'Marks,' said Pieternel through a mouthful of red pepper. 'And Sanger.'

Annie shook her head. 'He's not going to talk about them. But listen, Christa, if you tell him about my phone, it'll not looked so staged. Oh, and did I mention the press cuttings?' She explained the brief glimpse she'd had on that first visit and Webber's reaction to her when she asked about them. 'He might tell you stuff he wasn't going to tell me. They're press cuttings, for God's sake. Not state secrets. So …'

'That's him, now,' Christa interrupted. 'I'll tell you what, I'll see if I can patch you in. It'll be at least thirty minutes. Get yourselves somewhere quiet and mute your phone when I ring you.'

'No, Christa, don't …' But Christa had rung off.

Pieternel threw her an interrogative glance.

'You know Christa. Hates doing notes. I think she's going to ring us back and leave her phone on speaker so we can hear what he says for ourselves.' She picked up her fork and speared a meatball. 'Best not dawdle over this. It's not going to be a soundtrack to stimulate the appetite. And we don't want to be here. We'll go to your room.'

# chapter twenty three

Webber lay back into the soft mattress, savouring the feel of silk on his skin. This bed would cripple his back if he were to lie on it regularly, or even overnight. He knew that from painful experience. He ought to be exhausted. It had been a hell of a day, then he'd topped it with an hour's drive and a workout with Christa that must have burnt more calories than an hour in any gym. But it wasn't tiredness he felt. It was light headedness, a feel of the day's worries slipping off his shoulders, giving him space to recuperate. This was real relaxation, not like the show he'd put on for Klein.

His clothes and hers were scattered across the room where he'd flung them as he'd swept her from hallway to bedroom as soon as he'd arrived. He watched her now as she leant down to rummage through a heap of tangled material, checking her phone and tossing it back to the floor, coming up with his shirt which she slung casually round her shoulders, before slipping her arms into it, pushing aside the sleeves that flapped inches below her hands and padding off across the hallway to the kitchen. The clatter of the kettle coming to the boil played a foreground beat to the muffled roar of traffic. A siren cut in, its wail swelling from nowhere and shrinking to nothing in a beat. Not his problem. Nothing to do but lie here and drink her coffee for half an hour, then drive back home through the empty night time streets.

She called through from the kitchen; *Annie ... something-or-other.* He remembered that the two women got together when Annie Raymond was in the area. Christa had told him that before; the time she'd stunned him by producing Damien Marks's name out of left field. The Raymond woman had left something in the kitchen or left something in a mess. He wasn't interested; didn't give a monkey's about her.

The aroma of coffee preceded Christa's return to the room. She passed him a mug and then perched on the end of the bed. 'Annie said your lot had been to their office in London and taken a load of files.'

He sipped the hot coffee and ran his gaze down her from head to toe. His shirt sat lopsided on her shoulders, displaying the smooth curves of her body. It would hold the smell of her the whole way home. He wondered if she was miffed that no one had raided her office in Hull.

'I'll bet you didn't get all her surveillance records.'

OK, this comment had become a bit more interesting. He didn't let it show; took his time with another mouthful of coffee. 'Is that what she told you?' His tone was playful, as though the last thing on his mind was the Raymond woman and her shenanigans, which was hardly an act.

'No, she just said about the London office, but I know you've asked for her surveillance records. And I know what she's like. She's always months behind with her uploading. They'll be on her phone.'

He smiled as he reached out to take hold of her arm, applying gentle pressure, more an invitation than physical coercion.

She aimed an exaggerated glance at his watch where it lay on the bedside table. 'How late are you planning to be?' Her tone was severe but her eyes danced.

He hesitated because she was right about the time. 'What makes you so sure I've asked Annie Raymond for anything?'

'Because she's swapped phones.'

He laughed as though he couldn't care less, but now it was an act. He'd always known the Raymond woman was hiding stuff behind that cooperative façade. Not wanting to prompt her, he smothered a yawn and looked up towards the uncurtained window which glowed blackly back at him. He'd never been fool enough to trust Christa and after the last two days, he barely trusted himself.

'Her phone got wrecked, but don't get overexcited. It might have been an accident.'

'I'm not about to get overexcited for Annie Raymond.' He laughed at her turn of phrase, but the irony of the words struck him as soon as they left his mouth. Annie Raymond was the woman he'd establish as decoy; the one who'd set everyone's pulses racing with her revelation about Sanger.

'It got dropped or something.' Christa cradled her mug as she spoke, not looking at him but gazing out of the window. 'I've seen it. It's in pieces.'

Webber's smile was no less warm, but for a moment it wasn't for Christa. It was for the pieces of Annie Raymond's phone. She could wreck what she liked. His tech guys could get data off recycled ash. 'I suppose she didn't happen to throw it away here, did she?'

He turned his gaze towards the window again. It was a black sheen. Christa had never had curtains. 'No point,' she'd told him the first time he came here. 'I'm not overlooked.' He imagined the blank screen of the window springing to life showing his European colleagues sitting at the table in their video conference suite. He saw himself discussing dummy witnesses while he lay back on Christa's bed. The image made him smile, but made him uncomfortable, too. She hadn't answered him and he wouldn't push. He was aware of the sweat cooling on his body, and tipped his mug to look inside. It was empty. He had to be off in fifteen minutes or so and had an hour's drive ahead of him.

Taking the cue, she said, 'I'm getting more coffee. You want some?'

When she came back and handed him his cup, she said, 'How badly do you want to get your hands on Annie's phone?'

'Not as badly as I want to get my hands on you.'

She curled her lip at him, which was no less than he deserved for such a cheesy line.

He watched as she walked across towards the window, his shirt slipping off her shoulder, the material shimmering as it feathered her thighs, sliding tantalisingly upward as she reached to swat something high on the window. He struggled to keep his mind on Annie Raymond's smashed phone. Was she offering to get it for him?

As she turned to walk towards him, she casually pulled the shirt around her. Its thin material accentuated more than it covered. He reached forward and ran his finger round the curve of her breast, feeling her nipple harden under his touch. But she slapped his hand away and sat back on the bed. 'Who'd do that, Martyn, to a child?'

His desire for her dimmed as the images thrust themselves forward in his head. 'A psychopath. An inhuman bastard sick in the head. Someone who needs to be behind bars.'

'I'll get you Annie's phone,' she said. 'But I warn you, it's in pieces.'

This was crossing a line. They didn't discuss cases. But it was a child killing. Lines and boundaries blurred. He took her hand and squeezed it briefly. 'Thank you.'

'Martyn, she told me she'd seen some press cuttings. Has this guy done it before?'

His brief spark of anger focused solely on Annie Raymond. To Christa right now he felt only gratitude. He smiled at her and shook his head. 'There was a case ten years back. It might have been a copycat from a long time ago. But the guy was caught and gaoled. He died in prison.' Before she could say anything, he changed tack. 'How long have you known Annie Raymond's boss, what's-her-name?'

'Pieternel? A few years. I knew her when I worked in London.'

'She's ... uh ... fairly hard to find. I mean there's not much online.'

She shrugged. 'I've never looked. Why would I?' He wasn't sure if he saw an extra layer of wariness or if she was just getting bored.

'How long did you work for her?'

She shot him a glance but he made sure his attention was on his cup, as though the question wasn't really important.

'Coupla years, on and off. She taught me a lot.'

Not too much, Webber hoped. He'd yet to get a proper handle on Pieternel, hadn't found the real woman under all the aliases. The operation smelt of much more than a bog-standard PI set-up. At least Pieternel did. Raymond panned out with a bit of digging and he'd done the intel on Christa at the time of the documentary. 'What's her background?' he asked.

'Dunno. Never really thought about it. That copycat killing you mentioned, has it anything to do with anything that's happening now?'

She wasn't going to tell him anything. He doubted she knew much. He'd told her more than he should about the old cases, but nothing that wasn't in the public domain for anyone who knew where to look. 'Sins of the fathers,' he murmured.

'What do you mean?'

He laughed. 'I mean it's not surprising if some police officers end up a bit overbearing ... arrogant ... Look at the examples we get thrust in our faces every day. We shape up pretty damned well.'

She moved fast to jab her hand into his abdomen, making him flinch and clutch at his coffee. 'You didn't mean that at all. Don't you go all metaphysical, Detective Superintendent. You know I can't abide it.'

He laughed again, rubbing the back of his hand on the sheet to wipe away the coffee that had slopped there. 'How are you defining metaphysics, Miss Andrew? No, it's just that when you read about what some parents do, it's no bloody wonder their kids grow up maniacs.' His thought processes were skipping across aspects of the case, touching down briefly, making no sense in terms of the words that came from his mouth, but it never mattered with Christa. She wouldn't badger him for explanations the way some people did, though her response this time was severe.

'You're not excusing a child killer, are you?'

'Of course not, but sometimes you can see where it comes from. You remember all that research we did for the documentary?' He paused on a laugh. She'd done exactly zilch, just blagged her way to being able to say enough to look good in front of the cameras; the archetype of everything Klein complained about in a private detective. She'd been right of course. The way the production team flitted about changing the focus. By the time the programme aired, it was nothing like the one he thought he'd signed up to. There'd been no particular reason for him and Christa to meet more than a couple of times, but she'd used him to gather in the few facts she needed. He thought back to how he'd resented it when he'd realised. He'd acted the uptight arrogant copper to a T, until she'd teased him out of it. He'd talked about those old cases to her back then, lying on this same bed. 'How do you do it?,' he asked her. 'Flying through life doing nothing but what you please?'

'Hey.' She punched him lightly. 'I do my bit. I can work hard when I need to.'

'Yeah, right. Like for the documentary. Work hard at cherry-picking from other people.'

'I don't remember any complaints at the time. Anyway, what are you saying? Were those old cuttings about one of the documentary crimes?'

He shook his head. 'They didn't use that case.'

Her forehead furrowed in thought. 'What case? I don't remember. So is this current one linked to the old one, the one on the press cuttings?'

'I can't talk about current cases, Christa. You know that. But no, it's not.'

'So what's the old case?'

He yawned extravagantly. Typical of Christa to show an interest in the edges of the research now she had no need of it. He wondered if she were also doing a bit of fishing for Annie Raymond, maybe wanting some behindhand *quid pro quo* to assuage her conscience for the phone. 'Eastern Europe,' he told her. '17th … 18th century. Psychopathic father, two children. Well-to-do, powerful family. The kids were shielded from the worst of it, but then he killed the woman who'd been looking after them all. It wasn't their mother, but it was the woman who'd been their only day-to-day carer since they were born. I can't remember what she'd done to rile him. But he tortured her and killed her, slowly, in front of them. By slowly I mean over a few days.' The image of small Sam sat in his head; the trusting laughter, bath time with Daddy. He fought back a wave of cold anger that made him want to reach back through time and crush the life out of the man who'd done it, maybe before he could even father the children that he'd damaged so badly. 'The little girl went mad,' he told Christa. 'Couldn't live with what she'd witnessed. She turned it inward. Ripped herself to shreds – physically and emotionally. Ended up locked away somewhere. The boy seesawed between sanity and madness and ended up a brutal killer himself.'

'I don't remember any copycat case. What was it, someone killing a child-minder?'

'No, it was the son's murders they were re-enacting if anything.' He paused as he looked up at the black void beyond the window. Klein had had it to deal with ten years ago. The bizarre injuries aping the physical deformities of the original victim. All the talk of anniversaries. Klein had pooh-poohed that side of it. *Don't let that sort of garbage distract you, Martyn. Every day's an anniversary if you want it to be.* 'The only way the boy could live with what his father had done,' he told Christa, 'was to turn it into pleasure … gratification inside his head, to find enjoyment in the brutality. The worst had happened. He was never going to top what his father had done, but he spent his life trying to. You damage children and you nurture badness. It's a fact of life. Not a very nice one.' Phrases floated up from the recesses of his memory. What was it? *Extra fingers for extra hands … extra hands for extra prayers …?* Something like that.

'I don't remember any of this from the TV thing,' Christa said.

'No, they changed their minds about which crimes they were focusing on.'

'It must be pretty horrible living inside your head at times.'

He conceded the point with a smile. She was right.

'So is that what those press cuttings were about?'

'Christa. Shut up and come back to bed for ten minutes. Those press cuttings were nothing to do with anything. Annie Raymond's a nosey cow.'

'OK. Give me your cup. I don't want coffee all over the sheets.'

With a cup in each hand, she had nothing to hold the shirt. It billowed as she walked across the hallway towards the kitchen. Hands behind his head, he lay back and watched her through the open doorways. She had nothing to carry when she returned but she didn't bother about the shirt so he could watch her naked form as she meandered back to the bedroom. She paused to bend over and rummage through a heap of clothes.

'What are you doing?'

'Just making sure my phone's off. Don't want any interruptions, do we?' As she straightened up she gave him a sharp look. 'What's bugging you?'

He drew in a breath. 'There's a child killer on the loose, Christa. Your mate's outfit could have stumbled on something we need to know. She's cooperating with us … well, after a fashion. I'm not trying to stir up trouble for her or you, but I might need to get on to the organ grinder, and if I do there might not be time to fanny about.'

The pause was several seconds long. Eventually she said, 'If I give you a number, I want to know you won't use it unless you really

really have to. And there'd be no point anyway. Once she knows it's compromised, she'll bin it. But just for a one-off emergency, OK?'

Webber bit back a sarcastic response. Who did this Pieternel woman think she was, a bloody spook? 'Thanks,' he said. 'That's just what I'm after.'

He knew that what should really bother him was that this had become real, and home had become the pretence; that he just wanted to hold her for a few minutes before he had to leave. But he pushed the thought aside. Nothing would get out of hand. He'd deal with it when he had to.

◉ ◉ ◉

Annie sat at the desk, elbows on the polished surface, chin resting in her hands. Pieternel stood by the window, her back to the room. They were high above the city, and the hotel slept around them.

From Annie's phone, Christa's voice murmured, 'Don't want any interruptions, do we?' And the line went dead. Annie reached forward and clicked it off. She looked across at Pieternel, but her colleague seemed lost in thought. Annie was grateful to Christa for her timing, but amazed she'd got away with it, turning the phone on and off under Webber's nose.

The voices replayed in her mind. Christa had gone beyond her remit in offering to obtain the broken phone for Webber, but then Christa could never be relied on to stick to a script.

'Quite a neat move,' Pieternel's voice interrupted her thoughts. 'The phone thing. She gets brownie points and he has no reason to think you've set him up.'

'But now he thinks I was deliberately keeping things from him.'

'Well, not necessarily. She said it might have been an accident. And what was all that 18th century psychopath stuff?'

Annie shrugged. 'Apparently he's always been into stuff like that; origins of crime and all that. So Christa says. It's why he got involved in that documentary. How wonderful modern policing is; how awful it was in pre forensics days. That's his thing. They did a crime reconstruction. A Victorian murder. Showing how they'd have solved it if they'd had all the mod cons.'

'How did Christa get involved?'

'You know Christa. She got a sniff of the documentary and next thing she's muscled in, had the Thompsons on the local TV. It's no wonder they love her. I think that's where she first met Webber.'

'Annie, when Webber said the press cuttings were nothing to do with anything now, did you believe him?'

'No, I didn't. It's tied in with copycat murders somehow.' From where she sat on the floor, the view from the window was all dark sky, barely visible pinpricks of light all that showed of vast suns billions of light years distant. If she had the right telescope, she could distinguish the far-off stars from the relatively close planets. She might even see the craters on Mars. But even with the right telescope, she would still have to know where to look.

'I need access to the stuff Webber can get at; official information and databases,' she said. 'And I'd get to know what I'd missed about Damien Marks.'

'OK, by tomorrow, Webber'll have your surveillance files and he'll be able to find it if it's there.'

'Will he? I know Marks in a way that Webber doesn't. I've been on his coattails for months. I'll share the sodding the files, but if Webber would share what he knows with me, we'd find it – whatever it is – a hell of a lot quicker.'

'I daresay you're right, but it's not going to happen.'

'Not now that Christa's more or less told him I'm hiding stuff.'

'Come on, Annie. It was never going to happen. The best we can hope for is that if he unearths anything we need to know about whoever's targeting us, that Christa'll get it out of him. At least she's given us a way to get your files into the enquiry.'

'You've still to produce the right bits of smashed up phone.'

'That's a point. I'd better get on to the guys.' Pieternel sprang to her feet and headed for her phone where it lay on the dressing table tethered to its charger. As she picked it up, she turned back to Annie. 'If this is to be convincing, we can't let him find everything. A lot of that memory has to look like it's stuffed with things he can't get at.'

'Photos,' said Annie. 'Trash most of the photos. He knows what Damien looks like.'

# chapter twenty four

'No comment,' said Damien Marks.

*No comment ... No comment ... No comment ...*

The image showed more of the top of his head than his face, which he kept down, gaze fixed to the table, but he couldn't sit still. He shifted about, the metal chair legs scraping on the floor. His hand pulled at his collar, not that it was tight. He wore no tie.

Webber studied the screen. His prime suspect had been ill-at-ease in his no-comment bunker since bundled in there by his lawyer early in the proceedings. Webber needed him out again, in the ring sparring with his interrogators. They'd told him it wouldn't be long. That was why he was watching now.

A piece of paper was pushed across the surface into Marks's line of sight.

'Your work schedule says you called at this estate agency at 3 o'clock that afternoon, Damien.' The address was read out, the questioner relaxed, impassive.

Webber stared intently. He thought he caught the ghost of a nod preceding the routine, 'No comment.'

The brief was on edge, too.

'You recorded a two-hour meeting.' Just a statement of fact.

Again that almost imperceptible nod. Marks shot a quick glance across the table.

Then a subtle shift in body language from the questioner. Hands on the flat surface, leaning forward a little. 'So how is it no one in that office remembers you?' The tone sharp now, accusatory.

'She met me outside.' The words came quickly, a hint of triumph.

Webber's fists clenched as his mouth curved to a smile. He stared at Marks's lawyer; saw Marks glance round, too. Even through the grainy image he could read Marks's expression. *I've a simple explanation here, why shouldn't I use it?* Marks's questioner showed no emotion, just continued as though nothing out of the ordinary had happened.

'Who met you, Damien?'

Again Marks glanced at his brief, but he would find it hard to scramble back into his no-comment bunker while this topic was live. 'Her name's Miss Price. She was the land agent. I'd an appointment.'

'And why did she meet you outside?'

'It was chance, that's all. She was just coming out as I arrived. We went for lunch.' Marks had even worked up a measure of indignation.

'Tell me about the lunch, Damien. Where did you go? What did you eat?'

Webber watched the words tumble out as though from a breached dam. Marks couldn't say enough as his questioner led him into a detailed account of the café, the food, everything about the meeting except its purpose. He wasn't looking at his brief anymore, but Webber was. The man gave little away, but Webber could see the tension. Meanwhile, Marks ploughed on, convinced he was handling it just fine.

'And what was the purpose of your meeting with Miss Price, Damien?'

'Oh … Uh … Nothing really. Just routine.'

'Was it about this big property deal your colleagues have told us about?'

Webber saw shock light in Marks's eyes as he struggled to back pedal on his sudden volubility. 'No … uh … what big deal? Who said that?' His gaze raked the papers in front of his interrogators as though terrified at what might leap out at him.

'Then you tell me about the deal you were involved in, Damien.'

'No, I … It's … There's commercial sensitivity … It's all legit. I … I can't comment.' He turned to stare at his lawyer, a mute appeal for help. Too late, thought Webber, you're in the ring now.

Marks's lawyer was arguing for time out. Webber knew that if he were in there, he'd keep Marks and try to finish him off. He wondered about this property deal, hadn't made up his mind. Had it been a set-up to keep his colleagues quiet, to justify his huge salary? Or were they in on it, too? A cover-up of something more sinister. Certainly no one had produced evidence of any big deal in the offing.

They were winding up, reaching out to stop the recording, letting the fancy brief have his way. Webber was surprised but if they judged a break was in order, he wasn't going to argue. He'd put his best team in that room.

Marks had teetered at the edge for several hours, too far gone for any fancy brief to pull him back. He wished Klein was here to see this. Marks's annihilation was just a matter of time.

But then Klein, too, was on some kind of edge, and it wasn't just the job. There'd been no calls to or from Julia. Klein only mentioned her if they did first. Cracks in the Kleins' marriage? It was unthinkable. Where the hell was he, anyway? His status was ambiguous; here with Farrar's blessing but not under Webber's authority in any meaningful sense.

He stood up and stretched, walking out into the big office. A picture caught his eye, one of the few photographs they'd retrieved from Annie Raymond's phone. A shot of the inside of Marks's car, a shaft of sunlight obscuring the papers she'd tried to capture, but showing the gauges and instruments in sharp relief as though she'd attempted an arty shot. 'Is it right that the private investigator tried to destroy her phone so you wouldn't get these?' someone asked him. The rumour mill ground on.

◉ ◉ ◉

Olivia runs up the hill, puffing a bit because it gets quite steep, but she's determined to catch up with Ryan. It'll be dark soon and she'll have to run all the way home, but that's OK because it'll be downhill.

She isn't going to say she's not allowed or anything like that. She's just going to say, I'm not going. I'm not going on your birthday trip. She isn't even going to say, Stacy can go instead, because she doesn't care what Stacy does.

Auntie Enn gave her the idea. Auntie Enn sitting at the table. 'I'm not eating that.' Her mother saying, 'Oh Enn! What's wrong with it?' Olivia waiting for Auntie Enn to say, I don't like it or I'm not hungry or I feel sick. And Auntie Enn just saying, 'I'm not eating that.' It made her mum real mad, but Auntie Enn didn't have to eat her tea.

*I'm not going on your birthday trip.*

She has to catch him up and say it right now while she's not scared. Tomorrow she might be scared again. She thought that ghosts were the scariest thing, but her mum says there's no such thing. And when she thought it out, it was scarier that way round … the hands in the well, the face in the ivy, and hearing their voices. She has to stop to bend over because she's getting a stitch. The thought of the ghost hands being real hands makes a shiver go all the way through her.

◉ ◉ ◉

The office in Scarborough felt isolated, out on a limb, after the bustle and noise of the station in York. Ahmed fought a rising tide of annoyance. Kicked out of the York enquiry just as it took a dramatic turn. Salt in the wound that he hadn't even been back in time to witness the Cochrans' case careering to its grisly conclusion.

Both Cochrans, father and daughter, had already been arrested on suspicion of murder. Their victim, a man in his twenties who had disappeared four years ago, had been found at the bottom of the farm's disused well, a single blast from a 12-bore shotgun the clear cause of death. That much of the story had been splashed across the local newspaper.

'Just wait until the rest of it leaks,' one of his colleagues had said.

Leak was the word. He flicked through the paperwork. The Cochrans had been running a waste disposal side-line for years, tipping barrels of heaven alone knew what into the fissures in the cliff top. They'd used the well, too. And something they'd dumped down there had kept their crime in pristine condition.

Ahmed thought back to the incident that had catapulted him into the heart of Webber's enquiry. Janice's concern must have been that Billy Judd would unearth the waste, but she'd heard his emergency call. And once she knew he'd found a child's body, she'd taken off. He sat back and closed his eyes for a moment. It didn't feel like a complete picture.

Footsteps. The sound of a door opening. 'Oy, you can nod off in your own time, Constable.'

Ahmed looked up at the sergeant standing over him. 'No, I was just thinking. Janice Cochran. That knife. We got everything we could from the footage and you know what the pathologist said? Can't be certain it isn't the weapon that killed the little girl.'

'She certainly took off with it in a hurry.'

'And if it's not the murder weapon, what is it … was it? Why did she take it? She didn't take the gun.'

The sergeant gave him a hard stare. 'It's bad enough she got that blade on to the boat. I hope she wouldn't have had a prayer of getting a shotgun on board. And it's not that killing we're looking at.' He pointed to the file in front of Ahmed. 'Seems like the Superintendent wants his blue-eyed boy in York again by the weekend, but you're not going anywhere until that case is watertight.'

Ahmed tried not to look pleased. If Webber wanted him back, they could hardly say no. But he took the hint and buried himself in the case notes. If he was good enough that he was wanted on a complex case like Webber's, the Cochrans should be child's play.

◉ ◉ ◉

Olivia sets off again and pounds round the corner, but then skids to a stop quick as she can. Ryan's just up there in the road talking to his aunt. Olivia shrinks back into the shadow of the hedge. She doesn't like Mrs Fairclough. She has nasty starey eyes.

Mrs Fairclough has a really old woman with her, sitting in a wheelchair, all bundled in a blanket. They won't talk to Ryan for long. The old woman looks like she wants to get going. She's got real funny eyes, too. It seems like she looks right at Olivia with a big grin, showing a line of white teeth. Olivia's knees go a bit funny. She tries to push back into the hedge.

Olivia can't hear what Ryan's saying to Mrs Fairclough because of the breeze, but she hears the old woman OK. The old woman suddenly turns to Mrs Fairclough and shouts out, 'I want to go back now.'

◉ ◉ ◉

Ahmed could guess at the why. The Cochrans' victim had been an environmental protester, must have learnt what they were up to and confronted them or crept on to the farm to find evidence. One or other of them had shot him to shut him up, then tipped his body into the well. Somewhere in here would be the detail that would bounce either Janice or her father into a confession. Much easier all round to go ahead with an admission of guilt in the bag.

The murdered man had been reported missing by his girlfriend. But now Ahmed had found the girlfriend, the subject of her own missing person report just three months later. This one called in by worried parents, hundreds of miles away from the Cochrans.

No one had made the link at the time. The girlfriend's focus had been on an animal testing lab further down the coast. The Cochrans hadn't had a mention. But maybe she found something later. Did she have a go at conducting her own investigation? Had she gone up there to confront them? Webber still had a team at the farm. Ahmed reached for the phone. No harm in asking.

◉ ◉ ◉

Webber's thoughts turned to Myra Franklin. Forensics were clear. Her body had been in the boot of Marks's car, might have been there when the PI had been clicking her camera.

He wondered about the Raymond woman. She'd clocked a Miss Price, too, somewhere along the line. How well did she know Marks after all this time? Would she see anything different if she were standing here now looking at all this stuff, watching Marks squirm in the interview suite?

'Did we get anything off his mobile?' A woman at a desk by the window looked across at him as he studied the photos. 'The PI's records say he was forever on the phone.'

Webber gave her a wintry smile. 'All we found on his phone, other than his wife, were streams of calls to sex lines.'

Analysis of the calls had been frustratingly unfruitful. The numbers still in use were sleazy chat lines that panicked and disappeared when officially approached. 'These lines come and go like nobody's business,' they told him. 'Most of them aren't legit and some are used as anonymous message drops. They're just out for a quick buck, not properly registered or anything.' He didn't like it. It felt wrong. Smoke and mirrors.

Serious money in porn, he thought.

The reflective surface caught a movement. Klein. How long had he been here?

As he watched, Klein slipped into a side room. Something about his stance, slightly bent at the shoulders, made him look like an old man. Webber made to follow. He would put back the spring into his ex-governor's step. Marks was about to spill his guts and no fancy brief could stop him.

The doorway through which Klein had vanished gave on to a space little bigger than a cupboard. He'd caught both Klein and Ahmed skiving in there the other day.

He looked in. Surrounded by the packed shelves and boxes of paper, Klein had rested something on a narrow ledge. It looked like a page from an old file. Klein had his back to Webber and slowly shook his head.

Watching this gesture of defeat, Webber knew that Farrar had been wrong. Klein hadn't wanted to come back into the heart of this enquiry. He'd done his bit. He was here because he'd been asked; maybe thought he owed it to the victim. But he didn't. Klein had got his man; seen him die behind bars. It was wrong to have brought him back to torture himself over some copycat thing. He should be home with Julia. Maybe it was his decision to come over here that had caused the rift, and who could blame Julia for that? She knew better than anyone the toll it had taken of her husband the first time round. Klein needed to be with his wife, enjoying his retirement.

Webber felt a jolt of shock, suddenly aware of an almost imperceptible tremble in his colleague's hunched shoulders. He backed out of the small space, desperate not to let his presence be detected. Klein was crying. Taking in a breath, he marched back towards his office. Disentangling Klein from the case and getting him back home had become a priority.

◉ ◉ ◉

Mrs Fairclough turns to the old woman in the wheelchair and gives her a real nasty look. Two sets of starey eyes looking right at each other. Olivia watches. She's transfixed but she begins to think it might be better to sneak away and not wait for Ryan after all. Then Mrs Fairclough shouts in the old woman's face, 'Bloody go then, you can walk that far.'

Olivia feels her mouth drop open, her lips twitch. That is such a rude thing for a grown up to say to an old woman, it's like her mum saying it to Auntie Enn when Auntie Enn won't eat her tea. But her mum only says rude things about Auntie Enn to Dad, and she says them when she doesn't know Olivia is listening.

Olivia doesn't believe Mrs Fairclough will really make the old woman walk. So she's amazed when the old woman throws back the blanket and stands up out of the wheelchair. Mrs Fairclough and Ryan don't even look at her. And she doesn't look at them, because she has turned her big staring eyes towards Olivia. And she grins again and starts to walk forward.

Olivia feels her face crumple, feels her insides drop. A great wave comes at her. The starey eyes bore right into her. The line of white teeth gleam. Olivia's feet seem like they're glued to the ground, her hands feel like they're tied to her sides. Even the scream that she wants to make is stuck inside her throat.

Then she's pushed herself away from the hedge. Her legs work again. She's running and running, not even stopping at the road where cars might be coming. Diving over the wall because the gate's shut and if she stops even for a second, the bony hand will reach out and grab her from behind.

She pounds up the stairs, right to the top, and doesn't stop until she's flung herself into the den and pulled the curtain across.

'Olivia, gently up the stairs! ... Don't slam the door like that!'

She pulls in her breath in great gasps. The old woman wasn't a ghost. And she was the scariest of all.

# chapter twenty five

Not wanting to give the conversation an official air by having it in work hours, Webber had invited Ahmed for a beer in town on Friday evening. Ahmed was the only person he knew who had worked with Klein since his retirement but not before; the only one not bowed down under the baggage of say Farrar who had known Klein in his prime. It had been a spur of the moment thing, and Melinda had pointed out that Ahmed had probably taken it as an order, not an invitation, but they were here now, albeit Webber was unrehearsed in what he wanted to say.

'Uh … Useful result at the Cochrans' place,' Ahmed commented, his voice overly casual.

'Yes, Ayaan, you were right.' Webber gave him the acknowledgement he wanted to hear. And he deserved it. It had been on Ahmed's hunch that the second body had been unearthed from the underground labyrinth beneath the well.

'It's chaos up there now,' Ahmed told him. 'With the levels of seepage from the well system and the cliff top, they've had to shut off a huge area.'

Before the Cochrans could take centre stage, Webber said, 'Have you seen much of Len since you've been back here? I'm worried he's overdoing it. He's supposed to be retired after all.'

'Oh, don't worry about Len,' Ahmed said easily. 'He'll be pleased to be part of it. It's to do with the man he put away. He told me he was determined to see the case out.'

Webber felt exasperation rise. 'This is nothing to do with his old case, Ayaan. He saw that one out very successfully. The man was put away and he died in gaol.'

'Yes, but it's a copycat, isn't it? And didn't the killings start out just after the man died?'

This was an amalgam of information from Klein with a helping of Chinese whispers thrown in. 'No, it's not. I know Len has a bee in his bonnet about it, that's partly why I'm worried about him. But it isn't anything to do with his old case. The similarities are superficial. If it's a copycat then it's an arm's length one.' He felt his eyes lose focus as his mind ran back over the details the documentary team had uncovered. 'A hundred years or more,' he told Ahmed. 'A sick guy who tortured and killed people because he could. He turned his son into a brutal killer. The records are scrappy but he did ritualistic things with their bodies, shredding their fingers, decapitating some of them.'

'Some of them?'

'It was tied in with some archaic notion of sin. The similarities are unfortunate, the decapitation, the fact that they're children.'

Ahmed looked puzzled. 'Uh … someone lent me a DVD. The documentary, I mean.'

'No, they changed tack. I don't know why. Decided it was the wrong focus for their target audience, something like that. If you think detection has its frustrations, try working with a TV production company. But no, the thing is, it's nothing to do with Len's case. He got his man. There are no doubts.'

'And it's the recent killing we're looking at, not the one two years ago because we were wrong about a link with Marks.'

'Not that recent, Ayaan. We found her recently, but she was killed well over a year ago.'

'But what about the witnesses? Dead men talking. Doesn't it make a link of some sort? Just the fact that someone was after framing Marks?'

'They weren't framing Marks,' Webber said. 'Whoever it was

tried to frame anyone and everyone so the investigation would follow the wrong tracks until the trail went cold. It's not our case anymore.'

'So Marks turning out to be a killer is just a coincidence?' Ahmed didn't sound convinced and Webber couldn't blame him.

'I don't want Len burning himself out on this one.' Webber returned to his target topic. He needed Ahmed as an ally. Farrar had brought Klein in; he wouldn't want to push him back out. 'He's here because he was asked, but he shouldn't be doing these long hours. He should be home with his wife. It can't be very nice for her, all on her own.'

'You don't need to worry about that, Guv.' Ahmed said. 'Mrs Klein's come with him. They're staying together in York. She has family here.'

For a moment, surprise kept Webber silent, then he gave Ahmed a tight smile. 'Just bear in mind that he's putting more into this than he should. He's getting too involved and it isn't doing him any good. I need someone to keep an eye on him.'

This had to be a serious rift. Why else would Klein lie to Ahmed? Perhaps Ahmed knew Julia well enough that he might call round to see that she was OK while Klein was away. And Klein hadn't wanted that.

Could Julia be in York? Was that where Len was going on his long outings? Had they kept her presence a secret because she didn't want to be back in their lives? But why would Klein have put up with chaos at the Webbers if his wife was in the city? She'd had family here, Webber knew, but that was years ago.

'Believe me, Ayaan. He's not doing himself any good, but he might need some serious persuading to bow out. I'm relying on you to back me up.'

Ahmed looked alarmed. Webber toyed with telling him that Klein had ducked out of the office to cry over the case file, but it would feel like a betrayal so he kept quiet. He'd use it if he had to.

He pointed towards the window that let on to the street. 'Annie Raymond, the PI, she photographed Marks from across there. He sat in the place next door drinking coffee for just over an hour on the Saturday morning. Not that that helps. We need to place him on the North Yorkshire coast or find his accomplice.'

'How useful are the PI's records?'

'Not bad.' He tipped his head in acknowledgement of the detail she'd recorded, adding, 'Not the quality they'd have been if we'd had the resource to be behind him 24/7, of course.'

'But do they get him anywhere near the coast?'

'No, they …' He stopped. The files they'd had initially were stuffed with surveillance photos. The broken phone had yielded a few, but most were irretrievable. He saw them hanging askew from their magnets. Marks's car interior with documents strewn across the seats. He pulled out his mobile and dialled the home number of one of the tech guys. From the tone of the man's voice he was less than happy at an interruption to the start of his weekend.

'Photos?' he said. 'We got you all the ones we could. The rest had had it.'

'Can you estimate how many there were to start with, retrievable or not?'

'Hmm … maybe. If we went on size of the memory in … the relative number of … What are you after?'

'Based on the original set they sent across.'

There was a pause, then, 'Yeah … Yeah, you're right. Nowhere near enough, even allowing for that mashed-up card.'

As he closed the call, Webber found Ahmed staring expectantly. He raised his crossed fingers and treated Ahmed to a satisfied smile. 'The Chief Super'll go ape-shit.'

'About Annie Raymond's photographs?'

'No. About the overtime bill.' He thought again about the records from the PIs' office and the absurd charade about the smashed phone. He had to strike this iron while it was still smoking, before

170

anyone spirited away more of the evidence. 'I need the truth out of those two,' he told Ahmed.

Ahmed's expression showed his inner struggle to keep up with this incomplete commentary. Webber would explain in his own good time. 'Take this and keep it safe.' He passed across a copy of the number Christa had given him. 'It belongs to Annie Raymond's boss, Pieternel. But don't use it without my say-so. It's a one-shot thing. She'll bin the phone when she knows we have it. But I might need you to use it on Tuesday.'

'Tuesday?'

'Yes, I want a day to get a few things checked, but on Tuesday I want you in at the crack of dawn. Four AM. We're going on a trip.'

◉ ◉ ◉

The two-tone chime of the doorbell sounds to Olivia like a huge gong, too loud to miss. Sometimes Auntie Enn has the TV so high that her mum said she can't hear a thing over it. She holds herself still, but then her mum's footsteps are clack-clack-clacking down the hallway. She's shouting up the stairs, 'Olivia.'

And then Ryan's voice. 'Is Olivia ready?'

Auntie Enn's voice, too. Olivia wishes Auntie Enn would say about her being too young to go such a long way, but she's going on about something else now.

Ryan again. '… only we've not to hang about … Friday traffic …'

'Olivia! Come on.'

And it all just happens. She's downstairs and Ryan's got her case. Her mum says not to worry, she's going to love it and Ryan's mum and dad will be there to look after her. Everyone's saying goodbye and doing big waves because it's all a big treat. At the gate, there's a car, a big square one. It's full of people.

'That's not your car,' she says to Ryan, all the time thinking not about the car, but the people. That's not your mum and dad, is what she should say, but the words won't come out in all the fuss of him carrying her case for her and her mum telling her to have a good time and to behave.

'It's the youth club's people carrier, stupid,' says Ryan. 'How're we going to fit everyone in our car?'

Once they get going, it's not too bad. Ryan has let her sit right up front with him and the grown-ups. The grown-ups are from the youth club. Scary Mrs Fairclough isn't there and there aren't any old women in blankets. Ryan tells them, 'She's shy. She doesn't know anyone yet, so she's gonna sit up here with me.' It's all right because he keeps his voice down and no one but the grown-ups hear him, so she doesn't get teased. In fact, they're all playing some game of their own in the back, making a real racket. It sounds good, but when she tries to peep round Ryan to see what they're doing, he puts his arm right round her and says, 'Don't worry. I won't let them tease you.'

After a while, they stop for someone else and there's a bit of an argument. They all have to get out. Olivia isn't sure what's going on, but Ryan stays with her and keeps her away from the gang of boys who all start to fight on someone's lawn. She says to Ryan, 'If there isn't enough room, I can go back home.'

It's all shouting and grown-ups getting cross. Then Stacy's there and Ryan brings them both a Magnum, but says not to show the others because there aren't enough to go round, so they stay back, crunching on the chocolate coating and watching.

And in the end, it's all sorted out and they set off.

# chapter twenty six

Webber looked out over the London cityscape, the early light glinting from hundreds of reflective surfaces. It was a comfortable office, a pleasant place to relax after the long journey. The digital display on the window sill told him it was Tuesday and the digits clicked to 8:00 as he heard the outer door open and footsteps tap smartly across the polished floor.

'Pieternel, what's going on? Who's ...?' Webber saw shock whip the breath away from Annie Raymond and halt her progress with a physical jolt. He sat in her boss Pieternel's chair leaning back, legs crossed, fingers steepled, fixing her with a stony glare.

He saw realisation hit as she swung round. Ahmed was at the far side of the outer office, his eye on the man who'd let them in, who sat behind a desk looking scared.

'What the hell ...?' She swung back round on Webber. 'What's he doing out there? What are you doing? Where's Pieternel?' Again she turned her back on him and stormed out, repeating her question to her colleague.

'She's on her way, Annie.'

Webber moved the chair so he could watch her. She reached for a random piece of paper and flicked it, whilst tipping her head in his direction.

She was answered by a quick shake of the man's head and a mouthed, 'No warrant.'

Ahmed's footsteps padded across the floor behind her, crowding her, invading her space as Webber had told him to do. She looked through Ahmed and turned her glare on Webber. 'Right then. In that case ...'

Her colleague quickly raised his hand in an unmistakable gesture of caution. He murmured, 'I spoke to Pieternel. She said ... uh ...'

'She said to cooperate.' Ahmed finished his sentence.

Webber saw tension rise in every move Annie Raymond made as she ignored Ahmed and marched back to face him. 'I don't know who the hell he is,' she spat. 'And I don't know what the hell you think you're doing, but ...'

'That's Detective Constable Ayaan Ahmed,' Webber interrupted smoothly. 'And we're here to collect some information that must have slipped your mind first time round.'

'I don't give a damn who he is. And if you want information, you need a warrant.'

'I think we'll find that the first warrant covered it. I'm happy to wait for your boss if you'd rather, but I gather she's going to be quite a while.'

Webber watched her anger grow, half expecting a furious outburst. But whatever she itched to shout at him – *You didn't have a warrant first time round. We cooperated!* – she swallowed it and snatched a phone from her pocket, turning her back as she spoke into it.

'Pieternel, I'm in the office. Webber's sitting here like he owns the place. They don't have a warrant. What do you want me to do?' Ahmed kept step beside her. She clamped the phone tight to her ear.

After a moment, she clicked off the call, turned and stalked back again. Webber waited, staring into the middle distance. Her boss's workstation was within his reach but he'd learnt enough about them to know he'd trigger a meltdown if he tried to meddle with it.

She kept her tone even but he could see it was an effort. 'What is it that you want?'

He sat upright and gave her a smile. 'That's better. No point stringing this out if we don't have to, though it's no penance. It's a more comfortable office than mine.'

'I said what do you want?' she snapped, anger getting the better of her.

'My tech guys wasted a lot of time retrieving data from a broken phone.'

She shrugged a *so-what?*

'And I still don't have everything I need. I should bill you for that work. I'm here for the rest of the photographs.'

He watched her teeter at the brink of denying she had them, but before she could spout any garbage about an accident destroying her phone, he leant forward fixing her with a glare. 'Right now …' He enunciated each word carefully. 'I don't care what sordid little secrets you were keeping from me. I don't give a flying fuck! But you took months' worth of pictures of Damien Marks and his car. Seems to me that every time the man parked up, you took a shot.'

'Well, he always left stuff all over the seats.' Clearly the words were out before she considered them. She looked horrified that she'd been bounced into trying to justify herself.

'OK, so let's have the rest of them. All of them. You know the dates I'm interested in. More to the point, you know which photos are missing.'

He saw her hesitate, but knew he'd moved her way beyond the point where she could even pretend to pretend. 'Look, there was stuff on that phone to do with other things. We have to be hot on confidentiality in this game. It isn't stuff that would have helped you. Um … So it's Damien Marks's car you want, shots of the documents and so on.'

He nodded. 'And anything else, of course.'

'I couldn't find anything useful in his papers. Have you found something?' He'd really unsettled her for a question like that to slip out, but she turned away quickly not giving him the option of refusing to answer. 'Over here.'

He didn't let his satisfaction show. The trump card would have been to contact Pieternel on the number they weren't supposed to have, but he hadn't needed to. The Raymond woman would cooperate and he'd avoided hassle from Christa.

The pictures downloaded, flipping on to the display as thumbnails, filling the gallery and scrolling to screen after screen.

'Are they in date order?' Webber asked, leaning close to see the tiny images.

She nodded, saying tersely, 'The filenames give the dates. What do you want? CD? Memory stick?'

'Email them to me.' He held his phone in front of her so she could read the address.

'It'll take forever. Can't I put them on a stick?'

She had a point. 'Email everything from there …' He pointed to one of the thumbnails, '… down to …' He let her scroll down the list. '… to there. I'll take the rest on a pen drive.'

'All right,' she snapped. 'Then let me get on with it.'

He and Ahmed stood right behind her just in case she had any ideas about weeding anything out. The first couple of emails went off, each stuffed with as many pictures as it would hold, then he heard the ping of them arriving on his phone. Leaving Ahmed to monitor Raymond's actions, he opened them to check, not leaving anything to chance. And when she'd downloaded the rest of them on to the stick, he took it from her and passed it to Ahmed who attached it to his own phone via some gizmo.

Webber wasn't sure whether Ahmed could genuinely check the contents, but he made a convincing show of it. The Raymond woman didn't flinch, just said, 'You're not very trusting, Mr Webber.' He didn't grudge her a moment of childish satisfaction in stripping him of his rank.

'I've found it doesn't pay, Miss Raymond.'

'But we're on the same side here,' she burst out. 'I've no interest in protecting Damien Marks if he's guilty. I'm not his lawyer. All I'm contracted to do is find the truth.'

'And withholding evidence is your way of doing that, is it?'

She flushed and turned away.

# chapter twenty seven

It was getting on for midday when Ahmed drove up to the station in York.

'Drop me here,' Webber told him, undoing his seat belt and opening the door as Ahmed pulled up. As his boss strode off without a backward glance, Ahmed looked in vain for somewhere to park, no chance at this time of day, and swung the car round to search further afield. He smothered a yawn. The drive back had been tiring through the rush-hour traffic, and Webber practically a silent passenger, clicking through the images on his phone.

Len Klein had warned him. Webber would work him round the clock if he didn't watch out. Gets results, everyone said, but apt to go off at tangents. This one had been a several hundred mile tangent, and Ahmed hoped he wouldn't be called upon to justify the trip. He'd badgered Webber about why they had to go in person.

'What they handed over suggests their stored data is patchy. I don't believe a word of it. Smoke and bloody mirrors. They want to hide stuff from us but I don't believe it's anything to do with Marks, and I don't want to risk them trashing stuff for real if they see us getting close. So we need to be in close before they see us.'

'She might just have smashed her phone.'

Webber had shaken his head. 'I had that checked yesterday. The bits don't match up. It's been a rush job, quite a good one. But I don't want to get side-tracked into chasing bent PIs. Not yet.'

Ahmed had been uneasy, but he'd trusted that Webber knew what he was doing. And if he'd had any lingering doubts about the rumours of Webber and Annie Raymond, they'd evaporated in the events of the early morning. He played his part, making sure no one made contact to warn her, dogging her footsteps once she'd arrived, subtly harassing her. There had been quite a rush in seeing it all pan out.

It wasn't until they were on their way back and Webber beside him was clicking through the pictures, holding them to the light, peering closely, that he'd thought to ask, 'What are you hoping to find that we don't already have?'

The response surprised him. 'How the little girl's body got to the North Yorkshire coast,' but Webber hadn't elaborated, and simply grunted in reply to further questions.

Having crammed the car into a barely adequate gap, Ahmed raced back only to be stopped as he headed for the stairs.

'Ayaan, we've logged a missing kid. It's gone upstairs already but can you pick it up for Martyn?'

'I thought we weren't taking those anymore.' Ahmed paused to grab the details, but if his comment generated an answer, he lost it in amongst the bustle. Someone said, 'Who's that?' and he heard the words, 'Ayaan Ahmed ... Scarborough,' as he hurried away. All missing children from anywhere in Europe had been reported to the incident room since they'd made the link with the killing in Geneva. He thought it had been stopped now they'd dumped the Swiss connection, but maybe it had slipped Webber's mind. When he'd first seen them, he'd been aghast at the flood of reports, and then relieved at how swiftly the youngsters were found and reunited with their families, and then aghast all over again at the carelessness that had let so many children slip under the radar, however temporarily.

He ran his eye over this one. The girl was from York. That explained the report finding its way here, but she hadn't been lost in the city. It was a youth club trip; a weekend jaunt to France. He read about the mix up over transport and how one of the children was left behind. Olivia Lamb. Chances were she'd been found already. But poor kid, stranded in a foreign country, she must have been terrified, and only eleven years old. Nothing to connect it to the case here. Family liaison and contact with the French police had already been sorted. No alarm bells. He took the rest of the stairs in twos.

◉ ◉ ◉

With both the memory stick and his phone connected to computers copying photographs to the shared drive, Webber divvied up the job by date range, covering the ones they already had as well as the ones he and Ahmed had brought back with them.

He'd been fairly sure he wouldn't get a sniff of a proper analyst, but had envisaged pulling in a dozen people for an intense quarter of an hour to rake through the material and work out the full picture. But now, even with himself and Ahmed, there would just be four of them and it might take forever.

He couldn't begrudge the loss of manpower with one officer plucked straight out of the team for family liaison, and others following to bolster the search for the little girl left in France. With recent headlines over Myra Franklin, they couldn't be seen to skimp on resources for a missing child.

When Ahmed came in, he got them round a screen and pulled up one of the earlier photos. 'Marks's car, as we know, is like a mobile office. Because of the awkward angle, she often gets reflection on to the documents, so she's got in the habit of taking a whole stack of shots every time. But forget the documents and look at the dashboard.' He manipulated keyboard and mouse to expand the picture, bringing the instruments centre stage. 'OK, so it's not as sharp as it might be in this one, but it's readable. And a lot of them are crystal clear.'

'The mileage?'

'Exactly. We're going to get dates and mileage and we're going to find unexplained gaps. When he dumped the body, he gave the PI the slip, but the car's going to tell us when it made that trip. Log them all. Even if you can't see the dash, log the date. And if the clock's visible, log the time too. This isn't a job I want to have to do twice.'

'There's a hell of a lot of them.'

'Yes, so let's get going.'

Webber had given himself the stretch that covered the likely time the body was dumped, and he stayed out in the main office to work beside his team. It was less a gesture of solidarity than to stop anyone sweeping in and taking more of them away. He began to pull up the pictures one by one, enlarging, homing in on the digital display, recording the numbers.

He clocked up over thirty before the car gave him any indication it had moved, and then it jumped by twenty-five miles. So where had Marks been to start with? Where had he moved to? It would have to be cross-referenced with Raymond's written records. He glanced at Ahmed. The lad worked quickly; had a whole page of data already – Webber hoped he was being thorough – click, enlarge, scribble something down and on to the next. He was right of course. Get the numbers, don't try to analyse. Not yet. He'd already told them that; and hadn't followed his own instructions. He bent his head to the task again. There was gold dust in here, there had to be. Only with every shot of Marks's car dashboard, it seemed less and less likely.

The seconds blurred into minutes and hours. Webber straightened with a groan. He should let them go for a break, especially Ahmed who was visibly nodding over his keyboard. 'Ten more minutes,' he declared, making everyone jump. 'Then we'll have a break. But concentrate. We mustn't miss anything.'

Again he found it hard to follow his own orders; hard to focus on yet another lopsided car interior. This could have been done and dusted an hour ago. Where the hell was Klein? He'd had a reason not to want to put Ahmed on to this job; the lad had already driven 400 miles this morning; he'd struggle to stay sharp.

When it appeared, it was just another number. Eighty-four miles. Nothing exceptional. He clocked it and worked his way through several more. It was a 230 mile gap that jolted him. The ten minutes weren't up but he said, 'OK, give it a rest for a while.'

'You got something, Guv?' When Webber didn't answer at once, he felt all eyes turn his way.

'Yeah, maybe.' He looked at the figures he'd recorded. 'I'm in the period where Marks came to York. And I've just clocked a 230 mile gap that must have been his trip back home.' He ran his finger up the list. 'And there's a 211 mile one that got him here. But I have an 84 miles in between. Who clocks up 84 miles round York in a day, or rather at night,' he amended looking at the times. Between 2.20 AM and 10.30 AM, Marks had travelled 84 miles.

Ahmed, efficient as ever, had already leant across him to see the dates and was opening Annie Raymond's surveillance notes.

'It's about right,' Webber said, hearing his words came out in a flat monotone, pregnant with a sense of not tempting fate. 'York to where the body was found and back again.'

His colleague's voice from across the desk held no such restraint as he grinned and punched the air. 'That's it! Got the bastard!' The triumphant tone was enough to attract attention and bring people over. Webber heard someone say, 'They've got Marks dumping the body.'

He looked at Ahmed's screen where Annie Raymond's notes scrolled in a blur, then homed in on a date. They all looked to him for a lead, for official permission to celebrate. Not so fast. 'I think we have the night the body was dumped,' he said. 'But I'm not sure we have Marks.'

# chapter twenty eight

Webber noted Ahmed's sudden determination as he scrabbled through the notes, but didn't wait for him to find the answer. 'That night,' he said, 'is when Marks headed off from his B&B in the small hours and sat in an all-night services drinking coffee. It looks like his car went east to dump the body, but unless the PI fell asleep, Marks didn't go with it.'

'Maybe she's in it, too.'

He ignored that. Everyone knew they'd shone a spotlight on the private investigators. 'She might have failed to see the car taking off, but she did note the registration numbers of all the vehicles there that night. We've been through them. Give me the detail.'

It was Ahmed who pulled up the relevant note and turned his screen so Webber could see it. 'Smith, Cartwright, Levine and Nesbitt,' he read. 'Smith's the café manager. It says here they think Cartwright is probably Annie Raymond's second-guy. Levine's an old lady who doesn't drive but who lends her car out to the local church. Not unusual for it to be in that car park overnight. And Nesbitt lives just across the way. The café manager knows him, says he'll call in for a beer sometimes and leave his car. He might be Annie Raymond's sorry-guy.'

'What do we know about any of them?'

'Smith and Levine are squeaky clean but Cartwright and Nesbitt have records.' Ahmed scrolled to the next page. 'Cartwright's a retired plumber. Petty theft, drunk and disorderly. All a long time ago. Nesbitt much the same. Went off the rails when he was young, did a stint in a young offenders' institution, but seems to have kept his nose clean since then. He spent some years as a helicopter pilot for a medevac company.'

'OK, whoever took Marks's car might have parked away and walked in or they could have arrived after the Raymond woman went back to watch Marks.' He pulled in a breath, suddenly tired. 'Right, we need to take a break. There's more stuff to find in here and I want it all.'

He watched them head off. The atmosphere had changed in the blink of an eye. They were motivated again, back on Marks's trail, in reach of filling the gaps. Klein needed to know about this. It would give him a much-needed boost.

'I hope it's been worth it, Martyn.' Farrar was at his elbow. '*And* you've had people tied up all day on this new set of pictures, I gather.'

Webber took that emphasised *and* to encompass overtime, unnecessary trips and every other step out of line in his career, but his answer was upbeat. 'It looks like we've just put a date on when Marks dumped the body. Or anyway, when his accomplice did.'

A moment's silence. Farrar's expression showed a spark of triumph at the finding of a date, but his pursed lips said that he didn't want Marks to have had an accomplice.

'Show me.'

Webber showed him the pictures, the lists of numbers.

'How far is it to that services?'

'Not that far. There are enough miles unaccounted for to get that car to the coast and back.'

'So Marks'll claim he knew nothing about it.'

Webber laughed. 'What's his story? That he sat over a cup of coffee for four hours in a deserted all-night café a few miles from a comfortable hotel room while a random killer took a chance on using his car to dump the body?' It felt like a breakthrough, but it was too early to celebrate.

'Ah, Len. Just the man.' Webber looked round at Farrar's words. He hadn't noticed Klein come in. 'Good timing, Len. Looks like we have a bit of a breakthrough.'

'That's good news.' Klein shrugged out of his coat and slung it over a chair as he came to join them, looking the question at Webber, who gestured towards the computers whose screens had now blanked. 'New photos from the PIs' office. We might have a date for when the girl's body was dumped.'

Klein pulled out his glasses and leant forward to see, knocking the mouse to bring the monitor to life. It showed a shot of the car's dashboard. Webber pointed to the lists of numbers and explained what they'd found. Klein nodded. 'Good. Anything else?'

'Not yet, but we're not done.' Webber thought about his aim of getting Klein to go home, to make it up with Julia. The case had taken a positive turn. Send him home on a high. The problem was how to broach it.

'You've Ahmed and Len,' Farrar told him. 'And you can keep those other two for now, just till we see how this thing pans out.' He waved his hand towards the image of Marks's car dashboard. 'But if this little girl in France doesn't turn up soon ...'

'What little girl?'

Webber thought it an injudicious question from Klein, underlining that he'd been away from his post longer than he should. The station had had the story for hours. He gave a brief summary, ending, 'She wasn't at the hotel. They think she probably tried to find her own way to the ferry when they went off without her.' The words ran through his head; *if you were a serving officer, I'd be down on you like a ton of bricks, but you're not, so how about you just go home now? You've done your bit*. He sighed. Klein and Farrar were now swapping theories on what else they might get out of Annie Raymond's photos. He rubbed his eyes and smothered a yawn. The early start was catching up with him. His body wanted it to be at least seven o'clock in the evening; the light told him it was hours earlier. He should go and get a bite to eat if he wanted to be able to function at all this afternoon.

'This woman, the private eye,' Klein was saying. 'She's been following Marks for months, hasn't she?'

'Almost two years, one and off.' Webber nodded.

At the far side of the room, Webber watched a new set of pictures being placed on to one of the whiteboards. Stills from CCTV. A DI whose name he couldn't bring to mind placed the images, and was joined by a colleague who picked up a marker pen and began to write; the script too small to read from here. There were others watching. He saw their lips move but over the background hum of the office couldn't make out any words. It wasn't his case or it would be familiar enough that he'd lip-read the essence of their conversation. It was the little girl lost in France taking over what had been his incident room. A phone rang. A guy peeled off from the huddle to answer it, then beckoned across for someone to join him.

'What do you think, Martyn?' said Klein's voice.

Webber's attention was jerked back to the two men beside him. Klein looked at him expectantly. Farrar looked gobsmacked.

'Uh ... Sorry, Len. Run that by me again.'

'I said you should bring the woman in. She's the one who's been dogging the man's footsteps. Show her what we have ... the Geneva killing, the Franklin girl. She'll make connections we haven't had the time to see.'

No wonder Farrar looked taken aback. Klein was the last person Webber would have expected to make that suggestion. It wasn't a million miles away from what he'd thought himself the other day, though he hadn't come close to giving it serious consideration. 'Uh ... It's an interesting idea, Len.'

'Hasn't this woman caused us enough bother?' snapped Farrar.

'Well ...' Webber tipped his head in a yes-no gesture.

'Think about it,' Klein said. 'She came all this way when they ...'

'She'll not come here at her own expense again,' Webber interrupted. The issue of how she'd been so clued up on the enquiry was yet to be ironed out. He had a nasty feeling about that smashed phone and what they'd been hiding. If Christa was in the equation, he didn't want attention turning her way.

'Then pay her expenses.' Klein said, as though it was the most natural thing in the world.

Webber exchanged the ghost of a glance with Farrar who clearly thought Len was losing it. Easing him out might not be so hard after all.

'I mean it,' Klein said, his gaze steady. 'It'll bear fruit. You get too tied up in costs and budgets these days. Results are what matter.'

Webber was surprised that Klein kept pursuing it, but wasn't about to stop him. If he won the argument and got the Raymond woman here, it would be interesting to see what came of it. And if he didn't, then he'd lose Farrar's confidence and Webber would get him eased out and back home.

A cloud settled over him. Nothing in the body language from across the room suggested the little girl had turned up. There was still time for her to be found wandering the Paris streets unharmed, but the margins were narrow.

'I'm sorry, Len, I simply don't see it. And I don't think Martyn does either, even supposing he could keep his eyes open.'

'Uh … Sorry. I was distracted by what's happening over there.' He tipped his thumb towards the group across the room. 'It doesn't look like good news.'

They walked across. Webber found his gaze drawn to the whiteboard, its pictures now coming into focus. A posed school photo, the name *Olivia Lamb* written under it. Anonymous shots of vehicles, queues of people at customs check points. Webber watched as the Chief Super asked for an update. Then he glanced at the clock. The gap in which to find this girl closed in with every minute that passed. It was almost like physical pressure inside his head.

# chapter twenty nine

....................................................................................

Webber turned away from the board with its disquieting payload, and allowed his gaze to meet Farrar's. 'We need to be sure we have Marks tied in tight before we go after him again for this accomplice.'

Farrar narrowed his eyes at Klein, but his words were for Webber. 'Don't leave me with any loose ends, but be warned you'll be on your own with the young guy as soon as I need more manpower.'

...*on your own with the young guy* ... That was pretty close to publicly discounting Klein, but with attention all on the girl in France, no one else seemed to have noticed, not even Klein.

The ring of a phone jerked everyone into motion. People dispersed to their own tasks. Webber marched after Klein who was making for the door as he shouldered on his coat. 'I'm going for coffee and a bite to eat, Len. Join me.'

'Uh ... Thanks, Martyn, but no. I've eaten. I need to ...'

'I wasn't asking.' Webber kept his voice low but didn't disguise the tone of command. He heard an irritated grunt, but Klein's footsteps followed his as he strode away.

As they settled with their drinks, Webber said, 'We have no solid evidence the two cases are linked, Len. And there's no connection with your old case.'

'You don't believe that, Martyn. You know they're all linked. You need that private investigator back here, question her under caution if you have to.'

Webber took the time to draw in a deep breath. He wasn't sure why Klein had become fixated on Annie Raymond. It wasn't like him. But then he'd never known Klein estranged from Julia before. 'All we can say about Marks and the first victim is that he was in the same city and that someone went to some trouble to set him up. Wrong place, wrong time. That might be the top and bottom of it.'

'What about this new one, Martyn? The little girl in France. It's your job to convince John to bring that woman back here before it's too late.'

'You seriously want me to push for this new case to be seen as a linked abduction? On what grounds? Take a step back, Len. Look at it objectively. The cases aren't at all alike. And none of it has anything to do with your case. That's closed. There are no hidden anniversaries, no hidden killers commemorating anything. There are no real similarities.'

'There's the way the bodies were butchered.'

Webber tipped the remains of his coffee into his mouth before he spoke. 'Beheading is nasty … sick. But it isn't unique.'

'And the hands, Martyn. Don't forget the hands.'

'Also nasty, and also a way of delaying identification.'

'It's more than that. You know it is. The way the fingers were cut. That was unique.'

Webber rubbed his eyes and ran his hands through his hair. Suddenly it wasn't a case of persuading Farrar that Klein was losing it. Klein might genuinely have lost it. 'Len,' he said gently. 'That was your case. That was ten years ago. There was nothing like that in my case or the one in Switzerland.'

Klein looked him in the eye and Webber had to admit to himself that the man had never looked more sane. 'Last I heard, Martyn, neither you nor your Swiss colleagues were in any position to make that claim. Unless someone has turned up the hands in the past couple of hours, you can't possibly know.'

◉ ◉ ◉

The images blurred in front of Ahmed as a yawn overwhelmed him. His corner of the office lay still and quiet. When he'd sat down after lunch, the sun had been enough to bathe every corner in bright light, but over the following few hours it had faded. Someone had taken the trouble to click on the strip lights overhead, but not in his corner; maybe they hadn't noticed him there. From being centre stage, the work on Marks had plummeted down the scale; not even worthy of its share of the electricity bill. He wished Webber would come back from wherever he'd disappeared to, or Klein. His other two colleagues had been called away before they'd got started again.

He peered at the page beside him. It was the final page from his colleagues' work this morning. He'd created a spreadsheet with formulas to work out the gaps, so he could input date, mileage and time and have the software work out what needed to be flagged. He had the formulae colour coding the gaps. Once all the data was in, it would be the work of a moment to go back and see which bits to put under the microscope, which parts of Annie Raymond's notes to scrutinize. Putting the spreadsheet together had held his interest; inputting the numbers was a mechanical exercise. And he had the rest of the photos to do once he'd finished with this sheet. Tedious though it was, he had to get it right. It would be too much of a penance to have to go back through it all. He typed in the final number, put a line through the sheet and turned back to the stream of unfinished pictures. The team who interviewed Marks needed quality information, enough to rattle the man into telling them everything.

'Why are you working in the dark, Ayaan?'

His head shot up and he gave Len Klein a grin, watching him slip out of his coat. 'Just trying to get through this for Martyn.'

Klein smiled back. 'I warned you about him. He'll have you …'

'Yeah, yeah, working round the clock if I don't watch it. I know. Where is he, anyway?'

'I was with him when he had a bite to eat. Did he not come back here? And where are the others?'

Ahmed nodded in the direction of the busy end of the big office.

'What's the big fuss?' Klein asked.

'The missing girl. They've been trying to track down the other people who went on the trip. They haven't found them all yet.' Ahmed lowered his voice. 'Bit of a ruckus earlier.' He mimicked a quacking duck with fingers and thumb in an inadequate mime of the swell of raised voices and swearing that had originally made him sink lower in his forgotten corner.

'Well, anyway ...' Klein pulled a chair up close to Ahmed and sat down. 'I was talking to Martyn about your trip this morning; about the PI, the woman.'

'Annie Raymond,' Ahmed supplied through another yawn as he clicked on to another shot of Marks's dashboard.

'We need her help to get everything we can from this.' Klein gestured towards the screen in front of Ahmed.

'I could do with someone's help. Martyn wants it all written up for tomorrow.' Klein showed no signs of taking the hint, so Ahmed added, 'If you could do a batch and just write down the numbers I'll put them in the spreadsheet.'

'Just imagine if we'd had someone tagging Marks for all those months,' Klein didn't even seem to have heard. 'We'd have far more than a few pictures and some scrappy notes.'

'Well, we'd have had regular reports. And to be fair, she's not done a bad job.'

'Yes, but if she were one of us, she'd be here looking at the things we've found; she'd be putting it all beside her months of tailing Marks, getting to know him.'

'Yes, I suppose ...' Ahmed typed in a mileage figure, a date and a time. The gap popped up as 2.7 miles, black font, no warning colour coding. He clicked the mouse to move to the next image.

'So why don't we get her here and ask her?' Klein looked at him with a smile.

Ahmed laughed uneasily. Klein couldn't be serious. It was an absurd idea on so many levels. He grabbed for the easiest objection as he borrowed Webber's own words. 'The Chief Super'd go apeshit.'

'I doubt he'd notice. His hands are full with the kid in France.'

'Yeah, but …' Ahmed didn't quite want to say he thought it a daft idea, anyway not if Webber had approved it. Maybe he'd missed something. Klein glanced round as though to check who was in earshot. Ahmed watched him reach for the phone and turned back to his own task. If he didn't get a move on, he'd be here till morning.

It was Annie Raymond's name that pulled his attention back to Klein. Klein was speaking to her, arranging for her to come to York. And from the one side he could hear, Annie Raymond was not inclined to play ball. 'Think of the little girl,' Klein said into the phone. Ahmed felt uneasy, but if Webber had authorised it, who was he to … His train of thought crashed to a halt. It wasn't Webber's name that Klein was using.

'… that's right, DC Ayaan Ahmed. You met him this morning. I can see if he's available to talk to you now if you like.'

'No, Len!' Ahmed leant forward, his hand raised. Whatever Klein was playing at had to stop. Webber's words rang in his head, *He's not doing himself any good … relying on you to back me up*, and suddenly they made sense.

Klein ended the call and sat back. 'Don't worry, Ayaan. I'll take full responsibility if the shit hits the fan.'

'Well it will if you've got her to come here!'

Klein nodded. 'Don't worry. I'll be around to field her when she arrives, I'll make sure she doesn't bump into anyone she shouldn't.'

Ahmed felt stunned. 'When's she coming, Len?' He hissed the words, looking around to make sure no one could hear.

'Tomorrow, and don't look so worried.'

'What time?'

Klein shrugged. 'It won't be before midday. Don't worry about it, Ayaan. No one'll object when they see the results.'

'But, Len …'

'But nothing. Let's get on with this, shall we? We don't want to be here all night.'

Ahmed turned back to his monitor, but caught a flash of movement as the door opened. A weight lifted from him. It was Webber. Maybe Webber knew about it; maybe not, but he would dive in with a comment about Annie Raymond before Klein could say anything to stop him. He framed the words as he watched Webber pause to speak to someone. But before Webber came close, he heard his own name called from across the room. A woman held a telephone handset, her hand covering the mouthpiece.

'Ayaan Ahmed? That's you, isn't it? Member of the public asking for you. Won't give a name to anyone else.'

He lifted his hand in acknowledgement as the extension rang on the desk in front of him. This must be someone from Scarborough about the Cochrans. He didn't know any members of the public round here.

'Hello. Ayaan Ahmed.'

A man's voice said, 'You're the geezer in the paper, right? Inspector Ahmed?'

Ahmed was surprised. His name had appeared in an early version of the Cochrans' saga, but not with this phone number attached. Someone had gone to some trouble to track him down. 'Uh … yes, I'm *DC* Ahmed. Who's speaking?'

'I'll keep that to myself for now if you don't mind, but I've heard something you need to know. That photo in the paper. They've printed the wrong one. Don't know who it is, but it ain't her.'

'OK, which one exactly?' Ahmed didn't see that it mattered, except perhaps to the person wrongly labelled as Janice Cochran and to the newspaper who might have to print a grovelling apology.

'In the evening paper,' said the voice in his ear. 'Our lad's mate went to Paris with them. He told our lad you'd the wrong picture, and we thought someone ought to say, what with the lass not been found yet.'

Frantically Ahmed waved his hand to attract the attention of the woman who'd passed on the call. This wasn't for him. 'In that case, I'm afraid I'm not the person you should be speaking to ...'

The line went dead.

Someone flicked the switch and his gloomy corner was flooded with light. 'What was that about?'

Ahmed ran through the call while the woman scribbled notes and picked up her handset. 'It's OK,' she said. 'He hasn't hidden his number. But why did he ask for you?'

Ahmed said, 'No idea.' But a voice cut across him. 'Bloody hell, I'll tell you why. Look at this?' They all turned to see one of the new officers by the whiteboard brandishing a copy of the local paper. 'Evening edition just out,' he told them, holding up the front page. Ahmed saw Olivia Lamb staring out from the same photograph that was pinned to the board. Glancing at the text, the man read, 'The officer in charge of the enquiry into Olivia's disappearance, Inspector Ayaan Ahmed from Scarborough ...' All eyes turned to Ahmed.

'Ayaan, where did that come from?' Webber's voice held a note of resignation.

Ahmed stared round at them all. 'Don't look at me. I haven't spoken to anyone about this ... to anyone about anything, come to that.' A memory came to him of picking up the note about the missing girl as he'd rushed in after dropping off Webber; the crush of people; a voice saying, *Ayaan Ahmed ... from Scarborough.*

The phone on his desk rang again. Without thinking, he picked it up and saw Webber reach forward to click it on to speakerphone, raising his other hand for silence.

'Is that Inspector Ahmed?' boomed a voice through the speaker. 'It's about the missing girl.'

'Uh ... Yes ... No. The newspaper printed my name in error. Let me transfer you to the ... uh ... incident room.' With that *Inspector Ahmed* echoing through the silence, his mind blanked on the workings of the internal phone system; all he could think was that it wasn't the same as the one in Scarborough, and anyway, they rarely bothered transferring calls in that tight space. He held out the handset towards the woman who'd taken the first call. She shared a smile with her colleagues as she stepped across to click off the speaker and take the call.

Feeling all eyes on him, Ahmed stood up and walked across to look at the paper for himself. He was aware of Webber following and heard his governor's voice saying, 'Just to keep it simple, everyone's Inspector Ahmed for the time being. Don't transfer the calls to Ayaan. You've had most of my resources already. You're not having the rest by the back door. We'll get it sorted for the morning editions and the website.' Ahmed tried to feel relief that he'd avoided becoming the target of someone's wrath for the journalist's error, but felt only the discomfort of being the butt of the joke. By the time he was reaching for the front page to read the story, two more calls had generated exaggerated use of his name with its unearned promotion and laughter underlay the background talk.

The woman who'd taken the handset from him clicked it back into place. Without saying anything, she walked towards him. The buzz of conversation faded, leaving only the voices of the officers taking calls. Ahmed tried her read her face. All trace of amusement had been wiped away. She was the focus of attention as she walked to the whiteboard, whisking the page from Ahmed's hands as she passed him, and holding the black and white newsprint photo beside the colour print on the board.

'Similar call to the one you took,' she said with a nod to Ahmed. 'But that was one of the guys who *was* on the trip. We spoke to him earlier, but he hadn't seen the paper then. He didn't say wrong photo. He said that's not the girl who was in France with them.'

# chapter thirty

When Annie took the call that afternoon, she was nowhere near giving the Yorkshire police, North, South, West or Humberside, the benefit of the doubt over their methods or motives. Webber's early visit had left the place in turmoil and she'd resented shouldering the burden of sweeping up after him. Once Pieternel learnt that the Detective Superintendent and his Constable had left with their booty, she'd about-turned and headed for her original destination, leaving a battery of instructions and charging Annie with overseeing them.

By mid-morning, Annie had been smarting not only from Webber's high-handedness but Pieternel's too. She wanted her boss on the spot, having spent years not quite facing up to the darker side of Pieternel's dealings whilst knowing that the firm couldn't have flourished through bad times as well as it had on nothing but legitimate business.

She'd left at lunchtime, not because everything was done, but because she had an appointment with Heidi Marks and wanted fresh air, as well as a break and a friend to talk to. But when she arrived in the pub where they'd arranged to meet it had been to find Heidi veering between anger, fear and bewilderment, and in no state to be Annie's emotional prop.

'I've Pete coming round later,' she greeted Annie. 'I couldn't put him off. I don't want to see him. I don't want to see any of them.'

'Pete? You mean Damien's boss?' Annie wondered if the guy would be on his way to tell Heidi that Damien's salary was about to be axed. They hadn't fallen over themselves to support Heidi after the arrest. 'Did he say what it was about?'

'Oh, it's about all the questions from the police. What Damien was working on over the last year or so.'

Nothing much, thought Annie. He'd been on hand to close some of the firm's minor property deals, but had otherwise tracked aimlessly about the country not seeming to achieve anything beyond an occasional meeting. Not that the company itself was doing a lot now.

'How could he get us in this God-awful mess; how could he have been so stupid ...?' Heidi burst out, back on Damien, his boss forgotten. 'But what if ... what if it's ... Annie! I might have been married to a monster all these years.'

Annie made sympathetic noises as Heidi ranted on, landing where she always did these days: what the hell was going on and couldn't Annie make some kind of sense of it all?

Leaving Heidi with a few anodyne words of comfort, Annie had trailed back to the office, only to find herself at the end of an unexpected call from someone claiming to talk on behalf of Detective Constable Ayaan Ahmed.

'After the way he marched in here this morning,' she stormed. 'You expect me to drop everything and ...'

'Yes, yes. You're quite right. But please think of the little girl. It's only a few hours to York. You could be here before nightfall.'

Annie made no attempt to hide her astonishment. 'There's no way I could even think about being there before tomorrow afternoon, even supposing I had the time. Which I don't.' She wasn't sure why she gave any sort of hint that she might agree, but while she talked, she checked the calendar. Pieternel was coming in at midday, so that was tomorrow out. The man was quietly persistent and in the end Annie gave him a grudging promise to 'think about it.'

When he ended the call it was with profuse thanks and a murmured, 'See you tomorrow,' to which she simply grunted, knowing she'd been quite clear in giving no such commitment. When she told her colleague, he said, 'Oh, so you're off up North again, are you?'

'No! I don't run about at their say-so.'

'If it was the guy from this morning, I'm sure Pieternel would say ...'

'Yeah, well, stuff Pieternel! She can go swanning up there if she wants. And anyway it wasn't. It was ...' She paused; he hadn't given a name, just mentioned Ahmed and offered to bring him to the phone, 'some civilian worker or other.'

'Good, because the diary's rammed for tomorrow.'

They'd returned to their respective tasks, but throughout the afternoon, the phone call niggled at the back of Annie's mind. *Think of the little girl.* There was nothing she or anyone could do for Myra Franklin now.

Her fingers ran across the keyboard as she called up a search engine to check the local papers around York. The case might not get a mention now that Damien was in custody and contempt of court writs hung in the air.

The monitor loaded the online edition's front page. At first Annie felt nothing but mild surprise. A face stared out at her. A familiar face. She leant closer as though she wasn't already seeing it in perfect focus. Isolated words leapt out; *Olivia Lamb ... eleven years old ... missing ...*

'Hell, what's this about?'

It was the face that had stared back at her from across the darkness behind that house; the place sorry-guy's truck had been registered to. *Think of the little girl.* But surely he'd meant Myra Franklin.

'What is it?' her colleague asked from across the room.

'A little girl I saw in York. She's all over the papers.'

Snapping free from a moment of staring frozen at the screen, Annie grabbed the mouse and scrolled through the story, flipping to another of the papers, a bigger regional one.

*Local girl goes missing … Home Alone becomes Away Alone … Local Girl is left in Paris.* Few facts beyond the outline. The girl had been to Paris with some sort of school trip or Youth Club jaunt; the detail varied across the different reports.

But was this why Ahmed and not Webber had had someone ring her? There was a brief mention of Myra Franklin in a small paragraph on one of the sites, but no hint of making a connection. This was clearly an accident. The girl had been left behind. Careless and inadequate supervision, but not kidnap, not murder. It was coincidence, nothing more.

She thought back to the night she'd stood immobile, pressed into an ivy-covered wall, and seen the girl she now knew was called Olivia. And that other night, invisible in the darkness watching Damien Marks through plate glass; the inside of the café lit up; the truck in the car park.

Olivia, who'd gone missing in France, had been at the house where the truck was registered, the house in the sketch that Damien had thrown away. It wasn't a link that made any sense, but it was a link.

The guy on the phone said she could claim expenses for the trip. Suppose she could get to York by train, first class to be sure of a seat with room to work, and back again before Pieternel arrived. A check of the rail timetables showed the earliest train to York left King's Cross at 6.15, arriving at 8.30. If she were to get back for midday, she would have to catch the 9.30 from York. One hour to catch a cab to the police station, talk to Ahmed and get back again through York's rush hour traffic. It was a non-starter. And as he wouldn't expect her before midday, he might not even be there. She'd thought about it as she said she would; might even have made the journey if there'd been a bigger gap.

She stood up, stretched and walked the perimeter of the office space, staring out of the windows, focusing her eyes on distant buildings. For a moment she leant on the sill, her gaze tracking a flock of pigeons as they swooped low and dropped out of sight.

'Have you tried Pieternel again?' She tossed the question over her shoulder.

'Two minutes ago. Still on voicemail.'

With a sigh, she returned to her desk, found BBC Radio York and let Elly Fiorentini's voice play as a backdrop telling her the latest from North Yorkshire. A phone rang behind her.

'It's your number, Annie. Are you taking calls?'

'Not unless it's Pieternel.'

Her attention snapped back to her computer, whose speakers gave her the latest news from York. Olivia Lamb was the headline. There was worry, concern and liaison through Interpol, but the nub of the bulletin said, *Still missing*.

She heard her colleague get rid of the caller with a promise to 'tell Annie the moment she comes in.'

'Go on,' she said, as she heard the handset click back into place.

'A Mr Goodridge. Says you won't know him but he's a colleague of Damien Marks. Says he has to talk to you before tomorrow. He doesn't care how late it is when you call him.'

Goodridge. No, she didn't know him, but she knew who he was. He was Damien Marks's boss and one of the original partners in the firm; the Pete who had arranged to see Heidi. She looked at the sea of paperwork on her desk and held out her hand. 'Give me the number. Change is as good as a rest. I'm going cross-eyed with this lot.'

The phone was answered on the first ring. 'Hello, Pete Goodridge.'

'Mr Goodridge. Annie Raymond here.'

'That was quick! Thank you. Uh ...' She heard a door slam in the background. 'You don't know me but I'm ...'

'You're Damien Marks's boss these days,' Annie interrupted, wanting to cut to the chase. 'You used to be equal partners, but you bought him out. Now he works for you. I'm tight for time. What do you want?'

'I know you've been following him. I've … uh … talked to Heidi. I need to know if you found anything.'

Annie laughed without mirth. 'Ever heard of client confidentiality? I'll tell you one thing I found. You're paying him one hell of a wage for not doing much.'

'Yeah … he was … Uh … Can I trust you? I mean is this conversation confidential?'

'If you want it to be. And if you don't confess to a serious crime. Why?'

'This thing … that's happened to Damien. It could take the firm down with it.' Annie toyed with saying that she thought it was a years-old gamble on a land deal in Eastern Europe that was the real culprit, and that in her view, the firm was going down with or without Damien Marks's help, but she kept quiet. 'I want to help him,' Pete Goodridge went on. 'If he's innocent, that is. But I don't want to see the firm collapse. Not like this. And it's not some greed thing. We're talking wrecking people's lives if the company goes down right now. When I heard that Heidi had had you following him … She said you have surveillance pictures, him with other people. I need to know who they are. Look, if we're to save the company, I need to see you. Now. This afternoon.'

Annie looked at the chaos around her. 'Sorry, not a hope.'

'Then, this evening. Tonight. As late as you like.'

'Early tomorrow morning I might be able to give you …'

'That's the thing,' he interrupted. 'I won't be here tomorrow. I have to go to York.'

'York? Why?'

'To see if I can close out the deal Damien was working on. If I can, I might get Damien out of the shit as well as the company. But I need to know more about the people he's been meeting. And you're my last chance.'

Annie's colleague pushed back his chair, standing and stretching before heading for the outer office. She was on her own. No one to listen in. She wouldn't want Pieternel getting wind of this just now. 'Um … What time were you setting off?'

'Early. Before the rush hour.'

*Think of the little girl.* 'OK, how about you make it really early, give me a lift to York and we can talk on the way?'

'Yes, of course. That would be great. Only I might be staying over. It depends …'

'Don't worry. I only need a lift one way.'

◉ ◉ ◉

Pete Goodridge picked her up just after 4 AM. He was a tall man, fractionally taller than Webber, Annie judged, but of slighter build and with thinning hair. His car was an old-fashioned Jaguar, sleek, blue and comfortable. Traffic was light at this hour and they were on to the motorway without any holdups.

'Let's talk on the way,' he said. 'And then we'll stop for a bite when the bulk of the journey's behind us and you can show me your surveillance photographs. You have brought them, haven't you?' His voice sharpened as he gave a nod towards the case at Annie's feet.

'I've hundreds,' she said. 'And yes, they're all here.'

'Good. I was worried you might throw client confidentiality at me again.'

'No, that's OK.' She'd called Heidi the previous evening. Heidi had been unequivocal. 'Give him whatever you can. He says he might be able to help Damien.'

Pieternel had no idea where she was going. That was simply bad practice. They needed to watch each other's backs. An image hovered in her mind of posters that popped up from time to time all over the Underground. A pair of eyes in a car mirror, ordinary and yet chilling, under the caption, *If it isn't booked, it's just a stranger's car.* What if Damien was a player in some larger conspiracy and Pete Goodridge was a part of it? But he wasn't the one who'd tried to persuade her to come along. It was she who had asked him.

'You go first,' she said. 'Tell me what this is all about. Let me see if it chimes with anything I know.' She glanced across at him. He sat back, one arm straight on the wheel, eyes on the road ahead.

'Damien was chasing a big deal for us. The police have been sniffing round. They want to know what he was doing.'

'And haven't you told them?'

The pause told her that something had been held back. 'Look if he's guilty, we want no more to do with him, and if he was going round the country abusing kids then he wasn't out working for us. But if he was working for us, then … well, it's complicated.'

Annie saw his gaze flick to the mirror as they closed in on a convoy of lorries, easing back until a large bike roared past, and then accelerating to speed by. 'We've talked it through,' he went on. 'Damien was on the verge of a huge deal and might still be on the verge, but he's not there to close it. The firm's going to go under if this doesn't come off. We need to know.'

'I thought you were in trouble anyway.'

His gaze flicked towards her. 'Yeah, you're right. Don't quote me, but everything was riding on Damien pulling this one off.'

Annie thought about the man she'd followed for so long. The staid, boring, mostly predictable Mr Marks, and heard in her tone an incredulity she ought to have kept hidden. 'You had everything riding on Damien?'

'Like I said, it's complicated. We had a big deal from a few years ago that almost went sour.'

That would be the Eastern European land deal, thought Annie, as she queried, '*Almost* went sour?'

'There were some local difficulties.' His tone was light. If Annie hadn't seen the paperwork, she might be deceived. Shifting borders, legal ambiguity over ownership, dodgy dealings with corrupt officials. The contract that could have been the jewel in the crown had become the millstone that dragged them under.

'And Damien was going to put all this right, was he?' She kept her voice free of scepticism. He wasn't to know how much she knew already. And on paper she supposed there might be a way to retrieve this deal. It was the thought of Damien being the one to do it that stuck in her craw.

'Yes, he'd found the contacts. He was close to getting it in the bag.'

'And you've not told the police all this?'

'Well, yes and no. Damien kept things close to his chest. We genuinely didn't know much detail when they first asked.'

'So that's why you were paying him over the odds?'

'Oh yes, free rein. He was our only hope. It was a huge deal.'

The words were too casual. 'I'm sorry?' She let a level of impatience show under a tone of incredulity. She'd been on this man's coattails. He hadn't been chasing big deals. He'd been wandering about at random.

He sighed as though defeated. 'Well, we were paying him back his own money, if you must know. Well, not his own money, but money he generated. And it was all his idea.'

'What do you mean?'

'He'd set up some kind of consultancy and had the money go in to the firm. We paid him out of it. He was on to something. No one negotiates a consultancy fee at that level without something big behind it.'

Annie thought of the work they'd done on the firm's books. They'd missed this angle altogether. 'Out of interest, how were you recording this so-called consultancy deal?'

He gave her a wintry smile. 'We buried it in our estates side. Damien didn't want anyone knowing it was linked to his salary.

You have to realise, it was his deal that was going to get us all out of the shit.'

'You really believed that?' Annie couldn't help the question popping out.

'We were pissed off with him keeping it all to himself but he'd had a rough time, it was understandable, but we trusted him. I've known Damien for years. We go way back. And once he was getting close … Well, we were happy to let him run with it.'

Getting close? Annie blew out a sigh as she thought back to the early days of the case; finding out he'd sold his interest in the company and kept it from Heidi. The blackmail money, if that's what it was, looked like it came from outside. But Damien had had a rougher time of it than this man imagined. He'd relied on his trust of the old Damien, the pre-crisis Damien. The man she'd followed was someone else altogether; desperate to regain his peers' respect; maybe he'd had a breakdown.

'And what is it you want from me?'

'Some vital bits of the jigsaw. We've searched high and low. We can't go and ask Damien, but we grabbed his emails and things and we've dug out a lot. And I finally got some contacts and something concrete. He was due to be in York today. I'm turning up for his meeting. I have some names and I have context. What I don't have are pictures. If I'm to pull this off I have to know who these people are. I just wish Heidi had told me sooner.'

'Why York?'

'There's another deal. It's a set. All or nothing. We secure the York end and the rest will follow.'

'So these people who are expecting Damien, they'll have seen the news; they'll know he's under arrest and what he's charged with. Won't that put them off anyway?'

Pete Goodridge shook his head. 'I don't think so. They want the deal. It isn't only us it'll be good for. But I know what will put them off; the boys in blue crashing in mob-handed. That's why I want it sewn up before we hand over the rest of it.'

Annie felt her eyebrows rise slightly. She wasn't convinced by Pete Goodridge's idea of priorities.

'You realize what it means,' he went on. 'If Damien's innocent, then this might prove it.'

'Then why the hell hasn't he used it himself?'

'We think he doesn't want to scupper the deal. He was so close. He's waiting for us to get it in the bag and then he'll be able to give them the full story.'

It was a longshot and Annie said as much. 'I warn you I have hundreds of pictures, but barely any names. But you give me the names you have, and let's see if I recognize any of them. Then when we stop, we'll go through the pictures.'

He looked troubled and glanced at the clock on the dashboard. 'Hundreds? OK, if we make good time, we'll be able to stop for up to an hour.'

'Oh no, we won't! I need to do business in York and get back for my train.' She reached down for her laptop. 'I'll do some sorting. Most of them don't show anyone bar Damien. Now give me some names.'

As he nodded and began to speak, she knew he might be giving her the information she needed to scupper any hopes for his big deal. Her decision was whether or not to take all this straight to Webber or Ahmed. Pete Goodridge wasn't her client. Heidi Marks was. And Heidi's instructions were to get Damien out of this, money or no money. Goodridge might talk about this not being a greed thing but he missed a key point. If Damien were innocent, a killer was walking the streets. And another little girl was missing.

# chapter thirty one

It wasn't quite seven-thirty the next morning when Ahmed pushed his way into the office. The place buzzed with activity and it took him a minute to realize that Webber wasn't a part of it.

'Have you seen Martyn?' he asked the nearest person, who looked blankly at him for a moment, then shook his head with a glance at the clock. 'No, I shouldn't think he'll be in much before nine.'

Ahmed felt his lips purse in annoyance. *He'll work you round the clock if you let him.* He didn't mind that so much, but Webber had said he'd be in early to see what Ahmed's analysis of the photographs had produced. Hard work was what he'd signed up for, but he wouldn't have the piss taken.

Last night, in all the confusion around the missing girl's identity there hadn't been the chance to speak to Webber about Annie Raymond and Klein's phone call, but Klein had said, 'Don't worry, Ayaan. I'll have a word with Martyn this evening when he's in a better mood.'

He walked to the window scanning the car park for Webber's car as he half listened to a mini briefing on the missing girl going on behind him. They were trying to reconstruct her movements. At present the last confirmed sighting had been in York, so now no one was clear whose patch held the crime scene, but they talked as though there was no doubt about there being a crime scene somewhere; it wasn't an accidental mix-up. A sleek blue Jaguar pulled round into view. Not Webber.

A sudden clatter made him jump. One of the guys had shoved a clutch of papers on to a freestanding whiteboard, tipping the contraption off balance. One of the pages swooped down to land at Ahmed's feet. He bent down to pick it up.

As he straightened, he caught a movement from outside and smiled. It was Webber's car and by the looks of it, Klein was in the passenger seat. Then Ahmed saw something that turned his blood to ice. Annie Raymond marching towards the front entrance, raising her hand in acknowledgment to the driver of the Jaguar as it sped away.

Turning his back on the team who were retrieving the stand, he whipped out his phone and texted Klein.

*A Raymond @front desk.*

He watched Klein pull out his phone as he and Webber headed across the tarmac; saw alarm cross his colleague's face as he peered ahead. Then his hand was on Webber's arm. They stopped. After a brief exchange, Webber tried to give Klein his keys, but Klein appeared not to see him as he headed back towards the car. With an impatient gesture, Webber too retraced his steps. Ahmed watched Klein make great play of peering through the windows to examine the passenger seat and foot well, before pointing towards the back of the car. Ahmed could almost hear Webber's tetchy insistence that there could be nothing in the boot, but Klein stood his ground and Webber leant inside the car to release the catch. At once, Klein's phone was at his ear and Ahmed's phone rang.

'Get down there and get her out of sight,' hissed the voice in his ear. 'Round the side of the building, away from the office windows. I'll come and get her.'

'But Len ...'

'I haven't had chance to talk to Martyn yet. Just do it!'

Klein now had the car door open. With obvious irritation, Webber slammed the boot lid and marched round to see what he was doing.

Ahmed raced for the door, taking the stairs in reckless order as he leapt down. Annie Raymond was there, heading for the desk.

'Miss Raymond.' He was beside her, easing her round. 'This way. Good of you to come. You must have set off in the middle of the night.' He prattled on as he led her back outside. 'Len's just round here.'

'I got a lift. Who's Len? What's going on? Is it to do with this girl missing in France?'

'Len Klein. Retired Detective Chief Superintendent Len Klein. How long can you stay?'

'I have to be on the 9.30 train to London. I've no car so I'll need a cab. I trust that'll go on expenses with the train ticket.'

'Yes, yes. No problem. Are you sure it hasn't been delayed by that signalling problem?'

'Hell, what signalling problem? I have to be back in London by midday.'

Ahmed breathed an inward sigh of relief. The possibility of a delay had rattled her enough that she allowed him to lead her round the side of the building.

'If need be, we'll get you a car,' Ahmed said, keeping his fingers crossed behind his back.

'Oh ... OK then, so what's all this about?'

'Well ...' He tried to sound decisive. What was it all about? Klein had better be quick or she'd smell a rat and march back in there demanding to see Webber. 'We want you to look at some stuff. See if you can spot anything. After all, you spent a long time following Mr Marks.'

She looked at him as though he were mad. He knew he wore a false smile but wasn't sure what other front to put on. After a moment, she shrugged. 'Like what?'

'Uh ... well ...' He gestured with his hands, playing for time.

'I can tell you who that is,' she said. And he had to bite down on asking who. She was looking at the paper he still held in his hand.

He stared at it. It was the page that had fluttered to his feet. He hadn't even glanced at it, but saw now that it showed a less than clear profile of an old woman. 'That's Miss Price,' she told him. 'She's a land agent. Damien Marks met her a few times ages ago. It's all in my notes.'

Then Klein was beside them, trying to smile through his gasps for breath. 'Miss Raymond ... good of you to come ... want to ask you ... um ... show you a couple of things.'

'OK,' she said, 'but I need to be on that 9.30 train or have a car sorted out.'

'No problem. No problem,' Klein said, taking her arm. 'Could you fancy a good coffee? We won't get one of those here. Ayaan, Martyn wants you. I'll look after Miss Raymond.'

Ahmed spun on his heel and headed back inside. He leant across the desk. 'A blue Jaguar just dropped someone off. Can you get the reg off the camera and check it out for me?'

Webber would be upstairs now, would think he'd arrived before Ahmed. He knew it was childish to be annoyed about it, and when he told Webber about Annie Raymond's visit it would feel like he was doing it to get even. Klein had been a real support to him, but there were times lately when Ahmed wondered if he were losing the plot.

'There you are, Ayaan.' Webber greeted him distractedly as he flipped through a sheaf of papers, then reached for the phone.

'Martyn, there's something you need to know. It's about Annie Raymond ... and Len.'

'Go on. And what's that?' Webber's gaze rested on the paper that still hung from his hand.

'Oh ... It's from the board over there. It fell off. I should just ... But Annie Raymond's here. I have to tell you.' He turned and hurried over, holding out the page. 'Sorry, this is yours,' then spun round determined to catch Webber while he still had his attention.

Webber had followed him over. 'Annie Raymond? Where?' His tone was sharp as his gaze raked the office.

Behind him a voice was saying, 'Thank you, Inspector Ahmed,' to a ripple of amusement. He half turned back as he responded to Webber.

'No, not ...' He stopped as something threw a mental block across his train of thought.

He stared at the group that had laughed. They'd forgotten him already. The page was back up, promoted to the bigger board. Annie Raymond's voice ran through his mind. *I know who that is. That's Miss Price.* But on the board in front of him, it was labelled Mrs O'Dowd.

# chapter thirty two

Annie walked down the street side by side with ex Detective Chief Superintendent Klein, casting sideways glances at him as he chatted about the weather and asked if she was quite sure she didn't mind the walk; it was only a few minutes. Curiosity and coffee had been enough to persuade her this far. DC Ahmed had hustled her out; now Klein was getting her clear. She'd take bets Webber knew nothing about her visit, but why were they working behind his back? She thought about Pete Goodridge, with his insistence that Damien's big deal was for real. If that were true, then Damien might be innocent. Perhaps these two had cottoned on to something. And maybe Webber, arrogant oaf that he was, hadn't listened. She heaved a sigh, causing Klein to glance at her. She said, 'DC Ahmed said there were signalling problems and the train might be delayed.'

'No, that was a couple of days ago and anyway it wasn't on the London line. What time's your train?'

When she told him, he gave her a reassuring nod. 'Nine-thirty? No problem. We'll have you back in good time. I'll call for a cab before we get a drink.'

She wouldn't say so to Klein, but after seeing what he had to say, she would probably go back to the arrogant oaf with the full story, and to hell with Goodridge and his big deal.

'So why am I here?' she asked. 'Is it about the girl left in France? I looked up the news reports after you phoned. Only, I'm pretty sure I saw her last time I was in York.'

She tensed because when he asked for detail and she told him the address, he might cotton on that she'd read something she shouldn't have had access to, but he only said, 'You can tell me all about that later. For now if you'll indulge a retired copper and stay for a chat and a coffee, I'll show you something. It's me that's pressed for you to be brought here. There's too much emphasis on budgets for my liking these days. Corners get cut. You've been following Mr Marks in a way we haven't been able to. You're bound to have seen things we've missed. But the truth is that private investigators aren't in the best odour just now.'

'Are they ever?'

He gave a gentle laugh. 'But you didn't skimp on resources when you were behind Marks, did you? Or worry about mid-term management accounts or whatever the latest fad is?'

'Well, no, but I only take on the jobs that pay. You get stuck with everything. I mean who picks up the bill for a child murder?'

'We all do, as tax payers.'

'Then maybe our taxes aren't going in the right places.'

He smiled. 'You should meet my wife. You'd get on.'

She returned his smile. She would share a decent coffee with this dodderer and see what he had to show her. It seemed that this guy had more about him than Webber and his sidekick, Ahmed. At least he hadn't taken against her just for her profession. 'I thought you'd have stuff for me to look at back at the station.'

'I'm sure that'd help, too, but it's something else I really want to show you. You see, I dealt with a case a decade ago. My last big case before I retired. It was a child killer.'

'So you think it's some copycat thing. I heard ...' She tripped on her words. Those comments had been in the documents Christa had stolen from Webber.

Klein seemed not to notice her slip. 'Hmm ... Copycats,' he murmured. 'It's never straightforward, and sometimes it's simpler than you think. But I haven't anything concrete and modern policing methods don't allow for an old copper's instincts. There's someone I want you to meet … well, not meet, but see. I want to know if you'll recognize her.' He looked at his watch. 'We just need to be in the right place in twenty-five minutes time, and you'll get a grandstand view.'

'Twenty-five minutes is pushing it.'

'No, no. Don't worry. I'll have a cab ready. You tell me what you know about her, if anything, and that's all I'll need.'

'Who is she? What's the connection?'

He shook his head. 'I don't want to put anything into your mind. You might recognize her, but you might just recognize something about her. That's why I want you to have the opportunity to observe her.'

She watched him closely as she asked, 'You're doing this behind Webber's back, aren't you; you and Ahmed?'

He paused as though he might deny the accusation, but then shrugged and nodded.

'So what will Webber do when he finds out?'

'Nothing he can do to me. I'm not in the job any more. I used to be his governor. Did you know that? Here we are. We can get a decent drink here.'

He held open the door of what looked like a sandwich shop. Annie stepped inside to the smell of baking bread. It was too early for it to be busy, but they clearly plied their trade in bakery products rather than drinks, although there was a row of battered stools by an inadequate ledge in the window.

'How do you like your coffee?' Klein ushered her to one of the seats with old-fashioned courtesy that would have been better suited to a more comfortable establishment. 'And would you like anything to eat?'

She wasn't particularly hungry, but the smell of baking prompted her to ask for a croissant.

'Here you are.' He smiled as he pushed a plate in front of her. 'Coffee'll just be a moment. I'll ring for your cab.'

She felt her answering smile become fixed as she looked at the cargo on the paper plates. A fat sticky pastry sat on each. Either he'd misheard or he didn't distinguish between Danish pastries and croissants. She broke off a corner and put it in her mouth. It was as sticky, heavy and sweet as it looked. No way could she stomach the whole thing; she hadn't really wanted the croissant. She didn't want to rebuff his hospitality, so with a glance to make sure he wasn't watching, she ripped off a small piece, wrapped the rest in the serviette and shoved it in her pocket. He had his phone to his ear as he waited for their drinks. She watched with some dismay as a woman behind the counter shovelled instant coffee into polystyrene cups. If this was his idea of decent coffee, she wondered how bad it must be back at the police station. Klein closed the call and picked up the cups. 'That's your cab sorted,' he said as he brought the drinks across. 'It'll be waiting for you before nine. Plenty of time. And I asked him about rail delays. He said everything's running fine.'

'Thanks,' she said, grateful that he'd thought to ask. 'Is it coming here?'

'No, just up the road. We'll go there in a while.'

'That's where this woman is, is it? The one you want me to look at?'

'That's right. I suppose it all sounds a bit odd from where you're sitting.'

She laughed. 'You could say that.'

'The fact is I've had this case round my neck for more years than I care to remember.' Annie looked into the man's eyes. He seemed to age as he sat there in front of her, staring into the middle distance. Then he made an effort to pull himself back, gave her a half-hearted smile and added, 'Martyn Webber, too.'

'You've both been working on it for years?' she queried. 'So it goes back before Myra Franklin.'

He gave a short laugh. 'No, I meant I've had Martyn Webber

round my neck for years as well as the case. But yes, it goes way back.'

Something in his manner made her wonder if he was fishing for information on Webber and Christa. 'I saw some press cuttings,' she said, ignoring any secondary agenda. 'But they were too old to be the same case.'

'Yes, they were the start of it. Oh, you've nearly finished.' He gave a nod towards the sticky remnants on her plate. 'Would you like another one?'

'No, no. That was fine. Tell me about the press cuttings. How old were they?'

'1890s if I remember correctly. Like I said, it goes way back.'
\* \* \*

Ahmed raced in, taking the stairs in twos. He hadn't found Klein or Annie Raymond or anyone who'd seen them despite racing back out there within minutes of leaving them. He didn't want to face Webber with his failure but knew that every second of delay would make things worse. He had to pause to draw breath. His chest was burning with the fruitless sprint through the streets. If he burst right back in he wouldn't be able to speak. And Webber wasn't going to make allowances.

The spark had come when he'd said, 'Annie Raymond IDed it as a Miss Price,' pointing to the picture labelled Mrs O'Dowd. All hell had broken loose. He'd never seen Webber so angry. He'd demanded to know where Klein had taken her, but Ahmed didn't know. 'He just said they'd go for a coffee.'

'Where's the nearest coffee shop?' Webber had raised his voice and asked the room at large. Ahmed shrank smaller wishing he wouldn't involve everyone like this. They had work to get on with.

'Coffee's not bad right here,' someone had murmured, earning a withering glance from Webber who had ordered Ahmed out on to the street to search every coffee shop in reach and bring back Klein and Raymond pronto.

He'd been everywhere, and short of house to house enquiries, was out of options. He pushed through the big doors, hoping to see Klein had arrived back before him or that Webber was engrossed in something else. No such luck. All eyes turned his way. He shook his head and spread his hands wide in a gesture of apology.

He was aware of a voice saying, 'Don't blame Ayaan, it's hard to say no to a senior officer.'

Webber yelled, 'Len's not a senior officer, for God's sake. He's not even in the bloody job.'

'She said she had to catch the 9.30 back to London,' Ahmed remembered suddenly. 'We could get her at the station.'

Webber threw an impatient glance at the clock. Quarter to nine. 'What exactly did Len say to her?'

'He asked if she fancied a decent coffee, and he said you were looking for me.' Ahmed repeated the words as closely as he remembered them, aware that everyone was listening. It was as though they were all one team again. His gaze strayed to the board. *Mrs O'Dowd – Miss Price.* That's what had done it. He itched to ask someone what he'd missed while out chasing around, but not with that expression still on Webber's face.

'That jag you were asking about, Ayaan,' someone shouted across.

'What jag?' from Webber.

'A man in a blue jag dropped Annie Raymond at the front a minute before you and Len arrived.' Ahmed hurried across to get the information. 'Goodridge,' he said, surprised. 'It's registered to a Peter Goodridge. Isn't that ...?'

'Damien Marks's boss. Yes. What's that about? I want someone on to that firm. Find out what Goodridge is doing in York or who's in York with his car. Ayaan, get on to Raymond's outfit in London and find out what she's told them.'

A flurry of calls produced half a story. Ahmed didn't allow himself to be convinced by Annie Raymond's colleague who had expressed both surprise and concern to hear she'd been seen in

York, but the man had sounded sincere enough. Calls to Heidi Marks and Goodridge's firm filled in some gaps, but not enough. Someone identified and contacted the guesthouse where Goodridge was booked in for the night. They hadn't seen him yet.

'Wait!' Webber's sudden exclamation came like a finger on a pause button. Everyone froze. 'Decent coffee? Did you say Len said he was taking her for a decent coffee?'

Ahmed nodded.

'Right. I know exactly where they are. With me, Ayaan.' Webber strode to the door. Ahmed leapt up to follow.

Five minutes later, he followed Webber into a small bakery shop. The aroma of baking bread wafted tantalizingly over them, but apart from a woman in a tall hat manipulating a metal tray filled with pastries, the shop was empty.

'With you in a mo,' she threw over her shoulder as the door clicked shut.

Webber's gaze raked the small space. He jerked his thumb at Ahmed telling him to talk to the woman.

'We're looking for a man and woman …' Ahmed began.

'Grey haired, stocky?' the woman said. 'A lot older than the blond. They had coffee and pastries. They sat in the window. Only customers we've had today.'

Ahmed turned to Webber and saw him gazing at the waste bin. He stepped across to peer inside. The bin contained two crushed polystyrene cups and the screwed up remains of a couple of paper plates.

Webber's face was grim as he stared at the crumpled remains of Klein's and Annie Raymond's visit. Then he looked up towards the counter. 'When did they leave?'

The woman paused, then gave a shrug. 'Ten minutes. Give or take.'

◉ ◉ ◉

It was a gentle hill and felt deserted. The houses stood well back, hidden behind high walls and hedges. Tall trees spread branches out across the street. They'd left the main road behind them and the traffic noise was a faint background beat. Annie listened to Klein talking about problems with flooding which she found bizarre given the slope. Her eyes glazed as he explained about the old workings undermining the land. As he talked, she felt a light wind play through her hair. The rustling from the overhead leaves swelled as the breeze strengthened and the road narrowed to a single track lane.

'Do you know this place?' he asked, and looked mildly disappointed when she shook her head. She wondered if his old copper's instinct would lead them on a wild goose chase, but didn't care as long as she caught her train.

'All the houses look run down,' she commented.

'Yes, it's a shame. Now, keep close in to the wall as we go round here. It's not likely anyone's watching this way, but she won't come out if she thinks there are people around.'

Annie didn't ask who, because he'd already said he wanted her to come at this fresh, but as they rounded the corner, stepping from shadow into sunlight she realized she might know where they were. Something about the old-fashioned chimneys looked familiar. It was possible the house up ahead was the one on the flyer. Had they arrived at it by a more direct route than she'd taken the other evening?

Sturdy stone pillars held the rotten remains of a wooden gate, little more than a lacework frame. One stone sentry leant drunkenly towards its twin, bindweed and brambles making a sturdier defence than the skeleton gate.

This was the place she'd seen Olivia Lamb who was now missing in France. She started to speak, but Klein hushed her with an urgent gesture. 'Wait,' he whispered. 'We might be seen from the windows. We need to get under cover.'

He forced a gap through the brambles. After a moment's hesitation, Annie stepped through behind him. He pointed to one side, indicating the path they were to take. Instinctively she kept low, keeping a watch on the two windows that looked out this way. There was a patch of semi-cleared soil, partly enclosed by the curve of a privet hedge. He signalled with his hand to urge her under cover while he stayed at the edge peering through the tangle of branches.

'She'll come out of the side door.' His voice was low. She had to concentrate to hear the words. 'You need to be up here so you can see her, but stock still. Can you do that?' She nodded and he smiled. 'Yes, of course you can. You've had the training.' He tipped his wrist to look at his watch. 'A few more minutes.'

'I think …'

The urgent flapping of his hand silenced her. 'Back into the hedge, out of sight,' he hissed, then added, 'Mind the brambles,' pointing towards her feet in a gesture that belonged more to the courteous old man ushering her to a chair than to an ex-policeman conniving at an act of trespass.

He had his back to her now. His whole frame radiated unease. She tried to follow the direction of his gaze but couldn't see round him.

She eased herself into the embrace of the privet, its unkempt branches wrapping obligingly around her. Creepers grabbed at her trouser legs. She could only hope the crackle of the scrub as she crushed it underfoot was smothered in the rustle of the breeze. She was now sideways on to Klein. His face remained intent on something she couldn't see. There was a sudden scurry in the undergrowth. Instinctively she whipped her foot away, catching the flash of a small creature darting into the hedge bottom. The sudden movement had dragged the sharp brambles across her skin. She felt blood run down her ankle.

Klein stepped back. She saw him relax, and give a brief shake of his head.

'What?' She breathed the question as he stepped closer and his answer came at the same quiet level. 'Nothing … It was just … No, nothing.' He turned again to look round the curve of the vegetation.

His profile, staring at the house, was suddenly crumbling in front of her eyes. Her brain fought to make sense of it. Sharp tendrils turned his features into an inanimate silhouette. And as though someone had clicked a switch, the morning light was sucked upward in a kaleidoscope of twisting colours leaving nothing but an impenetrable inky black.

# chapter thirty three

Ahmed hurried behind Webber as they retraced their steps, threading their way through crowds of children heading for school. When they'd stepped outside the bakery, Webber had looked up and down the street. 'Where's he taken her, Ayaan?' Ahmed could only shrug as he pulled out his phone saying, 'I'll try again,' knowing it would go straight to voicemail. Listening to Klein's recorded message, he'd added, 'Len's found something, hasn't he? What is it?'

Webber had shaken his head. 'I don't know. I don't know if he's on to something or if he's chasing shadows.'

'Guv, how did you know about this place? Why would Len have brought her here?'

Again Webber had shaken his head. 'I know why he came here, Ayaan, but that's not the important bit. Where was he on his way to?'

And he'd marched off, leaving Ahmed to trail in his wake, the morning crowds preventing useful conversation until they were almost back, where Webber checked his watch as he flagged down a patrol car on its way out. He leant in to talk to the two uniforms inside, then turned to Ahmed. 'Hop in. They'll drop you at the station. Get her on the way to her train.'

Webber turned as they sped away. The back draught from the car set a polystyrene cup spinning in the gutter by his feet; a clone of those crushed cups back at the bakery. If he'd just got there a few minutes earlier. What was Klein up to?

Had Klein really found something or was he just obsessing while his marriage crumbled under him? On impulse, Webber pulled out his phone and searched through it. If Klein's home number were here he'd ring, but it wouldn't be. It had to be several phones ago that they'd been on the sort of terms where he would ring Klein at home. Even supposing Klein had persuaded the Raymond woman to go and meet Julia, they wouldn't be there yet. Except that Julia was in York according to Ahmed, so even if he had the number, he'd be ringing an empty house.

Surprised, he looked at the handset. There was Klein's home number. He hesitated but then tapped the button and lifted the phone to his ear, remembering it was always Julia's voice on the answerphone, and wondering how he would feel to hear it again. He glanced at the clock as he walked inside, the ringtone a rhythm to his stride. Not even an answerphone these days. He was taking the stairs in twos and about to give up, when there was a click and a voice spoke. The unmistakeable clipped tones of Julia Klein. It took a moment for him to realise it was Julia for real and not a recorded message. Mentally, he kicked himself. He knew the story of Julia coming to York was just a tale that Klein had made up for Ahmed.

'Julia? It's Martyn. Martyn Webber.'

'I know. I recognize your voice.' A pause. 'How are you, Martyn?'

'Uh … Yes, fine, thanks. So are Mel and the baby. We thought you might come across to York with Len. It would be good to see you.'

'Not sure I'm up to the journey these days. I was just on my way out. Len's not here. As far as I'm aware, he's still with you, but I'll tell him you rang.'

'Is he OK, Julia? I was … uh … a bit worried.' He struggled to get the words out, to vocalize his concerns to that cold, waspish voice that belonged to the days when Klein was solidly in charge.

'We're both fine, Martyn. Do remember me to Melinda. Now, if there wasn't anything else, I'm in a bit of a rush.'

And before he could respond, the line was dead.

He stood for a moment, then pocketed his phone and carried on up. Ahmed would get something out of the Raymond woman, though it was probably a waste of time because Klein would be back before him, might be upstairs already.

His priority now was to find out if they'd tracked down Mrs O'Dowd. Annie Raymond could easily have been mistaken, but if there were a link between O'Dowd and the Miss Price that Marks had been to meet, it needed to be untangled without delay. Suddenly the picture was in his mind of Klein in that side room, crying over the case files. To be exact – he'd been to check – over the old press cuttings. The very old ones from the 1890s.

He wondered if Klein's motives were more to do with warning off the Raymond woman, perhaps primed by Julia, than anything to do with the case, and felt annoyance with Klein for his meddling at a time like this. The man they'd arrested might not be the killer, and there was another child missing.

◉ ◉ ◉

It was getting on for mid-morning when Ahmed pushed his way through the doors, his gaze raking the office for Webber and Klein. No sign of the latter, but the office door at the far side of the space swung open and Webber strode out with Farrar close behind.

'Ayaan, did you find the woman at the station?' Farrar asked the question and Ahmed felt all eyes on him.

He shook his head. 'She wasn't there. There was another train at ten to ten and I waited for that, but she never showed up. Um …'

Farrar had turned away, but Webber peered into his eyes. 'Spit it out, Ayaan.'

Feeling horribly disloyal, Ahmed said, 'Len told her she could claim expenses for the trip. He might have put her in a cab.'

'Back to London?' Farrar spun back to face him, flinching as though at a sudden pain, but Ahmed had the impression these were minor irritations.

Farrar was telling someone to get on to the cab firms, see if they could find the woman. Up on the board, the picture he'd inadvertently shown Annie Raymond was now labelled *O'Dowd / Price*.

'Are we saying the cases are linked?' someone asked. 'What about Marks? Are we talking a paedophile ring?'

Webber spoke. 'The case for Marks acting alone has had the skids under it since we lost the link with Geneva. Forensics put the body in his car, but we've independent witnesses who put him in an all-night café miles away when the body was dumped.'

'Wait, do we know for sure the body was dumped that night?' Farrar chipped in.

'Pretty much. We've CCTV of the car on the A1039 heading Filey way. Angle's too high to get anything of the driver, but it's Marks's car.'

'And we believe the witnesses?'

'Well, the guy in the café pans out. He's worked there a long while, and Marks was in there for hours. It fits with the private investigator's story.'

'But Marks denies being there.'

'No, no. Mr Marks has changed his tune.' Ahmed was aware of heightened tension in the room. He wasn't the only one to whom this was news. 'His brief was incandescent. He just suddenly blurted it out. All part of his story of doing what he was told. He now says he was under orders to leave the guesthouse in the small hours and go to the café.'

'If someone wanted to use his car,' said a voice from behind Ahmed. 'Why didn't they take it from the guesthouse? Why the charade with the café?'

'CCTV,' Ahmed heard himself say, half turning. 'There wasn't any at the café. If anyone was seen driving the car away, it would have been Marks in York.'

'What about the other customers?'

'The guy at the café couldn't be certain which night. It was the PI's story that pinned that down.'

Someone pointed towards the *O'Dowd / Price* picture. The SIO on the missing child case stepped forward.

'We had one bit of luck. There was a level two security alert kicking in when the minibus carrying the children was due to board its ferry. All passports checked. We're not talking fine-tooth comb, certainly not for a youth club group, but we know what paperwork went through the system on the relevant days. And we have the footage of the boarding.' Ahmed felt a moment's relief for his having been out of the way. Better to be rushing about the streets than poring over reams of grainy CCTV images.

'According to the paperwork, Olivia Lamb was with the group when they left the country, but when they came back again, the girl with them was Stacy Gerrard.'

'Who's Stacy Gerrard?'

'School friend of Olivia Lamb.'

'So Olivia Lamb *didn't* come back from France?'

'That's what we thought at first, before we studied the footage, but we now know it was Stacy Gerrard who went out on Olivia's passport and came back on her own.'

'So Olivia didn't go at all?' asked Webber.

'Well, she might have.' The DI looked troubled as he went through it. The group had picked up Olivia from her home. Everyone was clear on that. She'd been in the front seat of the minibus with Ryan Davies. No one else had spoken to her. They'd stopped for their last pick-up which was for the couple who were to take charge while they were away. Stacy Gerrard had already been there. Her parents were hanging about to see that she got off OK. They saw Ryan and Olivia get off the minibus. Stacy went and joined them. They were standing quietly to one side, the two girls eating sweets. The rest of the group were bickering over the way the van was packed. 'And that's how they left them,' he finished. 'No one in that group knew Olivia except Ryan Davies and the Gerrards. And everyone bar the Gerrards thought there was only one girl there. Ryan Davies gave us a cock-and-bull story about both girls wanting to go, but he'd been told he could only bring one and he picked Olivia. Then she got cold feet right at the last minute and didn't want to go at all, and so he got Stacy to go in her place.'

'That can't be right ...' Ahmed muttered the words aloud as he imagined children that age arranging for a young girl to slip out to join a trip to France on someone else's passport.

'At that age, I wouldn't have picked a girl anyway,' murmured a voice in response. He nodded agreement though that hadn't been what he'd been thinking.

'And this couple who were supposedly in charge?'

'Distraught. Said they had no idea they had two girls there, but it was all very chaotic and the more I hear about it, the more it feels like Ryan Davies was a big part of the chaos.'

'Even so ...'

Ahmed heard his own scepticism echoed in the query. How could anyone make that sort of error?

'What have you got out of Stacy Gerrard?'

'Parents not so cooperative as the Davies, but she told us the same story. She'd told her parents she was going. Ryan had promised he'd get her a last minute place. She didn't know she'd be going instead of Olivia; claimed she'd not have gone if she'd known. She didn't speak out at the time because Ryan and Olivia told her that Olivia was "going in the car". When they arrived, she says Ryan told her to pretend to be Olivia because of the passport. She thought she wouldn't be allowed back home if she said who she was.'

The DI looked around, spread his hands in a gesture of helplessness. 'So far the adults pan out. They were careless, but that's about it. Those two girls aren't unlike. Same age, same height, same hair colour. At some point Olivia and Stacy changed places, maybe swapped coats. Ryan kept them apart from the rest of the group. But if Stacy got on the minibus after that final stop and Olivia didn't, which seems to be what happened, where did she go? She was the other side of York, but according to Ryan she had money to catch a bus.'

'What's the stuff about her going in a car?'

'According to Ryan that's the story he and Olivia made up so she could sneak off without Stacy telling anyone.

Ahmed eased his chair back. The sun had climbed to the point of spearing bright flashes of light into his eyes. He'd be in its full glare soon. He looked again at the photograph; *Mrs O'Dowd / Miss Price.*

'Where does this Mrs O'Dowd fit in?' he asked.

'In a former life, she was a junior school teacher in York. In the twenty years since she retired, she's travelled a lot, and she sometimes acts as a chaperone for young children, taking them back and forth between parents, that sort of thing. No record. She's squeaky clean. Can't find anyone to say a bad word about her. Quite the reverse, in fact. A model citizen. We haven't managed to talk to her yet, but she isn't due back in the country until next week.'

'So what has she to do with the trip?' Webber asked.

'We got O'Dowd in the passport check.' The DI's voice was grim. She was on the next ferry, chaperoning a little girl.'

'And you think it might be Olivia Lamb,' Webber said. 'Why?'

'We're waiting for footage,' the DI said. 'But the young girl with her was travelling on Stacy Gerrard's passport.'

# chapter thirty four

Annie surfaced from sleep, her body held by leaden tiredness, wondering why she should be waking so early. Oh yes, Pete Goodridge ... the trip to York ...

No, wait a moment, she'd been in his car ... what had he done to her? Panic bubbled up ... subsided. The old guy ... sticky confectionary ... watery coffee. Fragments came together ... walking up a hill ... a thick hedge ... brambles snagging her ankles, drawing blood. Memories pooled to a coherent whole right up to seeing his face in profile. And then ...?

Everything had closed in like a moonless night. But it had been morning. It was dark now. She couldn't see ... didn't know if her eyes were open or closed.

Keep calm. Breathe.

Her eyes began to work. She could feel them moving. She thought they were open, but all she saw were cold rivers of grey flowing through the air, a washed-out spiral that slowed as the dye leached away.

She thought she felt the sting on her leg where the bramble had cut it. Again, she tried to turn her head and this time there was movement. The grey rivers twisted and tangled. Real shapes through a heavy gloom.

Inside her head a coldly rational voice told her she'd been drugged. But how and when? And where was she now? Carefully, she clenched and unclenched muscles as they were returned to her control.

Klein had seen something. Had he got away? He was on his guard. *Of course you can. You've been trained.* His voice in her head. He was right. Let the training kick in. She had to concentrate only on her arms, and as soon as movement returned, haul herself to a sitting position and rub sensation back into her legs.

The more she moved, the more the gloom began to lift. The grey swirls coalesced and shimmied in and out of focus above her until frustration made her force her body into a violent twisting movement. As she wobbled almost on to her side, the swirls vanished. She flinched as stinging fires lit on the skin where it rubbed on the hard surface. It was a relief to know she could still feel pain.

She kept glimpsing that dab of colour. The colour of her jacket. The slightest movement and it ebbed and flowed, in and out of sight. Her eyes were adjusting. The surface of the ceiling was some kind of reflective material that showed whatever lay below.

With a huge effort she heaved her upper body partly away from the bed. Her hands slapped palm downwards, feeling restored. Smooth metal. She was lying on a smooth metal bed. Up above her the reflection swayed in and out of focus. She saw her body in outline, indistinct, strangely elongated. Multiple reflections. The ceiling was far from smooth, a patch of her jacket repeated endlessly.

As the first prickle of sensation touched her legs, a feeling of dread seeped in with it. Cold, hard, metal. A polished surface. Not flat but sloping inward. If she'd made it as far as a hospital, someone had pronounced her dead. This was a mortuary table. Her mind shrieked, *I'm alive,* but no words would come.

Deep inside her, a tiny voice of rationality fought desperately to keep back the panic. She knew she only had to work her throat a few more times and sound would come, but where was she and who would hear her?

◉ ◉ ◉

Webber paced the side of the room. The desperate search for Olivia Lamb had become a search for the elusive Mrs O'Dowd. He threw a glance towards her picture on the board but they hadn't written her first name up there and it hadn't stuck in his head. Mrs O'Dowd / Miss Price. The photos they had were inconclusive; grainy CCTV images or the distant shots taken by Annie Raymond. The only proper photographs they'd found so far were of Mrs O'Dowd as a teacher. A benign smiling face, two decades too young, sitting beside the later O'Dowd and Price images, that could have matched either, neither or both. Flurries of phone calls and enquiries were all painting the same picture. Mrs O'Dowd was a paragon, a saint, a woman who had dedicated her working life to the children in her care and who carried on caring after a well-deserved retirement during which she indulged her other passion for travel. As for the Miss Price that Marks had claimed to meet and who Annie Raymond had photographed, there was no trace.

The Raymond woman would be on her way back to London by now. He'd had Ahmed try her phone from an anonymous mobile, but she'd neither answered nor rung back. He needed to talk to Klein, but his phone too was still going to voicemail. He'd toyed with calling Julia again to find out where Klein might go. Where would he have stayed if not with the Webbers? That was a thought.

'Ayaan,' he called across and saw the lad leap to his feet and hurry over. 'Where did Len tell you he was staying?'

Ahmed's eyes narrowed in thought, but he shook his head. 'He didn't. He just said he and Julia had relatives in town. Guv, what about that mobile number you gave me? Shall I give that a try?'

Webber hesitated, but it wasn't Pieternel they were trying to reach. He shook his head, nodded Ahmed back to his desk and reached for the phone. A long shot but worth a try. He punched in his own home number.

'Hi, Mel. It's me. Has Len been back this morning?' In the background he could hear voices and laughter and the chirruping of a baby voice that sounded nothing like Sam. 'What's going on? Sounds like you're having a party.'

'It's the girls from up the road. We're taking the babies to the park. Len? No, I haven't seen him since he left with you. I can leave him a note, but we're heading out now.'

'No, no. That's OK. I just needed a word but he's not answering his mobile. You know what he's like.'

'Sure.' He heard the laugh in her voice. 'Anyway, I'd better be off. Oh, wait a minute, I forgot. He rang me earlier.'

'Len rang you? What for?'

'There was a bag of rubbish in his room. He'd forgotten to bring it down and he knew it was bin day.' She laughed again. 'Not that one small carrier bag was ever going to make a dint in this house, but that's what living with Julia Klein does for you.'

'What time did he ring, Mel? What was in the bag? Have you thrown it away?'

'Hey, just whoa there, Mr Detective. This is your wife you're talking to. It was a bag full of used paper hankies and a couple of newspapers as far as I could see. And no, I didn't rummage through it. And yes, I put it in the bin.'

'And have the bins been emptied?'

There was a pause, into which he heard her sigh. 'It wasn't the last thing I put in there. Two full bin liners have gone in on top of it and I know for a fact that one of them split as I threw it in.'

He softened his voice. 'But the bins haven't been emptied yet?'

'I can hear them at the top of the road, but sadly no, they're not with us yet.'

'Mel, I wouldn't ask if ...'

'Oh, for fuck's sake, Martyn, I'm not a moron. I know what you're asking. I'll get the bloody thing for you.'

He felt himself cringe at her tone. He would pay not only for the extraction of the carrier bag, but for making her swear in front of the baby. 'Thanks, sweetheart. I really wouldn't ask if it wasn't important. And ... um ... what time was it when he called?'

'Early. Not that long after you left.'

'How long? Half an hour, an hour?'

'I can't remember. I was busy.'

'Think, Mel, what were you doing when ...?'

'I know how it works, Martyn,' she snapped. 'Right now, I don't remember. And if you want this bag of rubbish, I need to go and get it now.'

'Thanks, Mel. You're a gem. You really are. I'll send someone for it.'

'I'm not waiting in. If they're not quick, they'll find it on the doorstep.'

As he ended the call, he became aware that Ahmed was at a barely discreet distance behind him doing the mini-jig that signalled something important to say. 'Ayaan, catch!' He tossed his car keys and Ahmed grabbed them one-handed out of the air. 'Hot-foot it round to my house and pick up a carrier bag of stuff. If no one's in, it'll be on the front step.'

He saw the mental change of direction as Ahmed opened his mouth to speak, paused to bite down on whatever he'd been going to say, then asked, 'What sort of stuff?'

'Probably nothing to justify what it's going to cost me, used tissues and last week's newspapers, but fetch it anyway. And what were you going to say?'

'It was just something I saw when we were in the PIs' office in London. I got a glimpse of the online diary. I think ... I'm not 100%, but I think they had a meeting at 12.30 today, Annie Raymond and her boss. It would explain why she had to get on the 9.30 train. Uh ... I mean, it's probably not important, but I just thought ...'

'Yeah, that's good, Ayaan. That could be useful. No harm in knowing where they'll both be in ...' He glanced at the clock. 'Just under an hour.'

As Ahmed left the room, Webber gave a brief shake of his head at his own paranoia. Klein had forgotten to bring a bag of rubbish downstairs. His mind played a scenario where Klein avoided producing his carrier bag while Webber was there to witness it, because they knew each other too well and some hint of awkwardness might show. No, it was paranoia plain and simple. It wasn't too late to call Ahmed back, to ring Mel and spare her the job of rummaging through garbage. But he made no move.

Looking round, he became aware that something had changed. No one was doing anything ostensibly different, but the tempo had increased. Something had arrived that had injected energy. He walked behind a group clustered round a monitor. More CCTV. The ferry terminal. An elderly woman and a young girl.

'O'Dowd?' he asked. Heads nodded but no one turned his way. 'And the girl, is it Olivia Lamb?'

'Not sure yet. They're doing some clever stuff with image software over there.' The speaker jerked his thumb over his shoulder, adding, 'But look at this. This is can't-put-a-foot-wrong O'Dowd. What do you think?'

Webber watched the sequence. It was fairly short, and as he watched the woman and child, it was as though he were watching two films playing side by side. In one there was nothing but an adult solicitously shepherding a child through a crowd; in the other was a woman very cleverly keeping her own and the child's face turned away from the surveillance cameras.

# chapter thirty five

With a huge effort, Annie propped herself on her elbows, but then had to stop, as breathless as though she'd sprinted up a hill. Each leg felt like a dead weight, but her arms had been the same only a few minutes ago. The shapes in the panel above her flickered in and out of view.

It was too much to hold herself up. With a defeated out-breath, she slumped on to the hard metal, gasping for air. The pattern above her broke into fragments that skittered away with the slightest movement, but she made out the outline of a body, patches of her jacket like splashes of paint across it. She lifted one of her arms, heavy as a lump of lead. The outline broke into pieces, disappeared and shimmered into place, slotting back piece by piece, a body with its arms by its side.

A hollow carved itself out inside her. It wasn't herself she could see. The flimsy ceiling panels were angled. There was someone else here. Someone lying on a table beside her.

Klein?

She let her head flop sideways. Nothing but inky blackness.

She took in two deep breaths, braced herself and then froze so the reflection would stay still. Daubs of colour, rags, the taut covering, the odd slivers of translucent grey that coalesced into a recognizable form. Hands. A pair of crossed hands, digits intertwined, the fractured reflection making dozens of fingers, an echo of the gruesome images from Christa's work on that documentary.

She looked at the image of the desiccated, collapsed body, skin stretched and dried, taut across its bones. An indistinct outline like a shadow blurring its contours as though etched into the metallic table top as the flesh rotted away. Its arms, sticklike, lay at its sides, divorced from the hands that sat crossed on its chest. And uselessly circling one wrist where there should have been a hand, she made out a rusted manacle attached to a heavy chain.

◉ ◉ ◉

Webber watched as Ahmed bustled back in, a black bin liner clutched in one hand. He could see from the lad's quick glances round the room that he'd returned with news. He watched those closest to the door wrinkle their noses, and caught the whiff of rotting garbage as he walked across. He hoped it was the right bag.

'She told me a carrier bag, Ayaan. Are you sure you have the right one?'

'Yes, Guv. Mrs Webber was there. She said it was falling to bits so she's put another bag round it.'

'OK, well, we won't open it up in here.'

'Good,' said a voice from behind. Webber ignored it.

'No, I know. I wouldn't have brought it in here, but I had a phone call on the way back. From the woman Annie Raymond works for. I thought you'd want to know.'

As he led the way to a side room, Webber asked, 'How bad is the actual carrier?'

'Pretty mashed up, I'm afraid.'

'OK,' He pulled a length of polythene sheeting from a cupboard and spread it on the table. 'So you had a call from the infamous Pieternel. What did she have to say?'

'She'd heard about Len's call yesterday and couldn't raise Raymond, so wanted to know if she'd been persuaded to come here. I ... uh ... Guv, does she have a surname?'

'Oh yes, there'll be a real person underneath all the aliases if you dig deep enough. I haven't got that far. What did you tell her?'

He pulled on a pair of latex gloves as Ahmed lifted the flimsy carrier with its noxious payload on to the sheet. As he fiddled with the knotted plastic handles, Ahmed explained how he'd given Pieternel chapter and verse on her colleague's plan to return on the 9.30 train. 'I told her I'd been at the station and hadn't seen her. I said she'd probably taken a cab and she'd be stuck in traffic somewhere.'

'How did she take it?'

'She was spitting. Wanted to know why Raymond's phone was going to voicemail.' Webber glanced up and caught Ahmed's eye where he saw his own unease reflected. On impulse, he slipped off one of his gloves and pulled out his mobile, punching in Klein's number. Voicemail. It was over three hours since anyone had heard a peep out of Klein or the PI.

'I told her we were dealing with a missing child case and we'd already had a child murder in the area, and if she knew anything, she mustn't hold it back.'

Webber nodded his approval, feeling mild surprise at Ahmed's level of assertiveness. 'Did you get anything?'

'Not really. She'd been on to Goodridge's firm and Heidi Marks. She didn't tell me anything new, but she gave me all the detail. She thought she was telling me stuff I didn't know. She's worried.'

'This business with Goodridge, some deal he's trying to close. It all sounds a bit disorganised,' Webber commented.

'I know. Pieternel said that, too.'

'When Len rang the Raymond woman,' he said. 'What exactly did he say about a missing child?'

'It was something like, Think of the little girl.'

He didn't want Annie Raymond to have known anything about Olivia Lamb, certainly nothing that motivated her to make the trip up here. She belonged to the Damien Marks case. The O'Dowd / Price conundrum was bad enough. He didn't want her making another bridge between Marks and the missing girl.

Ahmed pulled apart the top of the carrier bag and eased it on to its side spilling the contents on to the plastic sheet. As he watched Ahmed pick through the heap of screwed up paper, Webber wondered again why he'd thought there'd be anything to find. Was Klein chasing shadows from the earlier case or had he targeted the Raymond woman because he believed that he, Webber, was playing away with her? What he really wanted to do was have a trace put on Klein's phone, but knew it would be vetoed as a waste of time. He pulled on the gloves again and helped Ahmed to straighten out the crumpled papers.

'Why did he take her to that place, Guv? I heard him say they'd get a decent coffee, but ...'

'Len wouldn't drink decent coffee with a private investigator, Ayaan. He can't stand them, any of them. He thinks the whole profession should be outlawed. He'll have done what he had to do to get information out of her, but it'd have half killed him to break bread with one of the breed.'

'But what did he want out of her?'

Webber unravelled a torn piece of old newspaper, his mind making the match with a fragment that Ahmed was smoothing out. 'That's the million dollar question, Ayaan. It's ... Hang on ...'

Ahmed swivelled round his fragment and pushed it up against Webber's to complete the picture, saying, 'That's not last week's. Isn't it a copy of ...?'

Webber studied the cutting as he nodded. He recognized it from the old case file.

'Go through the rest of it, Ayaan. I need to have a word with the Chief Super. No interruptions.' Even without the impetus of a missing child, Webber couldn't overlook this. Klein was out of a job. He wondered if he'd be able to do anything for his old friend if it came to a prosecution. Ahmed had been wrong. It wasn't a copy. Klein had lifted the original document from the case file and tried to dispose of it in Webber's bin.

# chapter thirty six

Annie fought against the sense that she was trapped in a dream, because there would be no point in struggling, she could just lie here until she woke up … or faded away like her silent companion somewhere in the cloying inky blackness.

Somewhere at the corner of her vision there was a movement. At first, just another image in the darkness, but then there was a sound … words. She stared up towards what might be the corner of the ceiling. Fractured images shimmered.

With a jolt that brought her to full consciousness, she realised it was Klein's voice she could hear. She strained to make out the disjointed words. And within the snatches of light, she caught a glimpse of his face.

'Mr Klein?' she called out tentatively at first, but when his voice cut off abruptly, she called his name again. 'It's me. It's Annie Raymond.'

'What … what's happened? Where are you?'

He sounded woozy. The reflection broke up, swallowed into blackness, but she could hear him. He must only just be coming round from the drug. It was up to her to be strong for both of them.

'I don't know where we are,' she said. 'I don't know how long we've been here. Do you know what time it is?' In her head she saw the desiccated body uselessly manacled and wanted to add, what day … month … year?

He muttered something, seemed relieved that she was still alive. She made out the word 'hands'. The darkness pressed in. Without knowing what he was talking about or what he'd seen, she said, 'Don't think about it. Concentrate on getting feeling back in your arms and legs.'

'Don't think about what?'

'Don't think about the hands.' She heard the wobble in her own voice. Crossed hands. Too many fingers. 'What did they do to your hands?' This last was a whisper, not meant for his ears, but he answered as though he'd heard her.

'What hands? Where did you see them?'

'Here.' She felt rising hysteria, as though she were about to look down and see the crossed hands lying on the table beside her. 'Somewhere here. I don't know.' She gabbled the words out, wanting to deny having seen any hands at all.

'What do you mean? Where's here?'

'Uh … nothing. I don't know. It's nothing.' It wasn't nothing. It was a grotesque pair of crossed hands whose overabundance of fingers mocked her sanity. She mustn't think about them.

'I don't understand you. Where did you see the hands?'

'They're here.' Her voice broke as she gave in to the persistence of his tone. She had to stop thinking about the hands or she'd never be able to move.

'But where is here? How do you know? Where exactly?' He was being a policeman now, questioning, looking to snip off unfinished business. Maybe it was as important as he made it sound. He knew things she didn't.

'Here,' she said. 'There's a corpse on a table. The hands … they're … they're crossed …' She couldn't say the words because they painted pictures in her head. Irrational pictures. The drug was still in her system. Sometime soon she would have to nerve herself to get off this table and creep through the darkness of this cell to find a way out.

'What!' His exclamation was too sharp. It didn't match the words that had passed between them. What pictures were in *his* head? 'In the room with you? Crossed hands? Too many fingers?' His interrogation was urgent, but then collapsed into 'Oh God!' and silence.

◉ ◉ ◉

Webber glanced at the Chief Super's face and then looked down to flip through the papers in his hand. Farrar was shocked at Klein's behaviour, that was clear, but Webber wasn't sure if he'd go as far as to actively pursue him, to put a trace on his phone. They'd been friends and colleagues for a long time. Even now, the story barely sounded coherent. *Len's in trouble … he's got himself into something he hasn't been sharing …* Webber knew he didn't sound convincing because he'd yet to convince himself. But Klein had taken paperwork from those old case files and tried to dispose of it. That at least couldn't be clearer, but it didn't shed light on why.

When the knock sounded at the door, Webber cursed under his breath. He didn't want a diversion. He wanted a decision. When he saw Ahmed's face appear round the door, he felt a burst of anger. Ahmed of all people knew he didn't want to be interrupted.

'I'm sorry, Guv. It's the man we saw in the PIs' office in London. He won't speak to anyone but you. He sounds scared. I'm not sure he'll say whatever he wants to say if I put him off.'

Webber gave him a hard look. What would it have taken to go back to the phone, pitch his voice lower and say he was Webber? Neither of them knew the man from Adam. And how much insight did it need to avoid mention of their trip to London in front of Farrar? The lad was a strange mix of initiative and naivety.

'I'm sorry, John,' he said, turning away from Ahmed. 'I suppose I'd better take this.'

'Go ahead. I've heard enough for now. Keep me posted. And yes, I'll get that trace put on. I don't like the turn this is taking.'

Webber let out a breath he didn't know he'd been holding. His unease had been picked up and shared. He strode out into the big office as the voice behind him said, 'Ayaan, come in here. I've a job for you.'

Webber took a moment for a deep breath to quell an urge to snap before he spoke into the handset. 'Detective Superintendent Webber.'

'Uh … listen, I could lose my job calling you.' Ahmed had been right. The voice sounded scared. 'I can't raise Annie. Her mobile's going to voicemail. There's something that might … well, with it being a child missing. I've just looked at the York papers, the ones Annie looked at yesterday. It shocked her. The little girl, Olivia.'

The hint of a connection between Annie Raymond and Olivia Lamb lifted the hairs at the back of his neck. 'What did she know about the girl?'

'She told me she'd seen her the last time she was in York. And I think she looked up an address, but I wasn't really paying attention.'

Webber fought the dryness in his mouth to get out the words, 'Where? Where did she see the girl?'

'I don't know. The address she looked up. It must have been in her records, but …'

'Come on, spit it out. The girl's missing.'

'I … I can't find them. They're gone. All of them. Everything from this case has been wiped.'

'By whom? Who has access?'

'Only me, Annie and Pieternel. I haven't told Pieternel yet. We've had another break-in. She'll go spare when she finds out. I knew it didn't feel right when I got here this morning, but I thought it was just me. But when I saw the records were missing I played the cameras back.'

'*Another* break-in?' Webber interrupted. 'What went the last time?'

'Uh …' In the man's hesitation Webber read surprise that he didn't already know. 'Annie's records on the Marks case, but then your lot came asking …'

Webber leapt across a series of assumptions that could be checked later. Someone had targeted Raymond's files on Marks, but hadn't made it through the levels of paranoia employed by the firm and stolen only superficial copies. Was the man saying that in passing case notes to the police enquiry they'd alerted someone that the files still existed? He didn't like the feel of that at all.

'What did you see on the cameras?'

'Nothing. They'd been stopped and restarted. It was a professional job.'

'I don't suppose you reported the break-in.'

'Um ...'

He gave a tut of exasperation. Of course they hadn't reported it. 'Right then,' he rapped out. 'I'm going to get someone to call in on you and you're not to hold anything back. In particular, that address that Annie Raymond looked up. If you find it, get back to me at once.'

Webber put in the necessary calls to get someone out to the London office, but if it had been as professional a job as it sounded, finding that address would be needle-in-haystack territory. He didn't like it that Annie Raymond had seen Olivia Lamb; didn't like it that her records on Marks had been targeted; felt a general frustration that they'd been holding things back.

As he wondered whether to take this straight to Farrar, Ahmed reappeared, preceded by the whiff of rotting garbage. He hurried up, proffering something in his gloved hand. 'I found this, Guv.'

It was a small strip of paper singed brown down one edge. Webber peered at it closely, its fragility making him wary of touching it. It was blank. 'Anything on the other side?'

'Uh ... no.'

Webber waited a moment for an explanation, but when none was forthcoming asked, 'What did John want?'

'Oh, he's sending me out somewhere. I'm not to leave the office till he's ready. It's to do with finding Len but he didn't say what.'

Webber felt pleased at this confirmation that concrete action was being taken over Klein's vanishing act. *I can't raise Annie.* Klein and the Raymond woman seemed to have dropped off the radar at the same time. He looked again at the useless scrap still being held out for his inspection. 'OK, so what is it?'

'I'm not sure, but …' Ahmed's voice trailed off. 'Oh, and I'm afraid I've found a load more of the old cuttings.'

'Why afraid, Ayaan?'

'Well, they were all ripped up. Um … and I don't think they were copies. They must …'

Ahmed had cottoned on. Klein had taken more of the originals. He looked again at the singed strip. Not ordinary trash, not one of the local newspapers that had been stuffed in the bag. And not one of the old press cuttings. The lad was right. There was something oddly familiar about it.

◉ ◉ ◉

Ahmed, awaiting his summons from Farrar, sat at the edge of the group clustered round one of the desks. They'd been looking at interview tapes, reading transcripts, piecing together the hours during which Olivia Lamb disappeared.

Someone said, '… positive ID on the girl on the ferry with O'Dowd.'

He listened intently as queries and answers bounced back and forth confirming times and locations. '… positive ID … definite that it's her with O'Dowd on the ferry … arrived safely in Lyon … O'Dowd travelling south …'

It wasn't Olivia. Mrs O'Dowd had been with the girl she'd been employed to chaperone. She'd delivered her charge safely and continued on her way.

'So are you saying O'Dowd's legit?' Ahmed asked.

'The hell she is! That girl went out on Stacy Gerrard's passport.'

'Oh yeah, I'd forgotten that.'

'And that passport got back to Stacy Gerrard in time for her to come home on it. The girl and her mother look legit for now, but God alone knows where O'Dowd fits in all this.'

There was a pause before they dived back into the interviews and transcripts. Ahmed, trapped in no-man's land awaiting Farrar, leant to one side to catch a glimpse of the screen, seeing a small, wiry boy sitting with a man who was probably his father; both glaring at their questioners. As he watched, the image flicked to a small girl who looked wide-eyed with excitement. He wondered if it was Stacy Gerrard. For some reason, they continued to flip through the roll, staying no more than five or ten seconds on each interview. The minors were a mix of timidity and defiance, their parents much the same. The adult interviewees, from whose care a young girl had gone missing, were ashen and weeping.

Focus switched from the screen as they went back over old ground, arguing over minutiae, as if they were competing to see who could supply the most trivial scrap of information. Ahmed glanced towards the door. He hoped Farrar hadn't simply forgotten him.

He jumped and turned back as the DI behind him silenced everyone by banging his fist on the desk and declaring, 'It's the boy?' Behind the assertive tone, Ahmed could hear a question. Was what the boy? He didn't want to show how far behind the curve he'd fallen by asking aloud.

There was a moment's hiatus, into which one or two tentative comments were tossed. Ahmed saw an email pop up from a colleague in Scarborough. He ignored it as he listened.

'You mean because …?'

'But what about …?'

And then they were back in the thick of it, tossing the pieces back and forth, fitting them together, trying to pull them apart. This time the furore subsided almost at once. 'It's the boy,' the DI declared again, and this time it was a statement.

Ahmed was pretty sure he'd figured it. This painstaking check of the statements had led them to conclude that each account fitted everyone else's and fitted the known facts; all the adults, and even Stacy Gerrard who had swapped personas with Olivia Lamb. Everyone's account slotted into place in the minutest of detail. Everyone but the boy, Ryan Davies.

Ahmed sensed a growing excitement. Ryan Davies had let slip some tiny details, betraying a little more knowledge than he should have had about the time of Olivia Lamb's disappearance. He hadn't done badly in sticking to his tale, but he wasn't quite thirteen years old. They were a single interview away from a solid lead.

He pulled the keyboard towards him and opened the email, noting with resignation that he'd be back in Scarborough soon to tie loose ends on the Cochrans' case. It seemed remote. He felt far more connected to the investigation that was happening around him. Although the Cochrans weren't without their own uncertainties. How did Janice Cochran end up with the weapon that killed Myra Franklin? No one seriously doubted it now. It was the knife she threw overboard into the Humber. Someone might have worked it out. He picked up the phone to call back and get the latest, to find out exactly when he'd have to return.

'Hi, it's Ayaan. Just got your email. Can you give me a quick heads-up on what's new with the Cochrans?'

He watched out of the window, remembering the sight of Annie Raymond getting out of that blue car this morning. Where had she got to? And where was Klein?

Before he put the phone down, it was clear something else was happening around him. One of them had his head in his hands as though in despair. Another mini drama. This DI certainly liked to keep his team at boiling point. It took a moment to realise what he was hearing. Some glitch about the interview ... had the parents objected to their son being brought in again? No, it wasn't that. As he made sense of it, Webber crashed in behind him. 'What's happened, Ayaan?' Webber too was pushing his hands through his hair. 'What's this about another missing child?'

'It's Ryan Davies, Guv. He's run away.'

He told Webber the little that he'd gleaned. Ryan Davies had climbed out of a window and disappeared. The boy was officially missing.

# chapter thirty seven

Webber sat in his office, elbows on the desk, chin in his hands as the turbulent day drifted towards mid-afternoon. This Wednesday had no mid-week mood to it, just the sense of something racing away. Something they barely had a handle on.

Ryan Davies had run away to avoid being interviewed again. He must have done. Never mind that he'd gone before anyone had been back to the family. Did that mean some childish pact between him and Olivia Lamb? And if so, what had gone wrong? Where was she? He sat upright and took in a deep breath. These weren't his questions. There was a team out there working on it. Klein's obsessions had got to him. Could there be a link? On the face of it, it wasn't credible. Olivia Lamb's profile was all wrong. He thought about the way everything had come to focus on York; about the Raymond woman telling her colleague she'd seen Olivia Lamb whilst working a case for Heidi Marks. *I can't raise Annie …* No, thought Webber, and we can't raise Klein. In some way he couldn't get a handle on, Marks's original trip to York had been the catalyst to set a drove of hares running.

If there were a link, he had to find it. It was too late for Myra Franklin, but it might not be for Olivia Lamb. Five days since the last confirmed sighting. Five days was way too long. A movement made him look up. A young DC stood in the doorway, a piece of paper in her hand. Too many scraps of paper, thought Webber. Too much data, not enough information. He thought about the reams of detail in Annie Raymond's surveillance files, knowing there had to be a nugget of gold in there if he could but home in on it.

'What is it?' he said, wishing it was Ahmed who would at least have his own theories to pass on with whatever this was, instead of just wanting to hand it over and scoot back to the 'real' enquiry.

'It's to do with a Mr Goodridge, Guv. It's come out of something Ayaan Ahmed was chasing.'

He took the page from her. It said little but it gave him the contact details for Marks's firm in London. He picked up the phone.

As soon as he said who he was, words avalanched at him, a barely coherent jumble about school commitments and expenses claims.

'Stop!' he barked. 'Start again. Who sent a text to whom and what's the guesthouse to do with it? And why are you contacting me?'

'It's Pete. Peter Goodridge. He texted his wife to say he'd have to stay on an extra night, but when she couldn't get back to him, she rang us. She just wanted to know because they'd arranged this thing with the school–'

'And the guesthouse?'

'I rang them because we'd normally pay up front, rather than have people pay on their own cards, because then–'

'The guesthouse. What did they say?'

'Well, they said they'd already cancelled the booking, that Pete … well, they said, Mr Goodridge … had rung and cancelled it altogether because he'd decided to go back to London in the day. So I thought … Well, I didn't know what to think. He was telling his wife he was staying on and then cancelling. And he'd gone down there with that private investigator who turned out to have been following Damien. And Pete has to close out Damien's deal or we all go under … what with Damien arrested. I mean … but then we remembered about that DC Ahmed ringing about Pete and he was from York so we thought, if there's any funny business, well …'

'Where's Goodridge's meeting?'

'York.'

'Where in York!' Webber made no secret of his temper being on a knife edge.

The response came as a desperate gabble. 'We don't know. We've looked. Honestly, we've had all the files out. We've been trying to contact Pete. His phone's going to voicemail.'

'Names. Give me some names. Who's he meeting?'

'I don't know. Truly. Only Pete knows that. And he's taken all the files with him.'

'No one takes all the files these days. I suggest you start looking out the electronic copies and all the detail on that big deal and Mr Marks's consultancy arrangement because you'll be getting a visit shortly and if I find that any scrap of information has been withheld or destroyed, you'll be in the dock next to Mr Marks.'

The avalanche of words that assured him of their absolute cooperation from this point forward washed over Webber largely unheard. Ahmed had alerted traffic to Goodridge's car. As soon as he'd ended the call, he rang down to step up the urgency on finding the blue jaguar.

It was as he finished his next call to set in motion the promised targeting of Marks's firm, that his phone buzzed an internal call. 'Martyn, Chief Superintendent Farrar would like to see you in his office.'

◎ ◎ ◎

Loose bricks, uneven, wet with slime and slick like ice. Even clinging to the table, it was hard to stand. Gradually Annie worked out the terrain. A gully ran round the table, but there was a proper floor beyond it. She reached out with one of her feet to step across the gap. The ground here was smooth and sloped up. Gingerly she left the stability of the table and lowered herself to her hands and knees, pulling her foot out from the dank channel, feeling the loose bricks slip beneath her and screwing up her face as a rank smell rose from the slimy depths.

She moved her hands over the floor. It was a hard plastic coating, smooth but not uniformly so. Down at ground level, the dark remained impenetrable. She made to creep forward then felt something tug gently at her side.

Her insides scrunched in fear as she reached back, imagining grey lifeless fingers snagging at her clothing. Her hand met a bulge in the side of her jacket. One of her pockets was stuffed full. Every muscle tensed as she reached in touching a sticky, rubbery surface. Swallowing a cry of fright, she yanked her hand out, feeling bits fly from her pocket. Then she caught a whiff of chocolate and remembered the sticky pastry Klein had bought and how she'd shoved it in her pocket when his back was turned. She forced herself to hold still, to breathe deeply, to quell the thumping of her heart. She must stop jumping at shadows and find her way out of this place.

Cautiously, she moved forward. The smooth curves of the floor steepened until she found herself reaching up a wall that became close to vertical. It was as though she were inside the shell of a giant egg. She stretched up as high as she could, catching the glints of light from the ceiling panels, but unable to make out any coherent reflection.

It was impossible to move further, so she edged sideways. The smooth coating ran seamlessly from floor to wall. As she felt round it, she imagined a room coated in thick Araldite and inadequately levelled. A sudden slip took her foot over an edge. Her ankle twisted painfully on a heap of loose stones. She'd worked her way back round to the table. It was placed in some kind of dead end. She'd climbed off the wrong side.

Holding its surface for balance, she was able to stand and skirt around it. The curved walls pressed in on her, leaving barely enough room to squeeze past. No hint of a door or break in the coating.

At the other side, she lowered herself to hands and knees, feeling her way.

◉ ◉ ◉

Webber raised his hand to knock at Farrar's door. The shadows had begun to lengthen, a physical reminder of time running out. Obeying a curt command to come in, he stepped into the office as his boss yanked down the blind across the window with unnecessary force so that it jammed and hung lopsided, slats gaping open across one corner.

'You wanted to see me, John.'

'Shut the door, Martyn.' Farrar's voice as was as grim as his expression. He waved Webber to a chair beside the desk, shot him a speculative glance and then said, 'I don't like information leaking out of this station.'

Webber looked at him, surprised. Was this something new? He thought about the London PIs and the information they'd had at their fingertips. A wave of something like shame swept over him and he had to look down.

He supposed a part of him had been waiting for this moment since Monday when he'd looked full face at the business with Annie Raymond's files. A carefully doctored phone that Christa had happened to offer him. It would be naive to assume she hadn't known. And if she had known, did that put her in league with Annie Raymond's boss with her technological wizardry? He hoped not. He would have to rethink his whole history with her, where they'd been, what she might have got her hands on. He'd been careful since their affair started, but that was no reassurance. It was before that, when the documentary was underway, she'd been in all sorts of places. She'd been here in this building, passing chameleon-like and unnoticed under everyone's radar. Heaven alone knew what backdoor routes she'd opened for herself while she'd had the chance, and what he had unwittingly allowed her access to since.

As Farrar rifled impatiently through a sheaf of papers, Webber wondered if this would become the command to clear his desk, hand in his warrant card and take enforced leave pending investigation. The frustration would be unbearable. The missing girl needed every resource they could muster. Farrar had to see that. He wouldn't kick him out at this stage. Except Webber knew he would; he'd have no choice.

And yet, he *had* been careful, and despite her happy-go-lucky act, so had Christa. He thought back to her lewd approach when he'd joined her in the interview room in Hull. That hadn't been born of spontaneous desire; it had just been a ploy to keep him off balance, to show who really called the shots. For all her feigned indifference, she would have made quite sure there was no one watching from behind the mirror. Unless she'd deliberately betrayed him, he didn't see how anything conclusive about Christa could have come to anyone's notice. He looked back at Farrar determined to brazen it out if he could.

'Here,' Farrar slapped a sheet of paper on to the desk. 'Look at that.'

Webber picked it up. It was a printout of the inventory from Klein's old case file. So it had been digitized and Farrar had found it. For a second, relief was uppermost in his mind. This was nothing to do with Christa. With this list to show what had been in the original file, he could find out what that singed scrap … The thought stalled on Farrar's demeanour, which wasn't of someone seeing anything positive in this development. And then he looked closer. It was incomplete. Even with his scant knowledge of the file, he could see gaps. Those cutting he and Ahmed had pulled from the trash, for instance, no sign of them on the list.

'But this is …?' Webber struggled with which question would surface first.

'It's from the archive,' Farrar rapped out. 'Digitized soon after the case was closed. Don't ask about dates. They all match.'

'You mean it was doctored at the time it was archived?' Webber tried this for size and didn't like it.

'I've no evidence either way,' said Farrar, 'but I don't believe it was.'

'And the documents?'

'They'll have been scanned in at the time, too, but I'm not putting money on how complete the job was. The point is what's there now. It matches that list.'

Webber sat back and took a moment to think this through. The physical archive had been complete. He'd seen it himself. Klein had taken stuff and tried to trash it. Had he altered the contents list to match? No, it was worse than that. He'd been taking things since he arrived. They'd intercepted a single batch.

'I don't know the file well enough, John. We don't know what Len took out of it before that batch of press cuttings. And that thing that he tried to burn. That wasn't a press cutting; wrong sort of paper.'

'Any idea what it was?'

He had to shake his head. Something was at the edge of his mind but he couldn't catch it. 'I was wondering if any of the officers who worked on the original case were still around.'

Farrar pulled a face. 'I looked into that. Depressing. Retired and subsequently died for the most part. There's no one left of the team that might have been able to help us.'

'They can't all have retired,' Webber said. 'There was a young guy worked with Len, I've forgotten his name, but ...'

'RTA. M62,' said Farrar. 'Tyre blow-out I think it was. Only about six months ago. The point is, Martyn, the online archive has been tampered with.'

'Yes, I ...' Then Webber realised what Farrar was getting at. Klein's IT skills barely stretched to two-finger typing. He hadn't been working alone.

○ ○ ○

Annie inched along in the darkness until her fingers met a sharp lip that fell vertically downward. This must be the gully beneath a second table. Remembering the rank dampness of the gully under the table she'd been on, she eased close but didn't try to step into it. Reaching out blindly her finger ends met the cold solidity of a central leg and she was able to reach up to the table's edge and hold it as she stood up.

Running her hand gingerly forward, she felt the shape of an arm and braced herself for a cry of fright, but her touch provoked no reaction. The impression beneath her fingers was more of parchment than skin. This was the desiccated corpse with its severed hands crossed on its chest, not Klein. The reflection had reversed the layout of the room.

Keeping her touch at the table's rim to avoid contact with its grisly load, her feet clear of the gully, she worked her way to the end. But there she met the curvature of the wall. This table butted right into it. There was no way round. Again stopping to take in a breath, she tried to push away the images that danced in front of her eyes. This was not the time to let childhood demons back into her head. Carefully, she moved back along the table to the other end, only to find that this too butted into the wall, leaving no space to get past. She would have to go underneath.

It shouldn't be difficult to crawl under but Annie was loath to put her feet into the gully. She held the metal edge for balance, and reached out one foot, to try to bridge the gap. The stretch was too wide, the clearance too low. Remembering how slippery it had been beneath the original table, she lowered her foot gently, meeting that same feel of unstable blocks; the same slick surface.

The moment she disturbed the gully's bed, a stench reared up so foul that she instinctively twisted away, falling backwards, retching as she tried to cover her nose and mouth. Her feet skidded from under her and she landed painfully on her side.

Hands clasped to her face, fighting back the bile that rose in her gullet, she rolled face down to the unyielding floor as though to bury her head. Tears streamed down her cheeks, dripping from her fingers. Her heart pounded as her throat constricted. Every inch of her body shook. The odour of death swirled in the darkness, as a thousand rotting corpses danced in front of her tightly shut eyes. Any second now she'd feel the grasp of a bony hand round her ankle and it would pull her millimetre by millimetre across the smooth floor and down into their mass grave.

# chapter thirty eight

Webber stood firmly by Ahmed's integrity as Farrar gave him the third degree. Yes, Ahmed had worked with Klein, in some senses been mentored by his more experienced colleague. Klein had already been in post as a civilian nurturing the PCSOs when Ahmed joined up. The lad was guilty of no more than going along with him a step too far over the Annie Raymond business. Even then, he'd come straight to Webber, albeit a couple of minutes too late to intercept either Klein or Raymond.

'Not a peep from either of them since then,' Webber said. 'Not that I'd trust the PI outfit to get in touch.'

'I'll hear if either of their phones go live, but so far nothing.'

Webber noted the comment with interest. Someone was taking this more seriously than the evidence seemed to warrant if they'd sought authorization for Annie Raymond's phone as well as Klein's. He thought of the call he'd made before he came up here. 'Looks like there's another one to add to the list,' he said. 'Peter Goodridge, the man who drove the PI down here this morning. He's gone walkabout, too.'

'What do you mean? He was Marks's boss, wasn't he? What's happened?'

'We don't know much yet,' said Webber. 'Ayaan's had traffic looking for his car and I've just stepped up the urgency on that.' Webber outlined the information that he'd had from Goodridge's colleague. 'The B&B will let us know if he shows up but I'm not holding my breath. I've no idea whether it's some personal agenda or something significant. We know he drove the Raymond woman to York. Ayaan saw him drop her off.'

Webber shifted his chair to one side to avoid the shaft of sunlight that speared through the crooked blind. 'We've strong evidence against Marks, John, but I'm not happy with all these loose ends; signs of other people in the mix. How sure are we that Len put the right man away ten years ago? He's convinced there's a link.' Webber's mind turned to how close they'd come with Marks. What might have happened a few years down the line if Marks had been behind bars and the case closed?

'Len got his man. There were no doubts. You've seen the file. He confessed.'

'Marks wasn't far off a confession.'

'I'm not worried about Marks,' Farrar waved the matter away. 'Even his fancy brief can't keep Mr Marks together. We'll have everything he has to give before long … find out what he's been keeping to himself. Hasn't it occurred to you yet, Martyn? We need to chase the money.'

Webber looked up blankly. 'Money? What do you mean?'

Farrar sighed but didn't expand on his comment. Instead, he went back to Klein's old case, quizzing Webber on the theory of it having been a copycat crime. 'He would have meant the crimes they looked at in that documentary you took part in, wouldn't he?'

Webber thought back. Gruesome though the crimes had been, they were history. It all felt ephemeral and insignificant now. The biggest thing to come out of it had been meeting Christa and he didn't want any spotlights shining on that. 'Not really.' He answered Farrar's question. 'Len never spoke to me about copycats until he came on board with my case. Even then he was talking about ours being a copycat of his. He wasn't harking back to 19th century crimes. Well, except he seems to have run that theory past Ayaan. From what I remember of the old case file, the copycat theory was discussed at the time, but it never panned out as a viable hypothesis. Anyway, the documentary switched track if you remember. The cases that had similarities never got a public airing.'

'What about all the talk of anniversaries? That was certainly a live theory at the time, though I don't think Len ever went with it.'

'No, he didn't.' Webber let out a sigh. He hadn't noticed any references to the anniversary theory in his recent reading of the notes, but Farrar was right. Some talk about an anniversary rang a bell from his original scanning of the documents. 'No mention in the case notes now,' he said.

'Where the hell's he got to?' Farrar thumped the desk in a gesture of frustration and snatched up his phone. Webber could hear the even-pace of Klein's voicemail message from the handset before Farrar clicked it off and punched in another number which buzzed a busy signal. With a tut of exasperation he got to his feet, pointing one finger at Webber. 'Come with me. We're not finished here. I want to get to the bottom of these leaks.'

◉ ◉ ◉

Annie faced a stark choice. Either she find her way to the other side of that table or she must simply give up.

Her face felt wet from the tears that had streamed down; her limbs trembled. But the horror of what had risen from beneath that table had deadened something inside her. She would get out of here whatever it took. Very slowly, very carefully she began to feel her way, searching for the break in the floor that signalled the gully with its foul payload.

Then once again, she stood at the side of the table. With silent apologies she felt at the body wondering if it would crumble under her weight or burst open. It was hard to know if she was feeling skin or a cloth covering. Tight and dry. Her fingers felt their way to the chest and rested across its severed hands as she tried to make sense of their digits. More misshapen fingers than she could count with her own shaky hands, but all converging on just two wrists.

She had to do this. There might yet be dozens more tables and bodies to cross before she found either Klein or a way out. She must simply haul this body to the floor; get it out of her way.

Her hand knocked unexpectedly against the cold metal around the body's manacled wrist. The rusty chain, disappearing up towards the ceiling, brushed her face. The feel of it breached a dam she hadn't known she'd been holding back. The events of the day rushed up to overwhelm her; superstitions about the dead that she hadn't felt in decades rose up to bar her way. Her hand, already reaching forward to get a proper grip, to pull this body to the floor, froze.

A superstitious dread seeped down the scratchy metal chain. This victim had suffered too much abuse already. If she didn't show some respect, it would turn on her. She wrenched at the manacle. 'I'll free you from it,' she whispered. 'Just please let me pass.'

# chapter thirty nine

Farrar strode along the corridor, Webber at his heels hard-pressed to keep up. Farrar hadn't spoken since they'd left the office but the rigidity of his movements radiated displeasure. As he stopped to push open a door to speak to the people inside, Webber became aware of someone hurrying behind them. He turned to see the officer who'd been plucked out of his team for family liaison at the Lambs. She pulled on her jacket as she jogged towards them, her target clearly the staircase to the street. Farrar's head had disappeared round the door. Webber could hear him snapping at the room's occupants.

'How's the family doing?' he asked as she came abreast of them.

'Oh … you know. Not great. Better than they might be. In pieces of course.'

'Of course.' He tapped her arm lightly, a gesture of appreciation for her being good at that part of the job. She nodded as she headed off. He wondered how he would feel if he were in the Lambs' shoes; if it were Sam who wasn't there, wasn't anywhere. He shuddered and shook the image out of his head.

'Saints preserve us,' commented Farrar to no one in particular as he re-emerged. 'Tell me, Martyn, what do you make of Mr Marks and his big deal?'

Farrar was off down the corridor again. Webber set off behind him. 'God knows. The man's such a nonentity. Something's going on, but it's hard to imagine he has it in him to pull off anything big.'

'Oh, I don't know.' Farrar shot a glance over his shoulder that made Webber swallow involuntarily. 'He sold out his share in the company, kept it from his wife, ended up in a junior role, kept that from his wife. Then he negotiated a big salary rise for himself possibly on the back of blackmail. Deceit is quite a skill. It's not everyone can successfully deceive their wives as well as their work colleagues.'

Webber didn't know if there were a subtext or not and put all his efforts into taking the comments at face value. It was all to do with Marks. 'Not that successful,' he said. 'His wife put a private investigator on to him. The man's been manipulated, clearly, but he doesn't have what it takes to be negotiating multi million pound deals.'

'And where is he in the missing girl case?'

'Nowhere. I can't see how his history could have any link to Olivia Lamb. He was in custody when she went missing.'

'Why did he come to York?'

'Not to negotiate property deals, that's for sure. It looks like he was bringing his car here so it could be used to dump Myra Franklin's body. Exactly what he did and didn't know about it is still an open question.'

◉ ◉ ◉

The manacle wouldn't shift. The metal had melded to the severed end of the arm. Helpless, Annie felt her own tears splash down on her hands as she tried to prise it free. Then she made herself pause. She had to cling to rationality. She must find the inner resource to deal with this.

Hadn't she always prided herself on her years of training? There was always a way out. Follow procedures, go with what you know. But there were no procedures to follow. She knew nothing about being buried in a dungeon with a long-dead corpse. Then improvise, said the voice in her head. Go with what you know and then improvise.

As she let in the thought, she realized she did know something. She couldn't shift the manacle itself, but she recognized the mechanism with which it was fastened … a half forgotten conversation … one of her rare heart-to-hearts with Pieternel.

*Real torture, Annie … people use these things … no one's ever going to corner me again … Look at this … and this … and this …*

In her mind, Annie spoke to the corpse. *I can't get it off you. But I can twist the pin so it won't hold. Just as soon as they turn their backs, you shake yourself free. Please, it's the best I can do.* She bent over the corpse almost as though praying, feeling round the rusty metal of the manacle, scraping at it, twisting the mechanism. Too late, said her rational self. Way too late. But it had become a solemn promise. She would free it of this awful thing and it would let her escape.

◉ ◉ ◉

Farrar turned to Webber, paused as three uniformed officers went past, then said, 'If Marks has no link to the missing girl, then what's this business of Price and O'Dowd?' Before Webber could frame a reply, he added irritably, 'And remind me which one's which.'

'Price is the land agent,' Webber told him, 'and Mrs O'Dowd's the retired teacher, the paragon with the exemplary record. Price was one of Marks's contacts. O'Dowd's linked to the missing girl.'

'Do we know for sure they're one and the same person?'

'Not for sure, but Marks has identified the photo of O'Dowd as Price, and there's no trace of any land agent fitting Price's profile. We have O'Dowd's DNA so we'll know for sure when and if we catch up with either of them.'

'DNA? Where from? And if we're talking mix-and-match identities …?'

'No, apparently it's from way back. It's definitely O'Dowd's.'

'So where did that come from?' Farrar snapped as he marched

the last few strides back to his own office door which he pushed open.

'I don't know,' said Webber, entering behind him and pushing the door shut. He wanted to add, it's not the missing girl who's on my desk, it's the murdered one.

'What else links the missing girl to Marks?'

'Nothing that makes any sense. There's the private investigator, Annie Raymond.' Webber sensed tension as he mentioned her name. 'She saw the story on the news and told her colleague she'd seen Olivia when she was in York. I mean,' he spread his hands in a gesture of helplessness, 'in one sense, so what if she did? The girl lives in York. Raymond was here following Marks. Sometimes it really is just coincidence, but … I know they're looking at some kind of pact … the girl and Ryan Davies … hiding out while the French trip was on. But if so, something went wrong. The girl should have come home by now. So where did the PI see her? Why would she remember her? I'm thinking it was either somewhere odd or the girl was looking sneaky enough that it caught her notice. And what if that means it was somewhere to do with wherever she was planning to hole up?'

Farrar nodded and fixed Webber with a glare. 'Yes, those PIs,' he murmured.

'What about them, John?'

'I told you, Martyn, I don't like information leaking out of this station.'

Was Farrar accusing him of leaking information to the PIs? Webber felt anger rise. He and Farrar had worked together long enough for there to be a better bond of trust between them, whatever Farrar's suspicions. A part of him wanted to make a direct challenge, to get the accusation out in the open. It would be what he'd do if he were entirely innocent and got wind of allegations against him. But there in the middle of the equation sat Christa, and although confident there was no evidence on his boss's desk about their relationship, the strange business of Annie Raymond's phone held him back. The truth was that he wasn't 100% confident himself that he hadn't been the unwitting cause of a leak.

⊙ ⊙ ⊙

Taking care that her feet didn't slip into the gully as she hoisted herself up, Annie clambered on to the table then eased herself across the oblivious body, closing her mind to the gut-wrenching feel of bones snapping beneath her weight.

Once on the floor at the other side, she began to feel all around. A familiar shape met her outstretched hands. A semi-smooth surface rising up like the inside of a giant egg. She moved sideways, trying to be systematic. It didn't take long. This second table was welded into a dead end.

There was no way out, no break in the smooth surface. No third table. No Klein. Imprisoned now by the corpse as well as the dungeon … nothing left with which to barter safe passage.

Before the thoughts could take hold, she scrambled back to the table. If she didn't go right now, she'd never be able to do it. Clambering over the body a second time, feeling it crumble beneath her, she felt the futility of the pact she'd made with it to get past. How could she have wasted the precious minutes?

A new determination took hold. Forget superstition, forget what was behind her. Priority was to conduct a meticulous search of this part of the room between the two tables. The first time, crushed by incipient hysteria, she must have missed the doorway. She wouldn't miss it again.

⊙ ⊙ ⊙

The interrogation about the PIs had been thorough, leaving Webber feeling bruised. Farrar had unbalanced him from the off by homing

273

in on Christa, going right back to the documentary, asking questions about the involvement of the Hull PI firm. Had he seen her since? What was her involvement?

'I heard they had a missing child case so I checked up, but it wasn't until after the body was found that we realised they were one and the same.'

'So Len's theory is that if and when we find the girls' hands, they'll be the same as his case, is that right?'

'Or a copycat of the 19th century murders, which is what he ran past Ayaan.'

'The difference being …?'

Webber shrugged. 'The same shredded fingers in both cases, but as I remember from the early research on the documentary the older one was some ritualistic thing with the hands cut off and crossed on their chests. Extra hands for extra prayers.'

'I don't remember anything like that from the programme.'

'They'd changed tack by then. Different crimes, different focus.'

'Remind me, Martyn, what was the name of the private investigator, the one from Hull?'

'Uh … A Miss Andrew. Christa Andrew.'

Christa's name hung in the air as Webber looked into Farrar's eyes. Don't flinch … don't fidget … don't dive in with words to break the calm. He'd interviewed enough people over the years. He knew what the non-verbal cues for guilt looked like. But knowing wasn't the same as getting it right.

'Any link between her and the outfit in London?'

Play it straight. It was all about the case. 'Oddly enough, yes. Turns out she and Annie Raymond know each other. I checked again when I was in Hull after the body was found. That was when she let slip she knew Raymond and that she'd seen her in York, and she … uh … dropped out Damien Marks's name. That's the first we knew about the wife contacting a private investigator.'

'Why was it the first we knew?'

'She didn't want her husband knowing she had a PI on him, so she kept it away from the house. Separate pay-as-you-go mobile. No calls from the landline. All emails from her phone. Just one of those things.'

'And the Raymond woman was someone you already knew, was she?'

'No, I'd never heard of her. She'd worked in Hull years ago for the same outfit as Chr ... Miss Andrew, but no, she came to me. The ... um ... woman from Hull told her I'd been back to enquire about the custody case.'

Webber mentally sat on his hands. Farrar was focussing on Annie Raymond. He allowed himself a grunt of exasperation, an attempt to display annoyance at the laxness of private investigation. 'They didn't follow it up. Syeira Franklin had told them it was a boy, probably hedging her bets until she made up her mind, fishing to find out what it would cost. Then when she told them the child had come back, they just closed the file.'

'Remind me, what else did you get from them?'

'The parents' identities, not that we'd have found either of them alive even if we'd made the link sooner.'

Realising he hadn't been making eye contact, Webber looked up, meeting a cold and speculative expression from across the desk. Aghast, he found he'd not only rubbed his nose as his gaze dropped, but his finger was at his collar as though to loosen it.

'What is it, Martyn?' Farrar's tone was dangerously level.

As Webber cast about for something ... anything ... that wouldn't sound ridiculously defensive, it came to him that he had a perfectly good reason to be awkward about the Hull private investigators and their role. 'I didn't follow it up either, John. We'd never have known it was the same child if the Raymond woman hadn't chased it.'

'It's a sad fact they have more resource than us at times. Don't beat yourself up about it.'

'That's just it. She didn't have the resource. She chased it up because it didn't feel right, then she brought the information back to me.

'Who? Miss Andrew?'

'No. Annie Raymond.'

A pause. 'Shame she didn't follow her dad into a proper job. Did you know about her father?'

Webber felt himself well under the microscope now, but Farrar must know he'd done the intel on the PIs. 'Sergeant in the Strathclyde force, wasn't he? Retired some years ago.'

Another pause. 'She's good, don't you think so?'

Webber gave an irritated shrug, but then answered truthfully, 'Yes, she'd have been a good detective. It's a waste.'

'She's popped up here a few times now, hasn't she? How do you get on with her? Do you like her?'

For a moment, Farrar's agenda was overtaken by Webber's own concern over Klein and the missing press cuttings which collided in his head with the image of Annie Raymond evading his direct surveillance inside his own incident room. He found himself giving an instant and more honest response than if he'd taken a moment to think. 'No, I can't stand the self-righteous little cow. I've wanted to slap her since she first showed her face here.'

Farrar stared hard into his eyes. Webber pulled a face and murmured, 'Sorry, I shouldn't have said that. She's brought us some useful stuff. It's just that she irritates the hell out of me.'

Webber saw a smile of amusement spread across Farrar's face, the first crack in the grimness of his expression since the conversation had started. He felt his own lips curve to an answering smile. His dislike of Annie Raymond was too real, too substantive to be anything other than the whole truth of his relationship with her. Farrar had had the reassurance he'd wanted. Webber wondered why his dislike continued to burn so brightly. He ought to feel gratitude towards the woman. She'd not only cooperated with the enquiry, she'd been the perfect decoy for him yet again.

◉ ◉ ◉

A new sound pierced the darkness; the creak of a door opening. Annie stared. A line of light spread across the wall ahead of her. It began to seep into the room. Real light. Light she could see by.

Fear wanted to glue her gaze to the door that was opening out of the curved wall, out of a stretch she'd explored minutely, but she made herself look at everything. The other table. The dusty corpse, broken and dry. The ceiling, a mass of silver ribbons and wires. And in a high corner, the gleam of a monitor.

She lowered herself silently to the floor, where she crouched in the inadequate cover of the table and watched the thick door swing inwards. As a shaft of illumination speared through, tiny gleaming eyes shone out of the darkness in front of her. It was a tableau that lasted a fraction of a second. Three large rats had converged on the bits of pastry that had dropped from her pocket. Beyond them, coming through the opening, were a pair of legs in wide rubber boots. The rats scurried away, blurred streaks of fur flying up the smooth walls, as the boots danced a jig to a muffled gasp.

Petrified, Annie watched a pair of feet clump around the narrow walkway at the side of the room where moulded plastic curved around slimy broken bricks and gullies. If she could just get closer to the door, knock the booted legs aside and scramble through …

The line of brightness began to change, squeezed from the top. The door began to close, sucking the light out the room. No time to plan. She launched herself at the gap, her feet scrambling for purchase between the rickety bricks and smooth coating of the floor.

One huge boot was right in front of her; the other to the side, balanced on the curve. The floor played traitor by whipping her legs out from under her leaving her helpless. She looked up into an impossibly large pair of eyes, featureless and inhuman in their size. Huge ovals where there should have been a face.

The door slammed shut; the darkness sudden, complete. And she found herself tumbling as though tipped into a vat of liquid and shaken hard.

She threw her hands over her head and tried to curl into invisibility. Someone screamed. Deep down she knew the screams were her own. In the tiny space the noise deafened her.

# chapter forty

Webber clicked off the video link and sat back, absorbing the information he'd heard from his Swiss colleagues. He thought about Damien Marks and his extended stay in custody. He'd have to be charged soon, but it wouldn't be with murder. And Webber intended to fight any attempt on his lawyer's behalf to get him bailed. If Marks walked out of here, they'd never see him alive again.

Focus was all on the missing girl now, Webber's enquiry pushed to one side.

He looked out the recording of one of Marks's early interviews. The image flickered to life. It showed Marks looking smart, his suit uncreased. In the early interviews he'd bounced between overbearing confidence and semi collapse. And before his lawyer reeled him in, he'd been talking.

Webber fast-forwarded the recording.

'We've taken your car for forensic analysis, Damien.'

The shiny round face smiled condescension from across the table. 'I think the acquaintance is a little short for first names.'

'Is there anything you'd like to tell me, Mr Marks? You know that whatever's there to find, we'll find it. It'll be better for you if you tell me first.'

Marks shrugged. 'I've told you everything there is to tell.' A glance at his lawyer whose hard stare bored into him. The confident persona collapsed like a punctured balloon. 'No comment,' he muttered.

Webber paused the recording. Marks had acted like a prat until his brief got him together, but beneath the veneer, he'd been frightened and confused. Only it hadn't been about the car. Marks had still been reeling from the shock of his detention. Webber shook his head, annoyed with himself. Marks hadn't a clue what his car had been used for and he, Webber, should have seen it straight away, not just basked in the elation of positive forensics.

◉ ◉ ◉

With a brief knock at the open door, Webber stepped into Farrar's office.

'Ah, Martyn.' Farrar looked up. 'The Lamb girl, any news?'

'No.' Webber shaded his eyes against the afternoon sun that streamed through the broken slats of the window blind.

'Could there be a link with Myra Franklin or the Swiss child?'

Webber shook his head. 'I don't see how. Olivia Lamb's the wrong profile. She's an ordinary girl from an ordinary family. Myra Franklin and the other one were like strays. We'd never have known they'd lived if their bodies hadn't been found.'

'It's nothing to do with Len's old case, is it?'

Webber shook his head.

'Those witnesses in Geneva,' Farrar went on. 'Whoever did that wasn't just targeting Marks. They were setting up false trails, probably many more than we've found. That body was discovered by chance. Same as Myra Franklin. If it hadn't been for those flash floods, who knows where this case would be. But as soon as we started to home in on Marks, someone saw to it that he headed for York, and that his car was used to dump the rest of the body.'

In his mind's eye Webber saw the flickering image of Marks on the interview tape. 'The body was never meant to have turned up in Scarborough,' he said. 'Or York. I think she was set to turn up somewhere that matched with Marks's routine travels, not

Yorkshire at all. Someone gave Marks something that let him get back on his feet. Maybe it was blackmail, maybe something else altogether. He was set up for Myra Franklin. He didn't kill her.'

'That flies in the face of the evidence, Martyn.'

'I know. I'm relying on that to justify keeping hold of him.'

Farrar tapped his pen against the desk. 'Someone moved at lightning speed. They painted that Swiss hotel as the focal point, the conference, the attendees ... didn't put them all in the frame. It was subtle ... clever. Those dummy witnesses. I'll back you for now, Martyn, but if we're not going to charge him ...'

'Well, *we* can't charge him with murder, but ours isn't the only case.'

'Are you saying he's guilty of the Swiss crime?'

Webber nodded. 'Accessory after the fact, for sure. Maybe more.'

Farrar sat forward. 'Tell me.'

Webber summarised the call he'd had. 'Whether or not he was involved in the killing,' he ended. 'The Swiss have enough to show he was involved in the cover up.'

'OK, so where are we at the Swiss end of things?'

'There's a draft extradition request gone to the CPS. Once they've OKed it to go to the Secretary of State, they'll get their own arrest warrant.'

'Is this tied up in the money?'

'It must be, he was desperate, financially. I believe he was drawn in for money, and drawn in too deep to get out once he realised what had happened. It looks like he was sold the child's death as some sort of accident, collateral damage as it were. He certainly didn't know he was being set up to take the rap. If his version's to be believed, he was blindly following orders on the promise of a big property deal that would get him and his company back on its feet. And they had him by the short and curlies because of what he'd done in Geneva. He's bleating that he's been framed for the second murder to get him out of the way.'

'She wasn't killed so Marks could be framed,' Farrar said quietly.

'No,' said Webber, absently picking up a clutch of paperclips that had spilled on to Farrar's desk. 'It's killing for killing's sake. Whoever's responsible for the first child killed the second. I know, I know ...' He held up his hands to forestall objections. 'The links fall apart if it isn't Marks, but ... It's not to do with money or property. It's someone who likes to find anonymous children and slaughter them.'

'Marks's colleagues, where are we? Why is Goodridge in York?'

Webber imagined Goodridge gone to ground to clean up a crime scene. He tried to line up the ideas as he snagged together two of the paperclips. If only everything would link as easily. 'We've looked at Goodridge ... all of Marks's colleagues, but nothing's adding up. They're little league compared to what's been going on.'

*Follow the money.* The operation that orchestrated a diversion of the magnitude that had entrapped Marks needed huge resources. All those disappearing chat lines. *Money in porn.* He might be touching the tip of an iceberg but he wasn't near enough to make sense of it.

'The London PIs,' said Farrar. 'Tell me about the break-ins at their offices.'

'Frighteningly proficient,' Webber said with a cold smile. 'It smacked of a professional job to me.'

'Intelligence Services, maybe.'

Webber looked at him, surprised. 'Why would it be spooks?'

'What do you know about the boss of that outfit?'

'Not much. I never managed to find a real person under the aliases. Just Pieternel.'

'OK, well she's relatively harmless. You'll find her on such official paperwork as she needs as Mrs Nell Peters. That might be an alias, too. I haven't pulled in the favours I'd need to get more, and I'm not about to. She's not worth it. Getting involved with Marks was bad luck for her. She's into something bigger than she's comfortable with.'

'Whoever targeted her can't have been pleased either,' Webber said. 'They didn't get what they wanted first time round. Her systems kept them out. Where did she learn that stuff? You don't buy those sorts of skills by the metre.'

'She was Intelligence Services trained,' Farrar said, and Webber mentally slapped his forehead. Of course she was. How had he missed it? His fingers played with the tiny metal clips. At last a link that made sense. 'Not ours,' Farrar went on. 'Scandinavian. UNDK I think.'

'How come she went freelance?'

'There was some nasty business in South America, an operation that went pear-shaped. She went through the mill, spent time as a hostage. They got her out but she went her own way or she was pensioned off, I'm not sure. It was years ago. She set up her own business, took up with the Raymond woman and they've done OK.'

'So the last thing she wants is to get mixed up in that world again. No wonder she was so keen to cooperate.'

'Yes, once she got an idea of the scope of what they'd blundered into with the Marks case, she was all too keen to hand over everything they had. The PI from Hull, Christa Andrew, the one who was in the documentary, she worked in the London firm a few years ago. A bit of a protégé of the Pieternel woman. Did you know that?'

Webber hoped he didn't look as shell-shocked as he felt. More links clunked into place. The idea that Christa had a fraction of the talents of Mrs Nell Peters sent a shiver through him.

'It took serious money to pay for those false trails and for those raids on their office.'

What's the going rate to cover up the slaughter and dismemberment of a child, Webber thought sourly, but he knew it was the wrong question. All the witnesses had done was attest to various people being places they weren't. And as to getting rid of all Marks's records, ostensibly he was the killer already behind bars.

There were plenty of outfits who'd take money to trash a private investigator's records. 'But what the hell did the Raymond woman find that was worth going to those lengths to destroy?'

'I hope you're working on that one, Martyn.'

Webber thought of the reams of reports, surveillance records and photographs. He'd been through them. Ahmed had been through them. They might spend weeks going through them again and again without finding the speck of gold that was hidden in the mountain of detail. He picked another few paperclips from the tray on the desk. 'I need an analyst, John. Len's done a disappearing act and you've hijacked Ayaan.'

Farrar glanced at his phone. 'I'm hoping for a call from Ayaan in half an hour or so that might mean we get them both back again. Well, except you won't be getting Len back. That would mean overlooking the fact that he tried to destroy information and put you in the frame for it.'

'I wouldn't go that far,' Webber said, taken aback. 'He's staying in my house. He was just getting rid. I don't think he was after making it look like me.'

'Someone put pressure on him to do what he's done. Any ideas?'

Webber shook his head. The only person he knew to whom Klein routinely kow-towed was his wife, Julia, and that wasn't what Farrar was getting at.

'Well, I have a theory,' said Farrar. 'Pieternel, the London PI. We put pressure on her and she might have put pressure on Len. She doesn't want us delving into their business.'

'But how would she know anything about Len?'

'Look at all that's happened … all those false trails … databases tampered with. It reeks of an Intelligence Service operation. She'll have recognised that. Rogue operators. We train them. They go bad, sell their skills to anyone who can pay. We can't always put a stop to them when it happens. Don't get me wrong. I'm not saying the PI's a rogue operator, but she knows the business. She's paranoid over personal protection. She'd have known nothing about Len but she'll be canny enough to know he's the one to target.'

'But what could anyone get on Len? He's never put a foot out of line. Well ... before this business.'

'Says who? He came up through the ranks at a time when things weren't so tight. There'll be stuff in his past he doesn't want broadcast, and she'll have the contacts to dig. We put pressure on her and she didn't like it.'

Webber felt a growing unease as he played with the chain of paperclips, turned it in his hand, watched the links settle in a satisfyingly symmetrical pattern. It had been generous of Farrar to say 'we'. He'd been the one to put the heat on Pieternel. It had never occurred to him that she might target Klein.

'And don't forget, Martyn, someone's been tampering with our online records right here. I can't see why that would have been the Pieternel woman, but if it was ...'

Farrar left the sentence dangling. Webber's insides turned to ice. If Pieternel were behind the tampering with the online case file, her foot soldier could only have been Christa.

'So he's talking properly at last,' Farrar went back to Marks. 'We'd better see that we get everything we can out of him. If we have to bail him ...'

'We can't!' Webber heard himself interrupt more brusquely than he'd intended. Farrar looked at him with raised eyebrows. 'We can't let him go, John. If we let him walk, we'll never see him alive again.'

# chapter forty one

Webber ran his finger along the narrow strip, imagining a shiny feel to its surface through the plastic sleeve. It was thicker than ordinary paper, like an advertising leaflet. The singeing down its edge was the only mark. Nothing remained of whatever had been written on it. If Farrar were right, Klein had been pushed into destroying evidence and he, Webber, had had an inadvertent hand in it. And this, whatever it was, was something Klein had wanted rid of more than those old cuttings. He'd gone as far as to burn it before throwing it away, which meant he'd faffed about with naked flames in Webber's house, his hidden agenda trumping any thought of danger to Sam or Melinda. Webber's sympathies veered sharply away from his ex-governor. He thought viciously that he wished they'd left him to wreck his back on the uncomfortable couch rather than moving Sam's cot and allowing him a proper bedroom.

The cuttings Ahmed had retrieved from Melinda were the very old ones, the least relevant of all, but then he'd only caught up with Klein's manoeuvres late in the day. Webber pulled in a breath and began to read through them again, struggling to work out what Klein had tried to bury. He knew from the research done at the time of the documentary that the journalistic style had been considered a model of conciseness in its day, pioneering the populist tone that made the newspaper a commercial success, but to his 21st century eye, the articles were wordy blocks of text, hard to take in.

What could hold significance this long after the event? The personal details of the perpetrator and his victims were hardly going to be relevant when they were so long dead, but was there something in the manner of the murders? Klein had been fixated on the way the victims were butchered, particularly their hands.

Again he caught at the memory of dismembered hands crossed on the victims' chests. *Extra fingers make extra hands for extra prayers.* The pseudo-religious justification with its gruesome undertones came back to him, slightly longer than the quote he'd given Farrar. Those sliced fingers matched the injuries inflicted by the killer Len had put away, but the hands hadn't been with the bodies, they'd been found later. Certainly the reference that stuck in his mind wasn't in the information in front of him. That meant Klein had removed it earlier. Did that make it more significant? He looked again at what he had, but it was hard to pull anything concrete out of the flowery prose. Maybe it wasn't the content but for some other reason that Klein had done what he'd done? What had Farrar said? *... destroy information and put you in the frame for it.*

But why?

His mind ran across the themes of the research behind the documentary. His role had been to compare new policing methods with old, speculating on whether the 19th century crimes might have been stopped sooner either with present-day methods or with the tools they'd had available then. Part of his brief had been to laud the virtues of modern forensics, but he'd had to conclude that the killer could have been brought to justice earlier. It was less the tools and techniques, than the attitudes of the time that had shielded him. And money too, he thought. The financial angle hadn't been stressed at the time, just taken for granted. Rich people buying the privilege to butcher poor ones. That hadn't changed as much as it should have over the decades.

Farrar had half promised him specialist help when it could be spared, but he would focus it all on Annie Raymond's records. He wouldn't waste expertise on Klein's old case when there might be nothing to find beyond the demons conjured up in Klein's head, the shadows that had diverted him in the first place. And where the hell was Klein anyway?

He glanced round as he heard someone call Ahmed's name, saying, 'What is it? He's off on an errand for John.'

'Traffic,' the woman said. 'Ayaan was asking about a blue Jag. Someone remembers spotting it earlier, parked in a driveway. The guys are out on a call but they'll be back soon. I can get their patrol route if you want.'

At last! 'Yes, show me.' Webber sprang to his feet and marched across.

His gaze rested on the map, following the pointing finger as it traced a route through the city streets. '... not sure where ... I can call them up ...' Then his attention strayed from the woman's words, his gaze glued to a familiar street name. It took a moment to make the connection. He stared back towards the desk and that scrap of paper with its singed edge and blank surfaces.

Annie Raymond ... Marks ... Nothing to do with the old case. Klein had lifted this one from the live investigation.

His raised hand cut the woman mid-sentence. 'Get on to whoever spotted that car,' he said. 'I want the address where they saw it, and I want it now.'

He grabbed the nearest phone and punched in Farrar's extension. As the ringtone sounded in his ear, the door opened and Farrar himself strode in. 'John!' Webber called, diverting Farrar from his beeline towards the group at the far end of the room. 'John, look at this. I know what it was.' He pointed towards the desk where the singed strip lay in its plastic sleeve. 'It's not the old case at all. It was in the paperwork Annie Raymond handed over.'

'What? It was out of your case files?'

Webber nodded. 'It was a half-drawn sketch Marks threw in a bin outside a late-night services. Ayaan matched an address to it. I was looking at the map. The street name leapt out at me, but I can't remember the number. Goodridge's car was spotted earlier. We're just getting the exact address, but it's going to match. It can't be coincidence.' He turned back to the map and tapped his finger on the location.

Farrar leant forward to peer closely. 'That's not so far from where the missing girl lives.'

'I know. It's nowhere near where she was last seen but ...' He looked up at Farrar and saw his own puzzlement reflected in the Chief Super's eyes. Did that scrap of paper provide yet another link from Damien Marks to Olivia Lamb through Annie Raymond?

'Martyn, why is this the first I'm hearing about this place?' Farrar's voice was dangerously quiet as he took in what Webber told him.

'I don't know, John. She didn't know where it was, the Raymond woman. It was just a sketch when she handed it over.'

Farrar looked at the map. 'It's a long road. I want the exact address that was on that scrap of paper. Did you say Ayaan found it? Where did he get it from?'

Webber thought back. The memory was tangled in a time of frenetic activity. 'Yes, it was definitely Ayaan,' he said finally. 'But I don't know how he found it.'

'How did Len get it out of a live case file? Why didn't you miss it?'

Again Webber had to struggle for the memory. Hadn't Ahmed brought it to him? 'We need Ayaan. Where have you sent him?'

'Off on a long shot.' Farrar checked his watch. 'He might be driving, but ring him. We need to know.'

Webber picked up the phone, speaking as soon as it was answered. 'Ayaan, that scrap of paper, half burnt ... It's that flyer thing that Annie Raymond said Marks threw away. Night time ... late night Services.'

'Yes, you're right! Yes, of course it is.' He heard excitement through the speakerphone echo of Ahmed's tone.

'Can you remember the exact address that was on there, Ayaan?'

'Uh ... I think the road was ...'

'I've got the road. I need the house number.'

'No, sorry. I can't remember.'

'OK, we'll find out. And where did you get the address from?'

A pause. 'Um ... It was you who found the address, Guv.'

'Me? No, I didn't. I knew nothing about it.'

It was a longer pause this time, into which Webber eventually said, 'Spit it out, Ayaan.'

'I went into that side room, you know where ...?' Webber knew. It was the room where he'd caught Klein crying over the old case file. 'Len was there. He was writing the address on the paper, and I ... I thought he'd found something important. I asked him what it was, where he'd found it.'

Webber could imagine the bounce with which Ahmed had dived in to ask Klein what it meant and to congratulate him on finding it. Webber supposed Klein had been taken by surprise. The lad took everyone aback from time to time with his bursts of enthusiasm. But it began to spark something in his own memory. Hadn't he, Webber, somehow arrived in the equation at the critical moment?

'But you handed it to me, didn't you, Ayaan?'

'Yes. You came and asked us what we were doing.'

Webber's memory of the incident trickled back. He recalled snapping at them. *What are you two skiving in here for?* But there'd been something more urgent going on. If Ahmed had tried to explain, he hadn't listened properly. 'What did you say to me at the time, Ayaan?'

'I think I just told you that it was the address you'd given Len. You see, that was what he'd said to me, that you'd told him to check it out.'

'Yes, OK. Thanks Ayaan.' He ended the call. He hadn't taken the paper from Ahmed. He'd told him to put it on his desk; that he'd look later. And that was the last he'd seen of it. He supposed it was now ashes washed down the sink in his own bathroom.

He summarised the gist of the call for Farrar, ending, 'It was on my desk. He could have taken it any time. Anyone could.'

'Help me out, Martyn. I'm struggling to make a connection between Len's old case and this address.'

'I don't know. This is to do with Marks.'

'So where are we going here? Was the PIs' office raided to get rid of their copy of it?'

Webber shook his head. 'All they had was a scan of an unfinished line drawing. It wasn't the PIs who matched it to an address. It looks as though that was Len.'

As he looked up to meet Farrar's eye, the woman who'd brought the message was back. 'This is where they saw that car,' she said, handing him a piece of paper.

Farrar looked at it. 'That's nowhere near that road. It's the other side of the city.'

Webber stared at the words. Had he jumped to a spurious conclusion? Was it nothing to do with the torn strip after all? This was a completely different location, and yet familiar ...

'Nesbitt!' He felt a sudden surge of triumph as the link clicked into place. 'That's Nesbitt's address. He was there that night, too. He's the man Annie Raymond called sorry-guy.'

◉ ◉ ◉

Annie's eyes snapped open. The face in its awful mask had gone. She lay on her back, her muscles protesting the hard surface. It was as though a heavy blanket had been thrown across her. Too much trouble to move. Was this the same table, the same cell? Something had changed. The thought and the answer arrived together. She could see. The whole room was bathed in a dim light.

She'd been knocked out by something, but it had been fleeting. The gap in her memory felt small. A gloved hand reaching out ... a scratch on her skin ...

She remembered the garden. That scurrying in the undergrowth. It was the same image. That scuttling creature had been a gloved hand administering something quick-acting that needed no more than a scratch. The blood had run down her leg. It hadn't been a bramble. Someone had waited for them. In her mind, she saw Klein's face in profile, the puzzled expression as he thought he'd seen something. They'd drawn back into the bushes, back into the arms of … what?

The drug made her languid, but she knew she must fight it. Just now, raising her head would be like hauling up a ton weight, but that would wear off. And once she could lift her head she knew she'd be facing the door. If it wasn't already open, she intended to find a way to open it. Wearily she moved her hands to push aside the blanket that held her down.

There was no blanket. There was nothing. And only one of her hands obeyed the summons to move at all. A weird tingling played around her left wrist. There was no feeling in her hand. With a gasp that dispelled some of drug's calming effect, she reached across. Her right hand clasped the metal bracelet that encased her left wrist. Desperately she reached down and let out a huge sigh as she felt her hand intact below the metal band.

Manacled. Just like the corpse. Left to starve. Her free hand felt around the shackle and then on to the chain, tugging at it. As she did so, she could see the links move in the dim light above her, the chain crossing her line of sight and disappearing up towards the ceiling. She pulled in a breath and flopped her head to one side. There was the second table, now discreetly covered with a blanket that hid the body and fell right to the floor concealing the noxious gully. No chain disturbed the smoothness of the covering. She felt again at the metal around her wrist. Someone had wrenched it free of the corpse and locked it on to her.

She felt a spark deep inside as her right hand reached across again to explore the lock that held her. Her pact with the dead hadn't been for nothing. She'd tampered with the mechanism when she'd had two hands free to be able to do it. The spark became a small surge of triumph. She could be free of this bond within seconds.

For the moment she lay still. When she made her move, it had to count. What else did she have? She knew where the door was, and she still had the lion's share of a sticky pastry in one pocket. If she scattered it, she could bring back the rats. That booted figure had flinched as the rats had scurried.

Making a huge effort, she began to lift her head from the table, her stare moving inch by inch down from the ceiling, struggling to judge exactly where that line of light had run. The colour was an uneven yellowish brown, the surface itself a sort of resin, hard to guess its thickness. Irregularities made it difficult to decide which anomalies might be bumps in the coating and which could be the edge of a door.

Her neck ached as she raised her head, her gaze reaching down the far wall, from curved ceiling, to flat surface to …

No!

Shock jolted through her body. A figure stood at the foot of the table watching her. A pair of eyes stared impassively into hers. Annie felt her heart thump so hard it might burst from her chest. She gasped and fought for words.

She stared at the face, saw the mouth open. She took in the unemotional expression, listened to words spoken and sensed more than heard a question coming her way.

'Uh … yes …' She strove to articulate an answer. 'Yes … I'm awake now.'

The remaining languor from the drug and the strain on her neck were too much. Her head fell back, hitting painfully on the metal surface of the table. Shock made her breathing too shallow, threatening to bring dizziness. Through the dim lighting, the next question came at her, the sense of it lost in the image burnt into her mind of the slender figure who stood and watched.

Unemotional, expressionless, showing no fear or even much interest, holding vigil until Annie had come round enough to talk, Olivia Lamb stood and waited.

# chapter forty two

This was so surreal it was hard to believe it wasn't a dream and yet Annie had never felt so grounded, nor so scared. She was in a room with Olivia Lamb, the missing girl. The chain and manacle were heavy. She could scarcely move her left arm at all, but eventually managed to prop herself up enough to face the child. Olivia looked grey and wraithlike as she waited for Annie to recover. She also looked hostile. 'I know you're a ghost but I'm not scared and you can't get me anyway.'

Adrenaline pumped through her system. She saw the blank screen in a corner of the ceiling. That had been where Klein's face had hovered fleetingly. Someone was playing with them, watching them. She remembered the alien mask. Night-vision goggles. The whole room must have been bathed in infrared light, her movements visible to the hidden watcher. But she hugged a secret close. When she'd leant over that body in the darkness, her attention must have seemed to be on muttered prayers and apologies; no one knew she'd interfered with the mechanism on the manacle.

The door would open again at some point and when it did she would be ready to move. She reached her right hand awkwardly across, feeling at the metal round her left wrist, wondering if she could loosen it now discreetly and be ready to throw it off. But a movement stopped her. Olivia stared at Annie's shackled arm and took a step backwards, with a half glance behind her. To Olivia, Annie was the enemy, a ghost who might have supernatural means to escape. Olivia thought she was safe because of that chain. But the movement and the glance held hope for Annie. The child knew her escape route.

'This thing really hurts my wrist,' she murmured. 'I wish it weren't so tight.' But Olivia didn't relax until Annie moved her right hand away from the shackle.

'Who are you talking to?' It was Klein's voice, shaky and unexpected, out of the air, an echo behind it. She didn't want him butting in. Not now.

'I think we're being watched.' She spoke softly, not sure what line of communication was open between them.

'Why? Who's with you?'

'Electronic surveillance,' she said. 'I saw your face earlier, but it was on a screen.'

'Electronic …? Is that what it is? Wait a moment. There, is that it?'

A glimmer from above. The screen flickered to life, lines criss-crossing it. The image was blurred but it was unmistakeably Klein, three quarter face. She stared aghast. One of his eyes was a bloody mess, lines of red streaking his cheek.

'My God, what's happened to you?'

'Never mind that. Who were you talking to?' His tone was urgent now.

'It's Olivia Lamb, the missing girl.'

'I am not missing.' The words came forcefully from the figure at the foot of the table. 'I'm going home.'

'Olivia Lamb?' Annie heard a sudden uplift to Klein's tone. 'Then she's given him the slip. He's not here. No one's watching right now, but I can't get free. Olivia? Olivia, listen to me. Do you know your way out of here?'

'Yes, of course I do.'

'Then you must go now. Go home. Do you know your way home?'

'Of course I know my way. But I'm not going until she tells me.'

'For God's sake, tell the child whatever she wants to know. Let her get away at least. We don't have long.'

'But I don't know ...'

Olivia interrupted her. 'Tell me about the hands,' she ordered.

'The ...? Uh ... what do you mean?'

'Where are they?'

Annie felt her eyes flick towards the heavy pall under which the corpse lay, as Klein urged her again, 'Give her whatever she wants. Let her get away.'

'Over there,' Annie said. 'Under that blanket.'

With a tut of exasperation, Olivia's glance shot heavenwards. 'Not *those* hands. The other hands. Where did you see them?'

'I ... uh ... I don't know ...'

Olivia stared hard at her, as though annoyed that she wouldn't pick up an obvious hint.

'Um ... the hands ... I saw them ...' She had no idea where the words were going. She said them to see how Olivia reacted and watched as the girl nodded encouragement. 'At ... er ...' She waved her free hand in an indeterminate gesture.

'Do you mean in the water?' prompted the girl.

'Yes, in the water.'

For a moment, they stared at each other, then Olivia gave another exasperated sigh. 'What water? There's water all over.'

'Um ... Why don't you guess?'

'Miss Raymond, what in hell are you playing at? Tell the child what she wants to know and let her get out.'

Annie glanced up at the screen, seeing Klein flinch and clasp his hand to his face as a thick red gobbet rolled from his damaged eye socket down his cheek. She didn't know what to say. *She's the one who knows the answer not me*, was the obvious reply but she felt they were on a knife edge. Klein seemed to think no one was watching them, but that their captor, whoever it was, would be back soon. He could be wrong. He didn't look in any state to be making rational judgements.

Olivia knew something she wasn't telling. Annie couldn't begin to guess what or why. The manacle might not be the trap it was supposed to be but it was too tight around her wrist. Her arm would be useless if she didn't free herself soon.

'Shut up,' she hissed at Klein. 'Go on, Olivia. Guess about the water.'

'It could be the river or the ditch or the well,' intoned Olivia, opening her eyes wide on the word, well.

'In the well,' said Annie.

Olivia nodded. Klein's voice said, 'What do you mean, the well? What's …? Oh!'

At the exclamation, Annie's gaze shot up to the screen. 'What is it?'

'We have company,' Klein's voice hissed. 'Quick, can you …?' His voice cut out as the image tipped and blurred. She strained to see through the speckled fog that began to play on the screen.

A movement. Light flooded the room. She took in the open door … Olivia Lamb's small figure diving through it. With a gasp, she leapt for the floor, fingers scrambling to release the manacle. The chain clanked as it pulled taut, twisting her arm, yanking her sideways. Pieces of sticky confectionary flew from her pocket, flakes of pastry catching between her fingers and the pin as she struggled to release it.

The door slammed, cutting light and sound in an instant, leaving her half propped against the metal bed, feet floundering to avoid the loose rubble in the gully. The darkness was absolute. Then a new sound began to swell all around her. A light scurrying as the rats swarmed down the walls to find the feast.

◉ ◉ ◉

Webber climbed out of the car, tipped his thumb at a pair of speedcuffs hanging from the cigarette lighter and said, 'Don't leave those on show.'

The scramble to grab the cuffs and shove them into the glove box signalled to him that neither of his companions had even noticed them. They weren't familiar with each other, nor with the car. Farrar was pulling people out of the ether, trusting no one.

Webber felt frustration to be here with people he didn't know. Farrar had taken a team to Nesbitt's house, leaving Webber to cruise along this road and discover the house on the flyer. It hadn't been difficult. The odd-shaped chimneys stood out against the sky. He'd called it in and learnt that its sole official occupant was an elderly woman called Hannah Levine. And Levine was another name from that car park.

At this top end the street lay quiet, the house isolated. A patrol car had accompanied them and once sure of the address, Webber had studied the map and dispatched it to approach the house from a track that ran up behind. It was a long way round and they would probably have to do the last stretch on foot. He waited to hear they were in place. Farrar had made clear he didn't want a song and dance about this house or Nesbitt's just yet. The trail was insubstantial, but Goodridge had been to Nesbitt's and the footpath at the back of the house where Webber now stood led to the heart of the estate where Olivia Lamb and Stacy Gerrard lived.

The two constables, a man and a woman, waited discreetly by the car. He turned to them, speaking to the female officer. 'When we hear they're in place at the back, we'll go in. You go through the side entrance,' he added to the man, as he indicated the pair of stone pillars, one leaning drunkenly, bindweed and brambles engulfing the remains of a wooden gate. 'Keep an eye down the side. Chances are we'll find an elderly lady and nothing else, but it's a rambling old house. I want to know if our visit causes any waves.'

They nodded, and he wondered what they were heading into – the smoke and mirrors of Klein's old case or something relevant to the new one. He wondered, too, what Farrar and his team were finding at Nesbitt's.

A burst of static came from the woman's radio. She inclined her head to acknowledge the call. The guys at the back were in place and watching. As Webber looked up at the old-fashioned chimneys, a part of him wanted to call up a busload of officers in riot gear and a full forensic team. Somewhere in this tangle of cases lay something way too big to tackle with a routine knock at a door. But he had nothing to say this was it. The house wasn't far from the Lambs, but Olivia had last been seen the other side of the city. Klein had burnt the address – why? What could have happened to turn him from the unflappable dependable gov'nor Webber remembered into a man who would destroy evidence?

He waited to see that the constable would be able to fight his way through the undergrowth at the side entrance, noting with interest that the tangle wasn't as tight as it had looked. Someone had pushed their way through quite recently. The man picked his way, his gaze searching the terrain. Webber felt the crunch of gravel under his feet as he and the female officer marched up the main driveway and approached the front door. He looked doubtfully at a rusty bell push, pressed it anyway, but also raised the knocker and beat a brisk tattoo on the wooden panel. After a few seconds, footsteps could be heard from inside, a chain clanked and the door opened a few inches showing an unsmiling face beneath an iron-grey perm. Webber raised his warrant card, introduced himself and said, 'Are you Mrs Hannah Levine?'

'No, I'm her housekeeper.'

'And your name is …?'

She pursed her lips and fixed him with a severe look. 'If you are who you say you are, young man, you'll know that no sensible citizen gives personal details to strangers on their doorstep.'

Webber disguised his irritation behind a friendly smile. 'It's Mrs Levine we'd like to speak to.'

The woman's glare hardened. Webber thought he caught a shaft of disappointment that he hadn't made a fight out of knowing her name. 'She won't let anyone in without verification. I'll have to make sure you're who you say you are.' Without releasing the door chain, she lifted a mobile phone and punched in a number. They heard her say, 'There's a man and woman on my doorstep claiming to be from the police. She's in a uniform but he's not. I want to know ... Yes, just a moment.' Her face appeared again at the crack in the door and Webber held up his ID which she read into the phone. 'And yours,' she rapped out, scowling at his colleague who stepped smartly forward. Information gathered, the woman stood back into the shadow inside the house as she concluded the call.

The officer at his side leant close to Webber and murmured, 'Too tall for O'Dowd.'

Webber responded with a brief nod. He glanced into the unusual light blue of her eyes. She was better informed than the randomly picked officer she was supposed to be. He'd heard Farrar call her Suzie.

The housekeeper muttered that she would inform Mrs Levine of their visit, and disappeared into the gloom. Webber glanced at his watch. If he didn't hear footsteps return within half a minute, he was ready to kick the door in. He'd watched 27 seconds go by when the click-clack of heels on the tiled floor approached again. A burst of static from his companion's radio coincided with the clink of the chain. She stepped discreetly back to take the call as the woman opened the door and said, 'She'll see you, but you're not to tire her. She's not in the best of health.'

Webber followed her down the hallway to a gloomy sitting room. A small woman sat in an armchair, well bundled in blankets. Her hair was a mass of tight grey curls that Webber would have recognized as a wig even if it had been straight on her head. He supposed it had been hastily pulled on in honour of visitors. Beaming, she greeted him with, 'How do you do, Inspector ... what was it?' She turned milky eyes to the housekeeper who supplied, 'Superintendent Webber,' in a frosty tone. The old lady screwed up her eyes. 'Inspector Nesbitt?' she ventured, adding, 'Like Mrs Fairclough's cousin. He does our running about for us.'

One look at Hannah Levine was enough to know she hadn't been behind the wheel of a vehicle in a long time. It was understandable her ears had failed to catch his name and rank, but interesting that she would guess at Nesbitt. He smiled. 'That'll be Mr Nesbitt of …' He glanced at the housekeeper as he recited the address the other side of the city where Farrar had taken his team.

There was a certain rigidity in her expression as she stared back at him. 'Mrs Levine's hearing isn't what it was, and she mustn't be tired.'

'Detective Superintendent Webber,' he said again to the old lady, scrutinizing her as he held out his warrant card. Who did Hannah Levine remind him of? He couldn't catch the memory, but it wasn't O'Dowd or anyone connected to the case. The shape of her face, the way it lit up when she grinned at him made him think she must be someone's grandmother, some young officer whose features he knew well. He studied her as she peered at his ID. 'Inspector Nesbitt. What can I do for you? Do sit down. What about some tea?'

'Thank you, no.' Whoever she was, she was half blind as well as deaf, but keeping up a pretence. He looked round for his colleague but she hadn't followed them in. The housekeeper hovered in the doorway, casting glances back down the hall.

'We've had reports of children trespassing.' Webber raised his voice. 'Round the back of your house.'

'Kittens in the house?' The old woman looked towards her housekeeper for interpretation.

'Children,' the woman said. 'Trespassers.'

Hannah Levine nodded, with a confident, 'Oh, yes. That's right.'

Webber was sure she hadn't understood a word. He turned to the housekeeper. 'You've seen the news reports about the missing child, Olivia Lamb. We've had reports of children trespassing round the back. Breaking into cellars. She was one of them.' As he said the words, he wondered if they could be true. Had Olivia Lamb been here? Could this be where Annie Raymond had seen her? But no, that didn't add up because Annie Raymond had never had this address.

The housekeeper shrugged. 'We don't use the cellar. It floods.'

'You're at the top of a hill,' Webber objected.

'We're not. We're just the highest house on the lane. We get all the water from up there.' She gave a vague nod of her head towards the back of the house. 'We don't get the first of it, but when it's bad the place is unusable. You can look if you want, but I'm not having you traipsing about where I can't see you.' She shot another look down the hallway. 'You both stay where I can see you or one of you stays outside.'

Footsteps sounded down the corridor and Webber's colleague stepped into the room with a nod of apology. 'Can I have a word, Guv?' She leant close enough that he felt her breath on his skin as she whispered in his ear. 'Ayaan Ahmed called in for backup and an ambulance about ten minutes ago. He's found Mr Klein.'

# chapter forty three

Ahmed replayed Webber's call in his head. That singed strip; the piece of paper with its unusual weight and texture on which Klein had written an address. How had he missed it? And why had he believed Klein's story about it being Webber who had found the address? It hadn't even been a copy, for heaven's sake. Klein had been writing on the flyer itself. He wanted to recall a guilty start or a moment of alarm, but the image in his memory was of Klein's usual easy manner making him accept the bizarre circumstance as normal without a second thought. And now Webber would be off to that address without him, to find … to find what?

The North Sea appeared in front of him, a flat calm expanse placidly easing its way towards late afternoon. Almost there, but it was already way past the end of his shift and hardly worth returning to York, though he knew he would. If he'd been sent across to tie up the Cochrans' loose ends, that would be one thing, but being here at the whim of a Chief Super was another. Farrar had told him it might be a fool's errand; and just look, thought Ahmed, who the fool had turned out to be.

That piece of paper. He'd known it was significant. As soon as he'd pulled it out of the trash it had leapt at him. For starters Klein had burnt it which was more trouble than he'd gone to with the press cuttings. He wished he'd been the one to pin it down, but he wasn't surprised it should have been Webber. He'd never worked for anyone like Webber before. Never felt so constantly in need of being on his toes ready to absorb new information at a moment's notice. Webber changed tracks more than … what was that phrase that Klein liked to use? He couldn't remember. But it was exciting, stimulating. And everyone said it got results, though they didn't seem to like working with him. *Never know where you are … won't leave you to get on with it …* It just seemed so unfair that Webber should be taking a new team out to that address while he, Ahmed, drove too fast along the narrow North Yorkshire lanes, on the off chance that Klein might have returned home.

He'd been so sure he'd find an empty house that he might have turned round and headed back if he'd known sooner about the scrap of paper. But having arrived, knew he must do a thorough job. He'd even swung the car right in on to the drive, against Mrs Klein's express wish that visitors stick to the verge outside. She didn't like the gravel disturbed. She wouldn't be home. She was in York. They were both in York staying with relatives. Klein had told him.

Instead of approaching the front door to knock, he'd made for the nearest window and peered in, aiming to circle the house, checking the rooms as far as he was able, and planning to ring the doorbell for form's sake before he left.

Living room … Utility room … high window … no sign of recent use …

Kitchen with an old-fashioned TV. He'd smiled at the Kleins having a television in the kitchen after all their talk about TV junkies. And then he'd moved round, bringing the rest of the room into view.

All thoughts of televisions were wiped from his head along with the smile from his lips. Len Klein sat at the kitchen table, the side of his head a bloody mass.

He could barely track the sequence with which he'd leapt for the door, shouting to Klein, juggling his phone to rattle out an emergency call for backup and an ambulance.

For form's sake he grabbed the handle and wrenched at the door which didn't budge. He was sizing up the strength and position of the lock as he grabbed a stone from the rockery. Would his shoulder have enough force …? A good hard kick …? Smash through the glass panel with the stone …?

A shout made him pause. 'Ayaan, wait!' And he heard the sound of a key turning.

'Len!' He dived in to grab his colleague by the arm, his gaze scanning every corner for attackers. 'Who's here? Where?' He shot out the questions, not knowing whether it was safe to sit Klein back at the table to look at his injuries or if the perpetrator was still inside.

'It's OK … It's OK.' Klein's voice took a while to penetrate his frantic surveillance. 'I'm fine.'

'Of course you're not, Len.' Fine? Klein must be concussed. 'Sit down. Who did this? Are they still here?'

'Ayaan, stop. Listen to me. I'm fine. I did it myself. Dropped this from the shelf just now. I was about to clean myself up when you arrived.'

Next to the sink sat a large plastic tub, the inscription *Tomaten Ketchup 5kg* across its label, its lid resting at an angle. Klein shook off his hand and walked to the sink. He damped a tea-towel under the tap and applied it to his face. The cloth took on a bright red hue as his face emerged undamaged. Ahmed peered closely to convince himself there were no cuts, no swelling, then leant over the tub to draw in the smell of tomatoes.

He looked around at the unsullied floor and surfaces. 'I'm sorry, did you say you'd dropped it?'

'It didn't fall. I was getting it down to fill the ketchup jug. The lid was loose. I caught it but it splashed up into my face. Gave me quite a shock.'

'It looked like …' Ahmed peered again at Klein's face.

'What are you doing here anyway, Ayaan?'

'Chief Superintendent Farrar sent me. He thought you might have come back home. Len, why did you take that stuff, those press cuttings?'

'Ah yes, the press cuttings.' Klein's mouth curved to a smile but there was sadness in his eyes.

'Is Annie Raymond with you?'

'Annie Raymond? Why would she be with me? I put her in a taxi in good time for her train.'

'Well, it looks like she didn't get it.'

'Didn't I hear you call for backup, Ayaan? Hadn't you better cancel it? '

'Yes, I'm about to.' When he'd finished the calls, he said, 'Is Mrs Klein with you, Len?'

'Julia? No, she's still in York.'

'You know you'll have to come back with me.'

Klein nodded. 'Of course. Of course. I just needed some time to myself. I was barking right up the wrong tree, Ayaan. I thought I had a link … thought that private investigator had something. But I was chasing shadows. I'd have come back tomorrow morning. Just couldn't face it today. I'm getting old.'

Ahmed knew Klein was going to suggest they sleep on it, go back to York tomorrow. He felt bad that he was going to have to say no, they must go now. He practised words in his head as he watched Klein fiddle with the controls of the ancient television and run his hands over the surface of an old-fashioned microwave. He knew he wasn't even going to let Klein return in his own car. Watching his colleague … ex-colleague now, he supposed … as he played with the kitchen equipment, he saw an offer of a hot drink forming itself in Klein's head. He would refuse that, too. It was by the book from now on. No leeway.

'If you had the PI, Miss Raymond, in front of you now, Ayaan, what would you say to her?'

Ahmed shot Klein a glance. Klein knew the score. He wasn't going to make it difficult. There wouldn't even be the offer of a quick coffee. Ahmed had to look down as emotion pricked the back of his eyes. He and Klein had been close. He played along with the pretence. 'I guess I'd tell her to get in touch, first so we know she's all right and also she might be able to tell us more about … well, there might be more she can tell us.'

He'd almost let slip Goodridge's name. Not that it would have mattered but it had to be by the book now. If Klein noted the pause, he didn't let it show. He just peered at the blank face of the microwave as he ran the cloth over the side of his face again. Ahmed couldn't see any reflection in the battered surface but understood Klein's need to avoid eye contact.

'Did you get that, Miss Raymond?' Klein said as he took the cloth from his face and rubbed it over his hands. 'Detective Constable Ahmed would like to hear from you.' He turned and looked at Ahmed with a smile. 'Shame you can't hear her. She might have something after all.'

Ahmed smiled back. Klein might act relaxed, but he must be at breaking point. The nerves were showing. He'd said, shame you can't hear her instead of shame *she* can't hear *you*. He wouldn't point it out. 'OK, Len. We need to get going.'

\* \* \*

Klein injured? Webber's thoughts tumbled through a myriad of possibilities. That bitch, Raymond! What had she done? His young colleague murmured, 'Shall I chase it up? Find out more?' as her hand moved to the radio lying silently in its pouch.

Ahmed's call had come in ten minutes ago, she'd said. There was something reassuring about her composure. Farrar had hand-picked her. Webber wondered where from. He wanted to know more about Klein and Ahmed, but shook his head. He'd do this one himself. At least her offer to use the radio meant that nothing had elevated this to an emergency-calls-only crisis.

'Wait here with Mrs Levine, Suzie.' He strode down the dingy hallway and back outside clicking Ahmed's number into his phone. He had no idea what he would learn, but this wasn't a conversation to have in front of the house's inhabitants. He was aware of the suspicious gaze of the housekeeper following him as he as his colleague swapped positions, and wondered for a second if the hostility in her protective act was a little overdone. What was she protecting? He'd see to her in a moment.

Outside, the overgrown garden with its high bushes had begun to lose definition; the breeze had a chilly edge as it lost the sun's warmth. Listening to the ringtone in his ear, he caught sight of the man he'd sent to the side of the house, pacing its length, scrutinizing the windows, head tipped to speak into his radio. Farrar had hand-picked this team. They wouldn't relax their vigilance.

He stood by a patch of brambles that had been recently trampled. Had his guys done it? He didn't think so. The trailing fronds were flattened as though something had been dragged over them.

Ahmed's voice at last. 'Ayaan, where are you? How's Len? What happened?'

'It's OK guv, he's fine. I thought he'd been … anyway, he's OK. I'm at his house on the coast. Chief Superintendent Farrar sent me.'

'And the Raymond woman?'

'Annie Raymond? Len says he put her in a taxi about …' There was a pause into which Webber heard Klein's voice say he couldn't remember, but well in time for her train.

'What firm?'

Again there was a pause, then Klein murmuring, 'Oh, now wait a minute, was it …? Hell, I'll remember in a minute.'

'OK, never mind for now. Is Len's wife with him?'

'No, Mrs Klein is in York still. I'm not sure where. Len, do you want us to contact … No? OK. Um … I'm bringing Len back to York.' Ahmed's voice took on a hint of frost; it was the tone he'd used with the PIs in their office in London. Webber noted the phraseology – they weren't coming back together, Ahmed was bringing Klein. The lad had looked up to Klein. It must have been quite a blow.

'Good work, Ayaan. You're still at Len's house, yes? Just hang on there for a moment.' As he spoke Webber stepped back through the front door and headed down the hallway. The housekeeper was nowhere in sight, but he heard the old woman's voice say, 'I told you, Mrs Fairclough's nephew. I can't remember his name.' Her tone was tetchy.

Suzie looked up at him as he came in. In her hand she held a silver-framed photograph. 'Guv, look. Isn't that ...?' She turned it towards him.

Webber peered at it. Ryan Davies stared morosely out at him. The nagging sense of unease intensified. 'He's the housekeeper's nephew?'

'That's what she said.' Suzie looked round. 'Where is she?'

Webber shrugged a don't know. Mrs Fairclough hadn't gone past him. 'She must be upstairs or gone to the kitchen.' The presence of the photograph worried him more than her disappearance. If she decided to do a runner she'd be straight into the arms of one of the officers outside.

'Mrs Fairclough!' the old woman called from behind him. 'Mrs Fairclough! Where's Mrs Fairclough?'

Suzie went to her side, saying, 'What is it, Mrs Levine. Are you OK?'

'I need Mrs Fairclough.'

'I'll find her.'

'Give me a moment, Ayaan,' Webber said into the phone as Suzie left the room. He heard her calling up the stairs. He thought about that conversation he'd had with Julia Klein. It felt as though it were days ago but it had only been this morning. His gaze strayed to the photograph. 'Ayaan, can Len hear me?'

'No.'

'Good, I want to keep this call open. Stay with Len.' He took a step towards the doorway, pressing his phone to his shoulder as he called, 'Suzie? Are you there?'

She hurried back in, giving Hannah Levine a reassuring smile. 'I've called her, Mrs Levine. I'm sure she'll be along in a second.'

'She'll have to be,' muttered the old woman, casting worried glances towards the hallway.

'I need your phone,' Webber said. 'You're going to make a call and this is what you're to say.'

As he talked, Webber looked across at Mrs Levine. She stared eagerly and with small movements of alarm towards the door through which the housekeeper would return. She paid them no attention at all. He tapped the Kleins' home number into Suzie's phone and put his own phone back to his ear. He listened for the ring of a phone in the background. Nothing, just the faint buzz of the ringtone from Suzie's phone. He watched her as she listened. The phone had rung for ages last time, but had it been this long? Then he saw in her sudden stillness that someone had answered.

'Hello, is that Mrs Klein? This is Detective Sergeant Susan Harmer. I'm trying to contact your husband ... Uh ... yes, Chief Superintendent Farrar said ... I see ... Yes, well thank you for your time.'

'Please, what have you done to Mrs Fairclough? I need her badly.' The small voice from the sofa had real distress behind it.

Suzie exchanged a brief glance with Webber, mouthing, 'Where is she?' then went to crouch by the old lady. 'What is it, Mrs Levine? Is there anything I can do?

Hannah Levine's unfocused gaze shot towards Webber. He took care to feign focus on his phone as she lowered her voice. 'I need ... I need to go to the cloakroom. I need Mrs Fairclough with my frame.'

Webber discreetly cleared his throat to attract Suzie's attention before speaking quietly into his phone. 'Ayaan, has the phone rung while you've been there? The landline?' For Suzie's benefit he tipped his head towards the corner by the door where an aluminium walking frame stood.

'No,' said Ahmed. 'I ...'

'Well, don't mention it to Len,' Webber interrupted. 'Get him back here.' The calls were being diverted. Maybe Julia really was in York.

'Guv ... Is ...? Hmph.' The question died before it was born. But Webber had heard both steel and uncertainty behind Ahmed's words; the lad had shown no surprise and no reluctance about keeping Klein in the dark. The aborted question made clear that Ahmed still had no idea about Klein's role in all this. There was nothing Webber could say to enlighten him; he wished there was. Whatever Klein was up to, he wasn't happy about it. That much Webber would stake money on. Even so, he was relieved to read in Ahmed's tone that he was on his guard.

'Be careful, Ayaan. Watch your back.'

Suzie was by the old woman's side helping her as she hobbled towards the doorway on her frame, panting with the exertion, and saying, 'On the left just down the passage. Just get me so I can hold the rail. I can manage by myself from there. Where's Mrs Fairclough?'

Yes, thought Webber, where was the housekeeper? She'd been here when Suzie took the call about Ahmed. He eased his way past them, lightly tapping Suzie's shoulder and meeting her eye with the ghost of a wink. He didn't know her; hadn't seen her around before today. He wondered if she'd noticed her slip on the phone. Detective Sergeant Harmer. One of Farrar's foot soldiers for sure. There was something very Farrar about slipping a plainclothes officer into the enquiry by putting her in uniform as though she were somehow undercover.

He peered into the room on the left as he strode past. It was a narrow and gloomy old-fashioned cloakroom with coat hooks down one side, towels hanging over a metal bar. At the far end a half partition obscured the window and presumably the plumbing. He saw the silver gleam of the hand rails. Checking the room was instinctive. As he moved back outside, his mind was on Ahmed and Klein. And that silver-framed photograph of Ryan Davies. It shouldn't be difficult to find out exactly where the Kleins' calls were being diverted. He needed to talk to Farrar. Something inside him urged speed.

'There's a partition,' the frail voice came from behind him. 'Help me as far as that and there's a rail.'

Who did Hannah Levine remind him of? It hadn't seemed important but it was at the edge of consciousness and suddenly everything had become important. He flicked through the contacts screen for Farrar's number as he stepped outside.

An eruption of noise from inside the house spun him round. Suzie's voice. A strangled shriek. 'Help me!' Panicked. He took the length of the gloomy hallway in barely four strides.

She was there in the narrow cloakroom, doubled over, face creased in pain.

'Suzie!'

'No ... Guv ...' She struggled to get the words out as she tried to wave her hand towards the partition. 'Stop her. She's ...'

He understood. Hannah Levine. The old cow was after using the lavatory to flush away evidence. Evidence of what? And how had she managed to wind a fit young officer? He leapt to the partition ready to lift the old woman bodily and not too gently.

An old-fashioned toilet with a high cistern stood against the wall. Its flat face was patterned with flowers held in a badly-drawn hand. Petals and unconvincing bees wound their way down the pipe. The window was higher even than the cistern and tiny. The space was otherwise empty. Hannah Levine must have disappeared into the house. But how? She couldn't have moved fast enough to get out without him seeing her.

As he looked back he saw the deep shadow by the door. If she'd pressed herself to the dark panelled wall as he'd entered ... 'Don't worry, she won't get far.'

A groan snapped his attention to Suzie who half sobbed as she crumpled to the floor. In a second he was at her side. What had the old cow hit her with? Webber had barely registered that his hands were damp before they were wet and dripping. The blood was everywhere, soaking through his trouser leg where he knelt beside her; pooling on the floor; running down his arms … her arms …

He heard his own voice, an instinctive bellow for help from the officers outside as he ripped desperately at her clothing to find the injury, terrified it would already be too late.

It was the top of her leg. He couldn't feel anything in the wound, no sharp edge. He grabbed towels down from where they hung, and pressed wads of material on to her thigh. Thank God it wasn't her abdomen. The momentary relief vanished. With his whole weight on her, not caring if he crushed bones, he could barely stem the flow.

'Suzie! Suzie. Talk to me.'

'Oh God, what's she done? Never saw it coming.' The words had begun to slur.

'Suzie. You're going to be OK. Stay awake.' He daren't move either of his hands from their relentless pressure on what must be a severed artery in her leg … couldn't remember which pocket he'd shoved his phone into when she called out.

He yelled out again for help, heard running footsteps. Blood leaked, but at least it no longer gushed. Seconds could be vital.

She had a radio. The earpiece swung free by her shoulder. 'It's OK,' he told her. 'Hold on.' Shifting carefully in the awkward space, he moved his knee on to the thick towel wadding, and pushed down hard while he snatched her earpiece, clipped it to his ear and used her radio to make the call. The beat of running footsteps was loud now. He shouted again to guide them. His shouts … the pounding footsteps … Suzie's laboured gasps for breath. There were no other sounds. But for him and his team the house lay as still and quiet as if it were empty.

# chapter forty four

Ahmed stamped his foot on the brake with a muttered, 'Sorry,' to Klein beside him. The car swung wider than was compatible with safety round the sharp bend. Concentrate, Ahmed told himself, no time to surrender to tiredness no matter how stressful the day had been. He and Klein never normally had trouble getting a dialogue going, and he needed something to keep him alert at the wheel, but what could he say, what conversation could he initiate? He itched to interrogate Klein on the case notes, the press cuttings, on what exactly he'd thought he might learn from the PI, but he wasn't sure that was his territory. It was for the Chief Super to delve into all that. His job was to deliver Klein in one piece.

It was Klein who broke the silence. 'So you were back over here today, were you?'

'Not until the Chief Super sent me,' Ahmed replied. Klein was asking something he already knew. They'd been together in York at the start of the day. Maybe Klein had read his need for talk. He must have clocked how close he'd come to missing that turn.

'I meant have you been at the station over here catching up on the Cochrans?'

'No, I came straight to your house.'

'Ah, I thought John might have sent you because you were over here anyway.'

Klein was fishing to know how urgent the summons had been, but the Cochrans would be useful as a neutral topic. 'I'm coming back again tomorrow to sort the Cochrans. It's lucky I don't mind driving.'

'You're not up to date, are you?' Klein sounded surprised.

'Well, yes, unless anything new has come up in the past few hours.'

Klein laughed. 'Then you're way behind the curve, Ayaan. I called in on my way over.'

So Farrar's long-shot of sending him to the Kleins' hadn't been so long after all. He'd heard that Klein had called in to the local station. 'Go on. What's happened?'

'Turns out they took on a job about a week before Judd ploughed that field, waste to be dumped. The man insisted he do the dumping himself and paid enough over the odds that young Janice wasn't going to fuss. Just a bit of a sack, apparently.'

'What man?'

'Uh … Name of Nesbitt, apparently.'

'That's one of the names that … uh … that's what Janice Cochran said, is it?'

'No, this wasn't from the lass. I'm not sure who they had it from. The boyfriend, I assume. I don't think she'd have confided in her Dad. Seems she did the deal and met the guy on her own, took him up to the cliff. But then she blabbed about it. She prepped a bit of a hole. He tipped in this sack and poured some industrial paint down on top. He told her it was radioactive, but safe because of the way it was covered.'

'And she believed him?'

'Credulity stretches a long way for money, you know that, Ayaan.'

'So the murder weapon, the thing she threw into the Humber, did he dump that, too?' Ahmed tried to imagine Janice Cochran prying into something she thought was radioactive waste. She wasn't that stupid, surely.

'No. He gave it to her. He told her it was valuable treasure trove but that she mustn't try to sell it straight off. He suggested that she bury it on a different part of the farm, give it a few months to weather down and make out she'd found it. He warned her it'd spark a serious archaeological dig.'

Ahmed couldn't hold back a laugh. 'You mean she took the murder weapon as payment for disposing of the body?'

'Not entirely. He paid her as agreed. It was by way of a bonus. He said he had no way to sell it because he had nowhere he could legitimately have acquired it. He persuaded her that she might make a fortune on it. She took it because she's a greedy little thing, but of course she was stymied, too, what with all the stuff they had stashed about the place. She wasn't about to invite archaeologists on to her farm, not with those two other bodies there.'

The road ahead lay in darkness. And there would be precious few streetlights even on the long stretch of the A64 once they reached it. Ahmed had told Klein he didn't mind driving. It was true, he liked to be behind the wheel, but things were catching up with him – heavy traffic to London and back, the late shifts, the discomfort of an unfamiliar bed, and now the sight-testing gloom of unlit country lanes at night. There was a garage with a shop at the next junction. A can of Red Bull would wake him up.

He thought about Webber's frustration when he'd seen what Janice Cochran had thrown overboard from the ferry. Her involvement in the murder had put a spoke through all the logical lines of enquiry, but now it was all slotting into place. 'So this came from the boyfriend, did it? Has Janice Cochran been faced with it yet?'

'I don't think so. I imagine that's why they want you back tomorrow.'

Ahmed felt surprise along with a glow of gratification that they should wait for him before moving forward with this new development. He'd been the new boy for long enough. Maybe he'd earned his stripes now. As he slowed for the junction, he glanced to the far side. The forecourt lay in darkness, the shop windows shuttered. An exclamation of annoyance escaped his lips. 'I was going to call in to the garage for a drink,' he explained to Klein.

'There'll be something open further on,' Klein replied, adding, 'It doesn't look like old man Cochran knew anything about it.'

Ahmed grunted in response feeling his eyebrows rise a fraction. Billy Judd was the only one who looked to be fully in the clear. Cochran had been complicit in killing the protesters and hiding their bodies, though he could agree with Klein that he probably knew nothing about the buried child. If he had, he'd have made sure Judd went nowhere near that stretch. That part of the story had reached him. It had been some throwaway comment from the father about Judd being fool enough to plough the field to the cliff's edge that had catapulted the daughter to the nearest vantage point to look. Through the radio, she'd heard his emergency call. She must have had her doubts about the knife but had probably hoped to sell it until she heard what Billy Judd had found.

Ahmed kept his concentration on the road ahead. There would be shops along the route and some of those late-night services of the sort to which Annie Raymond had followed Marks that night. Klein was right and his careless response was reassuring. Ahmed wouldn't routinely stop the car for refreshments when he was taking a suspect in, but Klein wasn't about to run off, and if he tried, Ahmed was more than a match for him. That hot drink Klein had been on the point of offering might not be a bad idea for them both. Ahmed needed to stay awake and Klein must be pretty shaken up. He might not have been the victim of an attack but that had been an industrial-sized tub of ketchup that had almost fallen on him.

◉ ◉ ◉

Webber sat on an edging stone at the side of the drive. Night closed in fast now, but the house front shone under the beam of several spotlights. He felt poleaxed, stunned. The bustle and shouting had faded. The only other person on the drive was the paramedic with the fast responder car who'd been the first on the scene following his call. Webber had refused point blank to get into the ambulance, knowing they wouldn't stay to argue. The rush was to get Suzie to the hospital.

The paramedic was at his side again, offering to run him down to A&E. He gave a sigh and pulled himself to his feet, surprised to find himself accepting the man's arm to help him.

'I'm fine.' He seemed to have repeated the phrase again and again in the last half hour. He wasn't going anywhere.

He'd already called Farrar; or anyway, someone had. A team of CSIs was inside now. He'd told them about the cellars. The man he and Suzie had arrived with paced the garden impassively. Webber saw his silhouette grow to giant proportions as he walked through the path of the spotlights. The quiet felt unnatural … fake. It masked chaos. Farrar was with his team at Nesbitt's. That was where they thought they'd find Olivia Lamb and Ryan Davies. Nesbitt and the housekeeper, Fairclough, were cousins. Ryan Davies, too, somehow attached to both of them, to both addresses. Levine was part of the tangle, a great aunt or cousin several times removed. No one knew quite what might be here at her house, but Suzie hadn't been attacked for nothing.

The paramedic was taking another call. He'd have to leave Webber soon. One more repetition of *I'm fine,* would be enough. He knew he must be in shock to some degree but he was determined to stay with the action. As soon as he could, he would get himself to Nesbitt's. Nesbitt was the key; the one with the vehicle.

Webber played and replayed every second of his time at this house. The whole set up. Fairclough's disappearance. The old woman hobbling on her frame. In the panic of stemming the flow of blood, of hearing Suzie's voice swim in and out of consciousness, he hadn't got anything like a clear story from her. He wasn't sure that she knew who or what had hit her. It was possible that Fairclough had taken advantage of Levine calling for her and waited to incapacitate Suzie. But why? To divert Webber for long enough for them to get away, but where to? How had they got past him? Fairclough maybe, but the old woman wasn't play acting. She'd never have let Nesbitt's name slip if she had been. More to the point, why do it at all? They'd have made their enquiries and left. No, his best guess was that someone else had already been in the house and had hidden in the tiny cloakroom. Someone that Fairclough was protecting or was scared of. It began to explain her over-defensiveness. But it didn't explain the way they'd all disappeared. *We don't use the cellar … It floods … Look if you want … Is that what sprang them into breaking cover?* And maybe the someone else was Nesbitt. He hadn't been at his own house when Farrar's team had arrived there.

Things were winding down here. The CSIs hadn't found either of the children or any sign of them. The inhabitants had disappeared into thin air. He could tell from the comings and goings that the action was moving on. They would leave behind a skeleton team. Webber knew he wasn't functioning properly, that he'd have ordered another officer in his position down to the hospital. But he wasn't going there, and he wasn't going back to the station. He was going to Nesbitt's.

Only before he went anywhere, he had to make some attempt to wash off the worst of the bloodstains. He walked back up the drive towards the front door.

# chapter forty five

One of the CSIs sat on the floor of the big kitchen. Voices floated through the cellar door which was wedged open. Webber supposed they'd done some sort of preliminary work in the cloakroom where Suzie had been attacked, but the scramble had been to find the missing children if it wasn't already too late. Whatever Klein had done and whatever his motives, his certainty about a link was borne out now. Somehow the two cases had collided. The man on the floor gave Webber a brief glance but otherwise ignored him.

Webber's eye was drawn to the cellar entrance; the downward stairwell flooded with light. He judged from the voices it was just two people down there, making sure, double-checking. Webber turned his gaze back to the young guy sitting on the floor by the old-fashioned range, leaning sideways at the door to the small oven, his arm inside and reaching about. Aside from that initial glance he'd paid no attention to Webber, all his focus on whatever he'd found inside the cooker. It occurred to Webber that unless the man had very short arms, he was reaching further back than the oven seemed to go. As the man straightened to pull something out, his expression took on a grim satisfaction. Webber watched as he hauled out a thick cable. As though he'd caught a snake by its mid portion, the cable resisted attempts to do more than show its muscular middle coil. The man shifted on to his back, clicking on a small torch. He pushed the cable back inside to allow him room to work his head and shoulders through the door.

Webber pulled his attention away. If the man had found any

sign of a small body in there, he wouldn't be messing about with cables. He didn't even know what sort of warrant they operated under; how far they could legitimately extend the search. That look of satisfaction as the cable had come out into view had the stamp of a techno-geek all over it. Maybe Farrar had included this guy in the team in the hope of some extracurricular exploration while the house was empty of its legitimate occupants. He bit his tongue on a sharp command to stop pissing about with old cookers and get looking for the children. Not his team; not his call. And they wouldn't find the girl here so close to her own home. Nesbitt was the one with the vehicle. This house held its secrets but Nesbitt's place was the priority. Farrar had known that from the start. It was why he'd gone there himself.

In an alcove towards the back of the kitchen was a small sink with a mirror above it. Webber thought about asking if it was OK to use the facilities in the middle of the search. But if he were denied permission, he'd take no notice. And anyway, the geek should have stopped him at the door.

More blood had splashed on to his face than he'd realised. No wonder the paramedic had been so keen to get him into the ambulance. There was nothing he could do about his clothes. He rolled up his sleeves and held his hands and arms under the tap. The stains that had lost their brightness as they oxidised ran red again as Suzie's blood swirled down the sink. He splashed water over his face until the obvious signs were gone.

His plan to head across to Nesbitt's house would have to be postponed. Even with face and hands partly cleaned, his clothes were stiff with dried blood. He stood at the window and looked out over the back garden, overgrown but not impenetrable as though regularly tracked through. His mind kept jerking back to the fear he'd seen in Suzie's eyes; the terror as she realised she might be seconds from death. What if he hadn't heard her call out? He'd have gone back in to find an empty house and … He pulled in a couple of deep breaths. Tormenting himself with what ifs was as pointless as agonizing over if onlys.

His phone bleeped a Skype call. Farrar. As he opened the call, Webber strode back through the house and out of the front door. If he had to fight Farrar, he didn't want to do it with an audience.

Farrar's face appeared on the small screen, grim and unsmiling. 'I told you to get to the hospital to be checked over.' His tone was no more sympathetic than his expression.

'There's nothing wrong with me. I'd be wasting everyone's time. How's Suzie Harmer, have you heard anything?'

'Critical but holding her own. What the hell's going on, Martyn?'

Webber could only shake his head. He remembered the feeling he'd had earlier of something racing away from them. This was like testing for a damp patch and being hit by a tsunami. 'Who is Suzie Harmer? And the other guy you sent with her? Where did they come from?'

'Call them an unofficial hit squad. You've seen what's been going on. I need people I can trust to sort this out. Speaking of which, I want you back at the station since you don't need medical attention.'

'Why don't I join you at Nesbitt's, John?'

'Because I've just told you to get yourself back to the station!'

'OK, OK. What happened here tonight? I missed something. I should stay and find it.'

'There's a team there already. They'll find whatever's there to find.'

Webber looked up at the house, at its air of neglect that disappeared on close scrutiny. 'They weren't here with those two women ... to see what happened to Suzie. I need to stay.'

'Are you going to disobey a direct order?'

'Are you going to make me disobey a direct order?'

An exasperated glare. 'I'm one officer down already. The perpetrators haven't been caught. I can't afford protection for you. We're already stretched thin enough to break.'

'I'm not hurt, John. I'm fine. Whoever was here, they're long gone. God knows how but they're gone. There's no one here now but the search team.'

'Martyn, that's not the point. We don't have Nesbitt yet, but we've found Goodridge. The blue Jaguar was parked in one of the outbuildings here. He was in it. Unconscious unfortunately. He left in an ambulance about twenty minutes ago.'

'What about the PI, Annie Raymond? Any sign of her?'

'No, but what makes you think they were together?'

Webber looked again at the house. 'I don't know. I just think they're mixed up in the same thing. She came to York with him. She didn't get back on a train. They might have had it all arranged. Let me do one more walk through here, John. Suzie tried to tell me something after she was attacked. I'll lose it if I don't work it out now. This house has its secrets. It looks shabby, but it isn't. Everything's just so. The alarm system, the security cameras. It's set up for a siege.'

'All right, but I can't send you anyone else. Nesbitt's place has to take priority now we've found Goodridge.'

'John, do we have any idea if Olivia Lamb and her friends played up here … trespassed … whatever?'

'And if she did?'

'She knew Ryan Davies. And he's related to the women who were here. And to Nesbitt. And Nesbitt must be up here quite a bit. He runs their errands. Could Nesbitt have met Olivia at this house? I don't know. I'm trying to piece this together.'

'How important is it to know?'

It was hard to find the right words to answer. Something kept niggling him about that conversation he'd had when he was first in the room with Hannah Levine. *Trespassers … Children in the house.* 'I dunno, but … If we can find out where … uh … what this house is all about …' He blew out a sigh as he tripped on his words. The attack on Suzie had blunted his edge but he didn't want Farrar to see it. 'There's something wrong here, John. But maybe it's nothing to do with … maybe it'll turn out to be something else altogether.'

His words faded into a short pause and then Farrar said, 'I'm going to patch in the officer who's with the Lambs, but it'll be her call whether or not she puts the question to the parents.'

Webber nodded his thanks and marched back inside the house. He wanted quiet, not the sounds of the night around him when he talked to Olivia's parents.

The screen split and the DC's face appeared above Farrar's. Webber could just make out the impression of a staircase behind her as Farrar explained what he wanted, ending, 'But I don't want to spark a gang of vigilantes up to that house.'

'That's OK. I'll keep it low key. They'll be glad to be doing anything that might help, but I'll take her out to the kitchen. There's an elderly aunt with them who's a total nightmare.'

Farrar cut his video, so that the officer's face filled the screen for a moment before it became a swaying shot of floorboards and then carpet as she returned to the Lambs' living room. Webber heard voices but couldn't make out any words, then the carpet twisted and the picture made another journey to the lino of the Lambs' kitchen, showing Webber a brief shot of the back door, the window over the sink looking out on to darkness, then pivoting past cereal packets, shelves full of jars, turning its back on the window and facing Mrs Lamb coming through from the living room.

The face that appeared on Webber's phone looked haggard and grey. He took in the shadow of sleepless nights around her eyes, the lank lifeless hair. Even in this tiny image, the likeness to Olivia was marked. He kept his face close to the camera to avoid giving her any glimpse of a blood-stained shirt front.

'This is Detective Superintendent Martyn Webber.' He heard himself being introduced and clearly Mrs Lamb was not holding the phone because she put both her hands to her mouth as her eyes widened.

For a fraction of a second Webber didn't realise what he was seeing. Then shock coursed through him. What little colour she had drained from Mrs Lamb's face as though someone had opened a tap. For a second he thought her horror was for him. But she wasn't staring at the camera. Her focus was beyond it.

'Oh my God!' That was the officer's voice.

Before he could speak, the camera swivelled. A blur of jars, a box of Cheerios … white painted walls … And the back door, now wide open on to the darkness.

Webber's hand scrabbled for purchase on the wall. He barely made it to the wooden chair as his knees buckled.

The shot was unfocussed, the camera unsteady, but standing there framed in the open doorway, tiny and with that same lank unwashed hair as her mother, stood Olivia Lamb.

The words, 'I've come home and I want …' were drowned in a cry of 'Olivia!' and the screen blanked.

# chapter forty six

........................................................................

The house lay quiet. It wore its façade of shabbiness and decay, unabashed that its disguise was rumbled, that it fooled no one anymore. Voices came as a distant echo from the kitchen regions. Despite everything their focus was still on the missing child because it would take a few minutes for the message to reach them that she was safe, except for the one of the trio whose focus would remain on the minutiae, unravelling the electronics with a single-mindedness that made his colleagues jeer that he bled silicon not blood. He didn't lack sympathy, just empathy, and from the start had been exploring spaces that couldn't ever have held a child. He was now extracting coaxial cable from the recesses of a kitchen range that had never cooked food; uncovering electronics whose sophistication made his pulse race.

Webber sat on his own in the hallway. It was probably Farrar who had cut him out of the call as inessential. He couldn't blame him for that.

Olivia Lamb had turned up. Unhurt as far as Webber had been able to see, her voice clear and untroubled. *I've come home and I want* … His phone lay in his hand. He sat on the hard wooden chair feeling as though he might never summon the energy to stand. Olivia Lamb had come home.

After a moment, he put in a call to the station and spoke to the desk sergeant. The news of Olivia preceded his call.

'And Ryan Davies?' he asked.

'Yes, turned up on his own doorstep … must have been about

the same time she did. In a state, I gather … all tears and contrition. They say the little girl's just fine. It's been some childish prank that nearly went very wrong. They'll have learnt their lesson at any rate. What a relief, eh? Kids! You don't expect a good result after five …'

'How's Peter Goodridge?' Webber interrupted the flow. 'He was taken to hospital about twenty minutes ago.'

'Half an hour.' The sergeant stripped his voice of its upbeat tone. 'Certified dead on arrival, poor sod. Suicide, I suppose. But who knows what goes on in the minds of people like that.'

'And Sergeant Harmer?'

'Sergeant, is she? Must be one of Farrar's sidekicks. I thought as much. Critical. Any sign of the bastard who jumped her?'

'Not that I know of. Give me a call if anything crops up.'

Olivia Lamb back home. Ryan Davies back home. Peter Goodridge dead. Suzie Harmer hanging on. If the Raymond woman were mixed up in this, she'd be miles away and running hard. If she wasn't, she was probably lying dead somewhere.

He pulled himself to his feet and walked a few paces to stand in front of the small cloakroom where Farrar's sergeant, a woman he'd barely known, had been attacked and injured, maybe fatally. And on his watch. He remembered her air of calm composure; her breath on his cheek as she'd leant close to talk to him.

Hadn't he noticed something about the housekeeper as he'd headed out to call Ahmed? He reran the memory of her here in this hallway firing suspicious looks at him. He'd thought she was being overly defensive. No doubts on that score now. Suzie had tried to point towards that half partition. Had she been telling him that Nesbitt had been hiding there to ambush her? His replay of those few seconds didn't fit. She'd said, Stop *her*. Stop who? He'd assumed the old woman, but she must have meant Fairclough. *Stop her* … and she'd pointed at the partition. He shivered, couldn't push away the awful sensation of blood gushing through his fingers as he'd tried to staunch the flow. He would call in to see her later;

wouldn't let in the thought that she might not be there to see. And he wouldn't do flowers. He'd take her the news that her attacker was in custody.

He looked at his hands. Despite washing them, traces of dried blood still clung beneath his fingernails. His clothes were a write-off. With blood, you soaked it out immediately or it never came away.

The door to the small cloakroom swung open. They probably had more to do in here. They'd taped it off; wouldn't want him tramping through it, but that wouldn't stop him. However sluggish his brain, someone had to work out what had happened in this room. He skirted the stains on the floor as best he could and walked behind the half partition. The old-fashioned toilet bowl stood there as he remembered. He lifted the lid. The water shimmered as though reacting to the breeze outside. Webber idly ran his hands over the surface of the lid. It wasn't the cheap plastic he'd expected. Some kind of resin. It felt expensive. The pipe up to the high cistern with its badly-executed insects, flowers and handprint had something of the same disguise to it. Had anyone asked him for a description, he'd have portrayed an ancient bit of plumbing with cracked plastic seat and pipework in need of paint. It wasn't. It was pristine, robust. He stood on the toilet bowl to reach up and see inside the cistern. Tall as he was, it was a stretch. The front with its faded flower scene and outlined hand wasn't the work of some child decades ago playing with transfers and paint. The patterns were glazed in. The mechanism inside was modern, complex, not the simple ballcock he'd expected to see. He put his hand over the painted outline as he tugged the chain and watched the tank empty. The whole contraption shuddered, making him reach sideways to balance against the wall. Fresh water gushed in. Quick and efficient, but not quiet enough that something might have been flushed away in the time it took him to rush back inside when Suzie screamed. He stepped back to the floor. It didn't explain why Suzie had pointed this way, saying, Stop her. And it didn't explain where the old lady had vanished to.

Splashes of Suzie's blood had reached right across even beyond the partition. He could see the way it had run in lines between the floor boards. Inside the bowl, the water now lay still. Standing on the floor he had to tip his head back to look at the odd pictures painted into the porcelain of the tank. He tapped his foot and gave the partition an experimental kick. Then he crouched to rap his knuckles on the floor. It wasn't right. It didn't give him the echo of wood.

The water in the toilet bowl was shimmering again. The only thing that could be disturbing it was the activity of the team in the cellar, but the cellar couldn't possibly reach this far. And even if it did ... He leapt to his feet and ran through to the kitchen. The cellar door stood open, indistinct voices floated up. The guy by the range still sat there, now surrounded by trailing wires, his expression as captivated as Sam playing with his alphabet bricks.

'You on the floor,' he rapped out, jerking the man's attention to him. 'Leave those wires and come and have a look at this contraption.'

◉ ◉ ◉

The roads with their high hedges flashed past. The traffic had thinned to just a few cars. Ahmed thought back to Webber's call. He'd asked if the Kleins' landline had rung. Presumably he'd been ringing it from another phone. It had either been muted or diverted. He cast a brief glance towards his passenger and breaking a few moments of silence asked, 'Where's Mrs Klein? Does she know what you've been doing?'

'There are no secrets in a good marriage, Ayaan. I've told you that.'

It was true, Klein had said something of that sort when they'd been talking about the high attrition rate for marriage in the service generally. You don't have to give in to the games, Klein had told him, holding his own long-standing marriage to Julia as the exception to prove the rule. What rule exactly, Ahmed thought now, as he wondered for the first time how strong the Klein marriage actually was. No secrets in a good marriage? He was pretty sure Julia Klein knew nothing about her husband's shenanigans with the case files.

'And where are we with the little girl, Olivia Lamb?' Klein said. 'What line are they following?'

'I'm not in the picture on that one,' Ahmed said with a hint of frost.

'Come on, Ayaan. I just want to know if they're anywhere near finding the little girl.'

'See it from where I'm sitting, Len. The Chief Super sent me out to get you. He knows you took those press cuttings. That's like telling me to treat you like a suspect.' He stopped but then couldn't help the question coming out. 'Why did you do it, Len?'

'Are you sure you want to have this conversation, Ayaan?'

Ahmed paused but then nodded.

'OK, if you want to know. I thought it was tied up with my old case.'

'How?'

'My throat's dry. If you want me to talk, I need a drink.'

'Isn't there some water in the door?'

'Half a bottle. It looks weeks old.'

'There's a place about half a mile on. I'm going to stop there. I need a drink myself. But how could it be tied up with your old case? Everyone says you got the right man.'

'Yes, I thought so.'

'And he's dead.'

'Yes.'

This was like pulling teeth. 'What do you mean, you thought so?'

'The killings stopped once I'd sussed him. But then they began again. Waifs and strays.' Ahmed's mind turned to the small girl dead in Geneva, still unidentified.

'The man you put away was a recluse … a loner. I've read the file. He acted alone.'

'Did he?' The question was stark, bleak.

'What do you mean, Len? Don't play games with me. What is it?'

'Timing, Ayaan. When did the killings start up again?'

'Round about two years ago, but I'm not saying I agree there's any *again* about it. I don't see how there can be. What was the link you were chasing? What did you think the PI woman might have?'

The promised coffee stop loomed ahead. Ahmed saw Klein glance at the sign as he slowed the car, his hand poised to flick on the left indicator. Then his foot was on the gas, the car gathering speed again. He wasn't immediately sure what had made him change his mind. In part it was that he knew there was a bigger place just up ahead, not so isolated, just the other side of the next roundabout. 'I'm going straight to York, Len. If it weren't for who you are I wouldn't even be thinking about stopping.'

'Ayaan, please. I'm not going to do a runner. I need a bit of space to get my head together. It's the timing. The kiddies were safe as long as the man I put away was alive. That's what I was afraid of. That it was his death that triggered it.'

Ahmed felt uneasy about his own motives. He hadn't meant it when he said he wouldn't stop for a drink. It had been annoyance at Klein for being monosyllabic. But it seemed to have worked. Klein was clearly offering information in return for a comfort break. Even so, he shouldn't be having this conversation at all.

'How?' he asked. 'How could his death have triggered it?'

'They held a memorial service for him. Did you know that?'

'No, why would I? Who are they?' The roundabout grew from the gloom ahead, the lights of the pit stop visible the other side.

Other cars converged on the junction, a small mid-evening rush crowding around them like an escort.

'His family.'

'But Len ...'

'I know, I know. He wasn't supposed to have any family.'

Ahmed swung the car round the curve of the traffic island and flicked on his left indicator. To its steady ticking, he slowed and began to pull into the small slip road.

Was tiredness heightening his senses as Klein's words echoed in his head? From some backwater of his mind, a rational voice told him there was nothing to get excited about, but his gut was ahead of the action screaming that this was wrong. His only safe manoeuvre from this point was to snake the car round on to the tarmac of the car-park. Even if he decided not to stop, he was too far committed to do anything but drive in, round and back out again. The car behind was already pulling out to pass, boxing him in.

He wrenched the wheel, as he dropped a gear and floored the accelerator, fishtailing in an explosive spray of gravel as one wheel briefly grazed the verge. His teeth clenched as the car shot towards a rapidly closing gap.

A screech of tyres ... the long blare of a horn ... a frozen moment, everything focussed on the road ahead and the cars around him, judging the width, the angles, lightning predictions about how the obstructed driver would react.

In the adrenaline rush of a brief swerve and near collision, Ahmed caught a glimpse of the other driver's face, saw shock ... fear ... Anger would explode later. No one overreacted. Danger receded.

Klein's hand had snatched out for balance as the sudden move threw him against the door. For a few seconds, the only sound was the whine of the engine as they sped away.

'Ayaan, what are you doing?'

It was the question Ahmed was on edge to hear; the question

that should have reassured him. But the words came a second too late and a shade too gently. Klein should have sworn and shouted at him before he regained his equilibrium. It had been an unforgivably dangerous act.

The next junction was almost on them, just a couple of vans visible ahead, but even one slowing his path was too much now that Klein knew he wasn't going to stop. The siren's wail shattered the evening, pulsating light bathed them in blue as the car threw off its plainclothes and surged forward, vehicles scrambling out of its way.

# chapter forty seven

Webber's feet crunched on the vegetation. It encroached everywhere, leaving no clear paths. Artificial light shone unforgivingly on the face of the property, highlighting the inconsistencies; deepening the shadows. Mismatched brickwork, new dressed as old. Cultivated neglect, disguising a fortress. Still shaky from the attack on Suzie, he'd left the cloakroom to the geek, who had latched on to the workings of the plumbing as being at the heart of whatever the anomaly was. Webber had headed to the kitchen to get the other CSIs on to this new dimension to the cellar. They'd confirmed that no, they hadn't found anything yet that encroached far enough towards the front of the house, but noted what he said. 'You get some weird echoes in these rambling houses,' he'd been told, 'but we'll take some soundings in that direction. If there's a hidden cellar, we'll find it.'

They hadn't let him down there to see for himself. And these weren't obsessives who could be diverted; these were professionals who'd be on to Farrar to have him thrown out if he stepped out of line. He was confident they'd find whatever secrets were to be found. They might even find the two women holed up down there, but this house wasn't the focus. Everything pointed to Nesbitt's place. That was where he needed to go.

Outside in the night air, he couldn't throw off the feeling that he'd walked into this like a rookie. Worse, he'd walked a young officer into it with him. He could almost imagine the light breeze was Suzie's breath on his face as she'd leant close to whisper about Ahmed's call.

A crackle of undergrowth. He spun on his heel, senses at screaming pitch, ready to take out an assailant with his fists. It was the officer who'd driven here with him and Suzie. The man had tracked him from the shadow where he now emerged with a discreet cough.

Webber swallowed an urge to swear. He wanted them on their toes, alert to anyone crossing this land. He gave him a nod.

'Nothing out here,' the man said softly, his hand making a gesture that encompassed the whole property. It confirmed what Webber already knew. No one had come out of the house.

'If they're in there,' Webber said. 'It's a priest hole or hidden cellar, something like that. Possible, I suppose, but big enough to hold two maybe three people, and one of them an elderly woman? I doubt it. The CSIs haven't found anything.' His mind saw the geek in the cloakroom, not turning a hair at their tramping through a crime scene, brushing aside Webber's theories about the floor, and focussing his concentration on the plumbing.

'There are only three doors and we had those covered between us. Plenty of windows but …'

Webber took the point. He couldn't envisage Hannah Levine scrambling through one of the windows into the night with or without assistance. And certainly not in silence. But there had been a few moments when all attention was focussed on Suzie … 'I'm going to take the car,' he said. 'I can't do anything more here. Call in if you need transport.'

The man pulled the keys from his pocket and held them out, saying, 'Unless someone finds them, I'm here for the night.'

Webber drove across the city, thankful for the failing light. Anyone glancing into the car would take the dark stains for shadow. He would make a lightning stop at his own house, get some clean clothes and then head for Nesbitt's. He reached for his phone but changed his mind. Melinda might have gone to bed. He'd wait to see if the light was on before he called. He didn't want to walk in on her in this state.

He could see from the top of the road that their front room was lit up. As he watched, two shadows passed across behind the curtain. Damn, she had a friend in. He couldn't be doing with wide-eyed dismay and gasps of horror. He pulled up away from the house and killed the lights. Melinda could either get rid of the visitor or at least get her out of the way so he could slip in unnoticed to change. A comforting warmth enveloped him. He could rely on Mel. She'd play whatever role he asked and would save the questions for later.

He held the mobile to his ear, saw her shadow approach the window; her hand reaching for the phone. Something made her pull aside the curtain as she answered. He smiled. She'd sensed that he was close by. As he opened his mouth to speak, he glimpsed her companion.

He sat up with a start. Julia Klein! His mind raced as Melinda's voice said, 'Hello.'

Why? How? Why now? His mind's eye saw a kaleidoscope of faces: Suzie leaning towards him to murmur her assessment of the housekeeper, Hannah Levine smiling up at him; Julia's angular profile close to Melinda. Fingers of ice gripped tight inside him.

'Mel.' He kept his voice low, injecting urgency. 'Don't let on it's me. I know Julia's there. Pretend you're going to check on something. Leave the phone off the hook. Get upstairs. Stay with Sam. When I leave with Julia, get straight back down, lock the doors and don't open them to anyone bar me. Anyone! OK?'

There was a pause, longer than was comfortable. He heard her breathing. What had Julia been saying?

'OK ...?' she said, drawing out the word into a question. For a heart-stopping moment he didn't know if she would trust him or not. Then she murmured, 'Yes ... sure. Just a sec ... I'll check.' And he felt the breath rush out of him in relief. She would take him apart piece by piece later, but she'd recognized the import behind his words.

He thought about what he intended to do. When it came to taking him apart, she'd be queuing behind Farrar.

As her silhouette receded, he swung the car round and backed it into the drive. Leaving the engine running and the passenger door open, he reached for the glove box, grabbed the speedcuffs and strode towards the front door.

◉ ◉ ◉

Ahmed concentrated on the road ahead. He'd thrown off his tiredness as an unaffordable indulgence. Somewhere along the way his subconscious had done a lightning reconstruction of his companion's every move since they'd left the cottage, starting with Klein pulling on his gloves. Whatever Klein had planned, it had to be fast and effective. Ahmed had made no secret of being on his guard. He had no idea what the attack would be, but he knew where it would come from. Klein's right hand, apparently relaxed, was curled around something. And if Klein was sure he could subdue Ahmed quickly, all he needed was for the car to be travelling slowly enough for him to grab the wheel and the handbrake, knock it out of gear and to bring it to a safe stop. He'd let several chances go by, but that had been when he thought Ahmed would allow them a coffee break.

When his mobile sprang to life and he saw Webber's number on the screen, Ahmed's mind skated over whether or not to take the call, but Klein took the decision out of his hands by reaching across and answering it.

'Martyn? It's Len. Ayaan's driving, and like a bit of a maniac, truth be told. I'd rather he didn't have any distractions if we're to arrive in one piece … yes … OK.' He slipped the phone into its cradle and clicked it to speakerphone.

'Can you hear me?' Webber's voice crackled into the car, snappish and hard.

'Yes, loud and clear,' Ahmed said, noting from the background noise that Webber, too, was in a car.

'Len? Can you hear me?'

'Yes, why? Do you need a witness?'

'It's you I want to talk to. Ayaan's the witness. I'm with Julia. She's not too comfortable, I think her arthritis is playing up, so let's not string this out.'

Klein laughed. 'Come on, Martyn. Don't play games. What's this about?'

'Julia, have a word with your husband, will you?'

Ahmed allowed the car to slow a little. The only sign of life from the phone was Webber's breathing. He was aware of Klein beside him, a half smile curving his lips.

'Julia! Don't make me do this. Talk to Len.' Another pause and then a sharp cry. 'Oh, you bastard!' And even Ahmed recognized it as Julia Klein.

Klein jerked upright in his seat. 'What the hell? Julia …?'

'Sorry, Julia, but I need Len to know you're with me. Julia's beside me, Len, and unfortunately I felt the need to restrain her before we set off. You know how uncomfortable handcuffs can be, especially when they're behind your back.'

'You've cuffed her hands behind her back? You bastard! You've gone too far this time, Martyn. You're going to regret this.'

'Then let's not string it out.'

Ahmed heard Klein pull in a breath. He seemed to make some kind of effort before he spoke again, and when he did his voice had returned to its usual placid tone. 'What do you want?'

Lights appeared in the distance. They were approaching a village whose fishtail of a road would take some negotiating. Ahmed glanced at his passenger. The mild voice belied the deep flush on his face, the throbbing pulse at his temple. Klein was as angry as Ahmed had ever seen him. All his attention was on Webber's call. Ahmed slowed the car a little more.

'Marks's boss, Peter Goodridge, is dead,' said Webber, his voice flat. 'The private investigator's still missing. Julia and I are on our way to Mr Nesbitt's house. We're going to find out what's been happening.'

Ahmed was aware of a change in Klein's demeanour. He'd relaxed a little, but showed nothing in his voice which held its even tone. 'Of course, Martyn. We'll do everything we can. But please let Julia at least sit comfortably. What's she going to do to you? She's half your size.'

Ahmed wanted to warn Webber, but warn him of what? All he had to go on were Webber's words and Klein's reaction. And he must concentrate on the road. He glanced at Klein's gloved right hand and thought he caught a glint of silver. He raced the car round the curves of the sleeping village, causing a sudden explosion of flapping wings from birds roosting too close to the road. Klein was talking to his wife, telling her he'd be with her soon, not to worry. Ahmed took the final curve smoothly. Klein's attention was all on the phone. A long unobstructed stretch lay ahead of them. No other vehicles in sight. He could speed up, slow down, run the car sideways into the hedge if need be. He had no idea how Klein would react, but he'd be ready.

'Martyn,' he interrupted sharply. 'Nesbitt's is wrong. You're going to the wrong place.'

The spike in tension beside him was palpable. His peripheral vision showed Klein's right hand tightening around whatever he held. He began to swerve the car gently from side to side – making crystal clear there was no safe way to jump him at this speed. It seemed a long silence but Ahmed judged he'd travelled no more than 50 metres so it could only have been a couple of seconds.

'OK,' said Webber's voice. 'Change of plan. We're heading for Hannah Levine's place.'

Klein's sudden stillness told him that Webber had got it right now, whatever it was.

'That's it!' he called out just as Klein's hand snaked forward to cut the call. He hoped Webber had heard.

The phone call had changed the dynamic, stripped away the last vestiges of pretence. He couldn't get to York now. There was a wide sandy verge a quarter of a mile ahead. He would brake sharply, swerve to knock Klein away from him, use the sand to contrive a sudden stop. Then he'd cuff him, the way Webber had Julia Klein. Ahmed wished he'd done it before they set off.

A hundred and fifty metres ... a hundred ...

Two thoughts hit him simultaneously. He and Webber between them had upped the ante so Klein had nothing to lose. And he'd spent the last couple of seconds with all his attention on the road ahead.

The sting of a wasp ...

Klein's hand crashing down on his wrist holding it and the wheel in an iron grasp ...

A memory fusing with the scene ahead – *did you get that, Miss Raymond ... shame you can't hear her* – a tangle of colours spinning upward into a void.

# chapter forty eight

Ahmed's first thought was how good it felt to be lying down. But as soon as the thought arrived he wasn't so comfortable after all. His head had slipped off the pillow onto something hard, something curved.

A wheel ... a steering wheel. The pinprick of light wasn't a star, it was the dashboard.

He jerked upright, remembering.

Klein ...

He looked all around. Darkness outside, waving trees, tall hedges. Where was he? He saw a car's lights flash by. Not too far away but somehow above him and through a shield of vegetation. He'd been driving fast ... they must have crashed. Where was Klein? How long had he been here? He tried to sit back in the seat to bring the dashboard clock into focus but was brought up short as his wrist jarred against an obstruction. He'd been driving. Why was he sitting in the passenger seat? For a moment he stared without taking it in.

Klein had jumped him, brought the car here – where? Klein was gone. And before he'd left ... Ahmed felt the constraint, saw the gleam of the silver bracelet. He was handcuffed to the steering wheel.

His mind felt sluggish. There were things to do but he couldn't line them up. Get help ... get in touch with someone to let them know about Klein ... but who? How? The radio! His phone was gone from the cradle but he could get at the radio. It was awkward to reach across. The effort took all his concentration so it was a while before he realized it wasn't working. Klein had done something to it.

The glint of metal caught his eye. Keys. Klein had left the keys in the tray under the handbrake. How far could he drive like this? Sharp bends would stop him with his arm fixed behind the wheel, but he could get the car off the field and back to the road. Then maybe he could flag someone down.

Awkwardly, he clambered across. The engine sprang to life. He manoeuvred carefully. The ground was soft beneath the wheels, it would be all too easy to spin them in deep. It took a long time. He could feel the sweat beginning to trickle, but he eased the car off its soft bed and bounced it up a steep verge towards where he'd seen the lights.

He stopped when he made it to the side of the road. Which road? He opened the window wondering if anyone would stop on this lonely stretch. Voices up ahead ... shouting ... The road looked straight enough. He could probably drive that far, but would he be going into an ambush? He couldn't get his head round what had happened ... what it meant. And would anyone approach close enough to check his ID on this isolated stretch ...? If he had any ID on him. He felt in his pockets. At once his hand met the bulk of his wallet. It nestled against another familiar shape; his mobile. It hadn't been in his pocket. Klein must have put it there. Then Ahmed smothered a curse. His fingers could feel the shape of a handcuff key.

Unless he'd been unconscious for a long time, and he didn't think so, Klein hadn't wanted to engineer more than a brief delay.

He freed himself and climbed out of the car rubbing the feeling back into his wrist. Yes, he could see figures up ahead. He got back in and drove towards them, windows down, listening. No need to ask Joe Public for help now but he wanted to know what was going on. Was Klein still nearby? Had he, Ahmed, regained consciousness faster than expected?

A battered Ford Fiesta was parked at an angle on the grass verge. A woman stood next to it, phone to her ear.

'... she rang them from ... no, just the two ponies ... got them back now ...'

Across the road, Ahmed took in two more figures, both dishevelled. They carried ropes. He understood the story. They'd been rounding up some loose horses. He'd formed half an idea to stop and ask them where he was, but in the circumstances that would only generate suspicion. In all the unanswered questions that spun in his head, there was one thing he could be sure of. Klein hadn't escaped on a horse.

Leaving the equestrian crisis behind, he drove on until the lane stopped at a T-junction. A single wooden sign bore the unhelpful legend, Public Footpath. He stopped the car and made himself breathe deeply. He had his mobile. Why couldn't he focus? His brain seemed like cotton wool. Webber. He must call Webber to warn him that Klein had done a runner.

He stared at his contacts list. Nothing. It was empty. Klein had left his phone but had wiped it. And Ahmed knew the muzziness in his head wouldn't let anything out of his own memory yet, not even a number he'd called as often as Webber's. Where had they been when Klein jumped him? On the way to York. And where was he now? The phone would tell him. It was like pulling teeth getting his brain in gear, but he fought through the fog. He'd get there bit by bit.

The SatNav surprised him. Klein had driven them back towards Hull before he'd abandoned the car.

Out of nowhere, he recalled Klein's words; ...did you get that, Miss Raymond ... shame you can't hear her ... Klein had driven towards Hull. It was the people in Hull he must contact first, not Webber. It didn't matter that there was nothing left in the phone. The number for directory enquiries was etched by advertising into his brain.

It shouldn't have surprised him that he got through to someone he knew, but the possibility hadn't crossed his mind, so when the reassuringly avuncular tones of DC Tommy Marchant sounded in his ear, Ahmed had to blow out a breath to steady his own voice, almost as though he were about to cry. The drug Klein had given him had left him flaky and unstable. He focussed on rattling out as concise an account as he could.

'Len Klein?' Tommy Marchant expressed surprise without ruffling his air of calm acceptance. 'Who'd have thought it?'

'I don't know where he's gone, but there was something going on back at his house. Someone needs to get up there.'

Marchant replied with a grunt.

'What? What's the matter?'

'Nothing. Only I'm heading out to my sister's when I've done here. She's not far from the Kleins'. I can see I'm going to be volunteered for a bit of involuntary overtime. Your lot are stretched thin up in Scarborough tonight.'

Ahmed fought through the fog that clouded his head. 'Tommy, this is serious. I think the missing woman's there, the PI from London. You've got to watch your back. Look what happened to me.'

'Don't worry, Ayaan. We'll get on to it. Now, do you want me to call your governor?'

'I should do that, but my phone's been wiped. Can you get me his number?'

'No sweat. Give me a minute.'

◉ ◉ ◉

Webber had no illusions about Julia. One glimmer of an opportunity and she'd be away. He had a considerable weight and age advantage, but she had a card to play if she could find an ally. He acted way outside his legal authority, more like a thug than a policeman. All she needed was the right person to stop him – one of Farrar's team, someone who knew about the attack on Suzie; someone who would assume he'd gone slightly mad in the aftermath and needed medical attention. Well maybe he had, and maybe he did, but whatever clock was ticking down, it hadn't far to go.

He spared a thought for Ahmed, hoping he was OK. He'd not been able to raise him after the call shut off; the call where Klein had told his wife he'd be with her soon. He didn't want to do it this way but there was no time to take Julia in and question her under caution. And what would he use to hold her?

He was out of options, rolling the dice blindly, no idea how high the stakes had become. And what for? Not for Olivia Lamb or Ryan Davies; they were safe. Not for the anonymous child in Geneva or Myra Franklin; too late for them though there was a glimmer of satisfaction in having given one of them a name. Too late for Peter Goodridge, too. And he certainly wasn't doing this to further his career. If anything, he was doing it for Annie Raymond which had a certain irony to it.

He bumped the car up the gravel drive to Hannah Levine's front door, watching for the man he'd left pacing the garden. As soon as he saw him, he called out, identifying himself, telling him to check out a car that had turned into the road behind him. 'Probably nothing, but it came out of nowhere. See if it followed me up here.'

The moment the man's attention turned away, he dragged Julia out of the car and into the house. She could have called out, but probably thought it was no more than half a chance and she'd be better playing along until she had someone face to face. Bad call, Julia, he thought, that man was one of Farrar's.

Then they were in the hallway and Julia's chance popped out of the door to the small cloakroom, taking a stride towards the back of the house before Julia's cry spun his attention to them. Webber's thought processes dragged through treacle. He recognized the geek he'd left in there looking at the plumbing. Before he could speak, Julia, better prepared than he'd anticipated, stated her case with clarity. He froze. The geek stared at Julia, his brow furrowed as though she'd greeted him in an unfamiliar language. He gave her an awkward nod, then turned to Webber. 'There you are. Come and look at this.'

'Show me.' Webber pushed Julia before him into the room where Suzie had been attacked.

Thank the Lord for Asperger's, he thought, as the geek ignored Julia and showed him the door that opened up in the narrow space behind the partition. A new entrance to the cellar; the route that had allowed Hannah Levine and whoever else to disappear into thin air. Webber listened to a gabbled explanation about mechanisms, connections, things found here, things found in the kitchen.

When he pulled Julia forward, the geek said, 'You should probably wait. Could be anything down there,' but he wasn't going to stop them.

'You go and get the other guys,' Webber told him. 'The occupants could still be around. I'll need backup. And get on to Chief Superintendent Farrar. Any chance of lights down there?' As he spoke, he released one of Julia's wrists and brought her hands to the front of her body. Thug he might be, but he wouldn't risk her falling down a stone staircase with her hands tied behind her back. She held her hands palm to palm apparently resigned to the indignity.

Webber gave her a cold smile and switched them palm to back, not about to allow her a makeshift cosh however unlikely that she'd find enough force to do damage.

'There's lights,' the geek said, peering through the narrow gap, but I haven't found out where they're operated from. I've only just got it open and I ...'

'That's fine,' Webber interrupted. 'You go and get backup, tell the guys what's here. This part of the cellar can't join up with what they've already searched or they'd have found it.' Pushing Julia ahead of him and with only a thin torch beam to light the way, they started down. The spiral felt disorientating in the dark but the steps were shallow. At the back of his mind, Webber imagined Hannah Levine coming down here. It would have been slow progress and she'd have needed at least one person to help. They must have been on this staircase as he was desperately fighting to save Suzie in the room above.

At the foot of the stairs, Webber shone the torch all around. As far as he could see, there was a single corridor. 'I suppose it must be this way. Am I right?'

Julia Klein said nothing.

'You have the advantage of me, Julia. You've been down here before.'

'Have I?' He was pleased she'd chosen to speak but couldn't read anything from her snappish tone. He pushed her forward and started down the corridor. If there were hidden tunnels in any other direction he'd need the geek to find them. Alert for sounds or movement, he played the torch ahead as they moved forward. 'What are we going to find, Julia?'

'What do you think you're looking for?' Her voice was a sneer but at least she was talking to him.

In his head he thought, Levine, Fairclough, Nesbitt – any or all of them might be holed up here waiting. Did she know? She felt tense beneath his grip. Hardly surprising in the circumstances, but had her tension heightened as they pressed on? Was there fear as well? Fear didn't fit with her having allies ahead in the dark ready to jump him and release her. He answered her question, 'The private investigator from London, Annie Raymond. She's still missing.'

The response was a derisive snort. 'You're a scumbag, Martyn. A vile scumbag. I always said so. Melinda's far too good for you. She always will be.'

Webber paused and stared into the darkness ahead. He was beginning to feel a draught of cool air. 'Yes,' he said, conceding her point about Mel. 'I'm sure you're right, but for all that we have a good marriage. You can't stand that, can you, that we're good together?'

'A good marriage! You've just admitted you're playing about with that tart from London.'

'I'm not,' he said mildly. 'I barely know the woman.' He stopped. The neatly shuttered walls of the corridor ended abruptly and let on to a wider space. Damp, dank, no well-structured shape here. Cables and pipework, the underground workings of the house, criss-crossed the high ceiling. Webber caught glimpses of bundled silver wires and a disjuncture in one part of the wall as he played the torch beam round. It would reassure him to hear sounds of the geek and the rest of the team, but it remained quiet behind them.

'Don't make me laugh,' Julia spat out. 'Or should I say vomit? Why would you risk lives to save a woman you barely know?'

'It's my job,' Webber murmured but his attention wasn't on Julia. It was on the complex shapes all around them. It was as though a cavern had been roughly hacked out. He couldn't see into every nook and cranny but he thought this was a dead end. They must have hidden here and then slipped back up the staircase. It was a theory but he didn't like the feel of it. He hesitated at the edge of the new space.

'So it was a family thing, was it?' he asked her. When she didn't answer, he went on, 'Is Hannah Levine your aunt ... your elder sister? I know you're related. I recognised the smile of all things. Hard to believe I can remember you smiling at me, but I can, and it's Levine to a T.' His torch beam ran across the complex tangle of cables across the uneven ceiling. 'I suppose there've been some name changes over the years or you'd have been caught by the intel when Len joined up. How did you keep it all hidden?' He played the torch back down the corridor behind them and forward again. No one would take him unawares if he could help it. 'All down to money, wasn't it?' he went on. 'You and Len never went short of anything. You were clever about it, I'll give you that. I never gave it a second thought before now.' He paused to turn the light on to her face. 'Who was the patsy Len put away ten years ago?'

'Hannah's brother.'

The response surprised him, less for the revelation that this was another relation, than that she'd chosen to tell him. He'd seen all it was possible to see from the edge of the corridor. The thin beam of light from his torch wouldn't penetrate every corner. It was possible someone crouched in the darkness listening to them. Maybe Julia's decision to speak had been because she knew someone was listening; maybe she wanted to identify herself.

'Keep it in the family,' he said at random as he pushed her ahead of him out of the protection of the corridor. Then in a sudden burst of anger, 'You've got a bloody nerve trashing me to all and sundry. You and your family are child killers.'

'We are not.' He felt her shoulders stiffen as her back straightened. 'We saved those children, dozens of them. How many do you think would have died if Len hadn't intervened when he did?'

The timing fitted. When Klein made his arrest it had somehow put a stop to the killings. Then the man died and they'd started up again. He couldn't pause to puzzle it out now, but it didn't matter. His phone might be out of range of a signal down here, but it was recording everything they said for someone else to work out later.

'When was it going to end, Julia? How could you allow children to be swept up like litter?'

'We had a deal,' she said. 'Her freedom and no more killings. It was the best way. The only way.'

*Her* freedom? 'Who? Who was it … is it, Julia?' He didn't know why she'd started to talk, but knew better than to trust her motives. He wanted to shove her against the far wall where he could keep her at a distance, away from the escape route back down the corridor and far enough away that she couldn't take a swing at him. While her upper arm was in his grip, he couldn't use both hands for an investigation of that odd-looking wall near the entrance to the corridor. Its surface was smooth, not shuttered like the rest of the place. Some kind of box was attached. He might have risked letting go of her arm for long enough to check it out, but for a growing feeling that she was getting more and more desperate that he do just that.

Again he shone the torch beam all around looking for somewhere to secure one side of the cuffs. Nothing. Was he being paranoid? What could she do? Yet why the sudden release of information if not to disarm him? He had the torch; he could overpower her without breaking into a sweat; her hands were securely fastened together. But he couldn't shake off the idea that if he let go for just a second, she would dematerialise just as Hannah Levine had done. He looked again at the wall with the odd box thing attached. He needed the geek down here. Where had he got to?

'If you'd come to Len when that first child turned up,' Julia said, 'the gypsy girl's daughter would still be alive.'

And that was drivel. Both children had been dead for months when the first body washed up. She was talking to distract him, and it seemed that she said something every time his attention turned to that box of tricks over there.

'Why would I have come to Len? He was retired. It was nothing to do with him.'

'But you must have seen the similarities to his case. Even you're not that stupid.'

'Julia, even now I can't think of anything beyond superficial parallels.'

'Oh, come on. Shredded hands, crossed like that. How often have you seen that before?'

He bit back his response. Officially, no one had seen the murdered children's hands at all, let alone knew what state they'd be in. The phrase 'crossed like that' sent a shiver through him, because certainly no one knew anything about that. All he knew of it had been in a single uncorroborated report from over a hundred years ago.

'Why were their hands put like that?' he asked her.

'It gives a sinner the chance of redemption. Making them pray for eternity.'

'How were they sinners, Julia? They were children.'

'They were scavengers, Martyn, born into sin. It was wrong to do it, but it wasn't an evil act.'

He felt sick. Her tone was one of stating facts to someone who would find the truth distasteful. In his mind's eye, he saw Myra Franklin, smiling shyly in the one photograph they'd tracked down from Syeira's friend; and he saw her broken body scattered about the county. He'd take a bet it was her disappearance that was the root cause of both parents' suicides. Klein had lived with this woman. When had he found out? Why hadn't he done more than hatch his own private plans to stop the killings?

There was no way she expected him to pass on any of this. She was confident he wouldn't get out of here. Where the hell was his backup?

'How did you persuade Len to go along with it?' Behind his words he heard an echo of the horror he couldn't suppress.

Julia hesitated before she spoke. 'He wouldn't betray the family.'

Webber felt his mouth curl to a sneer. There was no truth in that. There couldn't be. Except that Klein *had* gone along with it. The grainy footage played through his head of Marks in his later interviews. Marks had gone along with it, too, and been in too deep to pull back by the time he realised the enormity of the trap that had been sprung around him. Had they done that to Klein? But Klein was no credulous fool like Marks.

'Len hated the killings,' Julia said. Something in her tone made bile rise in his throat, made him come close to pushing her away from him. Any revulsion she felt at their physical proximity was reciprocated in spades. What was she telling him? Of course Klein hated the killings. Hadn't he cried over the case file? It seemed obvious to Webber now. Klein had cried over all that had been done and couldn't be undone. It struck him she'd laid slight emphasis on the word, killings. Len hated the *killings*.

Was she trying to tell him Len had enjoyed the rest of it? Garbage! He thought about the obfuscation, the smoke and mirrors, the camouflage that kept everyone looking away. The retired Chief who everyone thought was past it. Webber didn't want to let in the idea that Klein had enjoyed running rings round them because it held a creeping credibility. And if Klein had hated the killings, he hadn't hated them enough, and others had revelled in them. The pictures in his head were from the documentary research, the original theme before they'd pulled it and focussed elsewhere; the boy damaged by a maniac of a father a century ago. The contemporary accounts had been almost too painful to read, the boy dodging his sister's route to insanity and finding his own; brutal, visceral pleasure in the butchery of the waifs and strays in his power.

'Where's the Raymond woman?' he snapped. Even if he didn't survive this for any reason, perhaps his phone would, and someone might find the missing woman before it was too late.

'Why should I tell you anything? Look at the way you've shackled me.'

He was certain now if he hadn't been before. She was trading information for the chance of freedom. But because of his supposed liaison with Annie Raymond, that particular nugget would be costly. How much freedom did she need and what would she do? He eased his grip slightly, as though he weighed her words, as though his concentration was beginning to slip. With luck he could coerce her into making her move too early.

'What were the anniversaries?' He changed tack.

'There were never any anniversaries. It was apprentices. Some fool misheard something. *If there are no anniversaries, it'll all stop.*' She laughed without warmth. 'Stop the anniversaries? Every day's an anniversary of something. It's the heirs they should have worried about. The killing gene.'

'Killing gene?' Again he found himself sneering at her. 'What are you talking about?'

'Why do you think Len and I never had children?'

She stared hard into his eyes. His heart thumped as the realisation hit him.

# chapter forty nine

Webber struggled to pull in air to breathe as it hit him like a physical blow. She was talking about the same family. Not a copycat. Not some pale imitator. The same family. The father who'd made a brutal killer of his son and driven his daughter insane. The documentary that had shifted focus, someone behind the scenes with the money to apply subtle pressure. The old press cuttings taken from the file. It had been staring him in the face. Personal details. Family connections. All those things that didn't seem like they could be significant so long after the event. They'd have led straight to Julia Klein, Hannah Levine, Fairclough, Nesbitt and even Ryan Davies, once someone had thought to dig.

But they couldn't be descendants, because … 'Those children were the last in the line …' He felt the propaganda in the lie as he spoke the words, and ended lamely, 'And there's no such thing as a killing gene.'

'It's all genes and baser instincts, Martyn, especially for someone like you who doesn't fight against it. I've heard your father was just the same, a different tart for every day of the week.'

His father? He stared at her, her face alabaster white in the torchlight. His parents had been happy like him and Mel. He thought of Sam. Sam would never hear a whisper of any discord between him and Mel. Glitches like Christa meant nothing. For the first time ever, it occurred to him that he had been the Sam in his parents' life. His fists clenched in involuntary preparation to strangle Julia here and now. Then he thought about the recording in his pocket that would be scrutinized by others and he pulled back from the bitterness he felt. 'Those children were the last of the line,' he repeated.

'No,' she said. 'Hannah's the last of them. The family dies with Hannah and me.'

'What about Fairclough,' he said. 'and Nesbitt?' *And the next generation, Ryan Davies.*

'They're not direct family,' she said dismissively.

He shone the torch around again, wondering where the attack would come from. She was still talking, giving him stuff, wanting him to let go. It was clear now there was no backup on its way.

Webber felt a trickle of sweat down his back. The temperature was rising.

'Olivia Lamb,' he said. 'Where did she come into it?'

'She came to no harm.'

He could feel the pulse at his temple; had to fight to keep his voice even. 'Why did you take her?'

When she didn't answer, he turned the torch beam to play across that strange box. Immediately, Julia said, 'They thought she'd found the gypsy girl's hands. She told Ryan. They just wanted to know. No one was ever going to harm her. She's a proper child with a family.'

*They were all proper children, Julia.* He wanted to shout it in her face, but the important thing was to keep her talking. The torch beam began to fade. It wasn't designed for constant use. He would have to turn it off soon to allow it to recover. 'And had she found the hands, Julia?'

She laughed. 'No, Martyn, she hadn't. But she'd seen someone else find them. You don't know, do you? It was your tart from London. She didn't trust you with that, did she? It might have been a whole different story if she had. The girl saw her in the garden here.'

Annie Raymond had found the hands? He didn't think so. She

wouldn't have kept quiet about that. But it explained the move to destroy all her records. So it had been here at this house she'd seen Olivia Lamb and Olivia had seen her, too. He wondered how she'd found the address. But it was Olivia Lamb who lived nearby, not Annie Raymond. What could people like Julia Klein know about how children's minds work?

'You were wrong, Julia,' he said. 'It was Olivia Lamb who saw Myra Franklin's hands. You pushed her too hard. She shoved the blame on to a stranger.' That was for the recording more than for Julia, but he'd take a bet he was right.

Her expression was briefly puzzled at the unfamiliar name. He daren't let her ask. One hint of her couldn't-care-less laugh for Myra Franklin and he'd kill her himself, right now. 'What about Ryan Davies?' he snapped.

'Mrs Fairclough said he was shaping up nicely. He got the girl for us.'

Despite the rising temperature, Webber felt a chill. *Shaping up nicely?* She kidded herself Ryan was being groomed to play his part in covering up the family crimes. She took pride in the way they'd kept the lid on it for so long. But deep inside she must know they were grooming the next generation's killer. She'd said, for *us*. Not for her, Hannah, but us, the family.

'Peter Goodridge?' A swing of the failing torch beam towards that box.

'He shouldn't have come snooping. He didn't deserve redemption. No one'll miss him.'

'He had a wife and family. He had friends. You've turned lives upside down killing him.'

'I didn't kill him.' He felt her stiffen; her indignation was real. 'Len and I have devoted our lives to controlling the killings. If you'd all just left us to it, everything would have been fine.'

'Ten years ago, it was Hannah Levine, wasn't it? She was the killer Len should have put away.'

Again, that was for the recording. He didn't need confirmation. He let the waning torch beam play close to her face, wanting to see her reaction when he asked about Fairclough and Nesbitt, because a woman as frail as Levine hadn't butchered bodies without help, not within the past two years, probably not within the past ten. It made his skin crawl to think that either or both of them could be in the shadows watching … listening … waiting for their chance when he let go of Julia's arm, or when the torch beam finally failed. But as her features flickered into view, they reminded him of something else. A CCTV sequence. O'Dowd … The ferry crossing … It had been Julia.

'Why did you take that girl out on Stacy Gerrard's passport?'

She shot him a raised-eyebrows glance, clearly surprised he knew. Then she laughed. 'Because I could.'

'What became of Mrs O'Dowd?'

'She was a good woman,' said Julia. 'She deserved redemption.'

He took that to mean she was dead … murdered. He thought about the child in Geneva … Myra Franklin … the victims from ten years ago … the panicked but meticulous cover-up, bankrolled by what? He remembered all those disappearing sex-lines whose numbers packed Damien Marks's phone, but supposed the porn empire was just the part of the iceberg above the water line. Did she really believe it was in her power or Len's to put a stop to it? Had she ever believed it?

It was uncomfortably hot now. His mind skated back across all that she'd said. There was no way to judge the truth of any of it. He didn't even want to try. But she'd given him one nugget. *Why would you risk lives to save a woman you barely know?* She thought the Raymond woman was still alive to be saved.

'Where's Annie Raymond, Julia?'

He never knew if she'd have answered him. She didn't have the time to draw breath before a voice boomed out of the darkness. 'Detective Superintendent Webber? Is that you?'

He jumped and spun round flashing the torch beam back towards the corridor. Nothing. No one. The voice was familiar. 'Yes, this is Webber. Who are you?'

'Tommy Marchant from Hull. Is that Mrs Klein with you?'

He'd let go of Julia's arm. The weak beam of light from the torch found her eyes. She'd stepped away from him. He grabbed her again.

'Tommy? What are you doing? Where …?'

'You know that Annie Raymond you just asked about? She's smallish with short blonde hair, isn't she?'

'Yes, why? Do you know where she is?'

'I can see her next to you.'

Again Webber spun round, flashing the torch. It was almost useless now. This time he kept his grip on Julia. 'Where? What are you talking about? I'm with Julia Klein.'

'I meant on the screen. One side it's you and Mrs Klein. The other's the blonde. She's tied to the ceiling, there's a chain and something round her wrist. Ah … hang on. Let's see what this is.'

As Webber stared round trying to locate the source of Tommy Marchant's placid tones, the cavern flooded with light, blinding him. He blinked, holding tight to Julia's arm. As his eyes adjusted, she came into focus in front of him. He pictured her a frail pensioner in the dock, her brief displaying pictures of the bruising on her arm from his grip, and he relaxed it a little. She glared at him. The small cavern was as chaotically-shaped as it had seemed in the dark. Shadows pooled in the misshapen edges where the light couldn't penetrate. The section he'd wanted to investigate looked even more out of place now the lights were on. A large plastic panel.

He flicked off the torch as Tommy Marchant's tones boomed around them again. 'Hello … Hello, Miss Raymond. Can you hear me?' A pause. '*You* can hear me, can't you, guv?'

'Yes. Where are you, Tommy?'

'I'm in Mr Klein's house. Ayaan Ahmed said … Oh, hang about

… What's this? No, I can't get this one to do anything. Can you hear the blonde?'

'I can't hear a thing except you, Tommy.'

'I've put the lights on in her side, too, and she's shouting for help, but I can't make her hear me. She's trying to get the thing off her wrist, but she's not having much luck. If she was close by, you'd hear her.'

'If she's in the house, the team upstairs'll hear her.'

'Upstairs? This is a bungalow.'

'I'm in York, Tommy.'

'In …? Oh hang about, I don't like the look of this. I've this flashing orange thing.'

Webber heard Julia's intake of breath. 'Julia, what does it mean?' He dragged her towards him as he spoke, pushing his face close to hers. He saw a flash of fear and disgust as she curled her lip.

'I told you you'd kill people. She's in there.' She made a move to gesture with her cuffed hands, indicating the plastic panel.

He stared at it. 'What do you mean?'

'What I say. That lever above the box will open the door. She's inside.'

Webber stared at her, then at the mechanism. Had she given him Raymond without him releasing her? 'Tommy. You need to get on to Chief Superintendent Farrar. Tell him we're in a cellar under the Levine house. There's a team of CSIs upstairs but for some reason they can't get to us.' As he spoke, he moved closer to the smooth wall, dragging Julia in his wake. She held back, a dead weight on his arm. He reached up and grabbed the lever. It wouldn't budge.

'You need to hold the catch back,' she said. There was a spark of triumph in her voice. It was a two-handed job. To work that lever, he'd have to let go of her.

'Tommy, I need you to find out what's happening in the house above us. I need to get someone down here to help.'

'Hang about, Guv.' A shade of worry overlay the placidity of

Tommy's tone. 'She's going frantic in there now, and I think I can see smoke.'

Smoke? Webber spun to face Julia, who raised her eyebrows and half shrugged in an I-told-you-so gesture.

Marchant's voice faded to a background echo, individual words indecipherable. Then it boomed around them again. 'The entrance thing closed itself and they can't get it open again,' he told them. 'They're at it with pickaxes and someone's gone for a big drill.'

'What about the other cellar? Is there a way in from there?'

Again, the words dwindled to a background babble. Webber thought he caught the name 'Levine' out of the echo, and felt Julia tense.

'They said to tell you they've found Levine. They're looking for how she got out, but she was a good way from the house. She's not making sense.'

Julia was suddenly still. Webber looked at her. Her eyes were unfocussed, calculating. 'So much for looking after the family, Julia,' he said. 'They've dumped your aunt.'

'Well, her mind's gone,' she murmured, but the news had shaken her.

'You need to find a way out,' Marchant's voice said. 'The smoke alarms are going barmy in the house, and it's getting real thick where Annie Raymond is.'

Julia gave an unconvincing laugh. 'I think we should listen in, don't you, Martyn? Top left button, Mr Marchant,' she called out. 'Hold it down and then click the silver switch underneath the console. We may as well hear her roast before it gets to us.'

Webber stared at her, fighting an impulse to smash her against one of the walls. She smiled. 'Don't look like that, Martyn. I'm giving you the chance for some last words with your lady love.'

'Thanks, Mrs Klein, but I don't think I will.' Tommy's unhurried tones embraced them. He might have been refusing the offer of a cup of tea.

'Oh, come on, Mr Marchant,' she urged. 'Don't be squeamish. Let Martyn speak to his lover.'

'It's not him I'm squeamish about, Mrs Klein. If I do what you say, I think I'll blow myself to kingdom come. Am I right?'

Webber saw the answer in her tight smile, and felt hollow inside. He'd missed that one. Thank heavens Tommy was on the ball.

'The smoke's getting quite bad in there, Guv.'

He reached out and put his palm flat against the plastic panel. It felt clammy but not warm. He looked at the corridor. That was the escape route, but it could take forever for the team to break through. Julia had a way out. He knew she did. Probably she could open the door from inside. He wished there was a way to talk to Tommy without her hearing him.

'Listen, Tommy. If Mrs Klein makes a break for it, the team need to be sure they keep that door open. I'm certain she knows how to work it. I want you to keep an eye on her. Watch my back.'

He jerked Julia across to the far side of the cavern, shoved her against the uneven woodwork, saying, 'Stay there.' He strode back to the lever, pushing back the catch. It was heavy and stiff, but once started, it moved smoothly to one side. He felt the surface give and before his eyes discerned any gap, the air was filled with Annie Raymond's shrieks.

'I can see the door opening her side,' Tommy Marchant said as choking fumes plumed out. The shrieks cut off abruptly. 'Righto, Miss Raymond. We'll have you out of there in no time. What are you doing, Mrs Klein?'

Webber tensed.

Julia's voice snapped, 'I'm sitting down. Getting away from the smoke.'

'Yes, she is. It's OK, Guv.'

'Help me out, Tommy. It's hard to see.'

'Directly in front of you, Guv. Watch your step.'

Webber made out Annie Raymond's form just ahead of him.

The smoke swirled. Instinctively, he crouched lower. 'Get down towards the ground,' he ordered.

'She can't,' Tommy Marchant said. 'Her wrist's tied.'

Webber grabbed a handful of clothing, pulling her towards him, working his hands roughly across her to find her shackled wrist. As his hand closed round the metal band, his heart plummeted. He'd assumed either a standard cuff that he could have unlocked in a second or rope that he could cut through. This was a manacle. The touch of the rusted metal beneath his fingers was enough to bring the image to his mind. He couldn't undo this with anything he had on him.

'How are the team upstairs getting on?' he shouted. 'I need bolt-cutters to get through this chain.'

Tommy cleared his throat. 'They're on their way.' his voice had become flat, impersonal. Webber read in his tone that he didn't think the team upstairs could beat the fire down below.

He raked through his pockets whipping out a linen handkerchief. 'Hold this to your face,' he ordered, reaching up through the smoke.

No response. Her weight slumped on to him. She'd passed out. He made a try at tying the cloth round her nose and mouth, not confident that it would stay there. He eased away letting her hang by her wrist. At least her face was closer to the floor.

Tommy's cough echoed his own as he ducked down to retreat to the cavern. 'Tell them we're going to open it from the inside,' he shouted. Julia would do this. She'd save them both rather than die down here.

'Shit, she's gone!' Tommy's voice hit his ears as he stared at the corner where Julia had been crouching to get away from the smoke. He looked all round.

'Where? Where did she go?' It must have been the corridor. He set off before Tommy spoke again.

'No, I'd have seen her.' His voice cut off in another coughing fit.

Lit up, the short length looked benign. Webber leapt for the curving stone stairs and raced up. Julia must be … His train of thought crashed to a halt as he grabbed at the walls to keep his balance. The staircase went nowhere. It stopped on a cliff edge with a drop down to the stone floor. Somewhere in the walls around him was a door that swung open to complete it. The air was clearer at this end, but the sting of smoke was in his nostrils. And Tommy's persistent coughing rang in his ears.

'Where the fuck is she?'

He leapt back down and strode towards the cavern, banging his fists on the wooden shuttering.

'Didn't go that way … sure she didn't …' Tommy's voice was rasping now.

'What's the matter with you?'

'Nothing …' the voice rasped out. 'There has to be a way out near where she was.'

His hand clasped over his mouth and nose, Webber ducked to hands and knees to get at breathable air. Tommy was right. That bit of a breeze. It came from somewhere.

'Yes,' he shouted. 'I've got it. It's small but it's a way through.'

'Then get … the hell … out, Guv. That … place is going … going to go up.'

'What's the matter with you, Tommy?' The man could hardly speak.

'It's … it's going up here, too. I … I can't … I can't stay much longer. Get yourself out!'

'The Raymond woman's still trapped.'

'Guv … She's past help. You can't see what I can. Get yourself out!'

Webber turned and headed towards the thick plastic door. The source of the smoke seemed to be inside the place where she was imprisoned. If he could free her and then slam the door, he'd win some time. He kept low and moved slowly, keeping his breathing shallow, taking in as little as possible of the acrid air.

Tommy Marchant's voice grew desperate as he choked out the words, begging Webber to go back, to save himself.

Webber inched his way towards Annie Raymond. He knew if he didn't make it out, history would have it that he went into a burning cell because he couldn't bear to leave the woman he was having an affair with. He mustn't leave Mel with that. But it was too late for explanations. The air was too thick. He couldn't speak, had no breath to waste on words.

He had a knife in his pocket. It would cut through rope, but not metal. What would it take to sever her arm? But if he could bring himself to try, he'd surely kill her. As a last resort he might knock her out cold before he left. What had Tommy said? *She's tied to the ceiling … a chain …* Maybe if he put all his weight on it, he could dislodge it from above. He'd have to stand right up into the thick of the smoke to try.

'Christ!' The exclamation came out of the air, with a crackle of fire. Webber's heart thumped hard in his chest. He cringed expecting a fireball to roll out of the smoke. Crashing … footsteps … They'd broken through from above. 'Here!' he called and gagged on a mouthful of smoky air.

The sounds cut off; mid step, mid crash. The echo he'd forgotten he'd been hearing was gone. Silence. Just the creeping smoke. The fireball had been elsewhere. Tommy?

Whatever link they'd had, it was broken. He was on his own.

Annie Raymond was on her knees, hanging from one arm, her other hand trying to hold the cloth to her face.

He drew in a mouthful of the slightly less acrid air at ground level, the trace of a vile stench turning his stomach. Then he reached up her arm to the chain and took a firm grip on it.

'Pin … The pin's loose …' It was her voice, close to his ear. She'd struggled to pull herself up so he'd hear her.

It took a fraction of a second to realise what she meant. The pin in the shackle. His hands grasped for her wrist. She was right. It hadn't been pushed home. He could free her, if he could just get the purchase to get both hands to it.

'Get your weight off it.' He half choked on the words, wasn't sure she understood him.

She was trying to pull herself up. Too slow. There was some kind of metal table. He bent down and heaved her up on to it, feeling the chain slacken. At once, his hands were at the mechanism, working the pin.

'Hold still,' he rasped in frustration, the smoke taking his throat in a stranglehold. He knew it was him yanking on the metal bracelet that made her jerk about.

The pin flew free and fell with a clatter. The metal band remained tight round her wrist. He wrenched it away; heard her scream out as he tore her arm free of it.

With her upper arm grasped in a tighter grip than he'd held Julia, he dragged her out through the plastic door and heaved it shut. Dropping her for a moment, he pushed his face close to the ground and tried to find air. A few half breaths would have to do. Not knowing if she were awake or comatose, dead or alive, he dragged her across the space and dumped her on the floor while he squeezed through the gap where Julia had disappeared.

He hauled her through behind him. No response. No movement, no whimper of pain or anything. Anger drove him on. Had he gone through this and she'd died anyway ...? Smoke had swallowed any vestige of light that might have crept through. The torch threw out an anaemic beam that lit floating strands of silver. The tang caught in his throat but it had lost its sharp edge. At the extremes of this fissure he could outpace it, even with Raymond a dead weight behind him. All he need do was find the way out.

The passage ahead narrowed. It was a trick of the failing torch. He looked back. The light from the cavern was a dull glow. Dropping Annie Raymond to the floor, he pushed ahead feeling his way with both hands. The walls closed in; wooden shuttering gave way to damp earth. There was no way through.

It was a dead end. He'd found this one gap in the chamber and scrambled down it without a second thought; without looking for other exits; without even scrutinizing the floor for scuff marks from Julia's feet.

The silvery strands curled around. The glow from the far end of the tunnel was hazy. It was too late to go back; to look for another way. The adrenaline rush that had brought him this far fell away. He sunk to the ground as the wisps of smoke caught his throat. His body would be discovered beside the lifeless heap on the ground. He'd never meant her to be this good a decoy. He couldn't go back. He no longer had the energy to lift himself, never mind her.

'Shit!' he called out in frustration.

'Martyn?'

He thought he imagined a voice answering him. A familiar voice. 'Tommy?' A section of the tunnel behind him lit up as though someone had opened a door in the roof.

'No, Guv. It's me,' said Ayaan Ahmed's voice. 'You need to get out of there.'

# chapter fifty

Annie looked up at Pieternel not sure if she was justified in her feeling of resentment that resonated with the dull throb of pain in her arm. She knew the medics were right to be wary with the painkillers. They didn't know what she'd been drugged with or how long it would be in her system. The bed was comfortable, the room clinically white. She'd insisted to the uniformed nurses that they leave the lights on, but they'd smiled and shown her the console by the bed. She had full control of the lights, the angle of the bed head, the TV.

She supposed she'd slept, but didn't feel rested. Every time her body relaxed into sleep, it jarred awake. She was back in that cell, reliving the awful realisation that she couldn't free her arm, that it would need two hands because the pin was old and misshapen. She'd pleaded with the ancient corpse. She'd kept her side of the bargain. Then the sting of smoke had hit her nostrils and she'd heard the panicked scurrying of the rats in the darkness as they flew up the walls to escape. When the place had flooded with light she'd been beyond anything except screaming for someone … anyone … to come and help her.

Beyond that, it wasn't clear. There'd been someone tugging at the chain. She'd found a last gasp to direct them to the pin. Then the terrible pain like fire up her arm.

She turned over in her mind what she now knew, couldn't get her head round the fact it had been Webber who'd hauled her out. 'Why was Webber there?'

'Who cares why?' said Pieternel. 'Just be thankful he found you.'

But she couldn't shake off the what-ifs. Webber was the last person she'd have expected to go the extra mile for her. He didn't like her. This would stalk her nightmares for months. 'He nearly died getting me out. Why did he do it?'

'It's his job,' said Pieternel, as though that made everything OK. 'He's a bastard but underneath it, he's basically just an old-fashioned copper. He'll never get beyond Superintendent. If you want to be angry with any of them, it should be the retired guy, Klein.'

'Yes,' Annie burst out. 'What sort of copper's Webber that he didn't see anything wrong? He worked with the guy, for heaven's sake.' She knew the comment was unfair, but after all that had happened, she smarted under a burning sense of injustice that wouldn't find a focus. 'I bloody heard him, you know,' she went on. 'The first time I went to that house. I told you I heard them talking. "For God's sake, Hannah!" Remember? It was his voice, Klein's. I should have recognized it.'

She slumped back on to the pillow. The edges of terror shivered through her every time she thought back to that swirling smoke, with only Webber between her and death. He could so easily have left her. She hadn't seen him since; wouldn't know what to say to him. Thank God for Pieternel whisking her away from the chaos of York A&E and into a private place miles away where he surely wouldn't take the trouble to visit, no matter what else he'd done for her. She couldn't bear the thought of lying helpless in a hospital bed with his bulk standing over her.

'Anyway,' said Pieternel, her tone closing the topic of Webber's part in Annie's rescue. 'I had a talk with the young guy, Ahmed. They think Will Stanley was promised a lot of money to reclaim his child. I guess he realised what he'd done when they dumped him and Myra vanished. He didn't even go back to Syeira.'

Annie didn't want her thoughts pulled from that dark cell.

She wanted to talk and talk until she'd banished it from her head altogether. But she looked up at her colleague. Pieternel was already bored. She gave in and asked, 'Didn't Will Stanley tell anyone?'

Pieternel turned to look out on to the manicured lawns of the clinic. 'Who knows? He certainly didn't go to the authorities. And who else would have been able to help him even if they'd believed him?'

'And when did you get to hear all this?' Annie grimaced as she tried to shift herself to a more comfortable position.

Pieternel turned back from the window to look her in the eye. 'I had the detail from DC Ahmed this morning when I rang him. But the fact is that he called my mobile while you were missing.'

It took a moment for Annie to understand Pieternel's narrow-eyed glance. 'Don't look at me. I didn't give him your number.'

'No, but he got it from somewhere. I'll have to get rid of it now.'

'But you just said you rang him.'

'That's right. I'd stumbled on some info that his Chief Super ought to know. Their online archive has been tampered with and they were thinking of putting us in the frame for it, but it was an inside job. A guy who'd worked with Klein. Not that they can do much now. He died on the M62 about six months ago; a tyre blow out, apparently.'

'Apparently?'

'Who knows? Not our problem.'

'And where did you stumble over all that?'

'I had to dig deep for it, call in some favours, but I want them off our backs. They can take it as a small thank you gift for getting you out of the shit. Quite generous in the circs. You realise this has landed us in it. We're going to have to do some serious restructuring.'

Annie blew out a sigh. She was too tired to think about it. She supposed someone would be back for another statement. Pieternel had let in a couple of uniforms to talk to her while she was still in York. She'd given them what she could and they'd taken samples from under her fingernails to see if they could identify the desiccated body on the second table. Just as long as no one else wanted a piece of her until she felt well again. 'Christa's going to dump Webber,' she said. 'He'll be no use to her, far too much on his guard after this little lot.'

'She won't have to. He's already dumped her.'

'Are you sure?' Annie was surprised. She'd have predicted that Christa would be the one to move first.

'Yes, I gave her the name to pass on to Webber. It'd have made more sense to him. But she couldn't get through. He'd blocked her number. Christa's not bothered. Said it saved her the hassle of doing it herself. She's got plans to get on to the TV company, thinks there's a whole new documentary to be done.'

That was Christa all over, flitting from one thing to another, never looking back. 'The little girl, Olivia Lamb,' Annie said. 'You were going to find out what happened to her.'

'She's fine. Back home.'

'But why was she there in the cell with me?'

'She'd seen something or found something. I'm not sure. But she'd told them it was you. She was supposed to get it out of you.'

Annie shuddered, remembering the strange interrogation about hands in the well. 'Why her?'

Pieternel shrugged. 'I don't know the details. Oh, and I've billed Heidi Marks. I've no idea if they'll be able to take any of that money back off her – proceeds of crime and all that – but I want our bit of it before the sharks get there.'

Heidi? Heidi felt like a long-ago client, not someone Annie had talked to two days ago. The case had mushroomed way beyond the boundaries originally set. 'You're closing the case, then?'

'It's like you told her, it's lawyers she needs now, not us. They've charged him with some makeweight thing in connection with Myra Franklin, but only so they can hold him. It'll be withdrawn.'

'So Damien Marks is out of the woods?'

'Er … no. I understand they're waiting for an arrest warrant for an extradition hearing. But anyway, no longer our problem.'

◉ ◉ ◉

Chief Superintendent Farrar clicked the handset back into its rest as he waved Webber into his office. 'OK, Martyn, I've let you sit about moping for the best part of the morning which, incidentally, I wouldn't have done if I'd been told sooner that you were here. Isn't it about time you saw sense and buggered off home or am I going to have to order you out?'

Webber drew in a breath to speak, but Farrar's phone rang again. With an exasperated sigh, he snatched it up.

He'd had to come into work. Home was too uncomfortable until he could get his head back together. Mel had come to fetch him from the hospital but she'd been spiky with the tales that Julia Klein had fed her. Chapter and verse almost on his affair with Christa, except she'd made the assumption the woman concerned was Annie Raymond. There had been no difficulty at all in proving that Julia's stories didn't add up, in showing that Annie Raymond had been hundreds of miles away from the locations of their supposed clandestine meetings. The hard part, the really hard part, was reconciling the guilt he felt inside with the injured innocence that he ought to feel. He didn't want Mel apologising to him for believing Julia's lies. He deserved the frozen edge of her anger for betraying her with Christa. With everything spinning in his mind, he simply couldn't cope with it. He'd come to work to get a break.

It was only now that he'd cottoned on to what had convinced Mel. It wasn't the facts of who had been where. Things like this were never about raw facts. It had been his complete indifference to someone's suggestion that he drop in to see the Raymond woman at the hospital before he left. Mel had seen the emotional honesty behind his disinterest. And until he could think straight again, he daren't trust himself around her. He might just blurt out the truth.

Farrar was wrong. He hadn't spent the morning moping. He'd been getting himself back up to speed. Marchant, the DC from Hull, had escaped the fire, though Webber wasn't sure what shape he was in. The guy had been *compos mentis* enough to call Ahmed to let him know where Webber and Annie Raymond were trapped. Suzie Harmer had made it through the night but he still didn't know who'd attacked her.

The news that Ahmed had solved the mystery of how Janice Cochran had acquired the murder weapon had initially given him a boost because it meant Ahmed had come through this unscathed. Then he'd learnt that the detail had come from Klein and he'd plummeted back to the depths. Klein had masked the story as second-hand, pretended he'd called into the station and heard it there. That it was true, and provided enough detail to corner Janice Cochran into admitting everything, did nothing to lift his spirits. He imagined Klein seeing it as some kind of advance *quid pro quo* for the carjacking and the thought sickened him.

Farrar hadn't invited him to sit but Webber was exhausted. Slipping into the chair brought a document into his line of sight. A physical reminder that this case would dog his heels probably forever. It was that half sketch that Klein had written on. A scan of the original must have survived. Marks had had that from Nesbitt, Annie Raymond's sorry-guy. It was to make sure he made it to the right house if they needed him to go there. He'd been lucky enough to be arrested before it came to that. Webber supposed Klein had written on it because he'd planned to confront someone, maybe even Julia. *Look how close they are ... We have to call a halt to this ...* Except that Klein could have called a halt at any time.

As Farrar finished his call, he tapped a pencil on the handset. 'It's a bloody mess, Martyn. And it's going to get worse.'

Webber, grateful Farrar had been diverted from ordering him home, nodded his agreement.

'Len Klein, of all people,' Farrar went on. 'And Julia! I've known them for years.'

Webber felt he hadn't known them at all. 'Just how far was he involved?'

'Julia must have known her own family secrets, but my guess is that she kept it all from Len until ten years ago. I'd like to think it came as a shock to her too when she worked out who the killer was. And of course it had been going on for a good while even then.'

'Who did Len put away?' he asked. 'Julia told me Hannah's brother.'

Farrar nodded. 'Julia's been a copper's wife long enough to know that lies are best disguised inside the truth. The brother got Levine out of Eastern Europe towards the end of the 1940s. Plenty of money and a string of killings behind them, masked by the havoc of war. It seems he was ready to take any risk to protect his sister. It's possible Len didn't know the extent of it until the brother died. Levine, Nesbitt and Fairclough took a trip to Switzerland. They called it a private memorial.'

'Private killing spree, more like. Len said something like that to Ayaan. They must have had poor little Myra Franklin in their sights by then, too.' So much done that couldn't be undone. Webber began to wonder if he'd ever summon the energy to get out of the chair, never mind back into the job. He thought back to the dark corridor, dragging Julia, her indignation when he called her a killer. 'Julia knew all about it. She called the children scavengers.'

'I know, I know. I suppose she tried to justify it to herself or she'd have gone mad.'

Webber grunted. He wouldn't class her sane, not the woman he'd been with yesterday. 'Len could have stopped it. He could have saved them all.'

'Myra franklin and the child in Geneva, yes. If he'd spoken out ten years ago, he could have saved them. But not the earlier ones.'

There'd been a gap between the net closing in and Klein making his arrest. The record said they'd interviewed the man, Hannah's brother, several times. Webber wondered. There was no one left to confirm or deny what was in the record. But Klein must have found out and somehow contrived to hold Hannah and her partners back while they did the deal. Hannah's freedom, no talk of apprentices and no more killings. A bit of time to build a convincing case of the lone killer and Len had his deal.

'He was complicit once he'd agreed to the cover-up,' Farrar said. 'That was the end point for Len. But I'm sure he genuinely thought he'd stopped the killings.'

Webber had seen the weight on Klein's shoulders as the new case had unfolded. 'And Hannah's brother's death freed them to kill again. Where did he think it would end? Did he think there was another deal to do?'

'I think it had become damage limitation, and clearly the idea of pulling the wool over everyone's eyes had its attractions. The ramifications will be awful, Martyn.'

Webber let Farrar's voice wash over him. The publicity and press explosion was already beginning to break on all their heads. He wondered how any of them would summon the stamina to cope with it.

'We've found Levine, haven't we? I didn't dream that.'

'Oh yes. She's in a secure unit. She was wandering down towards town. We'll get nothing from her. Dementia's had her memory. She's no more than a frail old lady, scared out of her wits.'

'Was there just the one way out of that hell-hole?'

'No, there were several. Geo-phys is on to what's left of the house.'

He thought about the three houses and the way they'd self-destructed; wasn't sure he wanted to know if they'd found bodies in the wreckage and asked instead, 'So Ahmed contacted Pieternel, did he?'

'You'd given him the number, apparently. It was in his wallet.' Webber nodded. He remembered passing across the scrap of paper. 'God knows what Len fed him,' Farrar went on. 'He got through to Hull via directory enquiries; never thought to dredge up a national emergency number he must have known from childhood. But anyway, Mrs Peters was worried enough about her colleague that she was ready to tell him anything he wanted to know. Looks like Annie Raymond had found the house before any of us.'

Webber had read the statement: the information Pieternel had given to Ahmed. He could track Raymond's footsteps by the detail of the night the she and the little girl had almost bumped into each other in the dark at the back of the house ... the track, the well, the ivy-clad walls, the outbuildings ... and the old coal chute that opened from the side of the path, that you wouldn't know was there if you weren't looking for it. He fought against a shiver of ice as pictures flashed in front of him; damp earth, floating silver strands.

Farrar was looking out of the window. Feathery cotton wool clouds hung in a blue sky. They're out there somewhere, thought Webber, all of them, under that same sky. 'Olivia Lamb's OK, is she?'

'She's fine, in better fettle than the boy. They thought they needed her to interrogate Annie Raymond about where she'd supposedly seen the severed hands. Olivia was the only person who saw Raymond face to face, with Len prompting remotely. And the only person who talked to Olivia face to face was the boy, Ryan. They kept her comatose until Ryan was back from France, then used him to tell her she had to get the PI to talk.'

Webber let out an exasperated sigh. 'They didn't have a bloody clue. You can't manipulate children like that.'

'Fingers crossed they can avoid lasting damage to the boy. But thank heavens they kept the girl out of it most of the time. She thought she was coming home the same night she'd left.'

In his head, Webber could hear echoes of Annie Raymond's

shrieks from the cell where she'd been shackled as the smoke billowed. He'd read the statement they'd had from her, about her desperation to escape and how she'd clambered across another body. It had never occurred to him to search further into that cell. Material from under her fingernails was at the lab now. He supposed the DNA would show it to have been Mrs O'Dowd.

'What was O'Dowd to them?' he asked.

'She was the paragon everyone knew her as, but we reckon those bastards cut short her retirement plans. She was always going to travel, but the thing about being a trusted chaperone to young children pops up suddenly after she'd been retired for about five years. It coincides with the death of her sister that left her with no family and no close friends i.e. no one to notice. It looks like Hannah's brother drew her in and slaughtered her so they could use her persona. It might well have been Julia in the role recently, but over the years, I'll bet there've been several Mrs O'Dowds and Miss Prices, too. Who knows? Maybe Mr Nesbitt'll tell us.'

'Nesbitt!' Webber felt his heart thump hard in his chest. 'We've found Nesbitt?'

Farrar smiled. 'We'll have him before the day's out. Thanks to a bit of lateral thinking from that DC of yours.'

'Ayaan? What's he done?'

'You know Len dumped him in the middle of nowhere,' Farrar said. 'Well, he got to wondering why. You'd think there'd be more options for a clean getaway at the edge of a city. He'd noticed a bit of a disturbance – loose horses – and he chased up the details, found the people involved. Something had stampeded the animals. The woman who alerted the owners thought she'd heard a helicopter landing or taking off. The description's sketchy but you know who has a private pilot's licence?'

'Nesbitt.' Webber heard the satisfaction in his own voice as he said the name. 'He worked for an aeromedical firm. I remember it coming up when we checked the vehicles.'

'Exactly. And notwithstanding a surprisingly large number of private helicopters in the area, airspace is too tightly controlled and the countryside's too crowded for impromptu flights to go unnoticed. If we could have chased this at the time, we'd have had them both, but Nesbitt's in the trap. I'd give him twelve hours tops and I've a gut feeling we'll get Fairclough at the same time.'

Webber laughed. Suddenly he didn't feel so tired. 'The first bit of advice Len ever gave me was to ignore loose horses.'

Farrar curled his lip. 'Well, it was his mistake to ignore them this time.'

Of course if Nesbitt had been tracking Klein and Ahmed, it put him out of the picture for the attack on Suzie Harmer. He must remember to ask about her before he left. 'What about Len and Julia?'

'They've had years to hone an exit strategy.'

'Yes, but no one plans for things to go as wrong as this. You said follow the money. Surely we know what to follow now. Goodridge's firm had a direct line to them.'

'Yup.' Farrar gave a satisfied smile. 'And for once Len would have no gripes about the level of resource that's going in to this, though I don't suppose he'll appreciate the irony. I'd give Len and Julia a week … maybe ten days. It'll be for the best. I'm sure Len would rather serve a few years in an English gaol than a life sentence on some ghastly beach thousands of miles from home.'

Webber's gaze shot up, but Farrar didn't meet his eye. Ex-job, involved in child killings? In Klein's shoes he'd top himself before he saw the inside of a prison. Maybe that was Farrar's idea of a best outcome.

'I suppose you've twigged that Julia was seeing to the insurance,' Farrar said.

A cold hand clutched at Webber's heart. 'Insurance?'

'She'd have sent Mel off on some errand, promised to sit with the baby, then disappeared with him. I'm sure they wouldn't have harmed the boy, but Len was tied up with Ayaan, I was taking Nesbitt's place apart and you had a team at the Levine house. They must have planned for one of their bolt holes to be uncovered, maybe even two, but not all three at once. She was lining up her hostage.'

Webber's mouth dried. He saw Julia's angular profile silhouetted behind the curtain in his front room. 'Julia had better hope I never get my hands on her again,' he said, his voice not quite steady.

'Your lad's safe, Martyn. I'm not saying this to upset you. I want to be sure you're not holding on to any illusions about Len Klein. You've known him a long time. Len was your boss at a key stage in your career.'

'Don't worry, John.' Webber ground out the words through clenched teeth. 'I'm well beyond that.'

'Look, we'll talk properly when you're back off sick leave. We'll have made some real progress by then.'

Webber looked up, surprised. 'I'm fine. I'm not on sick leave.'

'You are. I'll see you first thing Monday.' His tone brooked no argument.

Talk of sick leave reminded Webber. 'How's Suzie Harmer by the way?'

Farrar blew out a sigh. 'They had to operate and she lost a lot of blood, but she'll pull through. She's a good officer. You need to take better care of your people, Martyn.'

Webber felt his lips tighten. The accusation was doubly unjust since Farrar spent half his time demanding he stay behind his desk, from where he'd be in no position to look after them at all.

'Since you're not supposed to be here, you can clear off. And nip in to see her on your way home. She'd appreciate the gesture.'

'I don't know, John. I'm probably the last person she wants to see.'

'What is it with you and hospitals?' Farrar snapped. 'Call in and visit the woman and give her my best while you're there.'

Suzie Harmer looked very young and very vulnerable in her hospital bed, a world away from the efficient and robust officer Webber had first met not quite twenty-four hours earlier. Apart from a drip, she was no longer hooked up to any of the equipment that crowded the bed-head.

It was Klein who'd put her here, as surely as if he'd wielded the blade that had severed her artery. Ahmed too must be shattered by what had happened. He'd respected Klein. How would he cope with something like this so early in his career?

Suzie's eyes were closed. Her skin was smooth and white, almost translucent. Was it the blood loss or just that she was young and without make-up? The neat hairstyle he remembered had disappeared into a spiky tangle. Blood everywhere. He suppressed a shudder, replaying the panic of not being able to staunch the flow. Incredible to think the human body could lose so much and still survive.

Disjointed thoughts lazed across his mind as he looked down at her; he'd rung Christa on his way here, knowing that to end an affair on a blocked call was the road to serious hassle. She'd been friendly enough, polite, but somehow a stranger, surprised to hear from him. He'd always known she'd invested little in their relationship but it had been a mild shock to realise quite how close to zero the investment had been on her side. Hard to imagine how it had ever seemed so real, so vibrant, when it had all been a charade. It was a relief to have her out of his life, out of his head. Sure, she'd been a great antidote to the stresses of the job, but too high octane. It was relaxation he needed, not excitement. And if he never saw another private investigator in his life again, it would be too soon. Farrar was right, he needed a break, his judgement was shot to hell.

He wondered if Suzie minded that her hair was messed up. A wisp had strayed across her face. He reached out and moved it aside, his finger feathering her temple. She opened her eyes and looked up at him.

'How are you, Suzie?'

Her mouth curved to a half-smile. She gave him a strangely calculating look. 'I've been better. And it would be really good if you didn't treat me like a favourite daughter.'

'I'm not.' He laughed because she had a point.

'What's his name,' she asked, 'that DC from Scarborough? He's a bright-spark, isn't he? I wouldn't have thought of it.'

Webber smiled. For Suzie to know this, she must have had it from Farrar. He was pleased Ahmed had made such a good impression. 'Ayaan Ahmed,' he told her, 'and no, I wouldn't. I had a governor once who advised me to ignore loose horses.'

She took in a breath and lifted the hand that wasn't tethered to the drip line. Her fingers tapped his – *extra fingers make extra hands for extra prayers* – her touch light on his skin, the gesture unexpected, a thank you for what he'd done yesterday.

He should say something, but his brain felt sluggish. Farrar had been right to send him home. Thoughts of the Chief Super prompted him to say, 'John sends his best.'

'Those are from him.' Her gaze flicked towards a wicker basket on the table, a cascade of trailing greenery topped with red and yellow buds.

Webber glanced at them, remembering what he'd thought after the ambulance had taken her away. 'I wanted to bring you news that we'd arrested your attacker, only I don't know which one it was.'

'It was the housekeeper, Mrs Fairclough. I only had a glimpse. Have you got her?'

'It won't be long. A matter of hours. And with luck, we'll get her and Nesbitt as a set.'

'You could have brought flowers instead, you know.'

The patter of footsteps approached along the corridor. Someone to kick him out probably. They'd already told him just a couple of minutes.

'I came straight from the station.'

'Sure, and York hasn't a single florist between there and here.'

The door opened behind them. He laughed again as he raised his hand to say goodbye.

'Bye,' she said, that same calculating stare boring into his eyes, as though it wasn't him she was seeing.

*It's a bloody mess and it'll get worse.* Farrar's words. But suddenly it stopped bothering him. He was tired. That was all. A couple of days would free his head of the conflict of Klein's betrayal. Ahmed had already bounced back. Suzie Harmer, undefeated by her brush with death, was clearly hatching her own plans. Klein hadn't broken any of them.

Walking back through the city, Webber savoured the feeling of no deadlines on his shoulders, no crises demanding his attention. Despite the turmoil behind the scenes, none of it was his problem until Monday morning. Time on his hands. He'd come recklessly close to throwing away everything that really mattered, but he'd dodged the bullet, just. Things would be fine between him and Mel. They could take Sam to the playground. He grinned in anticipation of shrieks and giggles, tiny fists clutching at the sides of the slide. Lengthening his stride, he headed for home.

coming soon …

# Tiger Blood

When an ancient car is pulled from the depths of a flooded gravel pit and subject to modern forensic techniques, it looks set to tie the ends of a 30-year-old case. But the answers that emerge are not the ones that Detective Superintendent Martyn Webber expects.

# about the author

Penny Grubb is a novelist and an academic who teaches and researches creative and academic writing techniques. For six years to 2013 she was Chair of the Authors' Licensing and Collecting Society, the largest writers' organisation in the world. Her Annie Raymond mystery series has been published in the UK, USA and Canada. Buried Deep is her first police procedural. Penny is winner of an international crime fiction award from the Crime Writers Association.

Find out more about Penny at www.pennygrubb.com

Made in the USA
Charleston, SC
16 December 2014